Stan Lee Presents

THE ESSENTIAL
UNCANNY

D0878847

Volume 1

The Original X-MEN #1-24

4/28/00

ESSENTIAL UNCANNY X-MEN® Published by MARVEL COMICS; 387 PARK AVENUE SOUTH, NEW YORK, N.Y.
10016. Reprints X-MEN vol. 1 Nos. 1-24. Copyright © 1963, 1964, 1965, 1966 and 1999 Marvel Characters, Inc. All
rights reserved. X-MEN (including all prominent characters featured in this issue) and the distinctive likenesses
thereof are of trademarks of MARVEL CHARACTERS, INC. No part of this book may be printed or reproduced in any
manner without the written permission of the publisher. Printed in U.S. First Printing, September, 1999. ISBN #0-7851-
0730-4. GST #R127032852.

10 9 8 7 6 5 4 3 2 1

MARVEL COMICS

X-MEN #1 & X-MEN #2

WRITER:	STAN LEE
PENCILER:	JACK KIRBY
INKER:	PAUL REINMAN
LETTERER:	SAM ROSEN

X-MEN #3 & X-MEN #4

WRITER:	STAN LEE
PENCILER:	JACK KIRBY
INKER:	PAUL REINMAN
LETTERER:	ARTIE SIMEK

X-MEN #5

WRITER:	STAN LEE
PENCILER:	JACK KIRBY
INKER:	PAUL REINMAN
LETTERER:	SAM ROSEN

X-MEN #6

WRITER:	STAN LEE
PENCILER:	JACK KIRBY
INKER:	CHIC STONE
LETTERER:	SAM ROSEN

X-MEN #7

WRITER:	STAN LEE
PENCILER:	JACK KIRBY
INKER:	CHIC STONE
LETTERER:	ARTIE SIMEK

X-MEN #8, X-MEN #9 & X-MEN #10

WRITER:	STAN LEE
PENCILER:	JACK KIRBY
INKER:	CHIC STONE
LETTERER:	SAM ROSEN

X-MEN #11

WRITER:	STAN LEE
PENCILER:	JACK KIRBY
INKER:	CHIC STONE
LETTERER:	ARTIE SIMEK

X-MEN #12

WRITER:	STAN LEE
LAYOUTS:	JACK KIRBY
PENCILER:	ALEX TOTH
INKER:	VINCE COLLETTA
LETTERER:	SAM ROSEN

X-MEN #13

WRITER:	STAN LEE
LAYOUTS:	JACK KIRBY
PENCILER:	WERNER ROTH (as JAY GAVIN)
INKER:	JOE SINNOTT
LETTERER:	SAM ROSEN

X-MEN #14

WRITER:	STAN LEE
LAYOUTS:	JACK KIRBY
PENCILER:	WERNER ROTH (as JAY GAVIN)
INKER:	VINCE COLLETTA
LETTERER:	ARTIE SIMEK

X-MEN #15 & X-MEN #16 & X-MEN #17

WRITER:	STAN LEE
LAYOUTS:	JACK KIRBY
PENCILER:	WERNER ROTH (as JAY GAVIN)
INKER:	DICK AYERS
LETTERER:	ARTIE SIMEK

X-MEN #18 & X-MEN #19

WRITER:	STAN LEE
PENCILER:	WERNER ROTH (as JAY GAVIN)
INKER:	DICK AYERS
LETTERER:	ARTIE SIMEK

X-MEN #20, X-MEN #21 & X-MEN #22

WRITER:	ROY THOMAS
PENCILER:	WERNER ROTH (as JAY GAVIN)
INKER:	DICK AYERS
LETTERER:	ARTIE SIMEK

X-MEN #23

WRITER:	ROY THOMAS
PENCILER:	WERNER ROTH
INKER:	DICK AYERS
LETTERER:	ARTIE SIMEK

X-MEN #24

WRITER:	ROY THOMAS
PENCILER:	WERNER ROTH
INKER:	DICK AYERS
LETTERER:	SAM ROSEN

REPRINT CREDITS:

POLLY WATSON
REPRINT EDITOR

BOB HARRAS
EDITOR IN CHIEF

BRUCE TIMM
NEW COVER ART

THOMAS VELAZQUEZ
and
SUZANNE GAFFNEY
COVER DESIGN

MARIE JAVINS
COVER COLOR

JONATHAN BABCOCK
LETTERING
RESTORATION
& TOAD UPKEEP

SPECIAL THANKS

DAVE SHARPE & DAN CARR,
SCOTT "POND SCUM" ELMER,
ROGER BONAS and all the Guys
at Repro, COSMIC COMICS
and of course, THE TOADS.

GOOD OLD MARVEL COMICS

THE STRANGEST SUPER-HEROES OF ALL!

1 SEPT.

IND.

APPROVED BY THE COMICS CODE AUTHORITY

the X-MEN

MARVEL COMICS GROUP 12¢

IN THE SENSATIONAL FANTASTIC FOUR STYLE!

DON'T MISS THIS FABULOUS FIRST ISSUE!

X-MEN VERSUS MAGNETO EARTH'S MOST POWERFUL SUPER VILLAIN!!

EXCELLENT! NOW SPIN AROUND! FASTER! FASTER! PRETEND AN ENEMY IS SHOOTING AT YOU! YOU MUST MAKE YOUR-SELF AN IMPOSSIBLE TARGET!

AND NOW, AT MY COMMAND, RELEASE YOURSELF FROM THE TAUT WIRE AND EXECUTE MANEUVER "G"! YOU HAVE EXACTLY THREE SECONDS!

GO!

THREE SECONDS EXACTLY! WELL DONE, BEAST!

NOW FOR YOUR BALANCE DRILL! STEADY... STEADY! SLACKEN THE TENSION, CYCLOPS!

GOOD!! NOW, AS THE ROD BEGINS TO SAG, MAINTAIN YOUR BALANCE... ON ONE FINGER! HOLD IT! HOLD IT!

TOO FAST! YOU'RE SWAYING TOO MUCH! RECOVER... QUICKLY! NOW LAND ON YOUR FEET BEFORE THE ROD SNAPS BACK! CAREFUL... CAREFUL...

WHEW... HOW'D I DO, SIR?

YOU'LL RECEIVE YOUR GRADE TOMORROW! ALL RIGHT, ANGEL... IT'S YOUR TURN!

ARE YOU RECEIVING MY THOUGHT CLEARLY? GOOD! NOW, BE SHARP... TODAY WE TEST YOUR WING REFLEX! YOU DARE NOT MAKE A MISTAKE!

MISTAKES ARE FOR HOMO SAPIENS, SIR... NOT THE ANGEL!

3.

5.

HEY!! THAT'S NOT *FAIR!* YOU'RE OPENIN' THAT COTTON-PICKIN' *VISOR* OF YOURS *WIDER!*

ICEMAN, FOR THE KIND OF CAREER *WE'RE* TRAINING FOR, THERE'S NO SUCH WORD AS "FAIR"!

NOW *PROTECT YOURSELF!* MY ENERGY BEAM IS SMASHING THROUGH!

THIS IS *ONE* DAY I SHOULDA STOOD IN BED!

OKAY... TURN THAT BLAMED BEAM *OFF,* WILLYA?

ANGEL! BEAST! JOIN ICEMAN! TRY TO SUBDUE CYCLOPS!

WHUP!

THANKS, PROF! I COULD *USE* A LITTLE HELP!

IT IS NOT FOR YOUR SAKE ALONE, LAD! A FEW MINUTES OF ROUGH-HOUSE IS GOOD FOR *ALL* OF YOU...TO HELP YOU LET OFF STEAM!

THEN, SUDDENLY, MINUTES LATER, A SHARP COMMANDING THOUGHT PIERCES THE BRAIN OF EACH OF THE FOUR RAMPAGING YOUTHS...

ENOUGH! THE LESSON IS OVER! WE MUST TURN OUR ENERGIES TO *DIFFERENT* MATTERS! RETURN TO YOUR PLACES... *AT ONCE!!*

STUNNED BY THE FORCE AND EXPLOSIVE POWER OF *PROFESSOR XAVIER'S* MENTAL COMMAND, THE *X-MEN* RECOIL AND DRAW BACK, THEIR FRIENDLY FREE-FOR-ALL COMPLETELY FORGOTTEN!

WHEW! HE ALMOST BOWLED ME OVER WITH *THAT* ONE!

LET'S SIMMER DOWN AND SEE WHAT HAPPENS NEXT!

I CONGRATULATE YOU ALL! YOU HAVE MASTERED READING MY THOUGHTS PERFECTLY! AND NOW I SHALL RETURN TO NORMAL SPEECH COMMUNICATION!

YOU MAY BE INTERESTED TO LEARN THAT AT THIS VERY MOMENT I SENSE A TAXI APPROACHING OUR MAIN GATE! WITHIN THAT VEHICLE IS A NEW PUPIL....A MOST ATTRACTIVE *YOUNG LADY!*

7.

YOU'RE **RIGHT,** SIR! **WOW!** SHE'S A REAL LIVING DOLL!

A **REDHEAD!** LOOK AT THAT **FACE**...AND THE **REST** OF HER!

ALL OF A SUDDEN, I'M IN NO HURRY TO GRADUATE FROM THIS PLACE!

A GIRL...BIG DEAL! I'M GLAD I'M NOT A WOLF LIKE **YOU** GUYS!

I'M GLAD, TOO! WHO NEEDS THE EXTRA COMPETITION FROM ICEMAN?!

I WONDER WHAT SUPER-HUMAN POWERS **SHE** POSSESSES! SHE LOOKS NORMAL ENOUGH!

WELL, LET'S GO IN AND CHANGE, SO WE DON'T SCARE HER WHEN SHE FIRST SEES US!

COME IN, MY CHILD! I AM **PROFESSOR XAVIER!** I AM GLAD YOU RECEIVED MY MESSAGE!

IT ALL SEEMED SO STRANGE, PROFESSOR, AND SO... MYSTERIOUS! I WAS TO TELL NO ONE BUT MY PARENTS THAT I'M COMING HERE... AND YOU DIDN'T DESCRIBE THE COURSE OF STUDY!

WHAT KIND OF SCHOOL **IS** THIS, SIR? I HAVE A RIGHT TO KNOW!

I THINK YOU **ALREADY** SUSPECT, MISS GREY! YOU SEE, I CAN READ YOUR THOUGHTS QUITE CLEARLY... AND I KNOW ALL ABOUT YOUR UNUSUAL "TALENT"!

YOU, MISS GREY, LIKE THE OTHER FOUR STUDENTS AT THIS MOST EXCLUSIVE SCHOOL, ARE A **MUTANT!** YOU POSSESS AN **EXTRA** POWER.. ONE WHICH ORDINARY HUMANS DO **NOT!!** THAT IS WHY I CALL MY STUDENTS... **X-MEN,** FOR **EX**-TRA POWER!

AND HERE THEY ARE NOW! ALLOW ME TO PRESENT THEM TO YOU! FROM LEFT TO RIGHT WE HAVE **HANK McCOY,** KNOWN TO US AS **THE BEAST! BOBBY DRAKE,** NICKNAMED **ICEMAN! SLIM SUMMERS,** OUR HUMAN **CYCLOPS!** AND **WARREN WORTHINGTON THE THIRD,** WHO IS CALLED THE **ANGEL!** BOYS, THIS IS **MISS JEAN GREY!** SHE WILL BE KNOWN AS **MARVEL GIRL!**

WELCOME TO TO THE X-MEN, MISS GREY!

8.

HOW COME HE'S CALLING YOU *MARVEL GIRL*, MISS GREY? WHAT POWER DO YOU HAVE?

SHE HAS *ONE* VERY OBVIOUS POWER ...THE POWER TO MAKE A MAN'S *HEART* BEAT FASTER!

Y'KNOW SOMETHING, WARREN, IF I HAD *YOUR* LINE, I'D *SHOOT MYSELF!*

YOU'LL LEARN MORE ABOUT ME, BOYS, IN TIME!

WELL, NO TIME LIKE THE PRESENT! C'MON, SLIM, BRING THE LITTLE LADY A CHAIR!

HANK, I'D BRING HER THE WHOLE ROOM OF FURNITURE IF SHE ASKED ME!

THAT'S REALLY NOT NECESSARY, SLIM!

TH..THE CHAIR! IT SLID OUT OF MY HANDS!

YIIII!! HOLY SMOKE! WHAT'S GOIN' *ON?!!*

DON'T BE ALARMED, BOYS! I JUST THOUGHT I'D SAVE YOU THE TROUBLE!

ZZIP!

NOW, THEN, PROFESSOR, I BELIEVE WE CAN CONTINUE OUR INTERVIEW! AS YOU WERE SAYING...

I DON'T *GET* IT, SIR! WHAT HAPPENED TO THAT MOVING CHAIR??

PERHAPS YOU'D BETTER DEMONSTRATE A BIT *MORE,* JEAN!

VERY WELL, MY LIFE I'VE HAD TO *CONCEAL* THIS POWER OF MINE ...

NOW, I MUST ADMIT IT'S A PLEASURE TO BE ABLE TO PRACTICE *TELEKINESIS* OPENLY, WITHOUT FEAR OF BEING DISCOVERED! OBSERVE THAT BOOK!

BY THE POWER OF THOUGHT, I AM ABLE TO MOVE OBJECTS AT WILL!

BUT IT GETS BORING AFTER A WHILE, SO I'LL RETURN THE BOOK ...LIKE THIS!

9.

THANK YOU, JEAN! AND NOW LET ME TELL YOU MORE ABOUT MY SCHOOL...

I WAS BORN OF PARENTS WHO HAD WORKED ON THE FIRST A-BOMB PROJECT! LIKE YOURSELVES, I AM A *MUTANT*... POSSIBLY THE *FIRST* SUCH MUTANT! I HAVE THE POWER TO READ MINDS, AND TO PROJECT MY OWN THOUGHTS INTO THE BRAINS OF OTHERS!

BUT, WHEN I WAS YOUNG, NORMAL PEOPLE FEARED ME, DISTRUSTED ME! I REALIZED THE HUMAN RACE IS NOT YET READY TO *ACCEPT* THOSE WITH EXTRA POWERS! SO I DECIDED TO BUILD A HAVEN... A SCHOOL FOR *X-MEN!*

HERE WE STAY, UNSUSPECTED BY NORMAL HUMANS, AS WE LEARN TO USE OUR POWERS FOR THE BENEFIT OF MANKIND... TO HELP THOSE WHO WOULD DISTRUST US IF THEY KNEW OF OUR EXISTENCE!

DUE TO A CHILDHOOD ACCIDENT, I MYSELF MUST REMAIN IN THIS CHAIR, BUT THROUGH A MASTER CONTROL PANEL I HAVE MANY DEVICES AT MY COMMAND... AND THROUGH MY *MIND*, I AM ALWAYS IN TOUCH WITH MY X-MEN!

AND NOW, I LEAVE YOU TO GET TO KNOW EACH OTHER BETTER!

LET ME BE THE FIRST TO WELCOME YOU TO THE X-MEN, BEAUTIFUL! MMMMM!

OH!

HANK! TAKE YOUR PAWS OFF HER!

FOR THE LUVVA PETE!

OH, *BOY!* WHAT A *GAL!* I HOPE SHE KEEPS THAT BIG APE UP THERE *FOREVER!*

DON'T WORRY, WARREN! I'M NOT EXACTLY *HELP-LESS*, AS YOU CAN SEE!

HEY, C'MON! HAVE A HEART! I WAS ONLY TRYING TO BE *FRIENDLY!*

A FELLA COULD GET *DIZZY* UP HERE! LEMME DOWN, HUH? THIS IS EMBARRASSING!

VERY WELL, I'LL LET YOU DOWN!

THERE! YOU'RE DOWN!

WHUMP!

OOOFF!!

10.

I HOPE I WASN'T TOO ROUGH ON THE POOR DEAR!

NOT AT ALL, JEAN! WE DON'T USE KID GLOVES HERE! WE *HAVE* TO MAKE OUR TRAINING AS ROUGH AS POSSIBLE, TO PREPARE OUR-SELVES FOR OUR MISSION IN THE OUTSIDE WORLD!

THAT'S WHAT I'VE WANTED TO ASK! JUST WHAT EXACTLY *IS* OUR REAL MISSION, SIR?

JEAN, THERE ARE MANY MUTANTS WALK-ING THE EARTH... AND *MORE* ARE BORN EACH YEAR!

NOT *ALL* OF THEM WANT TO *HELP* MANKIND!... SOME *HATE* THE HUMAN RACE, AND WISH TO *DESTROY* IT! SOME FEEL THAT THE MUTANTS SHOULD BE THE REAL RULERS OF EARTH! IT IS OUR JOB TO PROTECT MANKIND FROM THOSE... FROM THE *EVIL MUTANTS!*

AT THAT VERY MOMENT, JUST SUCH A MUTANT PREPARES TO *STRIKE*... IN A SECRET LABORA-TORY NEAR CAPE CITADEL!

THE MOMENT IS AT HAND!

ALL MY MONTHS OF PREPARATION AND PLANNING SHALL NOW PAY OFF!

THE HUMAN RACE NO LONGER DESERVES DOMINION OVER THE PLANET EARTH! THE DAY OF THE *MUTANTS* IS UPON US!

THE FIRST PHASE OF MY PLAN SHALL BE TO SHOW MY POWER...TO MAKE HOMO SAPIENS BOW TO HOMO *SUPERIOR!*

THE MIGHTIEST ROCKET OF ALL IS ABOUT TO BE LAUNCHED! USING MAXIMUM SECURITY PRECAUTIONS, THE GOVERNMENT FEELS *NOTHING* CAN PREVENT ITS SUCCESSFUL FLIGHT!

BUT HERE, MILES FROM THE LAUNCH-ING SITE, I, THE MIRACULOUS *MAGNETO,* ALONE SHALL MAKE A MOCKERY OF THEIR GREATEST EFFORT!

11.

AHHH! I CAN FEEL THE IRRESISTABLE WAVES OF PURE MAGNETIC ENERGY SURGING FROM ME! NOW, BY EXERTING EVERY IOTA OF POWER, I CAN *DIRECT* THAT ENERGY UPWARD... UPWARD...

...UNTIL IT STRIKES THE SPEEDING MISSILE, CAUSING IT TO CHANGE DIRECTION...TO FALTER...TO LOSE ALTITUDE!

...TO BE COMPLETELY, IRREVOCABLY *DESTROYED.!!*

GENERAL, EVERY PHASE OF THE LAUNCHING WAS *A-OKAY!* THERE CAN ONLY BE *ONE* EXPLANATION... THE BIRD WAS *TAMPERED WITH!*

BUT *HOW?* EVEN A *MICROBE* COULDN'T HAVE PENETRATED OUR TOP SECRET SECURITY MEASURES!

THE NEXT DAY, THE SHOCKING NEWS IS TRANSMITTED TO A STARTLED PUBLIC...

INCREDIBLE! IT'S ALMOST AS THOUGH A DESTRUCTIVE *GHOST* IS RUNNING AMOK AT THE CAPE!

EXTRA! EXTRA! ANOTHER MISSILE *FAILS!* EXTRA!

DAILY GLOBE FINAL

SIXTH TOP SECRET LAUNCHING FAILS AT SEA!

PHANTOM SABOTEUR STRIKES AGAIN!

BUT THE WORST IS YET TO COME! LATER THAT AFTERNOON, AT THE HEAVILY GUARDED FENCE SURROUNDING THE LAUNCHING SITE...

KEEP THAT GUN *STEADY!* WHY IS IT *QUIVERING* THAT WAY?

W-WE'RE NOT DOIN' IT, SIR! IT...IT'S MOVIN' BY *ITSELF.!!*

SUDDENLY, LIKE A LIVING THING, THE MACHINE GUN LEAPS INTO THE AIR, SPINS AROUND, AND BEGINS TO FIRE WILDLY IN ALL DIRECTIONS!

RUN FOR COVER !! THE GUN IS OUT OF CONTROL !!

12.

BUT, THE MACHINE GUN IS NOT THE *ONLY* THING THAT SUDDENLY, MADDENINGLY SEEM TO GO AMOK!

RUN! THE TANK IS MOVING BY *ITSELF!* GANGWAY!

IT..IT'S *IMPOSSIBLE!* AND YET---IT'S ACTING LIKE IT HAS A MIND OF ITS OWN! LIKE IT'S *TRYING* TO MENACE US!

SWISH!

CLANK!

CLANK!

WITHIN SECONDS, THE ENTIRE INSTALLATION IS ALARMED, AS EMERGENCY MEASURES ARE SWIFTLY BROUGHT INTO PLAY! AND THEN...

SOUND THE ALARM! *CONDITION RED!* ALERT THE PENTAGON!

GENERAL! *LOOK!* ABOVE US...IN THE SKY!

APPEARING AS THOUGH BY MAGIC, OVER THE HEADS OF THE ASTONISHED TROOPS, HUGE LETTERS TAKE SHAPE...COMPOSED OF THE DUST PARTICLES FROM THE AIR ITSELF, SKILLFULLY MAGNETIZED INTO A MESSAGE BY THE UNSEEN MUTANT!

SURRENDER THE BASE OR I'LL TAKE IT BY FORCE!

Magneto

MAGNETO? WHO... *WHAT* IS MAGNETO??

GENERAL, WHAT DOES IT *MEAN?* IS SOMEONE PLAYING A GRIM *PRANK?*

YOU SAW THAT MACHINE GUN... THAT TANK... RAMPAGING OUT OF CONTROL! THIS IS *NO JOKE,* COLONEL!

THEY ARE STARTLED! *GOOD!* THE ELEMENT OF SURPRISE IS IN MY FAVOR!

BUT THEY'RE MAKING NO MOVE TO SURRENDER! PERHAPS THEY NEED *ANOTHER* DEMONSTRATION OF MY POWER!

I'LL DIRECT MY MAGNETIC IMPULSES INTO THIS ENERGIZER, TO INCREASE THEIR POWER, AND THEN I'LL LEAVE THE HELPLESS HOMO SAPIENS WITH NO ROOM FOR DOUBT!

13.

AN INSTANT LATER, INVISIBLE WAVES OF PURE, POWERFUL MAGNETIC ENERGY FLOW IRRESISTIBLY INTO AN UNDER-GROUND SILO WHERE ONE OF DEMOCRACY'S SILENT SENTINELS WAIT, AT THE READY!

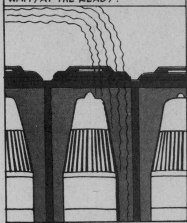

AND THEN, MANIPULATED BY A SINISTER INTELLIGENCE, MANY HUNDREDS OF YARDS AWAY, THE MAGNETIC FORCE LIFTS THE SILO HEAD, ACTIVATING THE MIGHTY MISSILE!!

DEMONSTRATING A POWER WHICH THE HUMAN BRAIN IS ALMOST UNABLE TO COMPREHEND, MAGNETO CAUSES THE GRIM ROCKET TO FALL INTO THE SEA MANY MILES FROM SHORE, NEXT TO AN UNMANNED TARGET SHIP!

BUT STILL, THE THOUGHT OF SURRENDER NEVER CROSSES THE MINDS OF THE FIGHTING-MAD BASE PERSONNEL!

SERGEANT! ORDER THE GUARD DOUBLED AT EVERY MISSILE CONTROL CENTER! ANY ROCKET DEEMED A MENACE IS TO BE DESTROYED INSTANTLY!

SOME POWER BEYOND OUR UNDERSTANDING IS AFFECTING OUR WEAPONS! WE MUST FIND THIS MAGNETO!

GENERAL, LOOK! THAT COMMOTION AT THE MAIN GATE! IT SEEMS THAT HE HAS FOUND US FIRST!

HOLD IT, MAC! IF YOU'RE LOOKIN' FOR A MASQUERADE PARTY, YOU'VE COME TO THE WRONG PLACE! BEAT IT!

WELL SAID, GUARD! WHAT A PITY YOU HAVE NO POWER TO BACK UP SUCH IMPRESSIVE WORDS! YOUR PUNY WEAPONS CANNOT STOP ME!

THEY CAN'T, EH? ONE LITTLE BURST OVER YOUR HEAD WILL SURELY CHANGE YOUR MIND!

HEY! WHA— WHAT GIVES? THE GUN WON'T FIRE! THE TRIGGER SEEMS LOCKED IN PLACE!

I CAN'T EVEN LIFT MY GUN! FEELS LIKE IT WEIGHS A TON!

14.

NOW I'LL MERELY ALTER MY MAGNETIC WAVES FROM POSITIVE TO NEGATIVE, SO THAT THEY WILL REPEL ANYTHING THAT COMES WITHIN RANGE! NOTHING CAN TOUCH ME AS I WALK TO MY OBJECTIVE!

WE CAN'T STOP HIM! CALL FOR RE-INFORCEMENTS!

I'M 'WAY AHEAD OF YA, PAL!

BUT, THE ADDITIONAL REINFORCEMENTS ARE EQUALLY POWERLESS TO STOP THE ONE-MAN INVASION OF THE STRATEGIC BASE!

IT..IT'S LIKE HE'S GOT AN INVISIBLE BARRIER 'ROUND HIM, HURLING US AWAY!

THERE! BY SIMPLY NARROWING MY MAGNETIC WAVES ALL AROUND THE LESSER HUMANS, I CAN KEEP THEM CONFINED TO THAT AREA UNTIL I REACH THEIR OFFICER-IN-COMMAND!

AND FINALLY...

HOLD IT, MEN! ALL RIGHT, WHO-EVER YOU ARE...IF YOU'VE SOMETHING TO SAY, YOU'VE GOT SIXTY SECONDS TO SAY IT!

WRONG, GENERAL! I HAVE ALL THE TIME IN THE WORLD! AND NOW, I, THE MIRACULOUS MAGNETO, CLAIM THIS ENTIRE INSTAL-LATION...IN THE NAME OF HOMO SUPERIOR!!

THAT DOES IT! TAKE HIM, MEN! WE'LL SHOW HIM THAT...

WHA...WHAT'S THAT?? WE CAN'T MOVE OUT OF THIS SMALL AREA! IT'S LIKE BEING ENCIRCLED BY AN INVISIBLE, LIVING FENCE!

THAT "LIVING FENCE" AS YOU CALL IT, IS THE SYMBOL OF MY GREAT POWER! IT IS A MIGHTY SHIELD OF MAGNETIC ENERGY!

AND SO I HAVE NOW ACCOMPLISHED MY FIRST OBJECTIVE! GENTLEMEN, CAPE CITADEL IS MINE!

15.

MEANWHILE, IN A DORMITORY ROOM AT THE WORLD'S MOST EXCLUSIVE PRIVATE SCHOOL, JEAN GREY IS ABSORBED WITH HER REFLECTION IN THE FULL-LENGTH MIRROR... THE REFLECTION WHICH REVEALS THE NEW *MARVEL GIRL!*

MMM, WHOEVER DESIGNED THIS UNIFORM COULD HAVE GIVEN CHRISTIAN DIOR A RUN FOR HIS MONEY!

WHERE DID THE NEW DOLL GO? OH... *THERE* SHE IS!

WOWEE! LOOKS LIKE SHE WAS *POURED* INTO THAT UNIFORM!

YOU AGAIN! HONESTLY! CAN'T A GIRL HAVE ANY PRIVACY AROUND HERE?

EASY, GORGEOUS! WE WERE JUST PASSIN' BY! DON'T GO GETTIN' 'MAD!

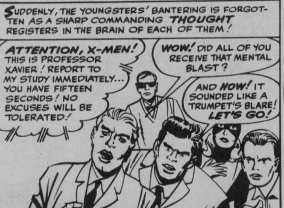

SUDDENLY, THE YOUNGSTERS' BANTERING IS FORGOTTEN AS A SHARP COMMANDING *THOUGHT* REGISTERS IN THE BRAIN OF EACH OF THEM!

ATTENTION, X-MEN! THIS IS PROFESSOR XAVIER! REPORT TO MY STUDY IMMEDIATELY... YOU HAVE FIFTEEN SECONDS! NO EXCUSES WILL BE TOLERATED!

WOW! DID ALL OF YOU RECEIVE THAT MENTAL BLAST?

AND *HOW!* IT SOUNDED LIKE A TRUMPET'S BLARE! *LET'S GO!*

EXACTLY FIFTEEN SECONDS LATER...

I COMMEND YOU FOR YOUR PUNCTUALITY!

YOU'RE SPEAKING ALOUD! THAT MEANS IT'S IMPORTANT!

I HAVE JUST HEARD A BULLETIN ON THE RADIO WHICH CONCERNS YOU!

I NEVER SAW THE PROFESSOR LIKE THIS BEFORE ...SO GRIM, SO INTENSE!

A CRISIS HAS OCCURRED AT CAPE CITADEL WHICH LEADS ME TO BELIEVE THE FIRST OF THE EVIL MUTANTS HAS MADE HIS APPEARANCE! THIS WILL BE YOUR BAPTISM OF FIRE! YOU ARE TO GO TO THE CAPE...AND DEFEAT HIM!

YAYBO!! ACTION AT LAST! GANGWAY!

CAPE CITADEL! WHATEVER THE MENACE IS, IT MUST INVOLVE OUR MISSILES!

WONDER WHO THE MUTANT BADDIE IS?

HAH! I CAN GET READY FASTER THAN THE REST OF YOU! ALL I HAVETA DO IS ICE UP AND PUT ON MY BOOTS!

16

AS FOR *ME*, IT'LL BE A PLEASURE TO GET OUT OF THIS HARNESS I HAVE TO WEAR!

HAVING A PAIR OF WINGS CAN BE MORE TROUBLE THAN YOU'D GUESS!

THESE RESTRAINING BELTS OF MINE KEEP MY WINGS FROM BULGING UNDER MY SUIT, BUT AFTER A WHILE THEY FEEL LIKE I'M WEARING A *STRAIT-JACKET!*

AHHH! THAT'S MORE LIKE IT! NOW I FEEL LIKE MYSELF AGAIN! NOW THE *ANGEL* IS READY TO SPREAD HIS WINGS ...AND *FLY!*

BUT THE TIME HAS NOT YET COME FOR THE ANGEL TO FLY! INSTEAD, THE BAND OF SUPER-HUMAN TEEN-AGERS ARE *DRIVEN* TO THE AIRPORT IN PROFESSOR XAVIER'S SPECIALLY-BUILT ROLLS ROYCE, WITH ITS DARK-TINTED WINDOWS!

BOY! IT MUSTA TAKEN A HEAP OF GREEN STAMPS TO BY A CHARIOT LIKE THIS!

NO JOKING, PLEASE! CONCENTRATE ON YOUR MISSION! REVIEW YOUR POWERS! YOUR FOE IS CERTAIN TO BE HIGHLY DANGEROUS!

MINUTES LATER, IN THE PROFESSOR'S REMOTE-CONTROL PRIVATE JET, THE *X-MEN* AND *MARVEL GIRL* ARE WINGING TOWARDS *CAPE CITADEL* AT NEARLY THE SPEED OF SOUND!

YOU MEAN THE PROFESSOR IS GUIDING THIS PLANE FROM THE GROUND... BY *THOUGHT IMPULSES?!* IT'S *UN-BELIEVABLE!*

LOOK, DOLL... WHEN YOU JOIN THE *X-MEN*, YOU REALIZE *NOTHING'S* UN-BELIEVABLE!

A SHORT TIME LATER, AT THE CAPE...

CEASE FIRING! IT'S USELESS! WE HAVEN'T ANYTHING IN OUR ARSENAL THAT'LL PENETRATE *MAGNETO'S* MAGNETIC FORCE FIELD!

TO ALL INTENTS AND PURPOSES, HE'S IN FULL CONTROL OF THE INSTALLATION, WHILE WE'RE ON THE OUTSIDE, LOOKING IN!

WITH DUE RESPECT, GENERAL, I REPRESENT THE *X-MEN!* PERHAPS *WE* CAN HELP!

X-MEN?! WHAT THE..?!

17.

19.

AND NOW, I'LL SWITCH TO *MAXIMUM POWER!* I CAN ONLY MAINTAIN THIS PRESSURE FOR A FEW SECONDS, BUT... *AHH!* I *DID* IT!

BEHIND THE FORCE FIELD, THE NATURAL ENERGY FEED - BACK WEAKENS THE STARTLED *MAGNETO!*

SOME POWER IS ATTACKING ME! SOME POWER AS SUPER - HUMAN AS MY *OWN!*

I WAS STAGGERED BECAUSE I WAS UN- PREPARED FOR ANY SUCH ONSLAUGHT! BUT NOW THAT I'M FOREWARNED, I CAN DEFEAT *ANY* FOE...NO MATTER *HOW* SUPER- HUMAN HE MAY BE!

BUT MAGNETO IS SOON TO LEARN THAT HE HAS MORE THAN ONE FOE TO CONTEND WITH! HE HAS THE FIGHTING BAND OF *X-MEN!*

CYCLOPS ALMOST KNOCKED HIM- SELF OUT, BUT HE GOT US *IN* HERE! NOW LET'S PROVE WE CAN CARRY THE BALL!

LOOK SHARP, *X-MEN!* YOU ARE FACING A DANGER- OUS ENEMY!

AHHH! NOW I SEE MY ANTAGONISTS! FIVE COSTUMED YOUTHS! SURELY ALL THEIR POWERS PUT TOGETHER CAN BE NO MATCH FOR *MINE!*

BUT I WILL LET THE BASE'S *HUNTER MISSILES* DO MY FIGHTING FOR ME! THEY WILL HUNT THE FIVE DOWN, ATTRACTED BY THEIR BODY HEAT!

INTERCEPTOR MISSILES

FIRE

AND SO, AT THE PRESS OF A BUTTON, *MAGNETO* UNLEASHES FIVE OF THE MOST SOPHISTICATED WEAPONS EVER CREATED... ALL ZEROED IN ON THE *X-MEN!*

19.

THE FIRST TARGET FOR THE MERCILESS MISSILES IS THE *ANGEL*, FLYING CLOSEST TO THEM!

GOT TO *DODGE* THEM, SOMEHOW!

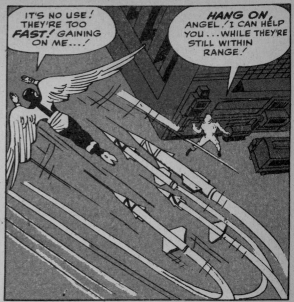

IT'S NO USE! THEY'RE TOO *FAST!* GAINING ON ME....!

HANG ON, ANGEL! I CAN HELP YOU...WHILE THEY'RE STILL WITHIN RANGE!

THESE *ICE GRENADES* MUSTN'T MISS! THEY'RE THE ANGEL'S ONLY CHANCE!

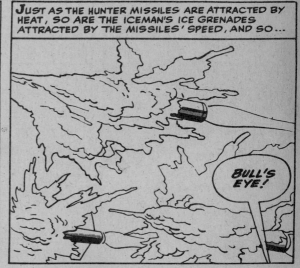

JUST AS THE HUNTER MISSILES ARE ATTRACTED BY HEAT, SO ARE THE ICEMAN'S ICE GRENADES ATTRACTED BY THE MISSILES' SPEED, AND SO...

BULL'S EYE!

IT *WORKED!* THE ICE COVERED THEIR NOSES, PREVENTING 'EM FROM EXPLODING! NOW, WITH THEIR GUIDANCE SYSTEMS KNOCKED OUT, THEY'VE GOT TO DROP TO THE GROUND!

BUT THERE IS STILL *ONE* MISSILE WHICH WAS NOT HIT...TOO FAR AWAY NOW FOR THE ICEMAN TO ATTACK!

CAN'T KEEP DODGING IT MUCH LONGER!

20.

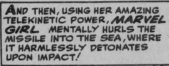

21

THE HEAT IS SO INTENSE THAT EVEN *I* CANNOT GET CLOSE TO IT! I MUST WALK CAREFULLY AROUND IT!

THAT *BEAM*... FROM BENEATH THE GROUND!! WHAT...WHAT DOES IT *MEAN?*

IT MEANS YOUR *FINISH,* MAGNETO!

CYCLOPS CREATED A TUNNEL FOR US UNDER THE BLAST WITH HIS ENERGY BEAM... SAVING US FROM THE IMPACT! AND *NOW..*

YOU HAVEN'T DEFEATED ME *YET!* I CAN STILL ESCAPE YOU, FLYING BY MEANS OF MAGNETIC REPULSION!

UGH! HE CREATED ANOTHER MAGNETIC FORCE FIELD! CAN'T FLY THROUGH!

DON'T WORRY, ANGEL! WE'LL BREACH IT IN NO TIME!

AND BREACH IT THEY DO! BUT BY THAT TIME ...

HE'S *GONE!* BUT WHERE...?

A MUTANT WITH *HIS* POWERS? HE COULD BE *ANY-WHERE!* BUT AT LEAST WE'VE BEATEN HIM FOR *NOW!*

YOUR BASE IS OPERATIONAL AGAIN, GENERAL! MAGNETO IS GONE!

UNCANNY! YOUR FIFTEEN MINUTES ARE NOT YET UP!

YOU CALL YOURSELVES THE *X-MEN!* I WILL NOT ASK YOU TO REVEAL YOUR TRUE IDENTITIES, BUT I PROMISE YOU THAT BEFORE THIS DAY IS OVER, THE NAME *X-MEN* WILL BE THE MOST HONORED IN MY COMMAND!

THANK YOU, SIR! AND SHOULD AMERICA'S SECURITY EVER AGAIN BE THREATENED, THE X-MEN WILL BE BACK!

WELL DONE, STUDENTS! YOU HAVE JUSTIFIED ALL OUR LONG HOURS OF TRAINING...ALL OUR SACRIFICES...ALL OUR DREAMS! AND NOW, RETURN TO ME, MY *X-MEN!*

23.

YOU HAVE JUST FINISHED THE NEWEST, MOST UNUSUAL TALE IN THE ANNALS OF MODERN MAGAZINES! BUT THE BEST IS YET TO COME! FOR FANTASY AT ITS GREATEST, DON'T MISS ISSUE #2 OF *X-MEN,* THE STRANGEST SUPER-HEROES OF ALL!

THE STRANGEST SUPER-HEROES OF ALL!

2 NOV.

IND.

APPROVED BY THE COMICS CODE AUTHORITY

the X-MEN

MARVEL COMICS GROUP 12¢

IN THE SENSATIONAL FANTASTIC FOUR STYLE!

I'VE BEATEN THE X-MEN BEFORE AND I SHALL DO IT AGAIN! BUT *THIS* TIME IT WILL BE... *FOREVER!!*

STAY BACK, ALL OF YOU! THOSE ARE THE ORDERS OF PROFESSOR X!!

THE X-MEN HAD TO FIND OUT...HOW DO YOU BEAT A MUTANT WHO IS..*UNBEATABLE?!!* A BOOK-LENGTH MARVEL CLASSIC: "NOTHING CAN STOP THE VANISHER!"...

2.

SORRY WE'RE *LATE*, SIR!

WE WERE DELAYED BY A...

I *KNOW!* I FOLLOWED YOUR PROGRESS *MENTALLY!* YOUR THOUGHTS WERE CLEAR TO ME! NO FURTHER EXPLANATIONS ARE NECESSARY!

MAY WE KNOW THE *REASON* FOR YOUR SUMMONS, SIR?

WHEN WILL YOU *LEARN*, ANGEL? HE'LL TELL US WHEN HE'S *READY!*

I AM READY *NOW!* ALL OF YOU, FACE THAT WALL! I SHALL PROJECT A SERIES OF MENTAL IMAGES FOR YOU!

WOW! WHO'S THE COSTUMED CLOWN? IS THIS A *GAG?*

SILENCE! NO TALKING!! NOT UNTIL I CONCLUDE THIS PRESENTATION!

YOU ARE LOOKING AT THE NEWEST MENACE TO HUMAN-KIND! HE CALLS HIMSELF *THE VANISHER!* I MENTALLY DETECTED HIS HOSTILE PRESENCE IN THE CITY EARLIER TODAY, AND I MONITORED HIS ACTIVITIES!

WELL, *WHOEVER* HE IS, WE'LL TAKE CARE OF HIM!

OOPS! SORRY, PROFESSOR! I FORGOT MYSELF!

"GIVE YOURSELF ONE DEMERIT, ICEMAN! NOW CONCENTRATE, MY X-MEN! I SHALL MENTALLY PROJECT THEIR *DIALOGUE* FOR YOU..."

BOY! WE GET ALL *KINDS* ON OUR BEAT! OKAY, BUDDY! WHY THE GET-UP??

THERE IS NO LAW AGAINST WEARING A COSTUME, AND YOU *KNOW* IT!!

NOW DIRECT ME TO THE METRO NATIONAL BANK! I INTEND TO ROB IT!

SURE, SURE! I KNOW... THERE'S NO LAW AGAINST HAVING *INTENTIONS*, EITHER! STEP RIGHT THIS WAY, ODDBALL!

5.

6.

AND *NOW*... NOW THAT YOU ARE *RELAXED,* AND OFF-*GUARD*...

QUICKLY! PRETEND THIS MISSILE IS THE *VANISHER!* MATCH ITS SPEED AND *CATCH* IT BEFORE IT ELUDES YOU!

SNNIK!

GOT TO CATCH IT! GOT TO!

CRAAAK!

I *FAILED!* IT...IT WAS TOO *FAST* FOR ME!

EXHAUSTED!! TOO GREAT A STRAIN...! CAN'T STAY ALOFT! ...MUST REST...

RETRIEVE THE ANGEL! BRING HIM TO ME! *INSTANTLY!*

HEART...BLOOD-PRESSURE... BOTH SATISFACTORY! BUT WE MUST BUILD UP YOUR RESISTANCE!

YES SIR!

THE ANGEL HAS HIGH POTENTIAL! WE MUST SEE THAT HE *ATTAINS* IT!

I'M YOUR BOY FOR HI-POTENTIAL, PROF! SAY, THAT SOUNDS LIKE A *BREAK-FAST* CEREAL!

VERY WELL, BEAST! I SHALL TEST *YOU* NEXT!

AW, I'M WISE TO THOSE OL' MECHANICAL HANDS! I CAN DODGE THEM *EASY!*

8.

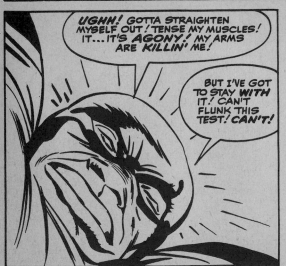

9.

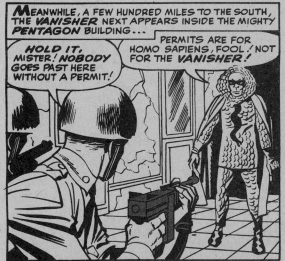

HAVEN'T YOU *GUESSED* YET?? AS A TRUE MUTANT...AS A MEMBER OF *HOMO SUPERIOR*, I HAVE THE ABILITY TO *TELEPORT MYSELF* TO ANY PLACE I CAN THINK OF...AT UNIMAGINABLE SPEED!

SO *THAT'S* HOW YOU VANISH...BY MENTALLY TRAVELING TO ANOTHER PLACE!

PREPOSTEROUS! PURE SCIENCE FICTION BALDERDASH! I DON'T BELIEVE A *WORD* OF IT!

THEN PERHAPS *THIS* WILL CHANGE YOUR MIND!

HE'S *GONE!*

AND HE'S SO SURE OF HIS POWERS THAT HE DIDN'T BOTHER TAKING THE PLANS *NOW!* HE PREFERS TO LET US *WORRY* ABOUT HIM FOR A FEW DAYS FIRST!

REMEMBER, IN A FEW DAYS THOSE DEFENSE PLANS SHALL BE *MINE!*

LATER, AFTER READING OF HIS INCREDIBLE EXPLOITS IN THE NEWSPAPERS, EVERY DENIZEN OF THE UNDERWORLD WHO ISN'T IN PRISON FLOCKS TO THE SIDE OF THE SEEMINGLY INVINCIBLE VANISHER!

NAME YOUR TERMS, VANISHER! WE'RE *WITH* YA!

SURE! WE'RE YOUR BOYS, PAL! YOU'RE THE BOSS!

HOORAY FOR THE VANISHER!

BACK, ALL OF YOU!

I HAVE AN ANNOUNCEMENT TO MAKE!

SHUDDUP, YOU GUYS!! THE VANISHER'S GONNA SAY SOMETHIN'!

IT IS ONLY *FITTING* THAT *HOMO SUPERIOR* SHOULD BE SERVED BY THE INFERIOR *HOMO SAPIENS!* THERE- FORE, I SHALL ALLOW YOU TO BECOME MY LACKEYS!

THREE CHEERS FOR THE *VANISHER!*

YEAH! WITH *HIM* ON OUR SIDE, WE'LL *NEVER* GO TO JAIL!

I HAVE ALREADY ANNOUNCED TO THE PENTAGON THAT I INTEND TO STEAL THE ARMY'S CONTINENTAL DEFENSE PLANS! I'LL GIVE THEM A WHILE LONGER TO MARVEL AT MY POWER, AND THEN...

BEFORE THEY KNOW IT, THE PLANS SHALL BE *MINE!* AND *THEN* I MAKE MY *NEXT* MOVE...THE MOST *DARING* MOVE IN THE HISTORY OF CRIME!!

11

12.

MINUTES, LATER, AFTER PROFESSOR X HAS RESTORED ORDER...

HOW'S *THIS* FOR AN EMERGENCY *GRAPPLE*?

FINE, BOBBY... BUT KEEP IT QUIET! THE PROF IS THINKING!

PROFESSOR X CALLING F.B.I. AGENT DUNCAN! DO YOU READ ME, AGENT DUNCAN?

AND IN THE NATION'S CAPITAL, AT F.B.I. HEAD-QUARTERS, SPECIAL AGENT FRED DUNCAN DONS A STRANGE-LOOKING SCALP DEVICE, GIVEN TO HIM BY THE AMAZING LEADER OF THE X-MEN!

IT'S EXACTLY FIVE MINUTES PAST THE HOUR, FRED...THE PRE-ARRANGED TIME! RECEIVING ANYTHING?

YES!! HIS THOUGHTS GROW CLEARER EACH TIME! THE MAN'S MENTAL PROWESS IS ALMOST UN-BELIEVABLE!

PLEASE RELATE THE LATEST DEVELOPMENTS CONCERNING THE VANISHER! YOUR PSIONIC HEAD-BAND WILL MAGNIFY YOUR BRAIN IMPULSES ENOUGH TO BE INTELLIGIBLE TO ME!

THE VANISHER HAS THREATENED TO STEAL OUR CONTINENTAL DEFENSE PLANS! WE ARE EXPECTING HIS ATTACK AT ANY MOMENT!

DEPARTMENT OF SPECIAL AFFAIRS

I SHALL CONTACT YOU LATER! OVER AND OUT!

I SUSPECTED THAT MIGHT BE HIS LIKELY NEXT MOVE!

ATTENTION, X-MEN! WE DEPART FOR *WASHINGTON, D.C.* WITHIN THE HOUR! REMAIN IN UNIFORM AND ASSEMBLE AT THE GARAGE WITHIN FIVE MINUTES! THAT IS ALL!

GUESS THAT MEANS WE TACKLE THE VANISHER! RIGHT, SIR?

WHAT CHANCE DOES HE HAVE AGAINST ALL OF *US*?

THIS IS *GREAT!* I'VE SOME NEW FLYING MANEUVERS I'M JUST ITCHING TO TRY OUT!

A SHORT TIME LATER, A McDONNELL XV-1 CONVERTIPLANE, WHICH HAS BEEN PUT AT THE DISPOSAL OF THE X-MEN BY THE DEPARTMENT OF SPECIAL AFFAIRS, TAKES OFF FOR THEIR ENCOUNTER WITH... *THE VANISHER!*

I FEEL LIKE A V.I.P. IN THIS SPECIAL MILITARY AIR TAXI! HOW ABOUT *YOU* GUYS?

WHADDYA *MEAN* YOU FEEL LIKE A V.I.P.? IF *WE* AREN'T IMPORTANT, WHO *IS*?!

I TRUST YOU YOUNGSTERS WILL *STILL* FEEL SO IMPORTANT *AFTER* YOU HAVE FOUGHT THE VANISHER!

13.

14.

15.

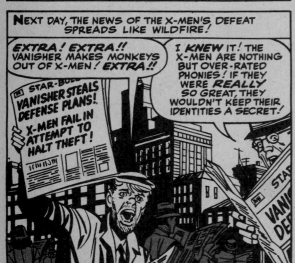

17.

"THIS IS A STROBE PROJECTION SHOWING THE VANISHER DIS-APPEARING! HIS DISAPPEARANCE WAS PHOTOGRAPHED AT A SPEED OF 20,000 FRAMES A SECOND!"

"NOTICE THAT EVEN WITH THIS SUPER-HIGH-SPEED CAMERA, IT IS ALMOST IMPOSSIBLE TO ANALYZE THE VANISHER'S ABILITY TO INSTANTLY TRANSPORT HIMSELF!"

"HIS SPEED IS SO UNBELIEVABLY FAST THAT IT DEFIES DESCRIPTION! THEREFORE, I HAVE CONCLUDED THAT THERE IS ONLY ONE WAY TO BEAT HIM! AND THIS IS MY PLAN..."

THE NEXT DAY, IN WASHINGTON, WHERE SIMILAR STROBE PHOTOS ARE BEING INTENTLY STUDIED, PROFESSOR X MAKES A HIGH PRIORITY CALL TO THE WHITE HOUSE, GIVING THE DETAILS OF HIS PROPOSED PLAN OF ACTION AGAINST THE VANISHER...

VERY WELL, SIR! I SHALL INFORM THE CHIEF EXECUTIVE OF YOUR CALL IMMEDIATELY! THANK YOU!

AND FINALLY, THE MOMENT OF DECISION ARRIVES! IN THE VERY CENTER OF THE NATION'S CAPITOL, THE X-MEN FIND WHAT THEY HAVE BEEN NERVOUSLY WAITING FOR...

LOOK! HE'S COMING NOW! IT'S THE VANISHER!

HE'S GOT A SMALL ARMY OF HOODS WITH HIM! YOU WOULDN'T THINK HE'D DARE!

THEY'LL BE NO PROBLEM FOR US TO HANDLE! IT'S THE VANISHER HIMSELF WE MUST BE WARY OF!

STAND FAST, X-MEN! REMEMBER OUR ORDERS!

I'LL GIVE YOU COSTUMED JUVENILES EXACTLY TEN SECONDS TO CLEAR OUT OF HERE, OR SUFFER THE CONSEQUENCES! MY BUSINESS DOES NOT CONCERN YOU!

I HAVE COME FOR MY TEN MILLION DOLLARS! THEY WILL NOT DARE TO REFUSE ME!

I DON'T LIKE IT! HOW COME THERE AIN'T ANY TROOPS OR GUARDS AROUND?

19.

AND THEN, SUDDENLY, SURPRISINGLY, UNEXPECTEDLY, ANOTHER FIGURE...ONE WHICH IS COMPLETELY UNKNOWN TO THE PUBLIC AT LARGE...

THE TIME IS *NOW*, MY X-MEN! ASSUME YOUR POSITIONS!

VANISHER, I GIVE YOU *ONE* CHANCE TO SURRENDER TO ME! OTHERWISE I SHALL HAVE TO COUNTER *YOUR* POWER WITH A FORCE WHICH IS FAR *GREATER*...FAR MORE *TERRIBLE!*

WHAT?? YOU?!! A HELPLESS HUMAN...ALONE AND DEFENSELESS, DARES TO THREATEN ONE WHO HAS DEFEATED THE *X-MEN??* LET ME *LAUGH* AT YOU...BEFORE YOU *PAY* FOR YOUR INSOLENCE!

LAUGH WHILE YOU *CAN*, EVIL ONE! FOR I AM *NOT* A HELPLESS HUMAN...BUT A *MUTANT*, EVEN AS *YOU!* AND YOU CANNOT EVEN *GUESS* THE EXTENT OF MY POWER...POWER WHICH IS EVEN *NOW* BEING DIRECTED *AGAINST* YOU!!

HIS EYES! HIS VOICE! WHAT IS IT THAT FILLS MY SOUL WITH DREAD? I MUST ESCAPE HIS PRESENCE! I MUST VANISH...BEFORE IT IS TOO LATE!!

WHA..WHAT HAS *HAPPENED* TO ME? I CANNOT CONTROL MY POWER!! *I CANNOT VANISH!!*

WAIT!! WHAT HAS BECOME OF ME?? WHAT AM I *DOING* HERE? WHO IS THIS MAN WHO FACES ME? TELL ME... PLEASE TELL ME... WHO AM *I??*

PLEASE...DO NOT HARM ME! I AM WEARY...SO WEARY! I MUST REST! I MUST THINK...HAVE TO LEARN WHO I AM... *WHAT* I AM??

I DON'T *GET* IT! ONE MINUTE HE WAS THREATENING US *ALL*...AND NOW.. HE'S LIKE A HELPLESS CHILD!

HE WILL TROUBLE US NO MORE!

BUT THEN, SENSING THAT SOME TERRIBLE MISHAP HAS BEFALLEN THEIR LEADER, HIS ARMED BAND OF CRIMINALS COME TOWARD THE X-MEN, THIRSTING FOR REVENGE!

IF THEY HARMED THE VANISHER, THEN WE LOST OUR MEAL TICKET!

GET 'EM!!

20.

NEXT ISSUE: THE X-MEN FACE THE GREATEST DANGER OF ALL, WHEN...BUT SEE FOR YOURSELF IN X-MEN #3...YOU'LL BE GLAD YOU DID!

SCOTT, YOU ARE PROBABLY THE MOST POWERFUL OF ALL MY X-MEN! YET, YOU ALWAYS SEEM SO GRIM-- SO UNSMILING! NOT LIKE THE OTHERS! THIS DISTRESSES ME!

SORRY, SIR! IT'S JUST THAT I WORRY ABOUT THE AWESOME POWER IN MY EYES! IF I SHOULD EVER FORGET TO SHIELD THEM, *ANYTHING* MIGHT HAPPEN! SOMETIMES I WISH I WERE *NOT* CYCLOPS!

SCOTT SUMMERS! DON'T EVER LET ME HEAR YOU SAY THAT AGAIN!

I DON'T KNOW ABOUT OL' GLOOMY-FACE, BUT *I'M* GLAD I'M THE *ICEMAN!* YES SIREE!

LOOK *OUT!* YOU *KNOW* I'M ALLERGIC TO SAWDUST!

LITTLE MAN, DID ANYONE EVER TELL YOU THAT YOU ARE A FEATHER-BRAINED FATHEAD? IF IT WEREN'T FOR THE FACT THAT I ABHOR VIOLENCE...

SORRY, BEAST, YOU'RE WASTIN' YOUR TIME! FLATTERY WILL GET YOU NOWHERE!

THAT MUSCLE-BOUND BOOK-WORM IS TOO *NICE* TO YOU, SHORT STUFF! THIS IS WHAT *I'D* DO IF YOU TRIED TO BUG *ME!*

HEY! WATCH IT! I JUST SHINED MY LITTLE BLACK BOOTIES!

THOSE WHACKY WINGS OF YOURS DON'T WORRY *ME,* ANGEL!

NOT WHEN I CAN FREEZE 'EM AGAINST THE WALL AS EASY AS PIE! *ESKIMO* PIE, THAT IS!

YOU REPULSIVE RUNT! WHEN I GET THROUGH WITH YOU, THERE WON'T BE ENOUGH OF YOU LEFT TO FILL UP ONE RUSTY ICE CUBE TRAY!

YOU TALK MIGHTY BIG, WARREN WORTHINGTON, THE THIRD... BUT I NOTICE YOU CAN'T THAW BOBBY'S ICE TRAP WITHOUT A LITTLE HELP!

STAY *OUT* OF THIS, CYCLOPS! IT'S BETWEEN THAT FROZEN J.D. AND *ME!*

2

BUT SUDDENLY, THE HIGH-SPIRITED TEEN-AGERS' HORSE PLAY IS INTERRUPTED BY A PIERCING TELEPATHIC COMMAND FROM PROFESSOR X!

FREE TIME IS *OVER!* RESUME YOUR PLACES! THE TRAINING PERIOD WILL CONTINUE!

IT'S *MARVEL GIRL'S* TURN NOW! ARE YOU READY, JEAN?

A MOMENT LATER...

IT IS TIME FOR YOUR *DEXTERITY* TEST, JEAN! HOLD THAT BLOCK OF WOOD MOTIONLESS IN THE AIR! GOOD! GOOD!

AND NOW, SEE HOW QUICKLY YOU CAN FIT IT THROUGH THE VARIOUS FORMS ON THE PRACTICE RACK! *GO!*

ISN'T THIS RATHER *SIMPLE* FOR ONE WITH MY ABILITY, PROFESSOR?

YOU KNOW THE RULES, GIRL! *NO TALKING* DURING TESTING PERIOD!

OH-- SORRY, SIR!

I *KNOW* THE EXTENT OF YOUR TELEKINESIS POWER AS WELL AS YOU, JEAN! BUT IT IS NOT YOUR *POWER* WE ARE TESTING TODAY...

...IT IS HOW SKILLFULLY AND RAPIDLY YOU CAN *USE* IT! *SEVEN SECONDS!* GOOD! A MARKED IMPROVEMENT!

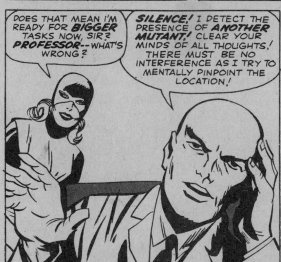

DOES THAT MEAN I'M READY FOR *BIGGER* TASKS NOW, SIR? PROFESSOR-- WHAT'S WRONG?

SILENCE! I DETECT THE PRESENCE OF *ANOTHER MUTANT!* CLEAR YOUR MINDS OF ALL THOUGHTS! THERE MUST BE NO INTERFERENCE AS I TRY TO MENTALLY PINPOINT THE LOCATION!

THEN, THERE IN THE SILENT CHAMBER, THE MOST GIFTED OF ALL X-MEN SENDS HIS UNCANNY THOUGHT PROBE OUT OVER THE COUNTRYSIDE, BLANKETING THE AREA WITH INVISIBLE TELEPATHIC EYES!

3

AND, MINUTES LATER...
DO WE GO GET HIM, SIR? WHERE IS HE?

I HOPE IT'S A FEMALE! ONE JUST LIKE MARVEL GIRL! MMMM BOY!

SLOW DOWN, ICEMAN! THE PROFESSOR HASN'T SAID IT IS A "HE" YET!

INTO YOUR STREET CLOTHES-- ALL OF YOU! THERE IS WORK TO BE DONE!

AND SO...
WHY THE RUSH, HANK? HE DIDN'T SAY IT WAS AN EMERGENCY!

ON THE CONTRARY, W.W.! FIRST ONE TO REPORT ESCORTS JEAN! AND THAT MEANS HANK McCOY!

THE HECK IT DOES! THIS IS MARVEL GIRL'S LUCKY DAY! I'M TEAMIN' UP WITH HER THIS TIME! GANG-WAY, SLOWPOKES!

COME BACK HERE, YOU FROST-BITTEN FLEA! SHE DESERVES A MAN, NOT A REFUGEE FROM A DIAPER FACTORY!

THEY ALL WANT TO TEAM UP WITH JEAN GREY, AS USUAL!

OF ALL THE GIRLS I'VE EVER MET, SHE IS THE ONE I'D GIVE MY HEART TO-- BUT I DON'T DARE! NOT WHILE I POSSESS MY DREAD POWER!

TOO BAD YOUR SPEED DOESN'T MATCH YOUR ENTHUSIASM, BOBBY BOY!

WHERE'D YOU COME FROM?!

BUT, UPON REACHING THE CHAMBER, THE X-MEN SUDDENLY STOP IN THEIR TRACKS, RESPECTFULLY, AS THEY SEE...

BE CAREFUL, MY DEAR! I CANNOT TELL WHAT POWERS THIS MUTANT MAY POSSESS! HE MAY BE A DANGER TO YOU!

DON'T WORRY, SIR! REMEMBER HOW WELL YOU'VE TRAINED US!

"DON'T WORRY"! AS THOUGH I COULD HELP WORRYING ABOUT THE ONE I LOVE! BUT I CAN NEVER TELL HER! I HAVE NO RIGHT! NOT WHILE I'M THE LEADER OF THE X-MEN, AND CONFINED TO THIS WHEEL-CHAIR!

SCOTT, DON'T LOOK SO GRIM! COME ON, YOU AND I WILL SEARCH FOR THE MUTANT TOGETHER!

WHAT? YOU WANNA GO WITH OL' PRUNE FACE INSTEAD OF LOVEABLE ME?

4

RELAX, YOU SECOND-RATERS! IT'S *MY* TURN NOW! THE *ANGEL* WILL ACCOMPANY HER IN OUR SEARCH FOR THE MUTANT!

THAT ARROGANT BRAGGART! ONE OF THESE DAYS HE'LL GO TOO FAR!

WARREN WORTHINGTON THE THIRD!! MUST YOU BE SUCH A SHOW-OFF?

HEY, HANK-- ARE WE GONNA LET THAT HIGH-FLYIN' HEEL GET *AWAY* WITH THAT?

WE DON'T SEEM TO HAVE ANY ALTERNATIVE, MY FROSTY FRIEND!

YOU CONCEITED CLOWN! I--I HOPE YOU GET YOUR PIN-FEATHERS CAUGHT IN A WRINGER!

I REALLY DON'T THINK YOU'RE WISE TO ANTAGONIZE THE OTHER X-MEN THE WAY YOU DO, WARREN!

DON'T LOSE ANY SLEEP OVER IT, BEAUTIFUL! REMEMBER, I'M THE *ANGEL!* THOSE EARTH-BOUND CHARACTERS CAN'T BOTHER *ME!* THEY'RE NOT IN MY CLASS!

SOME NERVE! HIM STEALIN' JEAN RIGHT OUT FROM UNDER OUR NOSES!

LET'S *FACE* IT, LITTLE FRIENDS! THE ANGEL *IS* THE GLAMOR BOY OF OUR SELECT LITTLE GROUP!

TRUE ENOUGH, HANK! BUT ONE DAY HE'LL REALIZE THIS IS NO *GAME* WE'RE PLAYING, BUT A GRIM, LIFE-AND-DEATH STRUGGLE!

LATER, GUIDED MENTALLY BY PROFESSOR X, THE OTHER THREE X-MEN SEARCH THE CITY FOR THE NEW MUTANT WHOSE PRESENCE THEIR LEADER HAS DETECTED...

GOSH! LOOK AT THAT FELLA BURNING A PAPER JUST BY HOLDING HIS HAND OVER IT! HE MUST HAVE AN X-POWER, LIKE US!

WHAT *LUCK!* I FOUND THE NEW MUTANT FIRST CRACK OUT OF THE BOX!

NO, BOBBY, HE IS NOT THE ONE WE SEEK! KEEP SEARCHING!

AW, RATS! HE'S USING A MAGNIFYING GLASS TO BURN THE PAPER! I SHOULD HAVE *GUESSED!*

MEANTIME, HANK McCOY SEEMS TO MAKE A DISCOVERY...

THAT MAN IS STANDING ON AIR! I'VE *FOUND* THE MUTANT! HE MUST HAVE THE ABILITY TO DEFY GRAVITY!

KEEPING VIGIL TILL THE SUN SETS, THE DECEPTIVELY GENTLE "BEAST" CAUTIOUSLY WALKS UP THE SIDE OF THE TALL BUILDING...

GOOD THING IT'S TWILIGHT! NOBODY'S APT TO NOTICE ME IN THE GLOOM!

5

BUT, UPON REACHING THE FOURTH FLOOR, HANK FINDS...

FALSE ALARM! HE'S MERELY SETTING UP AN ADVERTISING DISPLAY, AND STANDING UPON THE TRANSPARENT GLASS SHIELD WHICH WILL PROTECT THE SIGN!

AND, WHAT OF SCOTT SUMMERS, THE X-MAN KNOWN AS CYCLOPS? AT A NEARBY CARNIVAL...

CAREFUL, LAD! THE MENTAL EMANATIONS ARE STRONGER NOW! THE MUTANT IS VERY NEAR YOU!

THAT FELLOW-- HITTING THE TARGETS WITHOUT LOOKING! PERHAPS HE IS THE ONE WITH AN X-POWER --AN EXTRA POWER!

NO! IT'S JUST A FRAUD--TO LURE THE PUBLIC!

I'LL TEACH HIM A LITTLE LESSON WHILE I'M HERE--AND DRAIN OFF SOME SURPLUS ENERGY AT THE SAME TIME!

HOLY COW! THE JOINT'S HAUNTED!

AT THAT MOMENT, CYCLOPS HEARS THE SHRILL SOUND OF A BARKER'S RAUCUS PITCH...

ALL RIGHT, FOLKS, HERE'S OUR MAIN ATTRACTION! WHAT YOU'VE BEEN WAITIN' FOR!

THE ONE, THE ONLY, THE UNBELIEVABLE MARVEL OF THE AGE! FOR ONLY A QUARTER, THE FOURTH PART OF A DOLLAR, YOU CAN STEP INSIDE AND MEET--THE BLOB!

YOU WON'T BELIEVE YOUR EYES WHEN YOU SEE THE FEATS THE BLOB CAN PERFORM! SO HURRY, HURRY, HURRY-- THE SHOW STARTS IN FIVE MINUTES! DON'T PUSH--DON'T CROWD--THERE'S ROOM FOR ALL!!

THE BLOB! PERHAPS-- HE'S THE ONE--??

DON'T BUY A TICKET IF YOU'RE SQUEAMISH! STRONG MEN HAVE BEEN KNOWN TO FAINT WHEN THE BLOB PERFORMS! SO HURRY, HURRY, HURRY--

YES! IT IS HE! THE ONE CALLED THE BLOB!

I'VE FOUND HIM!

6

AND THEN, THE EXHIBITION BEGINS...

I WANT A HALF-DOZEN VOLUNTEERS --BIG, STRONG STRAPPING MEN!

YOU'LL WIN ONE HUNDRED DOLLARS IF YOU CAN MAKE THE BLOB MOVE!

ONE HUNDRED CLAMS!! WOW!

JUST TO MOVE FATSO THERE? IT'LL BE A CINCH!

BUT AFTER TEN EXHAUSTING MINUTES...

IT'S IMPOSSIBLE! WE CAN'T BUDGE HIM!

NO WONDER THEY OFFERED A HUNDRED BUCKS!! NATURE BOY HERE MUST BE NAILED TO THE FLOOR!!

SO HE'S THE MUTANT! HE DOESN'T SEEM SO GREAT TO ME! JUST A BIG, HEAVY GUY!

AND NOW FOR THE SECOND PART OF OUR DEMONSTRATION! THIS IS NOT FOR THE SQUEAM-ISH!! THE BLOB WILL STOP A RIFLE LOAD OF BULLETS WITH HIS BODY!! READY, TEX?

YES SUH! AH'M READY!

POW POW POW POW

SECONDS LATER, AFTER THE SMOKE HAS CLEARED!

FAKE! FAKE! HE WAS PROBABLY SHOOTIN' BLANKS!

WE WANT OUR MONEY BACK!

WAIT!! L-LOOK AT THAT!!

HE REALLY DID STOP THE SHELLS!!

THEY COULDN'T PENETRATE HIS SKIN!

WOW! HE'S TOSSIN' THE SHELLS AWAY JUST BY EXPAND-ING HIS CHEST!!

NEVER SAW ANY-THING LIKE IT! THE BLOB HAS A BODY LIKE SILLY PUTTY!! HE CAN DO ANYTHING!

7

LATER, AFTER THE EXHIBITION...

NO *WONDER* PROFESSOR X WANTS TO GET THE BLOB BEFORE THE EVIL MUTANTS CAN CONTACT HIM! HE'S FAR MORE POWERFUL THAN I SUSPECTED!!

THERE'S HIS WAGON NOW! I WONDER IF HE REALIZES HE'S A MUTANT??

MY NAME'S SUMMERS! MIND IF I HAVE A FEW WORDS WITH YOU?

IF IT'S A *TOUCH*, RUBE, YOU'RE WASTING YOUR TIME!

IT'S NO TOUCH, FELLA! HAVE YOU EVER HEARD OF -- THE *X-MEN*?

THOSE JERKY JUVENILES IN THE CORNY COSTUMES?? SURE, I HEARD OF 'EM! SO WHAT?

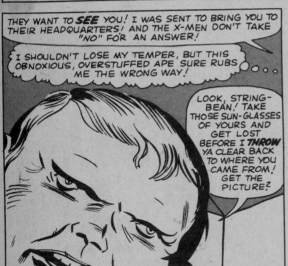

THEY WANT TO *SEE* YOU! I WAS SENT TO BRING YOU TO THEIR HEADQUARTERS! AND THE X-MEN DON'T TAKE "NO" FOR AN ANSWER!

I SHOULDN'T LOSE MY TEMPER, BUT THIS OBNOXIOUS, OVERSTUFFED APE SURE RUBS ME THE WRONG WAY!

LOOK, STRING-BEAN! TAKE THOSE SUN-GLASSES OF YOURS AND GET LOST BEFORE I *THROW* YA CLEAR BACK TO WHERE YOU CAME FROM! GET THE PICTURE?

PAY NO ATTENTION TO MY BOORISH FRIEND, BLOB! HE COULDN'T CONVINCE A DROWNING MAN TO TAKE A LIFE PRESERVER! BUT THIS LITTLE LADY AND MYSELF WOULD BE HAPPY TO DRIVE YOU TO THE X-MEN!

OUR CAR IS WAITING OUTSIDE...

WELL, WELL! *NOW* YOU'RE TALKIN' MY LANGUAGE! I'LL GO IF ME AND THIS CUTE TOMATO CAN SIT IN THE RUMBLE SEAT! HEH HEH!

HOLD ON THERE! LET GO OF THE LADY'S ARM!

LET *ME* HANDLE THIS!

IT'S TIME YOU LEARNED SOME *MANNERS*, TUBBY -- AND HERE'S YOUR FIRST LESSON!

HEY! WHAT THE --?!

8

YOU SHOULDN'T HAVE BEEN SO ROUGH WITH HIM, SCOTT! I'M SURE HE DIDN'T MEAN ANY HARM!

THAT'S RIGHT, DOLL! I'M JUST A BIG, FUN-LOVIN' KID, THAT'S ALL!

AND IT'S LUCKY FOR YOUR TWO SKINNY FRIENDS THAT I AINT MAD, SEE?

BECAUSE THERE'S *NOTHIN'* THAT CAN HURT THE BLOB!! DO I MAKE MYSELF CLEAR??

AND NOW THAT I MET RED RIDING HOOD HERE, I'VE CHANGED MY MIND! LET'S GO VISIT THE X-MEN!

AND SO, THE BLOB IS BROUGHT TO PROFESSOR X, AND CONSENTS TO HAVE THE EXTENT OF HIS STRANGE POWER TESTED...

I UNDERSTAND YOU CAN-NOT BE MOVED WHEN YOU PLACE YOURSELF ON ONE SPOT! LET US SEE HOW *TRUE* THAT IS!

START CRANKIN', MISTER! YOU'LL FIND OUT!

SNAP!

EXTRAORDINARY! YOURS IS A MOST UNUSUAL POWER! THE VERY MOLECULES OF YOUR FLESH REACT TO YOUR MENTAL COMMANDS AND SEEM TO PERFORM ALMOST ANY FEAT YOU DESIRE!

IN PLAIN ENGLISH I'M PRETTY TERRIFIC, HUH? HECK, I COULDA TOLD YOU THAT ALL THE *TIME*!

THIS CHUBBY LITTLE SHRINK-ING VIOLET NEEDS TO BE TAKEN DOWN A PEG OR TWO, PROFES-SOR! MAY I HAVE YOUR PERMISSION?

9

10

THEN, MOVING WITH STARTLING SPEED FOR ONE SO MASSIVE, THE BLOB MAKES THE FIRST MOVE, AS ALL FURY SEEMS TO BREAK LOOSE IN THE GREAT CHAMBER...

RATS! I *MISSED* 'IM!

HERE! YOU TWO *DESERVE* EACH OTHER!!

FALL BACK, MY X-MEN! REGROUP YOURSELVES! PLAN YOUR ATTACK CAREFULLY! YOU ARE BEING TOO CARELESS! YOU MUST WORK AS A *TEAM!*

I'VE GOT TO MOVE THE PROFESSOR AWAY! IF THE BLOB ATTACKS *HIM*, HE'S TOO VULNERABLE!!

USING HER ASTOUNDING POWER OF TELEKENISES, MARVEL GIRL HURLS THE PROFESSOR'S WHEEL CHAIR BACK OUT OF RANGE BEFORE THE BLOB CAN REACH HIM!

ONCE I GET MY HANDS ON YOUR *LEADER*, I'LL-- HEY! WHAT'S GOIN' ON??!

JUST IN TIME! NOW, WITH THE PROFESSOR OUT OF HARM'S WAY, WE CAN CONCENTRATE ON THE BLOB AGAIN!

BUT THEIR OPPONENT FINALLY DECIDES TO ESCAPE WHILE HE CAN...

OH NO YOU *DON'T!*

THE DOOR'S *HAUNTED!* IT SHUT BY *ITSELF!*

OUT OF THE WAY, JEAN! LET *ME* TACKLE HIM!

SL AM!

THOUGH THEY CALL YOU THE *BEAST*, YOUR STRENGTH CAN'T *NEARLY* MATCH MINE! *NOTHING* CAN HURT *ME!*

FAR BE IT FROM ME TO DOUBT YOUR VERACITY, BIG MAN, BUT I PREFER TO LEARN THINGS FOR MYSELF!

WHAM!

11

SATISFIED, MONKEY MAN?

LET'S JUST SAY YOU PROVED YOUR POINT, SON!

I'LL LOSE MYSELF DOWN HERE AND BE BACK AT THE CARNIVAL BEFORE THEY CAN FINISH PICKING UP THE PIECES!

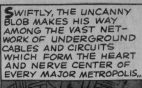

SWIFTLY, THE UNCANNY BLOB MAKES HIS WAY AMONG THE VAST NETWORK OF UNDERGROUND CABLES AND CIRCUITS WHICH FORM THE HEART AND NERVE CENTER OF EVERY MAJOR METROPOLIS...

MEANWHILE, BACK AT **X-MEN** HEADQUARTERS...

NO BONES BROKEN, PROFESSOR! GOSH-- WHAT'S *WRONG*, SIR??

MY FIRST MISTAKE! MY FIRST REALLY SERIOUS MISTAKE! I FOOLISHLY TOOK IT FOR GRANTED HE WOULD JOIN US...

I HAD YOU BRING HIM HERE! HE LEARNED WHERE WE ARE LOCATED, WHO WE ARE! IF HE TALKS, THE SECRET I HAVE SWORN TO DEDICATE MY LIFE TO WILL BE A SECRET NO MORE! *HE MUST NOT TALK!!*

CAN'T YOU DRIVE THE MEMORY OF WHAT HE HAS LEARNED FROM HIS MIND, SIR?

YES! BUT NOT BY LONG DISTANCE! HE MUST BE NEAR ME!! HE MUST BE BROUGHT HERE AGAIN!!

AND, REACHING THE CARNIVAL, THE BLOB'S THOUGHTS ARE TURNING IN THE SAME DIRECTION!

I KNOW THE IDENTITY OF THE X-MEN! THAT MEANS I'M *DANGEROUS* TO THEM! THEY'LL NEVER REST TILL THEY'VE RECAPTURED ME!

BUT I'LL OUT-SMART THEM! I'LL ATTACK *THEM* FIRST! I KNOW WHERE THEY ARE -- IT WON'T BE HARD!

CIRCUS

12

THE **BLOB!** WHERE IN SAM HILL HAVE YOU **BEEN,** YOU BRAINLESS LUMMOX?!!

SHUT YOUR MOUTH! AND **STAND UP** WHEN YOU SEE ME! THINGS ARE GONNA BE MIGHTY **DIFFERENT** AROUND HERE NOW!

FOR YEARS I THOUGHT I WAS JUST AN EXTRA-STRONG FREAK! BUT I FOUND OUT WHAT I **REALLY** AM! I'M A **MUTANT!** UNDERSTAND?! I'M ONE OF **HOMO-SUPERIOR!** AND THAT MEANS I'LL RUN THIS SHOW FROM NOW ON!! ANY OBJECTIONS??

N-NO!!

GET EVERYBODY TOGETHER!! ALL THE FREAKS, ACROBATS, PERFORMERS--EVERYBODY!! I WANT THEM HERE IN FIVE MINUTES! NOW HOP TO IT, YOU PUNY HOMO SAPIEN! **MOVE** WHEN I GIVE AN ORDER!!

AND SO...

FROM NOW ON YOU ALL TAKE ORDERS FROM **ME!** AND THOSE WHO **DON'T** WILL WISH THEY **HAD!** I'M GONNA MAKE YOU ALL **FAMOUS!!**

YOU'RE GONNA HELP ME BEAT THE **X-MEN!** I KNOW WHERE THEY'RE HIDDEN! WE'RE ATTACKING THEM!! YOU'VE GOT YOUR WEAPONS, AND YOU'VE GOT **ME!** WE CAN'T LOSE!

HEY, **LOOK!!** THERE'S ONE OF 'EM **NOW!** HE MUST BE **SPYIN'** ON US!! WHAT DO WE **DO???**

SHOOT HIM **DOWN,** YOU FOOL! HURRY!

BUT SHOOTING THE HIGH-FLYING ANGEL IS EASIER SAID THAN DONE! AND SO...

GOOD THING THE PROF HAD ME SPEND ALL THOSE HOURS PRACTICING MANEUVERABILITY ...DODGING GUNFIRE! BETTER REPORT BACK TO HIM, ON THE DOUBLE!

MINUTES LATER, BACK AT PROFESSOR X'S PRIVATE LAB...

GOOD WORK, ANGEL! IT'S AS I FEARED! HE'S PREPARING TO STRIKE AS SOON AS POSSIBLE!

THAT'S WHY I'M RUSHING TO COMPLETE THIS ELECTRONIC MASS INFLUENCER! IT WILL INTENSIFY MY OWN THOUGHT WAVES SO I CAN DRIVE ALL MEMORY OUT OF THE MINDS OF AN ENTIRE CROWD!

13

FOR THE PROBLEM IS NOW MORE DIFFICULT THAN EVER! WHEN THE BLOB ATTACKS WITH HIS CARNIVAL HENCHMEN, THEY WILL **ALL** KNOW OUR WHEREABOUTS--AND THEY MUST **ALL** HAVE THAT KNOWLEDGE ERASED FROM THEIR BRAINS!

ALERT THE OTHERS, ANGEL! EVEN THOUGH IT IS THEIR STUDY HOUR, HAVE THEM DON THEIR UNIFORMS---- READY FOR ACTION! THAT IS ALL!

YES SIR!

UP AND AT 'EM, HANK! THE PROF WANTS EVERYONE IN UNIFORM AND RARIN' TO GO!

ANGEL, ALTHOUGH YOUR COLLOQUIALISMS ARE EXTREMELY COLORFUL, THEY ARE COMPLETELY UNNECESSARY!

I WILL BE FULLY GARBED AND AT THE READY BEFORE YOU SHUT MY DOOR!

ADVANCED CALCULUS

INTO YOUR FIGHTING DUDS, JUNIOR! PROFESSOR X'S ORDERS!

SAY! WHAT HAVE YOU **GOT** BACK THERE! YOU WERE SUPPOSED TO BE **STUDYING!**

I **WAS!** I WAS, EH, STUDYING A PROBLEM IN, EH, KEEPING FOOD REFRIGERATED!

SURE! I WOULDN'T DOUBT YOU! NOW GET DRESSED!

SLAM!

HEY! WHAT'S GOIN' **ON** HERE??

SUFFERIN' SNOWBALLS! IT'S AN **INVASION!!** IT LOOKS LIKE THE WHOLE BLAMED **CARNIVAL** IS OUTSIDE!

AND BOBBY DRAKE IS ABOUT TO LEARN THAT THERE IS MORE TRUTH THAN FICTION TO HIS STARTLED EXCLAMATION!

THAT KID AT THE WINDOW **SEES** US, BLOB!

IT DOESN'T **MATTER** NOW! IT'S TOO LATE FOR THEM TO STOP US!

ATTACK! THIS IS THE END OF THE **X-MEN!**

14

15

16

17

BUT THE AMOUNT OF ENERGY REQUIRED FOR SUCH A HIGH-INTENSITY POWER BLAST TEMPORARILY WEAKENS THE POWERFUL CYCLOPS, AND...

NOW'S OUR CHANCE! *GRAB* HIM!

WITH *HIM* OUT OF THE WAY, THE OTHERS WILL BE EASY!

BROTHER, ARE *YOU* LIVIN' IN A FOOLS' PARADISE!!

I'LL JUST TOSS OFF A FEW ICE TORPEDOES AND --*HEY!* WHAT THE--??!!

THIS'LL TAKE CARE OF *YOU*, SMALL FRY!

THE BLOB WAS *RIGHT!* THESE INSULATED SUITS LET US GET NEAR THIS KID WITHOUT FREEZIN'!

I'VE GOT TO HELP ICEMAN!

BUT MARVEL GIRL SOON FINDS IT IS *SHE* WHO NEEDS HELP!

SURROUND HER! GOOD! NOW *SEIZE* HER! SHE CAN'T STOP *ALL* OF YOU AT ONCE!

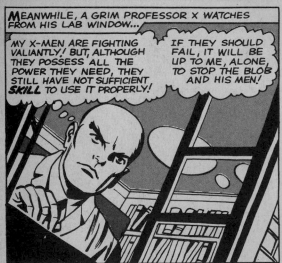

MEANWHILE, A GRIM PROFESSOR X WATCHES FROM HIS LAB WINDOW...

MY X-MEN ARE FIGHTING VALIANTLY! BUT, ALTHOUGH THEY POSSESS ALL THE POWER THEY NEED, THEY STILL HAVE NOT SUFFICIENT *SKILL* TO USE IT PROPERLY!

IF THEY SHOULD FAIL, IT WILL BE UP TO ME, ALONE, TO STOP THE BLOB AND HIS MEN!

MY LEGS ARE OF NO USE TO ME! I HAVE ONLY THE POWER OF MY *BRAIN*... AND THE HOPE OF COMPLETING THIS INTENSIFIER IN TIME!

18

20

THROW HIM DOWN *HERE,* TO ME! I'LL HANDLE HIM NOW!

NOTHING CAN BREAK THE GRIP OF THE BLOB!

THERE! YOU'RE THE *LAST* OF 'EM! I'VE BEATEN ALL THE X-MEN! ONLY HELPLESS PROFESSOR X REMAINS!

MINUTES LATER...

IF THE FOUR OF YOU STAY OUT OF TROUBLE NOW, I MAY LET YOU LIVE--FOR A WHILE LONGER!

AND DON'T EXPECT ANY HELP FROM THE *ICEMAN*-- HE'S GOT HIS *OWN* PROBLEMS RIGHT NOW!

MAKE ONE FALSE MOVE, JUNIOR, AND THAT CIRCLE OF FLAME WILL FALL, MELTING YOU BUT *GOOD!*

NOW *FOLLOW ME!* ONCE WE DISPOSE OF PROFESSOR X, ALL THE SECRETS--ALL THE POWERS OF THE X-MEN WILL BE *MINE!* THE WHOLE HUMAN RACE WILL BOW DOWN TO--THE *BLOB!*

SILENTLY, COMPLETELY MOTIONLESS, THE MAN KNOWN AS PROFESSOR X SITS AND WAITS FOR THE ATTACK WITH GRIM RESOLVE... AN ATTACK HE HAS BEEN FOLLOWING BY MEANS OF HIS AMAZING MENTAL PROWESS!

MY X-MEN HAVE BEEN STOPPED --BUT NOT FOR LONG! THERE IS STILL HOPE!

MARVEL GIRL, I AM SENDING MY THOUGHT TO YOU! YOU ARE NOT AS HELPLESS AS YOU THINK! DO EXACTLY AS I SAY...

21

YOU HAVE THE TELEKINETIC POWER TO MENTALLY MOVE AN OBJECT! USE THAT POWER TO REMOVE YOUR *BLIND-FOLD!*

WELL DONE, JEAN! AND NOW, LOOK AROUND YOU, QUICKLY! EVERY SECOND COUNTS! WE CAN *STILL* DEFEAT THE BLOB!

KEEP LOOKING! I CAN *"SEE"* WHAT YOU SEE BY PROBING YOUR MIND! *AHH! THAT* IS WHAT WE NEED! SEND YOUR TELEKINETIC POWER THROUGH THE WAGON WINDOW--QUICKLY!

SHARPO *WORLD'S GREATEST* KNIFE THROWER

PERFECT! AND NOW, THE REST IS UP TO *YOU!*

I WILL NOT FAIL YOU, SIR!

A SCANT FEW SECONDS LATER...

MARVEL GIRL! HOW DID YOU MANAGE TO FREE YOURSELF??

WE HAVE *PROFESSOR X* TO THANK! BUT I'LL EXPLAIN AFTER I FREE YOU ALL!

FINALLY...

THAT'S *HIM!* THE LEADER OF THE X-MEN! HE'S *HELPLESS!* GET 'IM!

BUT HOW CAN THE X-MEN'S *LEADER* BE HELPLESS??

DON'T QUESTION THE *BLOB!* JUST *OBEY* ME!

BUT, BEFORE THE BLOB OR HIS MEN CAN MAKE ANOTHER MOVE...

WHAT *HAPPENED??*

A SOLID WALL OF *ICE* FELL IN FRONT OF US!

WE CAN'T GET THROUGH!

ONLY THE *ICEMAN* COULD HAVE DONE THIS!! BUT HE'S OUR *PRISONER!*

DON'T *BET* ON IT, PAL!

22

AND THEN, A HUGE SECTION OF CANVAS SEEMS TO FLOAT THROUGH THE AIR, WRAPPING ITSELF AROUND THE STUNNED AND STARTLED ATTACKERS!!

WE CAN'T GET *OUT!* IT'S FOLDING ITSELF AROUND US!!

HELP!! THE X-MEN AINT JUST *MUTANTS* --THEY'RE *MAGICIANS!!*

SURPRISED, BROTHER BLOB? DON'T BE! YOU HAVEN'T SEEN *ANYTHING* YET!

I SAVED *YOU* FOR LAST! THE BOYS ASKED ME TO!

I BEAT YOU ALL *ONCE,* AND I'LL DO IT *AGAIN!* BUT *THIS* TIME I WON'T BE SO MERCIFUL!

BRAVO! SPOKEN LIKE A TRUE LITTLE *BLOB!*

STAY *BACK!* HIS GRIP IS *UNBREAKABLE* ONCE HE GRABS YOU! BUT I'LL SEE TO IT THAT HE NEVER GRABS ANY OF US AGAIN!

WHOOOM!

I WAS A *FOOL* TO ALLOW THOSE BUMBLING HOMO SAPIENS TO FIGHT YOU! WHEN I CLIMB OUT OF HERE, THE BLOB *PERSONALLY* WILL DEFEAT YOU ALL!

SORRY, CHUBBINS! WE'RE NOT *GIVING* YOU A SECOND CHANCE!

QUICK, STRETCHO! WE'VE GOT TO GET *OUT* OF HERE! LET'S *BLAST* OUR WAY THROUGH!

OKAY, X-MEN! THIS IS THE WRAP-UP! LET'S GET THOSE POP-GUNS AWAY FROM OUR FRANTIC FRIENDS!

EASY ON THOSE WALLS, BEAST! YOU'RE GIVING ME A *HEADACHE!*

YOU TRAVEL *YOUR* WAY, ANGEL-- AND I'LL TRAVEL *MINE!* I'M JUST A NON-CONFORMIST AT HEART!

23

USING HIS POWERFUL WINGS AS POUNDING WEAPONS, THE ANGEL KNOCKS THE GUNS FROM THE HANDS OF HIS ENEMIES, AS THE BEAST CAUSES THEM TO RETREAT IN PANIC!

BUT, THEIR RETREAT IS SHORT-LIVED, FOR ONE LOW-INTENSITY POWER BLAST BY CYCLOPS FORCES THEM TO HUDDLE HELPLESSLY IN A CORNER!

NO MORE! NO MORE! WE GIVE UP!

AND, AT THAT MOMENT, THE GRIM-VISAGED PROFESSOR X PRESSES THE "OPERATE" STUD ON HIS COMPLETED INTENSIFIER RAY--THE RAY WHICH INCREASES THE POWER OF HIS MUTANT BRAIN, TURNING IT INTO AN AWESOME WEAPON!

THIS IS THE MOMENT! WHEN THEIR RESISTANCE IS AT ITS LOWEST EBB!

MY THOUGHTS ARE YOUR THOUGHTS, BLOB! MY WILL IS YOUR WILL! YOU AND YOUR MEN HAVE NEVER HEARD OF THE X-MEN! YOU HAVE NEVER SEEN OUR HEADQUARTERS! YOU ARE ALL AS YOU WERE BEFORE WE FOUND YOU! MY WILL IS YOURS! MY WILL IS YOURS!

AND, WITHIN A MATTER OF SECONDS...

WHAT'S GOIN' ON? WHAT ARE WE DOING HERE?

I DON'T KNOW! BUT WE'D BETTER RETURN TO THE CARNIVAL BEFORE WE GET SACKED!

LOOKS LIKE YOU WIN AGAIN, SIR! YOU ENDED THE MENACE OF THE BLOB BY SHEER BRAIN-POWER ALONE!

NO, THE VICTORY IS NOT MINE ALONE! FOR WITHOUT YOUR COURAGE AND SKILL IN HOLDING OFF THE ENEMY UNTIL I COULD COMPLETE MY INTENSIFIER, WE WOULD HAVE BEEN ANNIHILATED! WE FOUGHT THE FIGHT TOGETHER, MY X-MEN, AND WE TRIUMPHED TOGETHER!

AND, SO ENDS THE TALE OF THE MUTANT WHO MIGHT HAVE ACHIEVED GREATNESS AS AN X-MAN, HAD HIS HONOR BEEN A MATCH FOR HIS POWER!

STEP RIGHT UP, FOLKS, AND SEE THE BLOB! ONLY TWENTY-FIVE CENTS! HURRY, HURRY!

WHAT A LIFE! ALWAYS ON DISPLAY FOR THE RUBES! OH WELL, IT'S BETTER THAN STARVIN'!

BUT THE BRAIN OF A MUTANT IS AN UNPREDICTABLE THING! PROFESSOR X KNOWS THAT SOME DAY IN THE FUTURE, THE BLOB'S MEMORY MAY RETURN...

BUT, WHEN IT DOES... THE X-MEN WILL BE READY! NOW, UNTIL NEXT ISSUE, FROM HOMO SUPERIOR TO HOMO SAPIENS --FAREWELL!

THE END

2

3

I'M READY NOW, PROFESSOR!

WAIT YOUR TURN, ANGEL! *MARVEL GIRL!* LOWER BOBBY TO THE FLOOR-- VIA TELEKINESIS--GENTLY--

YES SIR!

WELL DONE, JEAN! AND NOW, THAT WAS NOT YOUR TEST--*THIS* IS--RAISE THE LID OF THAT BOX CAREFULLY, AND REMOVE WHAT IS INSIDE! YOU MAY PROCEED...

EXCELLENT, JEAN! YOU HAVE LEARNED TO FOCUS YOUR TELEKINETIC POWER SO ACCURATELY THAT YOU DID NOT JAR THE BOX ITSELF! AND NOW...

OH, PROFESSOR --IT'S A *BIRTHDAY CAKE!*

YES, MY DEAR! A LITTLE SURPRISE FOR YOU ALL, FROM YOUR PROUD TASK-MASTER! IT HAS BEEN EXACTLY ONE YEAR SINCE OUR CLASS BEGAN AND I FELT THE DATE SHOULD BE CELEBRATED!

HMMPH! IF THIS HAD HAPPENED DURING *MY* TEST, THE CAKE WOULDA *EXPLODED* WHEN I TOUCHED IT!

MAYBE YOU JUST DON'T *LIVE* RIGHT, JUNIOR!

HERE, JEAN-- ALLOW *ME* TO CUT YOU A PIECE OF CAKE-- IN MY OWN WAY!

WHY, THANK YOU, CYCLOPS! BUT THAT'S A BIT LIKE USING AN *ELEPHANT GUN* TO KILL A HOUSE FLY!

BUT NOW WE LEAVE *PROFESSOR XAVIER'S SCHOOL FOR GIFTED YOUNGSTERS,* AND TURN OUR ATTENTION TO *ANOTHER* GROUP OF MUTANTS WHO ARE ALSO SEATED AT A TABLE! BUT, WHAT A WORLD OF *DIFFERENCE* WE SHALL FIND BETWEEN THESE TWO SUPER-HUMAN GROUPS...!

TOAD! MUST YOU CHOMP YOUR FOOD LIKE THAT?? MY *SISTER* HAPPENS TO BE AT THE TABLE, YOU OBNOXIOUS FOOL!

IT'S ALRIGHT, PIETRO! DON'T GET INTO ANOTHER FIGHT ON *MY* ACCOUNT!

IF THE TOAD IS ANNOYING THE MOST LOVELY *SCARLET WITCH,* I'LL PUT A STOP TO THAT!

IF YOU HAVE THE *MANNERS* OF A PIG, YOU MIGHT AS WELL HAVE THE *APPEARANCE* OF ONE, ALSO!

YOUR LITTLE TRICKS DON'T BOTHER *ME,* MASTERMIND! REMEMBER, I KNOW THEY ARE ONLY HYPNOTIC ILLUSIONS!

4

*"X-MEN VS. MAGNETO!" ISSUE #1--ED.

6

A SHORT TIME LATER, ON A ROUTINE LONG-RANGE TEST FLIGHT, THE SHARP-EYED *ANGEL* SEES THE ARMED VESSEL CRUISING BELOW...

THAT SHIP SEEMS *DESERTED* -- AND YET IT'S MOVING AT TOP SPEED!

IT'S AN OLD VINTAGE FREIGHTER! MIGHT BE A *TARGET SHIP*, OPERATED BY REMOTE CONTROL!

I'D BETTER LEAVE THE AREA BEFORE THEY START ZEROING IN ON IT!!

SOMETHING JUST FLEW BY! BUT NO SOUND OF ENGINES-- MUST HAVE BEEN A SEAGULL!

THUS THE TWO COLORFUL MUTANTS COME WITHIN YARDS OF EACH OTHER, THOUGH NEITHER SUSPECTS THE OTHER'S PRESENCE! AND THEN, A FEW HOURS LATER, BACK AT THE STUDY OF PROFESSOR X....

WELL, IF IT ISN'T LITTLE MR. MODEST!

YOU MAY APPLAUD IF YOU WISH, JEAN! I'M BACK!

I'LL BE READY FOR YOUR PROGRESS REPORT IN A MOMENT, ANGEL!

MINUTES LATER...

...AND THAT'S ABOUT *IT*, SIR! EXCEPT FOR SIGHTING THE SHIP WITH NO CREW! A PRETTY UNEVENTFUL FLIGHT!

AN UNMANNED SHIP, PROPELLED BY REMOTE CONTROL! STRANGE-- I WAS UNAWARE OF ANY NAUTICAL ARTILLARY TESTS AT THE PRESENT TIME!

HERE IS YOUR LAB EQUIPMENT, SIR!

YOUR HEART-BEAT IS SATISFACTORY --BLOOD PRESSURE NORMAL --JUST ONE THING DISTURBS ME --!!

WHAT *IS* IT, SIR?? SOMETHING WRONG WITH MY TESTS? I-I *FEEL* PERFECTLY WELL--!

NO, IT IS NOT *YOU*, WARREN! IT IS THAT FREIGHTER! I SEEM TO SENSE SOMETHING WRONG --SOMETHING STRANGELY OMINOUS ABOUT IT! CALL IT A *HUNCH* IF YOU WILL--!

7

MEANWHILE, ON A LONELY, UNCHARTED ISLAND IN THE ATLANTIC...

IT'S THE *LEADER!* HE'S *BACK!* HE'S *BACK!* AND HE HAS A *DESTROYER!*

STOP YOUR SNIVELLING, TOAD! INFORM THE OTHERS THAT I WANT TO *SEE* THEM!

BUT, MASTER--I HAVE MUCH TO *TELL* YOU! THEY QUARRELED AMONG THEMSELVES! THEY TRIED TO FIGHT EACH OTHER! I STOPPED THEM MYSELF! BECAUSE THE TOAD IS LOYAL TO YOU!

MASTERMIND! IS WHAT HE TELLS ME *TRUE??*

OH, I WOULDN'T CALL IT A *FIGHT,* MAGNETO! MERELY A DIFFERENCE OF OPINION!

DON'T *BELIEVE* HIM, MASTER! I WAS *HERE!* I *HEARD* THEM! HE TRIED TO HARM THE SCARLET WITCH!

YOU LOATHSOME *GARGOYLE!* I'LL *GET* YOU FOR THIS!!

WHAT?!! YOU *DARE* SAY THAT IN *MY* PRESENCE!! HAVE YOU FORGOTTEN THAT OUR PERSONAL FEELINGS ARE *NOTHING?!* IT IS THE *PLAN* THAT IS ALL-IMPORTANT!!

QUICKSILVER!! WITCH!! I WANT TO *SPEAK* TO YOU!

LOOK, MAGNETO-- YOU DON'T SCARE *US!* I'M TAKING MY SISTER *AWAY* FROM HERE!

NO! YOU CANNOT LEAVE! HAVE YOU FORGOTTEN *YOU,* MOST OF ALL, WHAT YOU *OWE* ME??

HE IS *RIGHT,* PIETRO! I *MUST* REMAIN AND SERVE HIM --UNTIL MY DEBT IS REPAID!

THEN I *TOO* SHALL STAY, WANDA--TO WATCH OVER YOU!

"HAVE YOU FORGOTTEN THAT DAY, NOT LONG AGO, WHEN I FIRST CAME TO YOUR VILLAGE IN THE HEART OF EUROPE? HAVE YOU FORGOTTEN HOW THE SUPERSTITIOUS VILLAGERS CALLED YOU A *WITCH* BECAUSE OF YOUR MUTANT POWER?"

WE *KNOW* YOU! YOU HAVE THE EVIL EYE!

NO! NO! PLEASE--

SHE IS A *SCARLET WITCH!* HER POWER MUST BE DESTROYED!

8

I WAS HALF-WAY ACROSS THE PRACTICE FIELD WHEN THE PROF'S SUMMONS ALMOST BOWLED ME OVER!

RUSTLE THOSE WINGS, FLYBOY! IT'S A RED ALERT!

WELL, WELL! WHICH ONE ARE YOU-- HUNTLEY, OR BRINKLEY?

SAY! WHAT'S HAPPENED TO THE PROFESSOR?

QUIET! HE MUST BE ASLEEP!

HE'S NOT SLEEPING, LITTLE FRIENDS-- HE'S IN A TRANCE!

YOU'RE RIGHT, BEAST! WE MUSTN'T WAKE HIM!

LISTEN! YOU CAN HEAR HIM WHISPERING!! HE'S COMMUNICATING WITH SOMEONE-- MENTALLY!

I KNEW YOU WERE TRYING TO CONTACT ME, MAGNETO!! I WILL NEVER TELL WHERE I AM, BUT WE CAN MEET ON A MENTAL PLANE! SEND ME YOUR THOUGHTS, AND I WILL AMPLIFY THEM...

AND THUS BEGINS THE WORLD'S STRANGEST MEETING --BETWEEN THE WORLD'S MOST POWERFUL HOMO SUPERIORS...

ONLY YOU AND YOUR X-MEN STAND BETWEEN THE MUTANTS AND WORLD CONQUEST! WHY DO YOU FIGHT US?? WHY US?? FOR YOU TOO ARE A MUTANT!!

BUT I SEEK TO SAVE MANKIND, NOT DESTROY IT!

WE MUST USE OUR POWERS TO BRING ABOUT A GOLDEN AGE ON EARTH-- SIDE BY SIDE WITH ORDINARY HUMANS!

NEVER! THE HUMANS MUST BE OUR SLAVES! THEY ARE NOT WORTHY TO SHARE DOMINION OF EARTH WITH US! YOU HAVE MADE YOUR CHOICE--FOREVERMORE WE ARE MORTAL FOES!

THE X-MEN WILL STOP YOU, MAGNETO! IT WILL BE MUTANT AGAINST MUTANT-- TO THE DEATH, IF NEED BE!! BUT MANKIND MUST BE SAVED!

LOOK! H-HE WOKE HIMSELF UP!!

PROFESSOR! WE COULDN'T HELP OVERHEARING! WAS THAT-- MAGNETO??

YOU KNOW WE'RE WITH YOU TILL THE END, SIR!

THIS TIME MAGNETO WON'T ESCAPE US!

10

11

WITHIN A SHORT TIME, MAGNETO SEIZES THE REINS OF GOVERNMENT, AND LOSES NO TIME IN FORMING A *REAL* ARMY MODELLED AFTER THE IMAGINARY ONE CREATED BY MASTER-MIND...

WE MUST GET OFF THE STREET! IT IS NEARLY CURFEW TIME!

THE BORDERS OF THE ONCE-FREE LITTLE NATION ARE CLOSED -- AND ALL ROADS LEADING IN AND OUT OF THE CAPTIVE STATE ARE HEAVILY-PATROLLED!

HALT! IN THE NAME OF *MAGNETO!* SHOW YOUR IDENTIFICATION!

HMMM... AN AMERICAN PROFESSOR AND SOME STUDENTS ON A GOOD-WILL VISIT FROM AMERICA!

WE HAVE ORDERS TO ADMIT SUCH VISITORS! THE LEADER FEELS THEY CAN BE FOOLED INTO THINKING HE IS A KIND AND BELOVED RULER!

YOU MAY PASS!

WHILE, WITHIN THE PRESIDENTIAL BUILDING, WHICH MAGNETO HAS CONVERTED INTO AN IMPERIAL PALACE...

HE DARED TRY TO AROUSE THE PEOPLE AGAINST *ME??* TAKE HIM TO THE DUNGEON!

I *LIKE* THE BRAND OF "JUSTICE" YOU HAND OUT, MAGNETO! IT'LL SHOW HOMO SAPIENS THAT *WE* ARE THEIR RIGHTFUL MASTERS!

SILENCE! THEY'RE *HERE* -- THE *X-MEN!* I CAN *SENSE* IT! THE MENTAL EMANATIONS OF THEIR LEADER ARE SO STRONG THAT I FEEL THEM IN MY BRAIN!!

SEE TO IT THAT QUICKSILVER, THE SCARLET WITCH AND THE TOAD ARE PREPARED! WE'LL LET THE X-MEN COME TO US -- LIKE FLIES ENTERING A SPIDER'S TRAP!

AND, A SHORT DISTANCE AWAY FROM MAGNETO'S PALACE...

IS IT TIME FOR US TO GET INTO UNIFORM NOW, SIR?

YES! THERE IS NO NEED FOR FURTHER DELAY! MAGNETO MUST HAVE DETECTED OUR PRESENCE BY NOW!

BUT I DETECT *OTHER* MUTANTS AS WELL AS MAGNETO! OUR MISSION IS MORE DANGEROUS THAN I FEARED!

12

THEN, TAKING PENCIL IN HAND, THE GIFTED LEADER OF THE UNCANNY X-MEN PREPARES THEIR BATTLE PLAN...

THIS IS HOW MAGNETO WILL BE ATTACKED! YOU WILL EACH APPROACH HIS HEADQUARTERS IN A DIFFERENT WAY!

HANK, YOU'LL BE THE FIRST!

FORGIVE MY OVER-ZEALOUSNESS, GROUP, IF I DON'T LINGER OVER A LONG GOODBYE!

IT IS A WASTE OF TIME GUARDING MAGNETO! WHO WOULD DARE ATTACK THE LEADER?

YOU ARE RIGHT! ALL OTHERS TREMBLE AT THE SOUND OF THE LEADER'S NAME!

STRANGE HOW HE TOOK OVER OUR ENTIRE GOVERNMENT-- SO SUDDEN, WITHOUT FIRING A SHOT!

LISTEN! DID YOU JUST HEAR SOMETHING??

FORGIVE THE INTRUSION, GENTS! I'M JUST AN INCURABLE PARTY-CRASHER!

BUT, MAGNETO HAS ALREADY ALERTED HIS OWN LOYAL MUTANTS, AND BEFORE THE BEAST CAN RECOVER HIS BALANCE, THE HIGH-JUMPING TOAD STRIKES!!

WHA--???

HAH! I HAVE STRUCK THE FIRST BLOW! HOW PROUD THE LEADER WILL BE!

BUT THE BEAST'S POWERFUL FINGERS SLAM AGAINST THE SIDE OF THE STONE RAMPART, AND THEN...

BETTER HANG ON HERE, HENRY, OLD BOY! IT'S A LONG WAY TO THE BOTTOM!

13

DON'T GO AWAY, LITTLE FRIEND! I'LL CLIMB BACK UP AND WE CAN GET TO *KNOW* EACH OTHER BETTER!

HE'S TOO STRONG! I'LL BOUNCE THESE ROCKS DOWN AT HIM, TO STOP HIM FROM REACHING THE TOP!

DON'T BOTHER, TOAD! THE *MASTERMIND* WILL SHOW YOU HOW TO HANDLE HIM...

SUDDENLY, THE CREVICES WHICH THE BEAST HAS DUG OUT IN THE MOLDY STONE WALLS SEEM TO *VANISH--* TO BE REPLACED BY A SMOOTH, GLASSY AREA WHICH PERMITS NO POSSIBLE GRIP...

CAN'T HOLD ON!!

SO SHOCKED IS THE HEAVY-LIMBED X-MAN, THAT HE LOSES HIS BALANCE AND BEGINS TO PLUNGE HELPLESSLY DOWN...

YOU SEE, TOAD? THERE ARE TIMES WHEN A CLEVER *ILLUSION* CAN BE MORE EFFECTIVE THAN MERE BRUTE STRENGTH!!

HE THOUGHT THE WALLS HAD TURNED TO GLASS!! THE *FOOL!*

THEN, AT THE OTHER SIDE OF THE CASTLE, THE SOUND OF GUNFIRE IS HEARD, AS THE NEXT X-MAN ATTACKS...

YOU FELLAS SURE HAVE A FUNNY WAY OF MAKING A GUY FEEL AT HOME!

BOY! I'D LIKE TO BE THE ONE WHO SELLS THEM THEIR BULLETS!! I'D GET RICH OVERNIGHT!

14

15

16

18

MINUTES LATER, AFTER UNTYING THE ANGEL...

THAT'S IT, BOBBY BOY! THE ICE IS REVIVING HIM!

HE'S COMING TO NOW! MAN, HE MUSTA USED SOME BLAST TO SEND THAT GENERATOR CLEAN THRU THE WALL!

OKAY--NOW LET'S FIND THE OTHERS! AND ESPECIALLY THAT RAT, MAGNETO!

MAYBE YOU BETTER TAKE IT EASY FOR A WHILE, CYCLOPS...

DON'T WORRY ABOUT ME, ICE-MAN! SAVE YOUR CONCERN FOR QUICKSILVER! HE'S GONNA NEED IT WHEN I CATCH HIM!

SUDDENLY, A WALL PLAQUE AND THE WEAPONS BENEATH IT BEGIN TO QUIVER STRANGELY...

AND THEN...

LOOK OUT, YOU GUYS! LOOK WHAT'S GOIN' ON!

DUCK, BOBBY! WE'RE IN THE LINE OF FIRE!

I HEAR YA TALKIN', PAL!

WEAPONS--FLYING THRU THE AIR AT US! IF I DIDN'T KNOW BETTER, I'D SUSPECT MARVEL GIRL--!

BUT, WARREN WORTHINGTON THE THIRD HAS HIT THE NAIL RIGHT ON THE HEAD, FOR...

LUCKY FOR ME YOU SAW ME FALLING AND LOWERED ME TO THE GROUND THRU TELEKINESIS, LITTLE FRIEND! BUT--WHAT ARE YOU DOING NOW?

OH, MY GOODNESS! I-I THOUGHT IT WAS MAGNETO'S MEN, COMING AFTER US!

19

I'M **SORRY**, BOYS! I DIDN'T REALIZE...

OKAY, GORGEOUS! NO HARM DONE! **SAY**-- WHERE'S THE **PROF**?

LAST I SAW, HE WAS OUTSIDE THE CASTLE! DON'T WORRY-- **HE** CAN TAKE CARE OF HIMSELF!

PERHAPS HE **CAN**, SCOTT-- BUT I'M BEGINNING TO HAVE DOUBTS ABOUT **OUR** ABILITY IN THAT DEPARTMENT!

SO FAR, WE'VE USED UP A LOT OF TIME AND ENERGY, AND ACCOMPLISHED **NOTHING**!

HANK'S **RIGHT**! WE DON'T EVEN KNOW WHERE **MAGNETO** RAN OFF TO!

HEY! SAVE THE PHILOSOPHY FOR **LATER**-- WE'RE IN THE SOUP AGAIN! LOOK WHAT'S **COMIN'**--!!

IT'S A RIVER OF BOILING OIL-- RUSHING RIGHT TOWARDS US! I HATE TO SOUND LIKE A WORRY WART, BUT-- **LET'S GET OUT OF HERE**!

IF THAT HOT STUFF GETS ANY CLOSER TO ME, I'M GONNA BE AN ICELESS ICEMAN!

IT'S COMING TOO FAST-- WE CAN'T OUT-RUN IT! AND LOOK--THERE'S A **STONE WALL** UP AHEAD!

CAN'T USE MY ENERGY RAY YET-- HAVEN'T FULLY REGAINED MY STRENGTH! WE'RE **TRAPPED**!

WE **CAN'T** END UP LIKE THIS! WE'VE **GOT** TO THINK OF SOMETHING! B-BUT **WHAT??**

THE FLAMES HAVE STOPPED COMING CLOSER! WE'RE SAFE--FOR **NOW**! BUT WE'RE LOCKED IN-- CAN'T GET OUT --CAN'T BREAK FREE!

THEN, SUDDENLY, ASTONISHINGLY-- RIGHT IN THE MIDST OF THE DEADLY FLAMES, THEY SEE--

DO NOT FEAR, MY X-MEN! THERE **IS** A WAY OUT!

PROFESSOR X!!!

20

H-HOW DID YOU DO IT, SIR??

QUITE SIMPLE! I SENSED YOUR PANIC AND CAME AFTER YOU! THERE WAS REALLY NO BOILING OIL--IT WAS BUT AN ILLUSION, CREATED BY ONE OF THE MUTANTS TO KEEP YOU PRISONER HERE!

WE WERE FOOLS-- DECEIVED BY A HYPNOTIC TRICK OF SOME SORT!

DO NOT REPROACH YOUR- SELVES! REMEMBER, THE EVIL MUTANTS ARE AS POWERFUL AS WE...AND WILL STOP AT NOTHING TO DEFEAT US, AND TO GAIN CONTROL OF MANKIND!

NOW THAT YOU'RE HERE, SIR, THIS IS IT! WE'LL FIND MAGNETO--AND FINISH HIM OFF!

BUT, WATCHING THE X-MEN FROM A PEEP-HOLE IN THE WALL, A BALEFUL EYE GLEAMS WITH NAKED HATRED AND FRUSTRATION...

BLAST IT! IF NOT FOR THEIR LEADER, THEY'D STILL BE CRINGING HELPLESSLY IN MUTE FEAR BEHIND MY MASTERFUL ILLUSION!

BUT WE'LL BEAT THEM YET! COME, TOAD--WE'LL REPORT TO MAGNETO!

MAGNETO WILL KNOW WHAT TO DO! THE GREAT MAGNETO IS MORE THAN A MATCH FOR ANYONE!

MAGNETO, THE X-MEN ARE STILL AT LARGE, AND...

SILENCE! I KNOW WHAT HAS OCCURRED! STAND ASIDE! I AM PREPARING THE ULTIMATE TRAP FOR THEM!

I AM WIRING TWO BOMBS! ONE WILL BE PLACED AT THIS DOOR, TO BOOBY-TRAP IT AND DESTROY THEM WHEN THEY ENTER!

AS FOR THE OTHER, THAT ONE WILL BE A NUCLEAR BOMB, CAPABLE OF BLOWING UP THIS ENTIRE NATION!

WE WILL FLEE NOW! IF THE SMALLER BOMB DOESN'T STOP THE X-MEN, THE LARGE ONE WILL--TAKING ALL OF SANTO MARCO!

BUT WHAT ABOUT ALL THE INNOCENT PEOPLE THAT WILL BE KILLED??

HAVE I NOT TOLD YOU-- THEY ARE MERELY HOMO SAPIENS--THEY WOULD KILL US IF THEY COULD! WE ONLY FIGHT IN SELF DEFENSE!

21

MAGNETO LEAVES *NOTHING* TO CHANCE! THIS ESCAPE SLIDE LEADS TO THE FREIGHTER -- AND TO SAFETY ON THE OPEN SEA!

I CAN'T BELIEVE MAGNETO WILL LET ALL THOSE INNOCENT PEOPLE BE HARMED! I JUST *CAN'T*!

FOLLOW ME, QUICKSILVER! EVERY SECOND COUNTS!

NO! THERE IS ONE THING I MUST DO FIRST! NO MATTER *WHAT* THE CONSEQUENCES!

LOOK! ANOTHER BOMB -- SET TO GO OFF!

QUICKSILVER JUST DESTROYED THE FUSE! HE *SAVED* US!

WAIT! COME BACK --!

NO! ALTHOUGH I COULD NOT ALLOW A NATION TO BE DESTROYED, MY PLACE IS STILL WITH *THEM!*

YOU ARE THE BETRAYERS OF HOMO SUPERIOR! EXPECT NO MERCY NEXT TIME WE MEET!

LET 'EM GO, SCOTT! THE *PROF* NEEDS US NOW!

PROFESSOR X! I ALMOST *FORGOT!*

HOW *IS* HE? HE'S ALIVE -- BUT SOMETHING *TERRIBLE* HAS HAPPENED!

HIS *BRAIN* SEEMS TO BE AFFECTED!

HIS *BRAIN??* BUT -- THAT'S HIS GREATEST *WEAPON!*

LEAVE ME! I'M NO GOOD TO YOU ANY MORE! THE EXPLOSION DEADENED MY MUTANT MENTAL POWER! I CAN NO LONGER READ MINDS -- OR THROW MY THOUGHTS! GO AFTER THE EVIL ONES -- FORGET ME!

FORGET *YOU,* SIR? *NEVER!* WE CAN'T DESERT YOU WHEN YOU NEED US THE MOST!

23

THERE GOES THE FREIGHTER! IT'LL BE OUT OF SIGHT SOON! THEY'VE GOTTEN AWAY!

BUT THEY'LL NEVER BE REALLY FREE! FOR NO MATTER *WHERE* THEY GO,... AS SOON AS THEY SHOW THEMSELVES, THE *X-MEN* WILL ATTACK!

IF THE PROFESSOR NEVER REGAINS HIS POWER, WE'LL BE ON OUR *OWN* NEXT TIME! BUT -- ARE WE STRONG ENOUGH WITHOUT HIM?

HE TRAINED US -- NOW WE MUST PROVE *WORTHY* OF THAT TRAINING! WE SHALL NOT FAIL HIM!

THE END

LEADERLESS -- FORCED TO FEND FOR THEMSELVES -- CAN THE FIVE MUTANT TEEN-AGERS MEET A RENEWED THREAT BY THE POWERFUL EVIL MUTANTS?? DON'T MISS OUR NEXT GREAT ISSUE!

X-MEN
THE MOST UNUSUAL TEEN-AGERS OF ALL TIME!

"TRAPPED: ONE X-MAN!"

Featuring: THE RETURN OF THE EVIL MUTANTS!

LAST ISSUE, WHILE BATTLING MAGNETO AND HIS EVIL MUTANTS, PROFESSOR XAVIER WAS INJURED AND SEEMED TO HAVE LOST HIS GREAT MENTAL POWERS! NOW, THE SADDENED X-MEN RETURN TO THEIR HEADQUARTERS...

SPELL-BINDING STORY BY: STAN LEE

DAZZLING DRAWING BY: JACK KIRBY

INKING: PAUL REINMAN
LETTERING: S. ROSEN

NEVER HAVE YOU, THE READING PUBLIC, BEEN SO INSTANTLY FASCINATED BY A GROUP OF SUPER-POWERFUL VILLAINS AS LAST ISSUE, WHEN YOU MET MAGNETO'S EVIL MUTANTS! NOW, WE PRESENT THEM AGAIN... MORE EXCITING, MORE UNPREDICTABLE, MORE DANGEROUS THAN EVER!!

X-668

AND NOW, LET'S JOIN THE X-MEN AS THEY RETURN TO THEIR SCHOOL BUILDING! ICEMAN FINDS THE DOOR LOCKED, AND...

I CAN'T GET MY KEY UNLESS I DEFROST! HEY, CYCLOPS...I CAN USE YOU!

HIT THE KEYHOLE WITH THAT POWER BEAM OF YOURS TO UNLOCK THE DOOR, HUH? HEY! NOT SO FAST! IF YOU MISS THE DOOR, IT'S GOODBYE ICEMAN!

BOY! IT'S GOOD TO BE BACK AGAIN! IF ONLY THE PROFESSOR WAS OKAY!

I'LL LIFT HIM INTO HIS SITTING ROOM! IT'S THE EASIEST WAY!

SLOWLY, JEAN...YOU'VE ALL THE TIME IN THE WORLD! DON'T JOSTLE HIM!

LET ME REMOVE HIS JACKET BEFORE YOU PUT HIM DOWN! YOU DID AN EXEMPLARY JOB, MARVEL GIRL!

NOW... SET HIM DOWN! GENTLY.. GENTLY...

I'VE CHECKED THE ENTIRE BUILDING! EVERYTHING'S AS WE LEFT IT! WE HAVEN'T BEEN DISCOVERED YET!

IT SURE SEEMS STRANGE TO SEE HIM SLEEPING THAT WAY, JUST LIKE ANY NORMAL HOMO SAPIENS! IT MAKES ME FEEL SO... ALONE...

I KNOW WHAT YOU MEAN, ICEMAN! FROM NOW ON WE WILL BE ALONE, FOR THE FIRST TIME!.. WITHOUT THE PROFESSOR TO GUIDE US AND HELP US!

HE'S SPENT COUNTLESS HOURS TRAINING US TO USE OUR POWERS, JEAN! NOW, WE'VE GOT TO PROVE WE WERE WORTHY OF THAT TRAINING!

WE'VE GOT TO CONTINUE HIS FIGHT AGAINST THE EVIL MUTANTS! BUT WITHOUT HIM TO LEAD US IT'LL BE AN UPHILL JOB, HANK!

WE CAN'T REMAIN LEADERLESS! PERHAPS WE SHOULD.. WAIT! I HEAR A SOUND IN THE DRIVE-WAY! A CAR IS APPROACHING!

2.

WHO *IS* IT, BEAST? HAVE THE EVIL MUTANTS FOUND US?

NO...IT APPEARS TO BE... IT *IS*...IT'S MARVEL GIRL'S *PARENTS!!*

I *FORGOT!* THEY *SAID* THEY'D DROP IN FOR A VISIT ON THE WAY TO THE WORLD'S FAIR SITE! QUICK...WE'VE GOT TO GET BACK TO NORMAL!

MOVE, GUYS! LET'S SHED THESE COSTUMES ON THE DOUBLE!

DON'T WORRY, JEAN! WE WON'T GIVE OUR SECRET AWAY!

IT'LL ONLY TAKE ME A FEW SECONDS TO DEFROST AND CHANGE FROM *ICEMAN* TO PLAIN BOBBY DRAKE!

IT'S GREAT THE WAY THE PROFESSOR DEVELOPED THIS HARNESS TO HIDE MY WINGS UNDER A SUIT!

SO ONCE AGAIN THE *ANGEL* BECOMES THAT DEVIL-MAY-CARE YOUNG BLUE-BLOOD, WARREN WORTHINGTON THE THIRD!

I'M ALWAYS RELIEVED WHEN I CAN DIVEST MYSELF OF MY COSTUME! ACTUALLY, I DON'T REALLY CARE FOR THE IDENTITY OF THE *BEAST!*

I MUCH PREFER BEING HANK McCOY, HONOR STUDENT...ALTHOUGH FATE NEVER LETS ME REMAIN THAT WAY FOR LONG!

I WONDER IF ANYONE WOULD DARE COME NEAR QUIET SCOTT SUMMERS IF THEY KNEW THAT WHEN I REMOVE MY PROTECTIVE GLASSES, THE DESTRUCTIVE POWER BEAM OF *CYCLOPS* IS UNLEASHED UPON THE WORLD!

AS FAR AS ANY OF OUR PARENTS KNOW, WE ARE ALL STUDENTS AT A PROGRESSIVE PRIVATE SCHOOL! AND ACTUALLY, THAT MUCH IS *TRUE!*

BUT, BEING NORMAL HOMO SAPIENS, HOW COULD MOM OR DAD UNDERSTAND THAT THEIR DAUGHTER, JEAN GREY, IS REALLY *MARVEL GIRL!*

HELLO, JEAN DEAR! WE'VE ONLY A FEW MINUTES, BUT WE *DID* WANT TO VISIT YOU!

MOTHER! DAD! WHAT A WONDERFUL SURPRISE!

3.

MOMENTS LATER, AFTER INTRODUCING HER "FELLOW STUDENTS"...

A REAL PLEASURE MEETING YOU, MR. AND MRS. GREY! WE'RE SORRY PROFESSOR XAVIER CAN'T BE WITH US, BUT HE'S, EH, UNAVOIDABLY DETAINED!

I UNDERSTAND, MY BOY! I FEEL I KNOW YOU ALL SO WELL! THE PROFESSOR WRITES TO US EVERY WEEK, TELLING OF YOUR PROGRESS! HE IS CERTAINLY A WONDERFUL MAN!

WHEN HE FIRST ASKED IF JEAN COULD ATTEND YOUR SCHOOL, WE WERE A BIT HESITANT! BUT THEN, WHEN WE WERE CONTACTED BY WASHINGTON, D.C., RECOMMENDING YOUR COURSE SO HIGHLY, WE KNEW IT WAS THE BEST THING FOR OUR DAUGHTER!

AND WE WERE SO IMPRESSED TO LEARN THAT SOME OF YOUR COURSES ARE CLASSIFIED TOP SECRET BY THE GOVERNMENT!

OH, WHAT INTERESTING SUN-GLASSES! I'VE NEVER SEEN THAT TYPE...

NO! DON'T TOUCH THEM!! I-I'M SORRY, MA'AM...IT'S JUST THAT I HAVE A SLIGHT EYE INFECTION! I'M SURE YOU UNDERSTAND!

MUST CHANGE THE SUBJECT QUICKLY, LEST WE AROUSE THEIR SUSPICIONS!

OH, I WONDERED WHY IT WAS SO EMPTY!

WE'D ENJOY SHOWING YOU OUR BUILDING, MR. AND MRS. GREY! THIS IS OUR GYM! WE'RE GETTING NEW EQUIPMENT NEXT WEEK!

CLEVER OF HANK! HE COULDN'T VERY WELL ADMIT THAT THIS IS OUR DANGER ROOM, WHERE WE TRAIN!

AND NOW, IF YOU'D LIKE TO SEE OUR LUNCHROOM, AND STUDY HALL ...

WAIT!! DON'T SHUT THAT DOOR!

TOO LATE! THEY FORGOT ABOUT ME! THE DOOR'S TIME LOCK HAS ME TRAPPED INSIDE!

BUT THE "DANGER APPARATUS" IS SET ON AUTOMATIC! THAT MEANS THE TESTING DEVICES WILL BEGIN TO OPERATE ANY SECOND!

THEY'VE STARTED! IT WAS THE BEAST'S TRAINING PERIOD NEXT! THESE ARE HIS SPECIAL SURVIVAL PROBLEMS! CAN I HANDLE THEM?

4

5.

LATER... SUCH A LOVELY SCHOOL! AND WHAT FINE, CLEAN-CUT YOUNGSTERS! IT WAS A MOST PLEASANT VISIT!

WE SHOULD BE PROUD OF OUR DAUGHTER! IMAGINE WINNING A FREE SCHOLARSHIP TO A GREAT SCHOOL LIKE THAT!

BUT AS MR. AND MRS. GREY DRIVE OFF, THEY FAIL TO NOTICE A SILENT, BROODING FIGURE WHO SLOWLY WALKS PAST THE MYSTERIOUS COMPLEX OF SCHOOL BUILDINGS...

SORRY WE COULDN'T SAY HELLO TO PROFESSOR XAVIER! HE'S SUCH A CHARMING MAN!

HE HAS MORE THAN CHARM, DEAR! SOMETHING ABOUT HIM GIVES A PERSON A FEELING OF CONFIDENCE IN HIM...HE ALMOST SEEMS TO KNOW WHAT YOU'RE THINKING!

I WOULD LIKE TO KNOW WHAT THE SCHOOL'S CONNECTION WITH THE GOVERNMENT IS! PERHAPS THEY'RE TEACHING A SPECIAL SECRET SCIENCE COURSE! OH, WELL, I SUPPOSE WE'LL FIND OUT SOME DAY!

AND AS THE CAR DRIVES AWAY, THE LONE PEDESTRIAN STOPS, SEARCHING, SEEKING, PROBING THE NEIGHBORHOOD WITH COLD MERCILESS UNBLINKING EYES...

FOR THIS IS THE EVIL MUTANT KNOWN AS MASTERMIND... WITH POWER TO CREATE IMAGES SO REAL THAT ALL WHO SEE THEM BELIEVE IN THEM! MASTERMIND, WHO OWES HIS ALLEGIANCE TO MAGNETO, LEADER OF THOSE WHO PLAN TO TAKE DOMINION OF EARTH FROM THE HUMAN RACE!

IT'S NO USE! THE X-MEN ARE TOO WELL HIDDEN! NO MATTER WHERE I SEARCH THERE IS NO TRACE OF THEM!

THEN, OPERATING A SMALL MAGNETIC DEVICE ON HIS WRIST, MASTERMIND CONTACTS HIS LEADER...

RESULTS STILL NEGATIVE, MAGNETO! AWAITING FURTHER ORDERS!

RETURN AT ONCE! WE SHALL TRY A DIFFERENT PLAN! THAT IS ALL!

THEN, MOMENTS LATER, IN A LONELY FIELD...

IT'S LUCKY THAT ALL OF MAGNETO'S PLANES OPERATE ON MAGNETIC ENERGY! THERE'S NO CHANCE OF ANYONE HEARING THEM!

TAKE ME BACK TO HEADQUARTERS, QUICKSILVER! I HAVE DECIDED TO RETURN!

YOU DON'T FOOL ME, MASTERMIND! I WAS TUNED IN TO YOUR WAVELENGTH! IT WAS MAGNETO WHO DECIDED...AS ALWAYS!

6.

MINUTES LATER, THE SILENT SHIP REACHES A JAGGED ASTEROID, CIRCLING THE EARTH! BUT, UPON DRAWING NEAR, WE SEE THAT IT IS MORE THAN JUST A SIMPLE ASTEROID... MUCH, MUCH MORE!

QUICKSILVER TO ASTEROID M! REQUEST PERMISSION TO LAND! OVER!

ASTEROID M TO QUICK-SILVER! PERMISSION GRANTED! FOLLOW LANDING PLAN B!

WITHIN SECONDS, TWO DRAMATIC FIGURES STEP THROUGH THE AIR-LOCK...

THEY'RE HERE, MAGNETO! I'LL GO AND WELCOME THEM!

LOOK OUT! IT'S THAT BRAINLESS TOAD!

DID YOU FIND THEM? DID YOU DESTROY THE X-MEN? TELL ME, TELL ME!!

MOVING AT DAZZLING SPEED, THE MUTANT CALLED QUICKSILVER EASILY AVOIDS THE TOAD'S UN-ORTHODOX "GREETING," BUT THE SLOWER-MOVING MASTER-MIND IS NOT SO FORTUNATE!

BLAST THAT UNBEARABLE FREAK! HE'LL PAY FOR THIS!

AT A SINGLE GESTURE FROM THE ANGRY MUTANT, AN IMAGE IS CREATED! AN ILLUSION WHICH SEEMS SO REAL THAT IT STOPS THE TOAD IN HIS TRACKS!

C-CAN'T MOVE! I'M ALL WRAPPED UP IN A HEAVY CLOTH! GET ME OUT OF HERE!! HELP!!

THEN, AS THE TOAD'S HYSTERICAL CRY REACHES THE EARS OF... MAGNETO...

MASTERMIND!! DISPEL YOUR ILLUSION! INSTANTLY! AT THE COMMAND OF MAGNETO!!

7

8.

OF *COURSE* I'LL TELL YOU! AND IF YOU FAIL... IF YOU MAKE ONE CARELESS MISTAKE... YOU'LL FACE THE WRATH OF *MAGNETO*, MOST POWERFUL OF *ALL* THE MUTANTS!

NEVER FORGET THAT... *ANY* OF YOU!!

NOT LONG AFTERWARDS, BACK AT PROFESSOR XAVIER'S SCHOOL...

SAY, SCOTT... THERE'S A GREAT *TRACK MEET* ON T.V. ! HOW ABOUT WATCHING IT WITH US ?

TRACK MEET! PROFESSOR X HAS *LOST* HIS POWERS! WE DON'T KNOW *WHEN* THE EVIL MUTANTS WILL STRIKE NEXT! AND ALL YOU HAVE ON YOUR JUVENILE MIND IS A *TRACK MEET!?*

OKAY! OKAY! I CAN TAKE A HINT!

SLAM!

AND *DON'T* COME BACK UNTIL YOU GROW *UP!!*

BOY! WOTTA *GROUCH!* THAT GUY THINKS IT'S A *SIN* TO SMILE OR HAVE ANY FUN!

DON'T TAKE UMBRAGE AT CYCLOPS, BOBBY! HE CAN'T ALTER HIS PSYCHO- LOGICAL MAKE-UP!

C'MON IN, HANK! HAVE SOME HOT CHOCOLATE! WAIT'LL YOU SEE THIS RACE!

THERE, PROFESSOR! YOU DON'T WANT TO GET A CHILL WHILE WATCHING T.V. ! YOU'LL BE MORE COMFORTABLE NOW!

POOR PROFESSOR X! HOW LAMENTABLE THAT HIS ONCE SUPER-BRILLIANT BRAIN IS NOW MERELY THAT OF A NORMAL HUMAN'S!

LOOK! THERE'S THE FELLA I WANTED YOU TO SEE! HE'S BRINGING UP THE REAR! DON'T TAKE YOUR EYES OFF HIM!

WHAT'S SO *SPECIAL* ABOUT HIM? HE'S THE SLOWEST ONE OF ALL! HE RUNS *TERRIBLY!*

IT'S NOT HIS *RUNNING* THAT'S IMPORTANT! KEEP WATCHING... YOU'LL SEE WHAT I MEAN ANY SECOND NOW!

9.

BUT WHAT ABOUT THE *PROFESSOR*??

DON'T WORRY ABOUT *ME*, MY DEAR! I'LL BE ALL RIGHT HERE! JUST REMEMBER.. I CAN'T FOLLOW YOU MENTALLY! I WON'T BE ABLE TO HELP YOU!

WE'LL DO OKAY, SIR! WE'LL MAKE YOU PROUD OF US... YOU'LL SEE!

MEANWHILE, AT THE STADIUM NEARBY, THE MOB GROWS ANGRIER BY THE MINUTE...

THE RACES WERE ALL *PHONY*! LET'S TEACH THAT FRAUD HE CAN'T TRICK *US*!!

WE'LL MAKE HIM *TELL* US HOW HE DID IT! IT *HAS* TO BE SOME KIND OF *HOAX*!

THEN, JUST AS THE SHOUTING CROWD IS ABOUT TO CLOSE IN ...

HEY! WHA...??

DON'T SQUIRM, FELLA! YOU'RE HEAVY ENOUGH!

HE'S TOO HEAVY! THE ANGEL CAN'T FLY FAR ENOUGH WITH HIM! I'LL HAVE TO HOLD THE CROWD BACK TO GIVE HIM A RESPITE!

TAKE A BREATHER, ANGEL! I'LL ACT AS A BUFFER FOR YOU!

THANKS, BEAST! I CAN USE THE BREAK!!

THEN, AS THE ANGEL TAKES TO THE AIR AGAIN...

THE CAR WON'T HELP US, MARVEL GIRL! THE CROWD IS PRESSING IN FROM ALL SIDES! WE CAN'T RUN THEM DOWN!

WHAT WILL WE *DO*? WE CAN'T LET THAT MUTANT BE TAKEN FROM US!

I..I CAN'T STAY ALOFT WITH HIM MUCH LONGER!

WE'VE ONLY *ONE* RECOURSE ... *RUN*!!

THIS ICE-WALL WON'T HOLD THEM BACK FOREVER!

11.

SEEING THE STRANGE, COLORFUL FIGURES RACING TOWARDS THEM, THE CROWD FALLS BACK FOR A MOMENT IN SHOCK, GIVING THE X-MEN AND THEIR FELLOW MUTANT A CHANCE TO GET CLEAR...

THERE'S A SUBWAY STATION JUST AHEAD... HURRY!!

HOP IN... *QUICKLY!* WE'LL HOLD THE DOORS OPEN! THIS WAS A VERITABLE *HAIRSBREADTH ESCAPE!*

ALL CLEAR! ONCE WE'RE IN THE TRAIN WE'LL BE SAFE!

L-LOOK! LOOK WHO IT *IS!!*

SEE HOW EVERYONE IS *STARING* AT US!

IGNORE IT, MARVEL GIRL! WE PAID OUR FARE JUST LIKE ANYONE ELSE!

THERE'S SOMETHING VAGUELY *FAMILIAR* ABOUT YOU, MY FRIEND! SOMETHING *DISTURBINGLY* FAMILIAR!

IMPOSSIBLE! I NEVER MET YOU BEFORE!

WAIT! NOW I KNOW! THE WAY YOU *HOPPED!* ONLY ONE MUTANT HAS THAT ABILITY... THE *EVIL ONE* CALLED... *THE TOAD!!*

DON'T, BEAST! YOU'LL *HURT* HIM... *SAY!* IT *IS* THE TOAD!

BLAST YOU! I ALMOST HAD YOU FOOLED!

BUT YOU CAN'T *HOLD* ME! I'LL ESCAPE FROM *ALL* OF YOU!

IT MUST HAVE BEEN MAGNETO'S SCHEME TO FIND OUR HEAD-QUARTERS! HE WOULD'VE SUCCEEDED IF WE HAD TAKEN THE TOAD *BACK* WITH US! *GET HIM...*

12.

DON'T BE ALARMED! THERE'S NO PLACE HE CAN HOP TO WHERE I CAN'T FLY AFTER HIM!

YOU'RE RIGHT, ANGEL! BUT JUST TO PLAY SAFE, I'LL SLOW HIM UP A LITTLE...LIKE *THIS!*

HAH! CLUMSY FOOL...YOU *MISSED* ME!

THAT WAS THE *IDEA*, PLAYMATE! I WANTED MY ICE DISC TO HIT THE FLOOR IN FRONT OF YOU! PRETTY NEAT, EH?

WHY DON'T YOU *ANSWER* ME? UNLESS YOU'D RATHER KEEP SPINNING AROUND THAT WAY! BETTER GET HIM, ANGEL...HE MUST BE DIZZY ENOUGH BY NOW!

NICE TRY, TOAD...BUT YOU DIDN'T REALLY THINK YOU COULD BEAT THE *X-MEN*, DID YOU?

SUDDENLY, AT THAT SPLIT SECOND, A STARTLING INCIDENT OCCURS! THE HUGE CLOCK IN THE MIDDLE OF THE STATION *FLIES APART*...AS THOUGH UNDER THE CONTROL OF SOME MIGHTY, WRATHFUL *MAGNETIC POWER!*

ANGEL!! LOOK OUT!! THOSE METAL PIECES ARE FLYING TOWARDS YOU LIKE *BULLETS!*

WHEW! GOOD THING THE PROFESSOR GAVE ME SO MUCH AGILITY-PRACTICE IN THE PAST!

AND THEN, ONE OF THE MOST AWESOME MENACES APPEARS ON THE SCENE...THE MERCILESS *MAGNETO!!*

THE TOAD ALONE IS NO MATCH FOR THE *X-MEN*...BUT MAGNETO *IS!*

13.

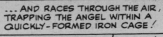

BUT THEN, THINGS HAPPEN WITH DAZZLING SPEED! THE LIGHTNING-SWIFT *QUICKSILVER* ATTACKS CYCLOPS FROM BEHIND, FREEING THE *TOAD!* SHOCKED, *MARVEL GIRL* TURNS AWAY FROM *MASTERMIND* TO COME TO CYCLOPS' AID...

RUN, TOAD! I'LL HANDLE CYCLOPS!!

OH, NO! I MUSTN'T LET CYCLOPS BE INJURED!!!

HAH! I'M SAFELY FREE OF THE GIRL'S POWER!

BUT *CYCLOPS* IS FAR LESS HELPLESS THAN IT WOULD APPEAR...

DON'T WORRY ABOUT *ME*, MARVEL GIRL! I'M NOT LETTING GO OF THE *TOAD!* AND QUICKSILVER WON'T HANG AROUND WHEN I AIM MY *POWER BEAM* HIS WAY!

KEEP YOUR EYE ON HIM! WATCH WHERE HE RUNS!

BLAST IT! I DIDN'T REALIZE HE COULD USE HIS POWER BEAM WHILE I WAS HOLDING HIS ARMS! I'VE GOT TO GET OUT OF RANGE!

ONLY MY GREAT SPEED IS SAVING ME FROM THOSE POWERFUL BLASTS! ANY *ONE* OF THEM COULD PUT ME OUT OF THE FIGHT!!

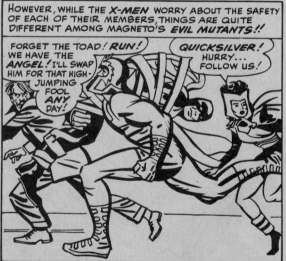

HOWEVER, WHILE THE *X-MEN* WORRY ABOUT THE SAFETY OF EACH OF THEIR MEMBERS, THINGS ARE QUITE DIFFERENT AMONG MAGNETO'S *EVIL MUTANTS!!*

FORGET THE TOAD! *RUN!* WE HAVE THE *ANGEL!* I'LL SWAP HIM FOR THAT HIGH-JUMPING FOOL *ANY* DAY!

QUICKSILVER! HURRY... FOLLOW US!

THEY'VE ABDUCTED THE *ANGEL!*

USING HIM AS A *HOSTAGE,* MAGNETO WILL HAVE AN INSURMOUNTABLE ADVANTAGE OVER US!

THE *BEAST* IS GAINING ON US! QUICK, MASTERMIND... WE NEED AN ILLUSION!

HE'LL NEVER REACH US! I'LL STOP HIM WITH... *THIS*...

15.

AT THAT VERY INSTANT, A CHARGING RHINOCEROS SEEMS TO COME HURTLING THROUGH THE ASTONISHED CROWD ...A WILD BEAST WHICH EXISTS ONLY IN THE IMAGINATIONS OF THOSE AFFECTED BY MASTERMIND'S UNCANNY POWER...

THE CROWD IS *PANICKING!* I CAN'T GET PAST WITHOUT INJURING SOMEONE! *MARVEL GIRL!* CAN YOU LIFT ME OVER THEM VIA TELEKINESES ??

I'LL *TRY!* OHHH, NO... YOU'RE TOO HEAVY! CAN'T LIFT YOU FAR ENOUGH!

MEANTIME, OUTSIDE THE TERMINAL, A MAGNETICALLY-POWERED SHIP SILENTLY DESCENDS TO EARTH...

AND BY THE TIME THE CROWD WITHIN HAS DISPERSED...

THEY'RE GETTING AWAY!!

I COULDN'T REACH THEM IN TIME! THEY'VE ABDUCTED THE ANGEL! I'VE *FAILED!!*

DON'T REPROACH YOURSELF, BEAST! WE'RE *ALL* TO BLAME! BUT THE BATTLE ISN'T OVER YET!

A SHORT TIME LATER, AT MAGNETO'S ASTEROID, ORBITING ABOVE THE EARTH...

TELL ME WHERE THE X-MEN'S HEADQUARTERS IS, ANGEL! ONCE I FIND PROFESSOR X, I'LL SET YOU FREE!

I'LL TELL YOU ONLY *ONE* THING, MISTER... DON'T HOLD YOUR BREATH WAITING FOR ME TO CRACK!

YOU YOUNG FOOL! DO YOU THINK I'LL LET YOU THWART ME *NOW?* ONLY *DEATH* WILL FREE YOU FROM ME! YOU'LL *HAVE* TO TALK!

MAGNETO! YOU CAN'T MEAN THAT! YOU NEVER TOLD ME THAT WE WOULD EVER DESCEND TO *MURDER!!*

16.

SPARE ME YOUR WEAK WHIMPERINGS, GIRL! I WILL STOP AT NOTHING TO ACHIEVE MASTERY OF EARTH... AND ONLY THE X-MEN STAND IN MY WAY!

I'VE GOT TO HOLD OUT! NO MATTER WHAT HE DOES TO ME, I MUSTN'T BETRAY THE OTHERS! NOT EVEN IF I PAY FOR MY SILENCE WITH MY LIFE!!

IN THE MOMENTS THAT FOLLOW, MAGNETO SUBJECTS THE TIGHT-LIPPED ANGEL TO HIS OWN UNIQUE FORM OF BRAINWASHING!

THOSE FLASHING LIGHT BEAMS WON'T HARM HIM PHYSICALLY, BUT THEY'LL PREVENT HIM FROM RESTING SO LONG AS HE'S HERE!

AND IT'S ONLY A MATTER OF TIME BEFORE THOSE HIGH-PITCHED SIRENS BECOME SO UNBEARABLE TO HIS EARS THAT HE'LL TELL ME ANYTHING I WANT TO KNOW!

FLYING TO THE CEILING WON'T HELP YOU, ANGEL! I CAN SEAL MY DEVICES BEHIND THAT METAL DOOR WHILE THE NOISE CONTINUES UNABATED!

I MUSTN'T WEAKEN! NO MATTER WHAT... I MUSTN'T WEAKEN!

AND AS THE HOURS TICK SLOWLY BY...

WHAT MANNER OF MAN IS THE ANGEL? WHAT IS THE SECRET OF PROFESSOR X'S TRAINING?? WHY CAN'T I BREAK HIS WILL?? WHY DOES HE RESIST ME??!!

MEANWHILE, AT A DESERTED PIER ON THE EAST RIVER...

WE CAN'T SET THE TOAD FREE... BUT WE CAN'T TAKE HIM TO OUR HQ IN CASE MAGNETO IS SCANNING US WITH SOME SORT OF MAGNETIC SPY DEVICE!

LOOK! SOMETHING SEEMS TO BE WRONG WITH HIM! SEE HOW HE'S TREMBLING!

I'VE GOT TO RETURN TO MAGNETO! I MUST RETURN!

HE KEEPS MUMBLING TO HIMSELF...

IT'S ALMOST AS THOUGH HE'S IN A VIRTUAL TRANCE! HE SEEMS OBLIVIOUS TO OUR PRESENCE... LIKE A MAN POSSESSED!!

LET'S LEAVE HIM ALONE! LET HIM TALK! WE'LL SEE WHAT HE DOES! IF IT'S NOT A TRICK, HE MAY LEAD US TO MAGNETO!

MAGNETO! I'VE GOT TO RETURN TO MAGNETO! SOMETHING IS LEADING ME TO HIM! I CANNOT RESIST!

DON'T LET HIM GO TOO FAR FROM US! IT MAY BE A RUSE! WE CAN'T AFFORD TO BE DUPED!

EASY, BEAST! HE WON'T GET AWAY FROM US!

GOSH, HE'S LIKE A GUY IN A TRANCE! IT'S REAL CREEPY!

17.

LOOK! HE HAD A HIDDEN MAGNETIC COMMUNICATOR UNDER HIS SOCK! HE'S CONTACTING MAGNETO WITH IT!!

AND MAGNETO GOT THE MESSAGE!! HERE COMES A DRONE PICK-UP CAPSULE... FROM ABOVE THE CLOUDS!

QUICKLY! WE'VE GOT TO ENTER IT WITH THE TOAD! EVEN IF IT'S A TRAP, WE CAN'T AFFORD TO SHIRK! IT MAY BE OUR ONE CHANCE TO FIND THE ANGEL!

AND WHEN WE DO FIND HIM, WE MUST PRAY THAT OUR POWER IS MORE THAN A MATCH FOR THE EVIL MUTANTS!

THERE'S MAGNETO'S HIDEOUT!! THAT ASTEROID ABOVE US!! THE CAPSULE IS BEING DRAWN TO AN OPENING BY A BAND OF MAGNETIC FORCE!!

SECONDS LATER...

TOAD!! HOW'D YOU ESCAPE THE X-MEN?? HOW'D YOU GET HERE??

I... HAD... TO... COME...

DID YOU HEAR THAT?? THEY WEREN'T EXPECTING HIM! IT'S NOT A TRAP! LET'S GO!!

FORGIVE THIS UNSEEMLY INTRUSION, MASTERMIND! BUT BEING WELL-BEHAVED LITTLE X-MEN, WE HATED TO TAKE OUR DEPARTURE WITHOUT SAYING GOOD-BYE!

ATTACK ME, WILL YOU?? LET'S SEE HOW WELL YOU FIGHT NOW... WHEN YOU FEEL YOUR LEGS TURNING TO DOUGH!

DON'T LET HIM STOP YOU, BEAST! IT'S JUST ANOTHER OF HIS ILLUSIONS!

MY BRAIN IS AWARE OF THAT... BUT I STILL CAN'T MOVE MY LEGS!

18

BUT YOU'LL FIND THAT *THIS* IS NO ILLUSION!

SHOULDN'T HAVE LOST MENTAL CONTACT, MASTERMIND! MY REFLEXES ARE FASTER THAN YOURS!

IF YOU THREATEN *ONE* X-MAN, YOU THREATEN US *ALL!* THAT GUN WILL NEVER MENACE US AGAIN!

BLAM!

QUICK, TOAD...TO MAGNETO! *WE* CAN'T FIGHT THEM ALONE!

TO MAGNETO!! HOORAY!! THE *LEADER* WILL SAVE US! THE *LEADER* CAN DO ANYTHING!

MAGNETO!! RIGHT BEHIND US! IT'S THE X-MEN!

QUIET, YOU EMOTIONAL FOOL! I HEARD THE ENTIRE THING! EVEN *NOW* I'M ARRANGING FOR THEIR FINAL DEFEAT!

BY MEANS OF THIS MAGNETIC INTENSIFIER, I HAVE INCREASED MY MAGNETIC POWER SO THAT I CAN MENTALLY CONTROL ANY METAL PORTION OF THIS ASTEROID! I'LL TURN MY ENTIRE HEADQUARTERS INTO A GIANT FLOATING DEATH TRAP!!

AND, TRUE TO HIS WORD, THE NEXT INSTANT...

CYCLOPS!! *LOOK OUT!* THAT PIECE OF METAL SHEETING IS DROPPING ON YOU AS THOUGH IT HAS A MIND OF ITS OWN!

MMPFF! CAN'T SEE... I'M ABLE TO BREATHE... BUT CAN'T USE MY POWER RAY!!

I..I CAN'T TEAR IT OFF!! IT'S TOO STRONG! I'LL TRY MY OWN MENTAL POWER...

BUT BEFORE SHE CAN MAKE A MOVE..

ALL THESE THINGS HAPPENING... CONFUSING ME...

BEEEEEEP!

CAN'T CONCENTRATE! CAN'T USE THE POWER OF MY BRAIN!

19.

20.

YOU THINK *YOU* CAN STOP ME?? YOU THINK YOU CAN STAND UP TO *MAGNETO,* THE MOST POWERFUL MUTANT OF ALL?!!

I'LL DO WHAT I *HAVE* TO IN ORDER TO PROTECT MY SISTER, WANDA... REMEMBER THAT!

BE CAREFUL, PIETRO! I FEAR WE ARE *STILL* NO MATCH FOR HIM!!

BUT, WE ARE DESTINED NEVER TO KNOW WHAT MIGHT HAVE HAPPENED NEXT, FOR AT THAT INSTANT, A MIGHTY *FORCE BEAM* BLASTS THE DOOR RIGHT OFF ITS HINGES!

WE FORGOT THE X-MEN! THEY'VE CRASHED THROUGH!

GET *BACK,* WANDA!! TAKE COVER! IT IS THAT ACCURSED *CYCLOPS,* AND HIS POWER BEAM!

QUICKSILVER, LISTEN TO ME! YOU'RE FIGHTING FOR THE WRONG CAUSE! DESERT MAGNETO...JOIN THE X-MEN!

I *HATE* MAGNETO...MORE THAN ANYONE KNOWS! BUT HE ONCE SAVED MY SISTER'S LIFE! I *MUST* SERVE HIM!

BUT DON'T YOU *SEE?* HE'S MAKING *CRIMINALS* OUT OF YOU AND THE SCARLET WITCH! IF YOU JOIN *US,* WE COULD..

NO MORE!! I'LL HEAR NO MORE! YOU'RE TRYING TO CONFUSE US! *YOU'RE* NOT OUR FRIENDS, EITHER! IF YOU *WERE,* YOU WOULDN'T FIGHT US! WE CAN'T TRUST *ANYONE!*

YOU WERE TOO CARELESS! YOU CAME TOO NEAR! NOW I'VE *GOT* YOU!

GIVE UP, QUICKSILVER! DON'T MAKE ME USE MY POWER BEAM ON YOU!

QUICK! PUT A *HEX* ON CYCLOPS!

THEY'RE TOO *CLOSE!* IT MIGHT HURT QUICKSILVER!

MEANTIME, THE OTHER X-MEN DESPERATELY TRY TO FREE THE CAPTURED ANGEL, REALIZING THAT EVERY SECOND SPENT PLACES THEM IN STILL GREATER DANGER!!

IT'S UNBREAKABLE GLASS, BUT I CAN FEEL IT GIVING! JUST A FEW MORE THUMPS MAY DO IT!

21.

HOLD IT, HANK! LET ME TRY IT... MY WAY! I CAN MENTALLY HURL ONE OF THESE HEAVY CHEMICAL TANKS AT THE GLASS WITH EVEN GREATER FORCE!!

YOU DID IT! HE CAN EXTRICATE HIMSELF NOW!

I KNEW YOU'D FREE ME!! BUT YOU'RE IN GRAVE PERIL! MAGNETO CAN TURN THIS ENTIRE ASTEROID INTO ONE GIANT DEATH TRAP!!

THE SUSPICION IS BEGINNING TO DAWN ON US THAT HIS MOTIVES ARE NOT THE FRIENDLIEST!

BUT, PERHAPS WE CAN INSTILL SOME OF THE MILK OF HUMAN KINDNESS IN HIS... SAY! WHAT HAVE WE HERE??!

DON'T LET IT THROW YOU! IT MUST BE ONE OF MASTERMIND'S IMAGES... WATCH! I'LL PROVE IT!!

AND, NOW, TALL, DARK, AND GRUESOME, WE'VE GOT A LITTLE SETTLING UP TO DO, SO WE MIGHT AS WELL GET STARTED!

HURRY, MASTERMIND... DON'T LET HIM GET YOU! TOO BAD YOU CAN'T HOP AWAY FROM YOUR ENEMIES LIKE THE TOAD!

NO! NO! STAY BACK!

BUT THE SOUNDS OF CONFLICT HAVE REACHED MAGNETO'S EARS, AND SO...

STOP YOUR WHINING, MASTERMIND! MY DART GRENADE WILL SAVE YOU!

X-MEN! LOOK OUT! IT EXPLODED INTO A THOUSAND FLYING DARTS!!

THEY'RE FASTER THAN I THOUGHT! THEY ALL SAVED THEMSELVES BY TAKING COVER! BUT AT LEAST I SLOWED THEIR ATTACK!

WAIT!! THAT RUMBLING SOUND!! CAN IT BE WHAT I THINK??!

22.

IT *IS*!! THE ASTEROID IS BREAKING UP!! DURING THE BATTLE SOMEONE MUST HAVE BRUSHED AGAINST SOME OF THE DETONATE BUTTONS!! BUT, I SHALL TURN THIS TO MY ADVANTAGE!

SAVE ME, MAGNETO! I DON'T WANT TO DIE!

SILENCE, TOAD! IT IS THE *X-MEN* WHO SHOULD BE FEARFUL! *THEY'RE* THE ONES WHO ARE DOOMED!

FIRST, WE MUST GET THEM TOGETHER, ON THE OTHER SIDE OF THE AIR LOCK!

AHH, THERE'S *CYCLOPS!* I'LL START WITH *HIM!*

NOW! BEFORE HE CAN USE HIS POWER BEAM!!

FORGIVE ME FOR ATTACKING YOU FROM BEHIND, BUT *WE* DON'T FIGHT BY ANY RULES!

THERE! STAY BEHIND THE AIR CHAMBER WITH YOUR WRETCHED PARTNERS! I LEAVE YOU TO EMPTY SPACE!!

MAGNETO, NO!! YOU'RE MAKING A *MISTAKE!*

IT'S NO USE, *TOAD!* HE DOESN'T HEAR YOU!

THE X-MEN *AREN'T* BEHIND THE AIR LOCK! THEY'RE STILL IN *THIS* SECTION WITH *US!*

THEN WE'LL FINISH *THEM* LATER! AT LEAST THE *CYCLOPS* WILL NEVER BOTHER US AGAIN!

BUT THE *X-MEN* NEVER DESERT ONE OF THEIR OWN, AND SO...

I'VE GOT TO FLY TO SCOTT BEFORE THAT SECTION CRUMBLES BENEATH HIM AND HE PLUNGES TO EARTH!

WAIT! I'LL *HELP* YOU!

THERE! I FASHIONED A TUBULAR *ICE BRIDGE* FOR YOU...IT'LL PROTECT YOU BOTH FROM THE BITTER COLD OUT THERE!!

23.

Panel 1: SCOTT! SCOTTY BOY! DO YOU *HEAR* ME? I'M COMING, FELLA! HANG ON!

Panel 2: Y-YOU WERE JUST IN TIME, WARREN! THE FRAGMENT WAS CRUMBLING... I COULD JUST BARELY KEEP FROM FALLING!!

YOU'RE OKAY, *NOW*, PARTNER! BUT WE'RE *STILL* NOT IN THE CLEAR! *BOTH* SECTIONS ARE STARTING TO SPLIT APART!

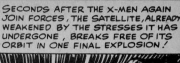

Panel 3: SECONDS AFTER THE X-MEN AGAIN JOIN FORCES, THE SATELLITE, ALREADY WEAKENED BY THE STRESSES IT HAS UNDERGONE, BREAKS FREE OF ITS ORBIT IN ONE FINAL EXPLOSION!

Panel 4: BUT, BEFORE DRIFTING OUT INTO AIRLESS SPACE, IT LAUNCHES A SILENT, MAGNETICALLY-POWERED ESCAPE SHIP... CONTAINING FIVE WEARY BUT TRIUMPHANT *X-MEN!*

NOT A SECOND TOO SOON!!

Panel 5: THEN, AS THE TEEN-AGERS REACH SAFETY...

IT'S *RISING* AGAIN... BY REMOTE CONTROL!

MAGNETO AND HIS MUTANTS MUST STILL BE UP THERE... IT'S RETURNING FOR THEM!

Panel 6: MAGNETO CAN CONTROL ITS COURSE *MENTALLY!* THERE'S NO TELLING *WHERE* HE'LL LAND!

IF THE EVIL MUTANTS SURVIVED, THIS WAS ONLY THE SECOND ROUND!! THEY'LL BE MORE DANGEROUS THAN *EVER!*

AND SO WILL *WE*, JEAN! WE *PROVED* OUR METTLE TODAY! BY OURSELVES!

Panel 7: FINALLY, UPON RETURNING TO THEIR SCHOOL...

I'LL GIVE THE PROFESSOR OUR REPORT...

NO *NEED* TO, SCOTT! I WAS WITH YOU ALL THE TIME... LISTENING TO YOUR THOUGHTS!

YOU MEAN... YOU HAVE YOUR MENTAL *POWER* BACK?!

Panel 8: I NEVER *LOST* IT! I ONLY *PRETENDED* TO, AFTER OUR FIRST BATTLE WITH THE EVIL MUTANTS!

BUT... *WHY*, SIR?

REMEMBER, THIS IS A *SCHOOL!* AND YOU CAN'T GRADUATE FROM ANY SCHOOL WITHOUT PASSING YOUR FINAL EXAM! WELL, YOU'VE ALL JUST *TAKEN* YOUR FINAL EXAM... JUST AS I PLANNED IT!

Panel 9: AND I'M PROUD TO SAY THAT YOU'VE ALL *PASSED* WITH FLYING COLORS! YOU'VE PROVEN YOU CAN THINK AND ACT FOR YOURSELVES!! YOUR TRAINING PERIOD IS OVER! *CONGRATULATIONS*, MY X-MEN!!

EDITOR'S NOTE: NOW THAT THEIR TRAINING IS ENDED, EVEN GREATER DANGERS AWAIT THEM! FOR THE STRANGE SAGA OF THE X-MEN IS JUST *BEGINNING!!* STAN AND JACK HAVE A MILLION SURPRISES IN STORE FOR YOU... SO BE WITH US NEXT ISH! *SEE YOU THEN!*

24.

MMM...BOY! IF THERE'S ONE THING I LIKE BETTER THAN PIE AND ICE CREAM, IT'S *MORE* PIE AND ICE CREAM!

I'LL JUST SHUT MY EYES AND ENJOY EVERY LAST... *HEY!!*

CLACK!

SOME WISE GUY IS GONNA GET HIMSELF A FISTFUL OF KNUCKLES IF... *JEAN!* WHAT'S GOIN' ON?!

BOBBY DRAKE!! YOU *KNOW* HOW PROFESSOR X FEELS ABOUT TABLE MANNERS! *NEXT* TIME USE YOUR FORK!!

GOSH, PROFESSOR... SOMETIMES WHEN I LISTEN TO ALL THE KIDDING AROUND, IT'S HARD TO BELIEVE WE'RE REALLY A GROUP OF *HOMO SUPERIOR* MUTANTS!

IT'S NATURAL FOR YOU TO FEEL THAT WAY, WARREN! AFTER ALL, EXCEPT FOR THE FACT THAT EACH OF US POSSESSES A UNIQUE SUPER-POWER, WE'RE NO DIFFERENT FROM ORDINARY HOMO SAPIENS!

I WONDER IF THERE ARE MANY *MORE* MUTANTS LIVING AMONG US WHOM WE DON'T SUSPECT?

I BELIEVE THERE ARE, JEAN! IN FACT, THAT'S OUR MISSION ...TO LOCATE THEM BEFORE THEY ARE FOUND BY THE *EVIL MUTANTS!*

HMM, SO MUCH HAS BEEN WRITTEN ABOUT PRINCE NAMOR, THE *SUB-MARINER,* LATELY! I WONDER IF HE, TOO, MIGHT NOT BE A MUTANT!

WHERE IS SUB-MARINER??

COAST GUARD PATROLS KEEP CONSTANT SEA-WATCH!

IF HE *IS,* WHAT A POWERFUL ALLY HE WOULD BE FOR THE X-MEN!! AND WHAT A DANGEROUS *FOE* HE WOULD BE IF HE JOINED *MAGNETO'S* EVIL MUTANTS!!

WE CANNOT CHANCE IT!! WE MUST *FIND* SUB-MARINER!

AS FATE WOULD HAVE IT, AT THAT VERY MOMENT, ON AN UNCHARTED ISLE FAR OUT TO SEA...

WE CAN DELAY NO LONGER! *SUB-MARINER MUST BE FOUND!*

BUT HE'S TOO STRONG, MASTER! WHAT IF HE WON'T OBEY YOU??

SILENCE, TOAD! HAVE YOU FORGOTTEN MY POWER?? HE SHALL OBEY *MAGNETO!!*

2.

SO FAR THE *X-MEN* HAVE FOILED ME AT EVERY TURN! BUT, WITH THE *SUB-MARINER* SERVING ME, I'LL DEFEAT THEM ONCE AND FOR ALL!

I SHALL CHOOSE MY MOST AWESOME WEAPONS! NAMOR WILL *HAVE* TO YIELD TO ME!

SUDDENLY, INCREDIBLY, ONE OF THE MOST FEARED OF ALL THE *X-MEN* APPEARS IN MAGNETO'S DOORWAY...

IT'S *CYCLOPS!* RUN, MASTER! HE'S RAISING HIS VISOR!!

BAH!! I'LL BLAST HIM TO SMITHEREENS FIRST!

THE RAY WENT RIGHT *THROUGH* HIM! WHAT *NEW* POWER HAS THE ACCURSED TEEN-AGER DEVELOPED?!

WITH NOTHING TO CHECK IT, MAGNETO'S MIGHTY RAY TRAVELS THROUGH THE GREAT HALL, PAST THE MUTANT CALLED *MASTERMIND* WHO RECOILS JUST IN TIME!

BUT ANOTHER OF MAGNETO'S ALLIES, SEEING THE DEADLY RAY, HAS BUT ONE THOUGHT IN MIND... TO MAKE SURE IT DOESN'T STRIKE HIS SISTER! AND SO, THE SUPER-SWIFT *QUICKSILVER* SUDDENLY STREAKS THROUGH THE CASTLE!!

WANDA! I'VE GOT TO REACH WANDA!

AND THEN, A SPLIT-SECOND BEFORE THE RAY CAN TOUCH HER, *QUICKSILVER* HURLS THE *SCARLET WITCH* TO SAFETY!!

PIETRO! YOU *SAVED* ME!!

WHAT *WAS* IT, PIETRO?? ARE THE *X-MEN* ATTACKING US AGAIN? HOW DID THEY *FIND* US?? WHERE IS *MAGNETO??*

I DO NOT KNOW, WANDA! BUT WHOEVER DARED DO THIS THING WILL *PAY* FOR IT! I HAVE PLEDGED MY LIFE TO GUARD YOU, MY SISTER!

3.

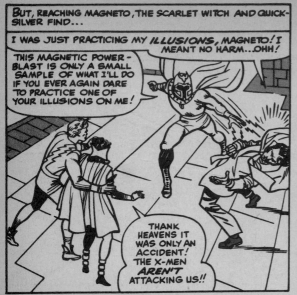

4.

THEN, IN THE SECLUSION OF HIS STUDY, THE MAN WITH THE MIGHTIEST BRAIN ON EARTH PREPARES TO SEARCH FOR SUB-MARINER, EVEN AS HIS ARCH-FOE *MAGNETO* IS DOING...

IF ONLY MY *PHYSICAL* BODY WERE AS FREE AS MY MENTAL IMAGE! BUT EVEN THE GREAT MUTANT POWER OF MY BRAIN IS NOT ENOUGH TO CURE MY HELPLESS FLESH-AND-BLOOD LEGS!

BECAUSE IT IS A PROJECTION OF HIS *MIND* WHICH IS TRAVELLING, IT CAN SURVIVE AS EASILY UNDER THE SEA AS IN THE AIR, AND SO THE DRAMATIC SEARCH BEGINS!

IF HE IS ANYWHERE IN THIS AREA, I SHOULD BE ABLE TO SENSE HIS PRESENCE!

BUT, BEFORE VERY LONG...

I *DO* SENSE ANOTHER PRESENCE... BUT IT IS AN *EVIL* ONE... COMING CLOSER.. AND CLOSER..

IT IS *MAGNETO!* IT CAN BE NO OTHER!!

HE, TOO, MUST BE SEEKING PRINCE NAMOR! BUT I SHALL NOT LET HIM FIND *ME* HERE!

WHEN NEXT WE MEET, IT SHALL BE AT A TIME OF *MY OWN* CHOOSING! I'LL RETURN TO MY STUDY AND LET MAGNETO FINISH MY QUEST FOR ME!!

A SHORT TIME LATER, LITTLE DREAMING THAT PROFESSOR X *KNOWS* OF HIS PRESENCE, *MAGNETO* APPEARS...

I'M GETTING *CLOSER* TO SUB-MARINER.. I CAN *FEEL* IT!!

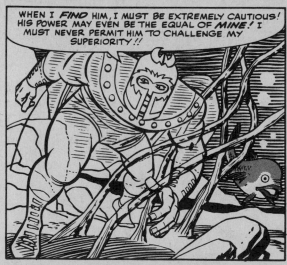

WHEN I *FIND* HIM, I MUST BE EXTREMELY CAUTIOUS! HIS POWER MAY EVEN BE THE EQUAL OF *MINE!* I MUST NEVER PERMIT HIM TO CHALLENGE MY SUPERIORITY!!

FINALLY, GUIDED BY THE EXTRA-SENSORY PERCEPTION OF HIS MUTANT BRAIN, MAGNETO SIGHTS HIS OBJECTIVE...

A REGAL CASTLE, UNDER THE SEA!! I'VE FOUND THE SUB-MARINER!!

5.

THERE HE *IS!* BUT...NEVER HAVE I SEEN SUCH *ANGER*... SUCH *INHUMAN RAGE!*

AGAIN THE FANTASTIC FOUR HAVE DEFEATED ME!! AGAIN THE GIRL I LOVE HAS SPURNED ME!!* THOUGH I AM PRINCE OF THE DEEP, MONARCH OF THE SEA, MY TITLES ARE HOLLOW...MY KINGDOM IS EMPTY AND MEANINGLESS!!

FANTASTIC FOUR #27...EDITOR.

WHAT DOES MY CASTLE MEAN?? WHAT USE IS MY *CROWN* TO ME?? THOUGH MY *POWER* IS ALMOST WITHOUT LIMIT, I LIVE HERE LIKE AN *EXILE!!*

THE HUMANS HAVE TAKEN FROM ME EVERYTHING I HELD MOST DEAR!! BECAUSE OF THEM MY PEOPLE HAVE DESERTED ME...ONLY YOU, A HANDFUL OF LOYAL FOLLOWERS, REMAIN!!

BEGONE!! THE VERY *SIGHT* OF YOU REMINDS ME OF MY BYGONE DAYS OF GLORY!!

BUT THOSE DAYS WILL RETURN *AGAIN!* AND WHEN THEY DO, PRINCE NAMOR SHALL RULE BOTH THE SEA AND THE *LAND*... EVERYTHING THAT LIVES ON EARTH SHALL PAY ME HOMAGE!

HIS ANGER IS TOO GREAT! I SHALL NOT APPROACH HIM YET! INSTEAD, I'LL GET *ANOTHER* TO DO MY BIDDING!

I DETECT A PRESENCE BEHIND ME...SO FILLED WITH EVIL, IT CHILLS MY BLOOD!

WHO... *WHAT* ARE YOU??

I AM *MAGNETO!* THAT IS ALL YOU NEED KNOW! I AM HERE TO GIVE YOU POWER BEYOND YOUR WILDEST DREAMS!

6.

I HAVE CHOSEN WELL! I CAN SENSE THE GREED, AND THE ENVY IN THIS MAN'S HEART! HE IS PERFECT!

HOW WOULD *YOU* LIKE TO REPLACE PRINCE NAMOR AS RULER OF ATLANTIS?!

ME??! HOW??

JUST DO AS I SAY!! GIVE THE SUB-MARINER A *MESSAGE* FROM ME! REPEAT IT EXACTLY AS I TELL YOU TO!

WHY SHOULD I *TRUST* YOU?? WHAT *KIND* OF MESSAGE?

IT IS A MESSAGE THAT WILL MAKE SUB-MARINER *LEAVE* HERE TO JOIN ME... AND WITH HIM GONE... A CLEVER MAN MIGHT EASILY STEAL POWER...!!

HMM!

MEANWHILE, BACK AT HIS HEADQUARTERS, PROFESSOR X COMES OUT OF HIS TRANCE...

GATHER 'ROUND ME, MY X-MEN... WE ARE ABOUT TO BEGIN A NEW MISSION!

OH, BOY! AT *LAST!!*

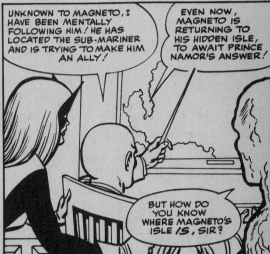

UNKNOWN TO MAGNETO, I HAVE BEEN MENTALLY FOLLOWING HIM! HE HAS MENTALLY LOCATED THE SUB-MARINER AND IS TRYING TO MAKE HIM AN ALLY!

EVEN NOW, MAGNETO IS RETURNING TO HIS HIDDEN ISLE, TO AWAIT PRINCE NAMOR'S ANSWER!

BUT HOW DO YOU KNOW WHERE MAGNETO'S ISLE *IS*, SIR?

"SOME DAYS AGO A FREIGHTER IN THE NORTH ATLANTIC REPORTED THAT ITS COMPASS SEEMED TO HAVE GONE MAD! I INVESTIGATED THE REPORT..."

"LATER, THE SHIP SIGHTED A MYSTERIOUS ISLE WITH A HUGE MAGNETIC DEVICE EMITTING STRANGE RAYS ... "

"AND THEN, BEFORE THE CREW COULD BE SURE THEY WEREN'T DREAMING, OR HAVING A MASS HALLUCINATION, THE ENTIRE FREIGHTER SEEMED TO BE LIFTED BY AN IRRESISTIBLE MAGNETIC FORCE, AND WAS FINALLY PUT DOWN FIFTY MILES SOUTH OF BERMUDA!"

7

I SURMISE IT WASN'T DIFFICULT FOR YOU TO PUT TWO AND TWO TOGETHER, PROFESSOR?

NOT AT ALL, HANK! AND NOW, WE'RE GOING TO CHARTER A SAILBOAT AND TAKE A LITTLE CRUISE!

AND IF WE HAPPEN TO FIND MAGNETO'S ISLE AT THE SAME TIME, WE'LL TRY NOT TO BE TOO SURPRISED!

A SHORT TIME LATER, THE STRANGEST CREW EVER TO MAN A SAILING VESSEL TAKES TO SEA, AND AFTER A FEW HOURS...

STILL NO SIGN OF LAND FROM HERE, PROFESSOR!

RETURN TO THE SHIP, ANGEL!

OUR T.V. CAMERA CAN "SEE" A GREATER DISTANCE THAN THE ANGEL CAN! LIFT IT AS HIGH AS POSSIBLE BY YOUR TELE-KINETIC POWER, JEAN!

YES, SIR!

NO LUCK, PROFESSOR! THE REMOTE CONTROL T.V. SCREEN STILL SHOWS NO TRACE OF AN ISLAND!

VERY WELL THEN! HANK, YOU MAY RETRIEVE THE CAMERA FOR US!

I'D BE DELIGHTED, SIR! I'VE BEEN PERFECTING THIS MANEUVER FOR DAYS NOW!

BEAST! LOOK OUT!! THE ROPE IS FRAYED! ...IT'S SPLITTING!!

CORRECTION... IT SPLIT!

I'LL GET YOU, HANK! OH... I...I CAN'T HOLD YOU... TOO HEAVY!

LEAVE IT TO ME, JEAN!

NOTHING LIKE A NICE SOFT, MUSHY PILE OF SNOW FOR A FELLA TO LAND IN!

LUCKY MARVEL GIRL WAS ABLE TO HOLD HANK LONG ENOUGH FOR YOU TO WHIP THAT SNOW UP, BOBBY!

8.

9.

A SHORT TIME LATER...

MAGNETO'S ISLE IS INDEED WELL HIDDEN! EVEN WITH DIRECTIONS IT WAS HARD TO FIND!

SUB-MARINER!! I KNEW YOU'D COME! I AM MAGNETO!! THIS IS MY ISLAND!

SILENCE!

NONE SPEAK IN THE PRESENCE OF ROYALTY WITHOUT FIRST BEING RECOGNIZED!!

BEFORE WE TALK, I SHALL SCOUT THIS ISLE AND MAKE SURE I HAVE NOT ENTERED SOME SORT OF HIDDEN TRAP!!

ALL I HEARD ABOUT HIM IS TRUE! HE IS EVERY INCH A MONARCH! AND HE'S SURE OF HIS STRENGTH!

BUT I MUST FIND A WAY TO INFLUENCE HIM...TO CONTROL HIM!

AH! YOU ARE WHAT I NEED! ONCE HE SETS HIS EYES ON THE SCARLET WITCH, HE'LL BE PUTTY IN OUR HANDS!

LET MY SISTER GO, MAGNETO, OR BY THUNDER, I'LL....!

SHE'S IN NO DANGER, QUICKSILVER! I MERELY WANT HER TO MEET SOMEONE!

IT'S ALL RIGHT, PIETRO! WE MUST TRUST MAGNETO! WE BOTH OWE HIM OUR LIVES!*

*X-MEN #4...EDITOR.

HOW NOBLE HE LOOKS...HOW SLIM, YET MUSCULAR! HE'S FASCINATING!

EVERYTHING ON THIS ISLE IS POWERED BY MAGNETISM!

WHY WOULD SOMEONE SO FINE, SO MASTERFUL, WANT TO ALLY HIMSELF WITH THE EVIL MAGNETO?? WELL, IT IS NOT FOR ME TO QUESTION!

I'LL APPROACH HIM...TAP HIM ON THE SHOULDER, AND THEN...OH, NO! I CARELESSLY MADE A GESTURE! IT WILL CAUSE MY HEX POWER TO OPERATE!!

10.

SUB-MARINER... LOOK OUT!

A BURST OF HIGH VOLTAGE *ELECTRICITY!*

HE'S RIPPING OUT THE CABLE WIRES WHICH I ACCIDENTALLY HEXED... WITH HIS *BARE HAND!!*

WANDA! WHAT HAPPENED?

IT IS ALL RIGHT, PIETRO! PRINCE NAMOR WAS SUBJECTED TO A DEADLY AMOUNT OF ELECTRICITY... AND IT DID NO MORE THAN JOLT HIM!

YOU WERE THE CAUSE OF THAT?

YES, BUT I DID NOT *MEAN* IT! SOMETIMES MY *HEX POWER* GETS OUT OF HAND! I AM THE SCARLET WITCH... AND THIS IS MY BROTHER, *QUICKSILVER!*

I STILL DO NOT TRUST HIM, WANDA!

SO *THAT'S* THE FAMOUS SUB-MARINER! HE'S JUST A MAN IN SWIMMING TRUNKS! WHAT A DISAPPOINTMENT!

SEE THE WINGS ON HIS FEET! HOW *SMALL* THEY ARE! OF WHAT *USE* CAN THEY BE?

FOOLS! HIS STRENGTH IS THAT OF A HUNDRED HUMANS!! HE HAS NO *NEED* OF COSTUME, OR WEAPONS! WITH SUCH AN ALLY BESIDE ME, I COULD CONQUER THE *WORLD!*

THEN, AT THAT VERY SPLIT-SECOND, A FLASHING, FLYING FORM SWOOPS PAST THE STARTLED GROUP OF MUTANTS...

THAT MEANS THE X-MEN ARE HERE!! THEY'VE *FOUND* US!!

LOOK! IT IS THE ANGEL!

SILENCE!! DON'T PANIC!! IF THE X-MEN ATTACK US, IT WILL BE THEIR GREATEST BLUNDER!! HERE, ON MY HOME GROUNDS, I CANNOT BE DEFEATED!!

11

A SHORT DISTANCE AWAY, AN ALARM IS SOUNDED...

HANK! ANGEL IS HEADING THIS WAY! HE NEEDS HELP!

HE'S COMING LIKE A *BULLET*! BUT DON'T WORRY...I'LL RETARD HIS PROGRESS!

GOOD WORK, NATURE BOY! HERE'S A LITTLE ASSIST FROM *ICEMAN* TO KEEP YOU FROM LANDING TOO HARD!!

FREEZING ON IMPACT, THE SPRAY OF ICE WHICH BOBBY DRAKE HURLED UPWARDS TOWARDS HIS TWO PARTNERS BECOMES A MAKESHIFT *SLIDE*, ENABLING THEM TO REACH THE SHIP SAFELY!

SORRY I DON'T HAVE TIME TO SEND YOU A *SLED*, FELLAS...BUT I GUESS YOU'LL FORGIVE ME!

THAT WAS QUICK-THINKING, HANK! THE PROFESSOR WAS PLEASED!

SPEAKING OF THE PROFESSOR...HE WANTS ANGEL TO REPORT TO HIM AT ONCE!

AND SO...

YOU WERE *RIGHT*, SIR! SUB-MARINER IS ON THE ISLE WITH MAGNETO!

THAT'S WHAT I *FEARED*! WE MAY ALREADY BE TOO LATE!

WHAT'S OUR NEXT MOVE, PROFESSOR?

WE CAN'T WASTE A MINUTE! WE'VE GOT TO HIT THEM *FAST*.. HIT THEM *HARD*! PREPARE FOR *ACTION*, MY X-MEN!

BUT, KNOWING THE POWER OF THE X-MEN, MAGNETO, *TOO*, PREPARES TO ATTACK, AS THE LARGEST MAGNET ON EARTH IS ZEROED IN ON THE X-MEN'S SHIP!!

13.

SUBJECTED TO A FORCE AGAINST WHICH THERE IS NO DEFENSE, THE STURDY SHIP IS TORN APART IN SECONDS!

ABANDON SHIP!

HANG ON, SIR! I'LL GET YOU... SOMEHOW!!

THE PROFESSOR!! WHERE IS THE PROFESSOR??

DON'T WORRY, ABOUT ME, HANK! MAKE SURE THE OTHERS ARE SAFE!

DON'T WORRY, SIR! WITH THE TRAINING YOU GAVE US, WE'LL ALL BE SAFE!

I'LL JUST TREAD WATER THIS WAY TO HOLD YOU UP TILL HELP COMES!

HAVE NO FEAR, BEASTIE DEAR... HELP IS HERE! I'LL MAKE AN ICY PLATFORM TO GET US TO MAGNETO'S ISLE!

MAGNETO WILL HAVE ONLY HIMSELF TO BLAME FOR WHAT HAPPENS NOW!

MINUTES LATER, UNARMED, BUT UNAFRAID, THE VALIANT BAND OF X-MEN APPROACHES THE MOST DANGEROUS ISLE ON THE FACE OF THE EARTH!

HEADS UP! WE'RE ALMOST THERE!

SUDDENLY...

HOLD IT! WHERE DID THIS WALL OF SPINE ROOTS COME FROM?? IT WASN'T HERE BEFORE?

BEATS ME, SCOTTY! IT'LL TAKE US FOREVER TO HACK OUR WAY THROUGH THEM!

BUT THEN, THE CLEAR, COMMANDING VOICE OF PROFESSOR X RINGS OUT...

IT WILL TAKE LESS TIME THAN YOU SUSPECT! WITHOUT STOPPING, WALK STRAIGHT INTO THE SPINE ROOTS! YOU FIRST, CYCLOPS!

YES, SIR... IF YOU SAY SO!!

14.

15.

16.

I CAN'T SHAKE THESE METAL PIECES OFF ME!! HE'S PRESSING THEM TIGHTER AND TIGHTER... MENTALLY!

I REALIZE NOW THAT I MISJUDGED YOU! ALL YOU POSSESS IS BRUTE STRENGTH! MY POWER IS MUCH GREATER... FOR IT IS THE UNIVERSAL POWER OF MAGNETISM!

BUT, AT THAT MOMENT, A SUDDEN BLAST ROCKS THE CHAMBER, JOLTING MAGNETO AND HIS TWO EVIL HENCHMEN AS THE VERY ISLE SEEMS TO QUIVER WITH THE FORCE OF THE BLAST!

AND THEN, BEFORE THE EVIL MUTANTS REGAIN THEIR BALANCE...

YOU WERE RIGHT ON TARGET, CYCLOPS!

ONE THING ABOUT YOU, SCOTTY... YOU SURE KNOW HOW TO MAKE AN ENTRANCE!

QUICK... RUSH THEM BEFORE THEY RECOVER THEMSELVES!

MAGNETO HAS FLED! WE'RE ALONE, MASTERMIND! QUICK, SAVE US FROM THE X-MEN!

I'VE GOT TO ACT FAST BEFORE HE GETS ME WITH THAT ACCURSED BEAM OF HIS!

GOOD! THE OTHER X-MEN ARE AT HIS SIDE NOW... THIS IS OUR ONLY CHANCE... AN HYPNOTIC ILLUSION WHICH CANNOT FAIL!

WHERE DID THIS SUDDEN FOG COME FROM?

IT WASN'T HERE A SECOND AGO!

IT'S ONE OF MASTERMIND'S ILLUSIONS! IT HAS TO BE!

ILLUSION OR NOT... WE CAN'T SEE!

I'VE GOT AN IDEA, GANG! EVEN THOUGH WE CAN'T SEE THEM... WE CAN ALWAYS TRY TO FREEZE THEM OUT! WATCH THIS!

17.

QUICK! THROUGH THIS IRON DOOR BEFORE YOU'RE FROZEN INTO IMMOBILITY!

THOSE BLASTED TEEN-AGERS WON'T EVER STAY BEATEN!

SCARLET WITCH!! HURRY! I'VE GOT TO SEAL THIS DOOR!!

NO! I WON'T LEAVE WITHOUT MY BROTHER! I CAN'T DESERT PIETRO!

HAVE IT YOUR OWN WAY, THEN! MY SAFETY IS ALL THAT MATTERS! ONLY THROUGH MY LEADERSHIP CAN HOMO SUPERIOR TAKE OVER THE EARTH!

WE DON'T NEED HER, MASTER! HER LOYALTY TO YOU ISN'T AS GREAT AS MINE!

LOYALTY! BAH! I RULE BY FEAR ALONE!

MEANWHILE, HEARING THE IRON DOOR SHUT, ICEMAN DEFROSTS THE CHAMBER, AND, AS THE ILLUSIONARY FOG FADES AWAY...

CAREFUL! WE'RE LOCKED IN HERE WITH SUB-MARINER AND THE SCARLET WITCH!

WHAT DO WE DO NOW?

KEEP CALM! WE'VE GOT TO PLAY THIS BY EAR!

WHAT HAVE YOU DONE WITH QUICKSILVER? I DEMAND THAT YOU RELEASE HIM!

YOU'RE IN NO POSITION TO IMPOSE DEMANDS ON US!

WITH MAGNETO GONE, THESE PIECES OF METAL ARE NO LONGER MAGNETIZED TO MY BODY! AND NOW...

THE SUB-MARINER COMMANDS YOU TO OBEY THE FEMALE! SET QUICKSILVER FREE!

LOOK, YOU PISCATORIAL PIRATE... YOU MAY BE MR. BIG WHEN YOU'RE IN THE BRINY DEEP, BUT YOUR IMPERIAL IDIOSYNCRASIES DON'T IMPRESS THE X-MEN!

FOOL! IT WILL TAKE MORE THAN A FANCY VOCABULARY TO STOP PRINCE NAMOR!

AND I'VE GOT MORE! I ALSO POSSESS SPEED AND AGILITY WHICH FAR EXCEED YOUR OWN!

18.

DON'T UNDERESTIMATE ME, NAMOR! DON'T MAKE ME USE MY *FULL INTENSITY!* THIS IS YOUR LAST CHANCE!

NAMOR TRIED TO *HELP* ME! I MUST RETURN THE FAVOR! I'LL USE MY *HEX POWER* ON THE FEARLESS X-MAN!

NO SOONER DOES THE *SCARLET WITCH* UNLEASH HER UNCANNY *HEX*, THEN THE VERY STONES SUDDENLY LOOSEN UNDER CYCLOPS' FEET, AND...

WHA...?? I LOST MY BALANCE!!

YOU *HAD* YOUR CHANCE, CYCLOPS! BUT NOW, BEFORE YOU CAN RECOVER YOURSELF, YOU'LL FEEL THE MIGHTY WRATH OF *NAMOR!*

HALT!

LOUDER THAN ANY HUMAN OUTCRY, THE IRRESISTIBLE *MENTAL COMMAND* OF THE MAN WHO SUDDENLY ENTERS STOPS EVERYONE IN THEIR TRACKS, AS ALL HEADS TURN... TOWARDS *PROFESSOR X!*

THERE IS NO NEED TO CONTINUE YOUR BATTLE! QUICKSILVER HAS NOT BEEN HARMED... AS YOU CAN SEE!

BUT WHY IS HE SO MOTIONLESS.. SO STILL? WHY ARE HIS EYES SO LACKING IN EXPRESSION?

HE IS UNDER MY *MENTAL CONTROL!*

NO! YOU MUST NOT DO THIS DREADFUL THING! *RELEASE HIS BRAIN!* LET HIM BE AS HE WAS!

I SHALL! YOU HAVE NOTHING TO FEAR! MY FIGHT IS NOT WITH YOU... NOR WITH NAMOR! *MAGNETO* IS THE REAL ENEMY! ALL OF YOU ARE BUT *PAWNS!*

PAWNS?!! WHO DARES CALL THE *SUB-MARINER* A PAWN?? *PROTECT YOURSELVES,* X-MEN! WE'LL *SEE* WHICH OF US ARE THE PAWNS!!

NO, NAMOR!! PLEASE..! NOT UNTIL QUICKSILVER IS HIMSELF AGAIN! NOT UNTIL PROFESSOR X RELEASES HIS MENTAL CONTROL!

MARVEL GIRL! PUSH THE PROFESSOR TO SAFETY! *WE'LL* STOP NAMOR!

STAND FAST, MY X-MEN! THE SUB-MARINER IS NO *MURDERER!* HE WILL NOT STRIKE IF WE DON'T PROVOKE HIM!

TOUCH PROFESSOR X, AND THE OCEAN WON'T BE BIG ENOUGH TO HIDE YOU, NAMOR!

20.

AND NOW, I SHALL RELEASE QUICKSILVER! I MUST KEEP MY MIND UNFETTERED, IN READINESS FOR THE BIGGER BATTLE WITH MAGNETO!

MAGNETO!! WHAT HAS HAPPENED TO HIM?? WHERE HAS HE GONE? WHAT WILL HE DO ABOUT PIETRO AND ME??

I FEEL AS THOUGH I'VE BEEN ASLEEP! MY HEAD FEELS NUMB...DAZED!

BAH! I WAS A FOOL TO HAVE COME HERE! THE SUB-MARINER NEEDS NO ALLIANCES! ALL SURFACEMEN ARE MY ENEMIES...WHETHER MUTANT OR NOT! I SHALL RETURN TO THE DEEP...WHERE I BELONG!

WHEN NEXT I RETURN, IT SHALL BE TO TAKE MY RIGHTFUL PLACE AS CONQUEROR OF THE AIR-BREATHERS, RECLAIMER OF THE SURFACE WORLD FOR THE ANCIENT EMPIRE OF ATLANTIS!!

PROFESSOR!! HE'S ESCAPING!

LET HIM GO! SO LONG AS HE DOES NOT JOIN MAGNETO'S MUTANTS, WE HAVE WON! HE CAN NEVER TRULY BE ONE OF US...HIS ALLEGIANCE IS TO ATLANTIS...OURS IS TO THE HUMAN RACE!

NOT SINCE I LOST MY HEART TO SUE STORM HAVE I SEEN SUCH A BEAUTY AS THE SCARLET WITCH! BUT I DARE NOT LOVE ANOTHER SURFACE FEMALE...I DARE NOT BECOME VULNERABLE AGAIN!

MEANTIME, MAGNETO, MASTERMIND AND THE TOAD REACH THE GIANT MAGNETIC DYNAMO WHICH ONLY THE LEADER OF THE EVIL MUTANTS HAS THE POWER TO OPERATE!

SO! NAMOR DARED TO CHALLENGE ME, DID HE? WELL, ANY MUTANT WHO ISN'T MY ALLY BECOMES MY MORTAL ENEMY!

I MUST MAKE CERTAIN HE CAN NEVER JOIN THE ACCURSED X-MEN! HE MUST BE SMASHED, ONCE AND FOR ALL!

BE CAREFUL, MASTERMIND! THE X-MEN ARE STILL AT LARGE! AND WE'VE LOST QUICKSILVER AND THE SCARLET WITCH!

HOW LITTLE YOU KNOW! ONCE NAMOR IS DESTROYED, THE X-MEN WILL BE NEXT! AND THEN, QUICKSILVER AND HIS SISTER WILL REJOIN US! THERE IS NO WAY TO LEAVE MAGNETO'S MUTANTS...EXCEPT BY DEATH!!

NOW BE SILENT! I WANT TO ENJOY NAMOR'S DEFEAT!!

SECONDS LATER, AS THE SEA PRINCE APPEARS ON THE GIANT MAGNET'S VIEWFINDER, MAGNETO ACTIVATES THE MIGHTY MACHINE, AND THEN...

I'M BEING ROCKED BY AN INVISIBLE FORCE...MORE POWERFUL THAN ANYTHING I'VE EVER FELT!! COMING FROM THAT PEAK...IT'S MAGNETO...OPERATING HIS MONSTROUS MAGNET!! I MUST FIGHT IT...I CANNOT BE BEATEN NOW!!

21.

IT'S FORCING ME TO THE GROUND... CRUSHING ME DOWN...DOWN...I'VE ONLY ONE CHANCE...ONE WAY TO STRIKE BACK!

FLEXING HIS MORE THAN HUMAN MUSCLES UNTIL THEY STAND OUT LIKE TAUT STEEL BANDS, THE SUB-MARINER SMASHES HIS TWO MIGHTY FISTS DOWN INTO THE GROUND WITH A FORCE BEYOND THE POWER OF HUMAN UNDER-STANDING!!

SO SHATTERING IS THE IMPACT THAT IT CAUSES THE ENTIRE ISLE TO QUIVER...AS THE GIGANTIC MAGNET PITCHES FORWARD, SHAKEN LOOSE FROM ITS ROCKY FOUNDATION!

WITHOUT A WORD, WITHOUT A BACKWARD GLANCE, THE AWESOME NAMOR RISES AND SLOWLY, IMPERIOUSLY, APPROACHES THE SEA...

THEN, WITH ONE BREATH-TAKING DIVE, THE RULER OF THE DEEP RETURNS TO HIS DOMAIN! THE OCEAN DEPTHS HAVE CLAIMED THEIR OWN!

AS FOR MAGNETO...NEVER BEFORE HAS SUCH ANGER, SUCH LIVID RAGE BEEN SEEN ON THE FACE OF THE EVIL MUTANT!

WE'VE LOST! NAMOR BEAT US!! HE... UGH!

SILENCE!! NO ONE BEATS MAGNETO!! HE MERELY ESCAPED MY VENGEANCE FOR THE PRESENT! TOAD! INTO THE MAGNO-SHIP!! HOP, YOU BRAINLESS GARGOYLE!

WITHIN SECONDS, MAGNETO'S SHIP, WITH THE TREMBLING TOAD AT THE CONTROLS, RAISES THE TWO MUTANTS MAGNETICALLY...

BUT WHAT ABOUT QUICK-SILVER... AND THE SCARLET WITCH?

THEY'RE COMING NOW...IN RESPONSE TO MY MENTAL COMMAND!

LOOK! OUR PRISONERS ARE ESCAPING!

I ALLOWED IT! UNTIL THEY JOIN US OF THEIR OWN FREE WILL, THEY WOULD BE USELESS TO US! SOMEDAY WE MUST LEARN WHAT MYSTERIOUS HOLD MAGNETO HAS OVER THEM!

I'M GLAD TO SEE THEM GO! THAT WITCH IS MUCH TOO ATTRACTIVE!

KNOW SOMETHING, JEANIE? SO ARE YOU!

HELP ME HOIST THE SAILS OF MAGNETO'S BOAT, MY FRIGID FRIEND!

SURE! EVERYONE YAKS AND I END UP DOIN' THE WORK!!

NEXT ISSUE: A STARTLING CHANGE OCCURS IN THE LIVES OF THE X-MEN! DON'T DARE MISS IT, OR WE'LL TELL THE PROFESSOR!

Then, after the memorable photo has been snapped...

PROFESSOR, I'VE BEEN WAITING FOR A CHANCE TO TELL YOU HOW MUCH I APPRECIATE ALL YOU'VE DONE FOR ME --AND FOR ALL OF US!

NONSENSE, SCOTT! ALL I DID WAS TAKE THE TALENT ALL OF YOU ALREADY HAD, AND CHANNEL IT IN THE RIGHT DIRECTION! YOU YOUNGSTERS DID ALL THE WORK!

DID THE PICTURE COME OUT OKAY, BOBBY?

DON'T ASK ME, PAL--ASK THE CAMERA!

BUT WITHOUT YOU, WE'D HAVE REMAINED MISFITS, IN A WORLD THAT COULD NEVER UNDERSTAND US-- WITH NO PURPOSE, NO GOALS!

PERHAPS WE SHOULD SEND A PHOTO TO MAGNETO, WITH A SUITABLE INSCRIPTION, SUCH AS: "ALWAYS THINKING OF YOU!"

NOW THAT THE CEREMONY IS OVER, I'D BEST RETURN TO MY CHAIR--

LET ME HELP YOU, SIR!

THANK YOU, JEAN! YOU'VE MASTERED YOUR TELEKINETIC POWER PERFECTLY!

JUST AS ALL OF YOU HAVE MASTERED YOUR MUTANT POWERS TO MY COMPLETE SATISFACTION! THERE IS NOTHING MORE THAT I CAN TEACH YOU!

SAY, PROF--I JUST NOTICED-- MY DIPLOMA'S A BLANK! THERE'S NO WRITING ON IT!

NATURALLY, MY UNCOMPREHENDING FRIEND! IT WAS JUST A PROP FOR THE PHOTO! YOU WOULDN'T EXPECT A DIPLOMA WHICH REVEALS TO THE WORLD THAT YOU ARE A FULL-FLEDGED X-MAN, WOULD YOU?

AS A MATTER OF FACT, I DO HAVE DIPLOMAS FOR YOU WHICH TESTIFY THAT YOU'VE SUCCESSFULLY COMPLETED YOUR NORMAL PREP SCHOOL CURRICULUM--AS INDEED YOU HAVE DONE!

2

AND NOW, I SHALL NOT BORE YOU WITH LONG SPEECHES, BUT I MUST TELL YOU THIS--YOU ARE EACH *MORE* THAN MERE HOMO SAPIENS --YOU ARE THE FORERUNNERS OF *HOMO SUPERIOR*--SUPERIOR MAN! YOU EACH HAVE A PRICELESS EXTRA MUTANT POWER TO BE USED FOR THE GOOD OF HUMANITY--

AND, YOU MUST *STILL* KEEP YOUR X-MEN IDENTITIES SECRET, FOR THE WORLD OF ORDINARY HUMANS IS NOT YET READY TO ACCEPT YOU--WHILE *MAGNETO* AND HIS BAND OF *EVIL MUTANTS* STILL SEEK TO DESTROY YOU! AND NOW, IT IS TIME FOR ME TO BID YOU FAREWELL--

FAREWELL??!!

YES! I HAVE MANY UNFINISHED TASKS WHICH I MUST NOW TURN MY ATTENTION TO! SO, I MUST LEAVE YOU FOR A WHILE! BUT, BEFORE I GO, I SHALL APPOINT ONE OF YOU AS *GROUP LEADER*, TO ACT IN MY BEHALF TILL I RETURN...

MEANWHILE, IN A LONELY RAMSHACKLE MANSION WHICH STANDS HIGH UPON A WINDY HILL, HALF-HIDDEN AT THE EDGE OF TOWN, ANOTHER CONVERSATION TAKES PLACE...

WELL, WELL! IF IT ISN'T THE BEAUTIFUL BUT HAUGHTY *SCARLET WITCH!* TO WHAT DO I OWE THE HONOR OF THIS VISIT?

DON'T *FLATTER* YOURSELF, MASTERMIND! YOU KNOW I DID NOT COME TO SEE *YOU!*

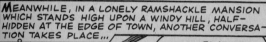

MAGNETO HAS SUMMONED ME! WHERE *IS* HE?

HE HASN'T *ARRIVED* YET! BUT, WHILE WE'RE ALONE, I HAVE SOMETHING TO *SAY* TO YOU, MY LOVELY ONE!

NOTHING YOU CAN SAY WOULD INTEREST ME --AND YOU *KNOW* IT!

WANDA, YOU ARE A *FOOL!* WITH *YOU* BESIDE ME, WE COULD ACCOMPLISH *ANYTHING!* TOGETHER, OUR POWER MIGHT EVEN EXCEED *MAGNETO'S!*

YOU *LIE!* YOU HAVE NO *REAL* POWER--MERELY THE GIFT OF CREATING *ILLUSIONS!* BUT, I CARE NOT FOR POWER! ONCE I HAVE PAID MY DEBT TO MAGNETO, I HOPE TO *LEAVE* THIS DREADFUL BAND--TO BE FREE AT LAST!

BUT SEE WHAT I COULD *DO* FOR YOU! AT THE SLIGHTEST GESTURE, I GIVE YOU A *PALACE* TO RESIDE IN-- I CAN SURROUND YOU WITH LUXURY!

WHAT DOES IT *MATTER* IF IT IS MERELY AN ILLUSION? IT WILL ALWAYS SEEM REAL TO YOU!

NO! WITH *YOU*, EVEN A PALACE WOULD SEEM LIKE A HOVEL TO ME!

3

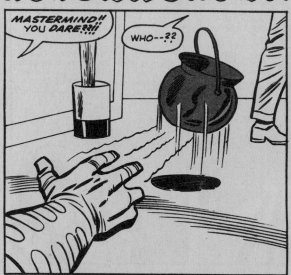

4

I *SHALL* WORRY-- AS LONG AS WE MUST SERVE MAGNETO! BUT HEAR THIS, EVIL ONES-- IF ANY HARM EVER COMES TO MY SISTER--YOU SHALL ALL ANSWER TO *QUICKSILVER!*

I HAVE PLEDGED THAT *NONE* SHALL BE HARMED, SO LONG AS YOU OBEY ME IMPLICITLY! AND NOW, ENOUGH OF THIS CHARADE! THERE IS *WORK* TO BE DONE!

REMEMBER, BEFORE WE CAN FIND A WAY TO CONQUER AND RULE THE INFERIOR *HUMANS* WHO INHABIT OUR PLANET, WE MUST FIRST DEFEAT THEIR SELF-STYLED PROTECTORS--THE ACCURSED *X-MEN!* AND I HAVE DEVISED A NEW PLAN TO DESTROY THEM!

HAH! I *KNEW* YOU WOULD STRIKE BACK AGAIN, MASTER! MIGHTY MAGNETO FEARS *NOTHING!*

SILENCE, TOAD! KEEP YOUR CACK-LING COMMENTS TO YOURSELF TILL I AM DONE!

WHILE BACK AT THE X-MEN'S SECRET SCHOOL...
SCOTT, WOULD YOU ACCOM-PANY ME TO THE WEST WING?

CERTAINLY, SIR!

STRANGE! THIS IS THE ONE SECTION THAT HAD BEEN "OFF-LIMITS" TO US!

I IMAGINE THAT YOU HAVE LONG WONDERED WHAT IS *KEPT* IN THIS DARKENED, LOCKED SECTION OF THE SCHOOL!

YES SIR! WE HAVE ALL BEEN CURIOUS ABOUT IT FOR MONTHS!

THEN, AFTER THE LIGHTS ARE TURNED ON...
GOSH! WHAT *IS* ALL THAT??

SOMETHING I'VE BEEN WORKING ON FOR A LONG LONG TIME! YOU ARE THE ONLY OTHER PERSON WHO WILL SHARE MY SECRET!

IT IS ACTUALLY A COMPLEX E.S.P.* MACHINE WHICH I CALL *CEREBRO,* FROM THE LATIN "CEREBRUM" MEANING "THE BRAIN!"

ITS SOLE PURPOSE IS TO AID IN DETECTING NEW MUTANT BRAIN WAVES-- TO HELP US TO LOCATE OTHER MUTANTS--BOTH GOOD AND EVIL!!

*E.S.P.: EXTRA-SENSORY-PERCEPTION-- *EDITOR.*

5

THESE WIRES LEAD DIRECTLY TO MY PRIVATE OFFICE, TRANSMITTING ALL E.S.P. DATA AS SOON AS IT IS RECEIVED!

BUT, SIR, WHY DO YOU *NEED* THAT MACHINE? I THOUGHT YOU COULD DETECT OTHER MUTANTS BY THE POWER OF YOUR BRAIN ALONE!

TRUE, SCOTT! I PERSONALLY HAVE LITTLE NEED FOR SUCH APPARATI! BUT, WHILE I AM GONE, THE ONE WHO *REPLACES* ME WILL FIND IT MOST USEFUL!

THE ONE-- WHO *REPLACES* YOU??

EXACTLY! I HAVE DECIDED THAT *YOU*, THE X-MAN KNOWN AS *CYCLOPS*, SHALL BE GROUP LEADER UNTIL I RETURN!

ME?? BUT, SIR-- THE *BEAST* IS A BETTER SCHOLAR-- WHILE *ANGEL* IS MORE AGGRESSIVE, AND--!

BUT IT IS *YOU* WHO POSSESSES THE RARE QUALITY OF *LEADERSHIP!*

MY DECISION STANDS!

AND SO, EARLY THE NEXT MORNING...

IMAGINE! NO DUTIES FOR US "OL' GRADS" TODAY! LET'S HAVE A REAL CELE-BRATION!

TOO BAD THE *PROFESSOR* CAN'T JOIN US-- BUT HE'S ALREADY LEFT!

ITS A PLEASURE TO BE DIVESTED OF THE ENCUMBRANCE OF OUR X-MEN UNIFORMS!

I WISH YOU'D LEARN TO SPEAK *ENGLISH*, HANK!

HEY, LET'S GO FIND SCOTTY BOY!

THE LIGHT'S ON IN THE PROFESSOR'S STUDY! LET'S SEE IF-- *SCOTT!* BEHIND THE PROF'S DESK!

I JUST REMEMBERED --PROFESSOR XAVIER SAID HE'D CHOOSE A *GROUP LEADER*--

OF *COURSE!* IT WAS THE *LOGICAL* SELECTION!

CONGRATULATIONS, CYCLOPS!

THANK YOU! COME IN PLEASE!

I WANT YOU TO KNOW THAT I DIDN'T *ASK* FOR THIS ASSIGNMENT! IN FACT, I DIDN'T DESIRE IT! I HAD BEEN THINKING OF *LEAVING* THE X-MEN!

LEAVING THE X-MEN?? WHY, SCOTTY?

YOU KNOW HOW I FEAR THE POWER BEAM WHICH EMANATES FROM MY EYES--!

I SHUDDER TO THINK WHAT WOULD HAPPEN IF IT EVER ACCIDENTALLY GETS OUT OF MY CONTROL! I HAD HOPED TO VISIT VARIOUS DOCTORS-- TO SEEK A CURE!

BUT, THE *PROFESSOR* CONVINCED ME IT IS MY *DUTY* TO REMAIN-- TO USE MY POWER AGAINST ALL EVIL-- NO MATTER HOW I DREAD THE TASK!

6

WE KNOW HOW YOU FEEL, SCOTTY! AND WE'RE WITH YOU ALL THE WAY, PAL!

OH, SCOTT--WE ALL UNDERSTAND! BUT YOU MADE THE RIGHT DECISION! WE'VE STUDIED TOGETHER SO LONG, WORKED SO HARD--WE JUST CAN'T SPLIT UP NOW!

THE WAY SHE LOOKS AT HIM! HOW CAN HE BE SO UNMOVED? CAN'T HE SEE HOW SHE FEELS ABOUT HIM??

WHY NOT JOIN US, SCOTT! IT MIGHT BE GOOD THERAPY FOR YOU!

I'D LIKE NOTHING BETTER THAN TO BE WITH YOU-- BUT I MUST REMAIN HERE, TO LOOK AFTER THINGS! THE PROFESSOR WOULD WANT IT THIS WAY! I--HOPE YOU ALL HAVE-- A GOOD TIME!

OKAY THEN, SCOTTY! IF ANY EVIL MUTANTS COME KNOCKING AT THE DOOR, GIVE US A WHISTLE!

WE'LL BE BACK BEFORE DINNER, SCOTT!

I KNOW THE COOLEST LITTLE COFFEE SHOP IN GREENWICH VILLAGE, WITH THE DREAMIEST WAITRESS!

WELL THEN, LEAD ON, MAC-DUFF!

THEY'VE GONE! AND HERE I SIT-- ALONE! NOW, FOR THE FIRST TIME, I CAN REALIZE HOW IT MUST HAVE BEEN FOR THE PROFESSOR, ALL THOSE LONG MONTHS-- ALWAYS APART-- ALWAYS ALONE...

SLOWLY, THOUGHTFULLY, THE X-MAN KNOWN AS CYCLOPS SLIDES THE TOP PANEL OF HIS DESK BACK, REVEALING AN ARRAY OF COMPLEX ELECTRONIC CONTROLS...

NOW TO LISTEN TO THE STEADY DRONE OF CEREBRO'S "VOICE"...

BEEP! BEEP! BEEP! BEEP!

--UNABLE TO LEAVE MY POST UNLESS AN ALARM IS SOUNDED-- AND YET, DREADING THE MOMENT I HEAR THAT ALARM, FOR IT CAN ONLY MEAN--THE MENACE OF-- MAGNETO!

BEEP! BEEP! BEEP! BEEP! BEEP!

MEANWHILE, AT A NOISY CARNIVAL AT THE EDGE OF TOWN...

THIS IS THE ONE PLACE I CAN APPEAR IN PUBLIC WITH IMPUNITY! ALL WHO SEE ME THINK I AM MERELY ANOTHER COSTUMED PERFORMER!

SIDE SHOW

7

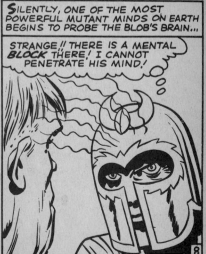

HEY! WHO IN SAM HILL ARE *YOU,* MAC?? WHAT ARE YOU DOIN' WITH MY PERFORMER??

WHO AM I ??

I AM-- *POWER!!*

BUT *YOU* MAY CALL ME-- *MAGNETO!!* MARK THAT NAME WELL, HOMO SAPIENS -- SOON YOU, AND *ALL* YOUR INFERIOR KIND SHALL PAY IT *HOMAGE!!*

I DON'T KNOW WHAT YOUR GAME IS, MAC, BUT IF IT'S A *FIGHT* YOU WANT, YOU CAME TO THE RIGHT PLACE!!

FOOL! YOU *STILL* DO NOT COMPREHEND THE AWESOME FORCE YOU ARE DARING TO CHALLENGE!

HEY, RUBE!

SECONDS LATER, IN ANSWER TO THE TIME-HONORED CARNY BATTLE CRY, A GROUP OF HUSKY ROUSTABOUTS CHARGE THE MIGHTY MUTANT!

LET'S *GET* THAT COSTUMED NUT!!

BUT, BEFORE THEY CAN REACH MAGNETO--

NO ONE MAY TOUCH THE *MASTER!!*

LIKE A HUMAN BOUNCING CANNONBALL, THE INCREDIBLE HIGH-JUMPING *TOAD* LEAPS BACK AND FORTH, UP AND DOWN, SCATTERING THE DAZED ROUSTABOUTS LIKE TENPINS, WITH SPEED AND AGILITY SECOND ONLY TO THAT OF THE *BEAST!*

MAGNETO MUST *NEVER* BE HARMED!!

THEN, BEFORE THE STUNNED CARNY MEN CAN RE-GROUP THEIR FORCES, A SPEEDING, CAREENING, LIGHTNING-SWIFT FIGURE RACES THRU THEM SO QUICKLY THAT ONLY A HAZY BLUR CAN BE SEEN!!

HEY! WHAT'S GOIN' *ON* HERE!

LOOK OUT! THERE'S *ANOTHER* ONE!

9

POSSESSED OF A SPEED MANY TIMES GREATER THAN ANY NORMAL *HOMO SAPIEN* COULD HOPE TO ATTAIN, THE MUTANT *QUICKSILVER* STARTLES AND CONFUSES THE STUNNED HUMANS!

IT AINT *POSSIBLE!* HE'S SO FAST YOU CAN HARDLY *SEE* HIM!

AND THEN...

HEY!! LOOK WHAT HAPPENED TO MY STAKE DRIVER!!!

MINE TOO! W-WE MUST BE *DREAMIN'!!*

THIS AINT A *DREAM!!* IT'S A LIVIN' *NIGHTMARE!*

OUTTA *NOWHERE* --A *VOLCANO*-- ERUPTIN' RIGHT ON THE CARNY GROUNDS!!

SO! YOU CALL MY GREAT POWERS MERE *ILLUSIONS*, DO YOU?? SEE HOW THEY THROW AN ENTIRE GROUP OF FIGHTING MEN INTO SHEER PANIC, MY LOVELY!

BUT YOU CANNOT THROW THOSE ACCURSED IMAGES EVERYWHERE AT ONCE! EVEN *NOW* SOME ROUSTABOUTS ARE APPROACHING FROM BEHIND THIS WAGON!

THROWN OFF BALANCE BY THE SURPRISE ATTACK, MASTERMIND MOMENTARILY LOSES CONTROL OF HIS ILLUSIONS, AND RUNS IN PANIC...

GRAB THOSE TWO! THEY'RE IN LEAGUE WITH THE OTHERS!

NO! DON'T *HURT* US!

QUIET, YOU SHAMELESS COWARD!

MY OWN *HEX POWER* IS ENOUGH TO SAVE US! ALL I NEED TO DO IS CAUSE CONTINUAL *MISHAPS* TO BEFALL OUR ATTACKERS!

HOLD IT UP, YOU GUYS! DON'T CHASE 'EM ANYMORE! THEY'RE TOO *MUCH* FOR US!!

10

MINUTES LATER, MAGNETO AND HIS MUTANTS ARE FINALLY ALONE WITH THE BLOB...

I OFFER YOU A CHANCE TO *JOIN* MY BAND! YOU CAN BE ONE OF US, TO SHARE OUR TRIUMPH OVER HOMO SAPIENS!

MISTER, I DON'T KNOW WHO YOU ARE, OR WHAT YOU WANT-- BUT I DON'T NEED *ANY* OF YOU!

STOP! CONSIDER YOUR WORDS! IF YOU ARE NOT *WITH* US-- THEN WE MUST TREAT YOU AS AN *ENEMY!*

I CANNOT LEAVE YOU HERE, ON THE CHANCE THAT THE X-MEN MAY ONE DAY RECRUIT YOU TO JOIN *THEM!* I MUST-- *WHAT??* YOU DARE L'AY A HAND ON THE PERSON OF *MAGNETO* ??!!

LOOK, RUBE-- I'M GONNA SHOW YOU THAT *NOBODY* SCARES THE *BLOB!* NOT EVEN A BUNCH OF BIG-TALKIN' COSTUMED CLOWNS!

SUDDENLY, AN IRRESISTIBLE MAGNETIC IMPULSE AFFECTS THE UTILITY PIPES DIRECTLY UNDERGROUND, AND THEY SNAP TO THE SURFACE WITH TITANIC FORCE!

FOOL! BE GRATEFUL I HAVE ONLY DEIGNED TO USE A *FRACTION* OF THE LIMITLESS MAGNETIC POWER WHICH I POSSESS!!

AND THEN, A CAPRICIOUS *FATE* ENTERS THE PICTURE, AS THE FORCE OF IMPACT JARS LOOSE PART OF THE MENTAL BLOCK WHICH PROFESSOR X HAD PREVIOUSLY PUT OVER THE BLOB'S MEMORY--!*

I REMEMBER NOW! I'M A *MUTANT!* THE X-MEN ARE MY ENEMIES! THEY WERE AFRAID I'D JOIN MAGNETO! BUT I *WILL*-- I *WILL* JOIN HIM!!

*SEE X-MEN #3 "BEWARE THE BLOB!" --EDITOR.

AT THAT VERY INSTANT, AT *X-MEN* HEADQUARTERS, A SIREN BEGINS TO HOWL LIKE A BANSHEE AS THE NAME OF THE *BLOB* LIGHTS UP UNDER THE OTHERS ON A MASTER CONTROL PANEL!

KNOWN HOSTILE MUTANTS

MAGNETO

TOAD

ASTER-MIND

UICK SILVER

ET WITCH

BLOB

UNKNOWN

WHEEEEE

THE *SIREN!!* THE BLOB'S NAME-- BURSTING INTO LIGHT! IT CAN ONLY MEAN *ONE* THING--!

HIS *MEMORY* HAS RETURNED! HE'S JOINED THE EVIL MUTANTS!

THE PROFESSOR IS GONE! IT'S UP TO *ME* TO TAKE COMMAND! I DARE NOT FAIL!

I'VE GOT TO CONTACT THE OTHERS! I'LL CHECK THEIR DESTINATIONS IN THE SIGN-OUT BOOK! I CAN REACH THE *ANGEL* THRU HIS CAR RADIO--!

11

15

BUT, THE POWERFUL BLADE SNAPS TO SHREDS AT THE FIRST IMPACT AGAINST THE BLOB'S UNCANNY FLESH!!

A LOT OF GOOD *THAT* PIECE OF TIN WILL DO YOU!! YOU'RE FIGHTING THE *BLOB* NOW-- THE ONE ENEMY YOU CAN'T EVER BEAT!

THERE'S *NO ONE* THE *X-MEN* CAN'T BEAT, MISTER-- AND DON'T YOU FORGET IT!! WE PROVED THAT *ONCE,* THE LAST TIME WE MET--! UHH!

SURE-- BUT YOU HAD PROFESSOR'S X'S *BRAIN* TO HELP YOU! *NOW* HE ISN'T HERE-- AND ONCE I GET MY *HANDS* ON SOMETHING, *NOTHING* CAN PRY THEM LOOSE!

ARE YOU AWARE THAT YOU TALK ALMOST AS MUCH AS *I* DO, BLOB? ALTHOUGH YOUR VOCABULARY IS NEITHER AS VARIED NOR AS ERUDITE!

WHUP!

THE BEAST'S ATTACK WOULD HAVE BOWLED OVER A HIPPO, BUT THE BLOB TOOK IT! NOW HE'S GOT THEM *BOTH*! PERHAPS I CAN MAKE HIM RELEASE THEM BY RAISING HIM TELEKINETICALLY--!

I *WARNED* YOU --*NOTHING* CAN BREAK MY GRIP! NOTHING!

NOT EVEN THE WEAK ATTEMPT OF *MARVEL GIRL!*

IT'S *USELESS!* HIS FEET STICK TO THE GROUND-- PULLING IT UP *WITH* HIM! I-I CAN'T RAISE HIM ANY HIGHER!!

JEAN!! YOU SHOULDN'T HAVE *STRAINED* YOURSELF AGAINST IMPOSSIBLE ODDS LIKE THAT! LEAVE HIM TO *ME* NOW!! ONLY MY *POWER BEAM* CAN BEAT HIM!

BOY! YOU'VE GOT *ONE* QUALIFICATION FOR A GROUP LEADER, SCOTTY! YOU'VE SURE GOT *CONFIDENCE!*

16

BUT, THE EVIL *MAGNETO* CHOOSES THAT VERY INSTANT TO LAUNCH HIS PREVIOUSLY-PREPARED ATTACK--!

EVERYTHING IS *PERFECT!* THEY'VE BEEN DECOYED INTO THE RIGHT POSITION! NOW I'LL MAGNETICALLY RELEASE MY WAITING *TORPEDOS.!!*

R--KEEP OU--

CYCLOPS.!! THEY'VE LAUNCHED *TORPEDOS* AT US.!! *QUICK--* YOU'VE GOT TO DESTROY THEM WITH YOUR POWER BEAM.!!

I *CAN'T* BOBBY.! IF MY BEAM HITS THEM, THEY'LL *DETONATE--* FINISHING US ALL.! THERE'S ONLY *ONE* THING TO DO--

CREATE A CURVED ICE TUBE-- *QUICK.!!* THE WAY YOU'VE DONE IN PRACTICE SESSIONS.!

I *READ* YOU, LEADER MAN.!! WHY DIDN'T *I* THINK OF THIS?!!

WHOOPS.! THERE'S ONE THAT GOT AWAY.!!

BUT I'LL JUST PUT SOME *ICE WHEELS* AROUND IT, LIKE *THIS.!!* NOW *WATCH--!*

NEAT, EH? IT JUST ROLLS HARMLESSLY AWAY.!

BOBBY! LOOK OUT-- BEHIND YOU.!

17

Panel 1:

MOVING WITH THE SPEED OF THOUGHT, THE DYNAMIC *CYCLOPS* BLASTS A HOLE UNDER ICEMAN'S FEET, DEEP ENOUGH FOR BOBBY TO DROP BELOW THE PATH OF THE DEADLY MISSILES!!

OWW WAH!!

DUCK, KID-- DUCK!

Panel 2:

THEY'RE TOO FAST-- TOO CLEVER FOR MY TORPEDOS! BUT, IF I CAN GET THEM WITHIN REACH OF *YOU,* BLOB--!

I *TOLD* YOU I COULD HANDLE THEM! JUST GET THEM OVER TO ME-- LET ME GET MY HANDS ON *ALL* OF THEM!!

Panel 3:

BUT, UNLIKE THE *BLOB,* THE QUICK-THINKING *BEAST* HAS HIS *WITS* TO RELY ON, AS WELL AS HIS STRENGTH--!

I'LL CONCEDE YOUR SUPERIORITY IN AN ARM-WRESTLING MATCH-- BUT LET'S SEE HOW YOU COPE WITH SOME SUDDEN *MUD* IN YOUR EYE!

Panel 4:

TAKEN UNAWARES, THE SLOWER-WITTED BLOB RELEASES HIS UNBREAKABLE GRIP AS HE FOLLOWS THE NATURAL IMPULSE TO RUB HIS EYES!

WHA--?? CAN'T *SEE!!* GOT TO GET THE MUD OUT OF MY EYES,!!

Panel 5:

BUT, INSTEAD OF RACING OUT OF REACH OF THE BLOB, THE BEAST ONCE MORE MAKES AN UNEXPECTED MOVE, WHILE HIS GARGANTUAN OPPONENT IS STILL OFF-BALANCE--!

EUREKA! I THOUGHT THIS MANEUVER WOULD SUCCEED!

EVEN *YOU* CAN'T MAINTAIN YOUR STANCE WHEN DEALT A BLOW WHICH YOU HAVEN'T PREPARED YOURSELF FOR!

WUP!

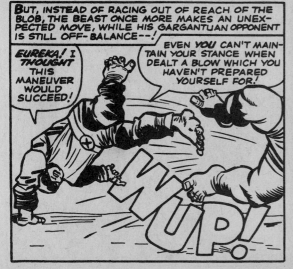

Panel 6:

BLAST THE LUCK! THOSE X-MEN NEVER SEEM TO KNOW WHEN THEY'RE BEATEN! I'LL SHIELD MYSELF FROM THE *ANGEL* WITH A FLYING TORPEDO BARRIER!

18

19

BUT MAGNETO'S COMMAND COMES TOO LATE! HIT WITH THE SCARLET WITCH'S HEX POWER, THE BEAST AND CYCLOPS CANNOT STOP THEMSELVES FROM COLLIDING INTO EACH OTHER!

THUMP!

OHHH!

I'M FREE! NOTHING WILL EVER CATCH ME NOW!

THEN, THE DARING ICEMAN, TRYING HIS OWN STRATEGY FOR RESTRAINING THE POWERFUL BLOB, SEES THE LIGHTNING-SWIFT QUICKSILVER APPROACHING--

THERE, CHUBBINS! THAT OUGHTTA HOLD YOU FOR A WHILE-- AT LEAST TILL I CAN SLOW DOWN OL' CRAZY-LEGS THERE!

BUT, SO UNIMAGINABLY SWIFT IS QUICKSILVER, THAT EVEN THE COMBINED EFFORTS OF ALL THE X-MEN ARE NOT ENOUGH TO CAPTURE THE SPEEDING MUTANT!

WELL DONE, PIETRO!! I KNEW THEY COULD NOT CATCH YOU, MY BELOVED BROTHER!

FALL IN BEHIND ME NOW! THE BATTLE LINE IS DRAWN-- WE'RE ALL TOGETHER IN A BODY-- JUST AS MAGNETO'S MUTANTS ARE-- THIS IS IT-- THE FINAL ATTACK!

JUST SAY THE WORD, CYCLOPS! WE'LL MAKE THEM THINK WATERLOO WAS A SOCIAL TEA PARTY!

HEY! STOP FLAPPIN' THOSE WINGS OF YOURS, ANGEL! YOU'RE TICKLIN' MY EARS!

BUT, BEFORE ANOTHER MOVE CAN BE MADE, THE GARGANTUAN BLOB EXPANDS HIS ENORMOUS BULK UNTIL THE BLOCK OF ICE WHICH CONFINED HIM SHATTERS WITH A DEAFENING ROAR!

BAROOM!

YOU HAVE USED EVERY POWER YOU POSSESS AGAINST ME, AND FAILED! NOW, IT'S MY TURN-- BUT WITH THIS ONE DIFFERENCE --THE BLOB SHALL NOT FAIL!

WAIT! DON'T MAKE ME BLAST YOU WITH MY POWER BEAM! STOP! WE'VE NO REASON TO FIGHT! WHY SHOULD YOU SERVE MAGNETO? HE'S ONLY USING YOU--

HE'S NOT STOPPIN', SCOTT!

20

AT LAST! THEY'RE ALL IN ONE GROUP! NOW MY TORPEDOS CAN FINISH THEM ALL OFF!

BUT--THE BLOB!! HE'S THERE WITH THEM, TOO!!

THAT'S HIS HARD LUCK!! HE'S SERVED HIS PURPOSE!!

NO!!

YOU CAN'T! YOU MUSTN'T!

LOOK OUT!

I'LL SHIELD YOU, JEAN!

QUICK--BEHIND THE BLOB--ALL OF YOU!!

MAGNETO!! NO! DON'T-- STOP!! OHHHH!

SECONDS LATER...

IT'S ALMOST INCOMPREHENSIBLE!! HE TOOK THE FULL BLAST OF THREE TORPEDOS, AND WAS MERELY KNOCKED OFF HIS FEET!

IT'S IRONIC! ONE OF OUR MOST DEADLY ENEMIES SHIELDED US FROM A FATAL BLAST!

WHILE HIS OWN ALLY WAS WILLING TO LET HIM DIE WITHOUT A SECOND THOUGHT!

STAY BACK, JEAN! THERE'S NO TELLING WHAT HE'LL DO NEXT!

I HAD EVERYTHING FIGURED PERFECTLY! BUT THE BLOB SPOILED MY PLAN! HE WAS IN THE WAY!! AGAIN I'VE FAILED!!

MAGNETO, I KNOW YOU SAVED MY LIFE ONCE--AND BECAUSE OF THAT, I OWE YOU MY ALLEGIANCE! BUT I CAN'T TAKE ANY MORE OF THIS SENSELESS CARNAGE --I CAN'T--!

EASY, WANDA! DO NOT LOSE CONTROL! WE SHALL TALK OF THIS LATER!

REALIZING HE IS IN DANGER OF WEAKENING THE HOLD HE HAS OVER HIS MUTANT BAND, MAGNETO MAKES A SUDDEN GESTURE, AND ONE OF THE MOST UNIQUE VEHICLES ON EARTH APPEARS...

QUICK! INTO THE MAGNA-CAR--ALL OF YOU! THIS DAY HAS NOT BEEN A TOTAL LOSS, FOR I HAVE LEARNED ONE THING--

21

PROFESSOR X WAS NOT WITH THEM TODAY-- NOT EVEN *MENTALLY*, ELSE I WOULD HAVE SENSED HIS BRAIN WAVES! THAT MEANS THE X-MEN FIGHT *ALONE* NOW! THERE-FORE, I SHALL PLAN MY STRATEGY *DIFFERENTLY* FOR OUR NEXT BATTLE!

CYCLOPS! THEY'RE GETTING *AWAY*!

NOT *THIS* TIME! I'LL *BLAST* THEM TO THE GROUND!

WAIT! THE *SCARLET WITCH*-- SHE'S *ABOARD* ALSO!

YOU'RE *RIGHT*! AND HER BROTHER, *QUICKSILVER*! SOMEHOW, I CAN'T BRING MYSELF TO BELIEVE THAT THEY ARE AS EVIL AS THE OTHERS!

WELL, PUDGY-- IT LOOKS AS IF YOUR PALS RAN OUT ON YOU, EH?

PALS?? THE BLOB HAS NO PALS!! I REALIZE THAT NOW!

WHY DON'T YOU JOIN *US??* WE'VE NO NEED TO BE ENEMIES!

YOU COULD RECEIVE *X-MAN* TRAINING! AND PERHAPS, IN TIME, IF YOU QUALIFY--

NO! I'M THRU WITH MUTANTS-- THRU WITH FIGHTING *OTHER* PEOPLE'S FIGHTS! I'LL NEVER TRUST ANYONE AGAIN!

I SEEM TO REMEMBER SOMETHING THE PROFESSOR ONCE SAID-- LONG AGO--

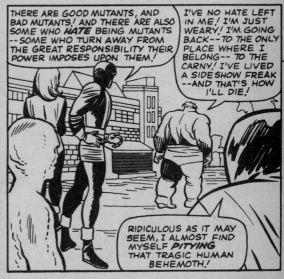

THERE ARE GOOD MUTANTS, AND BAD MUTANTS! AND THERE ARE ALSO SOME WHO *HATE* BEING MUTANTS --SOME WHO TURN AWAY FROM THE GREAT RESPONSIBILITY THEIR POWER IMPOSES UPON THEM!

I'VE NO HATE LEFT IN ME! I'M JUST WEARY! I'M GOING BACK-- TO THE ONLY PLACE WHERE I BELONG-- TO THE CARNY! I'VE LIVED A SIDESHOW FREAK --AND THAT'S HOW I'LL DIE!

RIDICULOUS AS IT MAY SEEM, I ALMOST FIND MYSELF *PITYING* THAT TRAGIC HUMAN BEHEMOTH!

I SURE HOPE HE NEVER CHANGES HIS MIND! I WOULDN'T WANNA HAVE TO FIGHT *HIM* AGAIN!

SCRATCH ONE WHIRLY-BIRD, X-MEN! THIS WRECKAGE IS BEYOND REPAIR!

WELL, I GUESS WE'LL HAVE TO PHONE FOR A *TAXI!* UH OH-- I HAVEN'T ANY CHANGE IN MY POCKETS-- IN FACT-- *NO POCKETS!*

KNOW SOME-THIN'? WE'RE GONNA FEEL LIKE *NUTS* WALKING HOME THRU THE STREETS LIKE THIS!

HAVE NO FEAR-- *ANGEL'S* HERE! I'LL FLY AHEAD AND HAIL A TAXI FOR US!

WHILE YOU'RE AT IT, BORROW THE FARE! YOUR "GROUP LEADER'S" *BROKE!*

--- *THE END*

AND SO ANOTHER X-MAN ADVENTURE BECOMES HISTORY! BUT, WILL WE SEE *MORE* OF MAGNETO'S EVIL MUTANTS? WILL WE SEE *NEW* DANGER AND SURPRISES? *WILL* WE?? ARE YOU *KIDDIN'??!* NOW, TO ALL YOU HAPPY HOMO SAPIENS-- SO *LONG*... TILL NEXT ISH!

22

YOUR SPEED WAS BETTER THAT TIME, WARREN... BUT YOU MUST ALWAYS REMEMBER TO WATCH OUT FOR ANY *TRAPS* YOU MAY BE FLYING INTO!

ATTA BOY, SCOTTY! *THAT'LL* KNOCK SOME OF THE CONCEIT OUT OF THAT HUMAN PARAKEET!

CAREFUL WHERE YOU'RE WAVING THAT ELONGATED ICEPICK, BOBBY!

W.HOOSH

AW, C'MON, SCOTT! THAT'S NO FAIR! YOU'VE GOT ALL OF PROFESSOR X'S GADGETS TO USE AGAINST US, AND ALL *WE'VE* GOT ARE OUR OWN POWERS!

THAT'S THE PURPOSE OF THIS TRAINING, WARREN! YOU CAN'T CRY *FOUL* IF AN UNEXPECTED WEAPON IS USED AGAINST YOU BY *MAGNETO*, OR ANY OTHER FOE, CAN YOU?

HAH! THAT'S TELLIN' HIM, CYKE, OL' BOY!

WHAT ARE *YOU* GLOATING ABOUT, ICEMAN? *YOU'RE* PART OF THIS TRAINING PROGRAM *TOO*, YOUNG FELLA! NOW *QUICKLY...* DEFEND YOURSELF!

HUH?? WHA...?? WHERE...?? HEY! LOOK OUT! DON'T!

IS *THAT* WHAT YOU WOULD SAY TO A SUDDEN ATTACK BY THE *BLOB*, BOBBY?? HASN'T THE PROFESSOR TOLD YOU *ALWAYS* TO BE ON GUARD!?

NOW, STAND WHERE YOU ARE AND PRACTICE REFINING YOUR ICE CRYSTALS, AS I'VE SUGGESTED!

OKAY, TEACH! ... WATCH *THIS!*

EXCELLENT! BY INCREASING YOUR DEGREE OF COLD, YOUR BODY BECOMES EVEN *MORE* ICY, MAKING YOU ALMOST TRANSPARENT!

YOU'RE BECOMING A REGULAR *SUE STORM,* KIDDO!

AW, SHUDDUP, ANGEL!

2.

JEAN, PROFESSOR X WOULD BE *PROUD* OF YOUR PROGRESS IN CONTROLLING YOUR TELEKINETIC POWER!

CAREFUL, NOW! LET'S SEE HOW QUICKLY YOU CAN RUN THE THREAD THROUGH THE PUNCH-BOARD IN A REGULAR PATTERN!

EXACTLY SIX SECONDS! THAT BEATS YOUR PREVIOUS TIME! NOW GET IT DOWN... LET'S EXAMINE IT!

EXCEPT FOR ONE STITCH WHICH YOU DROPPED, IT'S FLAWLESS! YOU CAN REST NOW!

IF ONLY I COULD TELL HER THE WORDS I *REALLY* WANT TO SAY! HOW GORGEOUS HER LIPS ARE... HOW SILKEN HER HAIR IS... HOW I *LOVE* HER! BUT, I DARE NOT...

I HAVEN'T THE RIGHT! NOT NOW, WHEN I'M SUPPOSED TO BE THEIR *LEADER!* I CAN'T LISTEN TO MY OWN HEART! I MUST BE DETACHED... UNEMOTIONAL! I... I'D BETTER GET BACK TO MY *JOB!*

YOU WERE DAY-DREAMING, HANK! SEE HOW I TOOK YOU BY SURPRISE! I DIDN'T EXPECT THAT OF *YOU!*

NOR DID *I* EXPECT SUCH AN UNCALLED-FOR MANEUVER FROM *YOU,* CYCLOPS! I WAS UNDER THE IMPRESSION OUR TRAINING PERIOD HAD BEEN CONCLUDED!

OUR TRAINING CAN *NEVER* BE ENDED... AND YOU *KNOW* THAT, HANK! OUR ENEMIES GET STRONGER EACH DAY... AND WE MUST ALWAYS BE ABLE TO MATCH THEIR *OWN* EVIL PROGRESS!

YOU WIN, LEADER MAN! BUT, IF I DIDN'T KNOW YOU BETTER, I'D FEAR THAT YOU'RE BECOMING DRUNK WITH POWER!

PERHAPS I *HAVE* BEEN WORKING YOU ALL TOO HARD! IT'S JUST THAT I WANT TO BE WORTHY OF THE CONFIDENCE PROFESSOR X HAS SHOWN IN ME! ANYWAY, THAT'S ALL FOR NOW! YOU CAN HAVE THE AFTERNOON OFF!

WHAT ABOUT YOU, SCOTT? WON'T YOU JOIN US?

I'M AFRAID I *CAN'T,* JEAN! I STILL HAVE MORE WORK TO DO!

OH, SCOTT... IF ONLY YOU FELT ABOUT *ME* AS I DO ABOUT *YOU!* BUT YOU DON'T... YOU JUST DON'T!

3.

Panel 1:

LATER, ON THEIR FREE TIME PERIOD, WE FIND THE *BEAST* AND *ICEMAN* HEADING FOR A LITTLE GREENWICH VILLAGE COFFEE SHOP...

MUCH AS I LIKE BEIN' AN X-MAN, I SURE CAN'T WAIT TILL EACH TRAINING PERIOD IS OVER!

MY SENTIMENTS EXACTLY, BOBBY BOY!

Panel 2:

BUT, TURNING A CORNER, THE TWO YOUNG MUTANTS SUDDENLY SEE...

HANK, *LOOK!* WHAT'S GOIN' *ON??* WHAT'S EVERYONE SO *EXCITED* ABOUT???

I DON'T *KNOW!* BUT, JUDGING BY THE DEGREE OF THEIR APPREHENSION, I'D SAY...

WAIT! NOW I SEE! IT'S *UP THERE! LOOK*, BOBBY... ATOP THE WATER TOWER, ON THE ROOF OF THAT BUILDING..!

Panel 3:

IT'S A LITTLE *BOY!* HE'S *TRAPPED* UP THERE!

HE MUST HAVE CLIMBED UP... AS A PRANK! BUT NOW HE'S *FRIGHTENED*.. HE CAN'T MAKE IT DOWN! BUT... HE CAN'T HOLD HIS GRIP *FOREVER!*

Panel 4:

PERHAPS I CAN REACH HIM IN TIME... BY RUNNING UP THE SIDE OF THE BUILDING!

HANK... IF YOU *DO*, YOU'LL GIVE YOUR IDENTITY AWAY! THE CROWD WILL GUESS WHO YOU ARE!

Panel 5:

NO TIME TO WORRY ABOUT *THAT*, BOBBY! HERE *GOES!*

LOOK! DO YOU SEE WHAT *I* SEE ??

IT..IT ISN'T *POSSIBLE!*

Panel 6:

IT'S POSSIBLE, ALL RIGHT... FOR A *MUTANT!*

YOU MEAN..??

OF *COURSE!* IT MUST BE... *THE BEAST!* WHAT A SHAME, NONE OF US HAD A CHANCE TO SEE HIS *FACE!*

4.

REACHING THE TOP OF THE WATER TOWER IN MERE SECONDS, THE POWERFUL, SOFT-SPOKEN *BEAST* GENTLY SOOTHES THE TERRIFIED YOUTH IN FRONT OF HIM...

EASY... EASY... DON'T BE FRIGHTENED! I'LL GET YOU... JUST REACH OUT YOUR HAND... SLOWLY... SLOWLY...

I..I'M AFRAID TO OPEN MY EYES... I GET *DIZZY* WHEN I DO! BUT... I'LL REACH OUT TOWARDS YOUR VOICE!

EXACTLY TWO SECONDS LATER...

YOU'LL BE ALL RIGHT NOW, YOUNGSTER!

TOMMY! YOU'RE *SAFE!*

NOW I'VE GOT TO MOVE TOO FAST FOR THEM TO GET A CLEAR VIEW OF MY FEATURES!

DID YOU SEE HOW HE RACED UP AND DOWN THAT BUILDING... LIKE A HUMAN *GORILLA!*

I'VE HEARD THERE ARE *MANY* SUCH MUTANTS IN HIDING... WAITING TO TAKE OVER THE WORLD!

DID YOU SEE HOW HE RAN *PAST* US?? LIKE HE WAS *AFRAID* OF US ...LIKE HE *KNEW* HE'S OUR *ENEMY!*

HE PROBABLY SAVED THAT KID JUST TO THROW US OFF GUARD... TO MAKE US THINK MUTANTS AREN'T *DANGEROUS!*

BUT HE CAN'T FOOL *US!* C'MON... LET'S *GET 'IM,* BEFORE HE LOSES HIMSELF IN THE CROWD!

BUT, FAST AS THEY ARE... ANGRY AS THEY ARE... THE UNTHINKING MOB CAN'T POSSIBLY KEEP PACE WITH THE SUPERBLY TRAINED TEEN-AGERS WHO RUN PAST THEM AT BREATH-TAKING SPEED...

WE CAN'T STOP THEM!

CAN'T EVEN SEE WHO THEY *ARE,* THE WAY THEY HAVE THEIR FACES COVERED!

MINUTES LATER...

HANK! BOBBY! WHAT *HAPPENED??*

I'M *THROUGH,* SCOTT! I'VE HAD IT!

A MOB... ALMOST *CAUGHT* US!

5.

I'M *THROUGH* RISKING MY LIFE FOR HUMANS...FOR THE *SAME* HUMANS WHO FEAR US, HATE US, WANT TO *DESTROY* US! I THINK MAGNETO AND HIS EVIL MUTANTS ARE *RIGHT*...HOMO SAPIENS JUST AREN'T *WORTH* IT!

YOU'RE TIRED, HANK.. ALL UPSET OVER WHAT HAPPENED! YOU DON'T *MEAN* WHAT YOU SAY!

I'M IN FULL POSSESSION OF MY FACULTIES, SCOTT! I MEAN EVERY WORD! I'M *RESIGNING* FROM THE X-MEN!

BUT, HANK.. ALL YOUR TRAINING... YOUR WORK.. YOU CAN'T JUST TOSS IT ALL ASIDE!

CAN'T I? JUST *WATCH* ME! FROM NOW ON I'LL USE MY POWERS TO HELP JUST *ONE* PERSON...HENRY McCOY...YOURS TRULY! THE HUMAN RACE CAN GO FLY A KITE!

BUT WHERE WILL YOU GO? WHAT WILL YOU DO??

DON'T WORRY ABOUT *ME*, FELLA! I'LL GET ALONG! IF THE HUMAN RACE IS GONNA BE MY ENEMY-FINE! BUT *I'LL* MAKE THE RULES FOR MY NEXT FIGHT!

HANK..KEEP IN TOUCH WITH US! CALL IF YOU NEED ME! TAKE *CARE* OF YOURSELF, YOU BIG, BAD-TEMPERED LUG!

SECONDS LATER, AS SOON AS HE FINDS HIMSELF ALONE ONCE MORE, CYCLOPS ACTIVATES HIS SENSITIVE CEREBRO MACHINE...

I COULDN'T PERSUADE HANK TO REMAIN! THAT MEANS...I'VE *FAILED* AS LEADER!

THIS IS OUR MOST SERIOUS SET-BACK! I'VE GOT TO CONTACT *PROFESSOR X!* THE LOSS OF AN X-MAN IS TOO IMPORTANT FOR ME TO TRY TO HANDLE *ALONE!*

SLOWLY, THE THOUGHT IMAGE OF PROFESSOR XAVIER IS CONVERTED INTO A VISUAL IMAGE ON THE GLOWING SCREEN, AND THEN...

I'VE MADE *CONTACT!*

PROFESSOR, THIS IS CYCLOPS! WHERE *ARE* YOU, SIR?

I AM IN THE HEART OF THE BALKANS, IN EUROPE... DESCENDING INTO AN ALMOST BOTTOMLESS CAVE!

THEN, AFTER CYCLOPS HAS RELATED THE SITUATION, THROUGH MENTAL TRANSMISSION...

WHAT DO I DO, *NOW*, SIR?

NOTHING! HE WILL *NOT* JOIN MAGNETO'S EVIL MUTANTS! YOU DID ALL YOU COULD!

6.

BUT... WHAT OF YOUR MISSION...?

I CANNOT TURN BACK! I AM ON THE TRAIL OF LUCIFER! I SHALL TELL YOU ABOUT IT ONE DAY ---IF I RETURN! FAREWELL, CYCLOPS...

THEN, AS SCOTT SUMMERS TRIES TO PLAN HIS NEXT COURSE OF ACTION ...

I'M LEAVING NOW, SCOTT!

AND, IF YOU WANT MY ADVICE, YOU'LL DISBAND THE X-MEN! HUMANITY ISN'T WORTH THE TROUBLE!

HANK! YOU'RE NOT GOING TO...JOIN MAGNETO???

WHAT I DO CONCERNS ONLY ME FROM NOW ON! GOOD-BYE!

ONE WEEK LATER, A NEW WRESTLING PERSONALITY EXPLODES ON THE T.V. SCREENS THROUGHOUT THE NATION! CORNY AND COLORFUL, HE SOON BECOMES A TOP-DRAW WRESTLING VILLAIN, PLAYING THE HEAVY UNDER THE LOGICAL NAME OF...THE BEAST!

BOOO, BEAST!

AT THE RATE I'M GOING AS A PRO WRESTLER, I'LL BE A MILLIONAIRE IN A YEAR!

LOOK AT THE BIG HAMBONE!

UNUS WILL MAKE MINCE-MEAT OF HIM TONIGHT!

AND, AS AN ACROBATIC WRESTLER, I CAN HOP AROUND ALL I WANT TO WITHOUT ANYONE SUSPECTING I'M A MUTANT!

THERE HE GOES! WOW! LOOK AT 'IM JUMP!

SO WHAT? HE WON'T BE ABLE TO LAY A HAND ON UNUS!

LADEEES AND GENTLEMEN...THE MATCH YOU'VE BEEN WAITING FOR! THE NEW APE-LIKE SENSATION OF THE NATION...THE BEAST... VERSUS THE GREAT, THE UNBEATABLE, THE UNTOUCHABLE CHAMPION OF ALL TIME... UNUS!

7.

NOT FOR NOTHING AM I CALLED UNUS, THE *UNTOUCHABLE!*

IT...IT JUST ISN'T *POSSIBLE!* AND YET... IT'S REALLY *HAPPENING!!*

GOWAN BACK WHERE YOU *CAME* FROM, BEAST!

WHY DON'TCHA GIVE UP, YA BUM?!!

NOBODY CAN BEAT UNUS! YOU HAVEN'T GOT A CHANCE!

BOOO! WHERE'D *YOU* EVER LEARN TO RASSLE??

THERE'S *MORE* TO UNUS THAN THESE HYSTERICAL FANS *SUSPECT!* HE POSSESSES SOME SORT OF AWE- SOME *POWER!*

IT'S TAKING YA SO LONG TO CLIMB BACK IN THE RING THAT THE REF'S COUNTING YOU *OUT!* UNUS WILL WIN *AGAIN!*

THAT FACE IN THE AUDIENCE! IT *IS*... IT *HAS* TO BE...*MASTER- MIND!!* ONE OF MAGNETO'S EVIL MUTANTS!

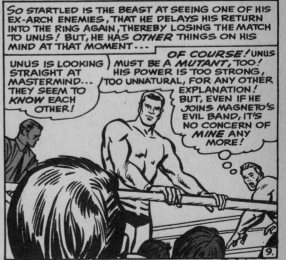

SO STARTLED IS THE BEAST AT SEEING ONE OF HIS EX-ARCH ENEMIES, THAT HE DELAYS HIS RETURN INTO THE RING AGAIN, THEREBY LOSING THE MATCH TO UNUS! BUT, HE HAS *OTHER* THINGS ON HIS MIND AT THAT MOMENT...

UNUS IS LOOKING STRAIGHT AT MASTERMIND... THEY SEEM TO *KNOW* EACH OTHER!

OF COURSE! UNUS MUST BE A *MUTANT,* TOO! HIS POWER IS TOO STRONG, TOO UNNATURAL, FOR ANY OTHER EXPLANATION! BUT, EVEN IF HE JOINS MAGNETO'S EVIL BAND, IT'S NO CONCERN OF *MINE* ANY MORE!

9.

A SHORT TIME LATER, AFTER THE MATCH...

UNUS, I'M YOUR TRAINER...YOU CAN TELL ME! HOW DO YOU KEEP ALL THOSE OTHER GUYS FROM LAYIN' A HAND ON YA??

SHUT UP, MAXIE...AND BEAT IT! I'VE GOT BUSINESS TO DISCUSS!

WELL, MASTERMIND? WHAT'S MAGNETO'S VERDICT? CAN I JOIN YOUR GROUP OF MUTANTS?

NOT SO FAST, UNUS! MAGNETO HAS BEEN DISAPPOINTED BEFORE!* HE WANTS TO MAKE SURE HE CAN TRUST YOU!

*SEE X-MEN #7 "RETURN OF THE BLOB!"...STAN

HE'S CONVINCED THAT YOU'RE A REAL MUTANT...AND HE FEELS YOU'VE GOT PLENTY ON THE BALL...BUT HE WANTS YOU TO PROVE YOURSELF!

HOW? WHAT CAN I DO?

WELL, IF YOU WERE TO FIND THE X-MEN FOR US, FOR EXAMPLE...OR EVEN TO BEAT ONE OF THEM...!

LATER, AS UNUS THOUGHTFULLY WALKS THROUGH THE STREET...

OF COURSE I COULD BEAT ONE OF THE X-MEN...OR ALL OF THEM! NOTHING CAN DEFEAT ME! BUT WHERE DO I FIND THEM? I'VE NEVER EVEN SEEN ONE IN PERSON!

MC 2417

AT THAT POINT, FATE HERSELF STEPS IN! FOR UNUS ACCIDENTALLY STUMBLES ONTO A BIG BANK ROBBERY WHICH IS IN PROGRESS AROUND THE CORNER...

GUNMEN! ROBBING THE BANK! COME TO THINK OF IT, I CAN PUT THAT MONEY TO BETTER USE THAN THEY CAN!

MOVE...BEFORE THE PLACE IS SWARMIN' WITH COPS!!

ALL WE HAVETA DO IS MAKE IT TO THE GETAWAY CAR ACROSS THE STREET!

BANK

10.

BUT, THE STARTLED CRIMINALS ARE NEVER DESTINED TO *REACH* THAT WAITING CAR! AT LEAST, NOT WITH ANY STOLEN MONEY!

I'LL TAKE THAT MONEY BAG!

IF MAGNETO *DOESN'T* ALLOW ME TO JOIN HIS BROTHERHOOD, AT LEAST THIS MONEY WILL HELP LAUNCH ME ON MY *OWN* CAREER OF CONQUEST!

HEY, *LOOK*, CHARLIE! MY BULLETS DON'T EVEN *TOUCH* 'IM! THEY JUST GO FLYIN' AWAY!

DON'T YA KNOW WHO THAT *IS?* IT'S UNUS, THE *UNTOUCHABLE!*

AND, AS THE BULLETS MISS THE UNCANNY UNUS, THEY RICOCHET BACK FROM THE NEARBY WALLS, CAUSING THE GUNMEN TO FLEE FOR THEIR LIVES!

LET'S GET *OUTTA* HERE, BEFORE WE'RE HIT BY OUR OWN SHELLS!!

MEANWHILE, A POWERFUL, PRIVATELY-OWNED HELICOPTER IS RAPIDLY APPROACHING THAT SAME AREA...

WHAT MAKES YOU THINK THERE'S A NEW MUTANT AT LARGE, CYCLOPS?

PROFESSOR X'S CEREBRO MACHINE DETECTED HIS PRESENCE ...AND THE READINGS SEEMED TO INDICATE THIS NEIGHBORHOOD!

IT JUST DOESN'T SEEM THE SAME TO BE HEADING INTO A NEW ADVENTURE WITHOUT THE *BEAST!*

WE ALL FEEL THE SAME WAY, WARREN ...BUT LET'S CONCENTRATE ON THE JOB AT HAND NOW!

LOOK! SOMETHING'S GOING ON DOWN THERE!

THE *BANK'S* BEEN ROBBED! YOU LAND THE CHOPPER...I'LL GLIDE DOWN UNDER MY OWN POWER AND LOOK AROUND!

11.

THAT BIG FELLA WITH THE MONEY BAG...HE MUST BE ONE OF THE ROBBERS!

STAY WHERE YOU ARE, BUDDY! I WANNA *TALK* TO YOU!

WHAT A STROKE OF *LUCK!* NOW I WON'T HAVE TO *FIND* YOU BEFORE I CAN POLISH YOU OFF!

SO, YOU *ARE* ONE OF THE ROBBERS!! WELL, I'LL TEACH YOU NOT TO MAKE IDLE THREATS TO AN *X-MAN!*

STRANGE...HE DOESN'T SEEM THE LEAST BIT WORRIED! HE'S CALMLY FOLDING HIS OUTER CLOTHES!

IF I'M GOING TO BECOME ONE OF MAGNETO'S ALLIES, I MIGHT AS WELL DO MY FIGHTING IN A DISTINCTIVE COSTUME!

THUS, AS THE OTHER X-MEN LAND IN THEIR WHIRLYBIRD, *ANGEL* IS THE FIRST TO RECEIVE A SAMPLE OF UNUS' FEARSOME POWER!

THE WAY WARREN WAS HURLED FROM THAT MUSCLE MAN BEFORE HE COULD TOUCH HIM, TELLS ME ALL I NEED TO KNOW! WE'VE *FOUND* OUR MUTANT!!

STAY *BACK*, ALL OF YOU! I'LL TACKLE HIM WITH MY *POWER BEAM!*

UNNHH!

THIS IS USELESS! MY ENERGY BLASTS BOUNCE AWAY BEFORE HITTING HIM...AND THEY'LL HIT ONE OF *US*, IF I DON'T STOP!!

YOU SEEM TO BE THE LEADER...SO *YOU* SHALL BE MY VICTIM!

I DODGED HIS *FIRST* BLOW, BUT I CAN'T DODGE FOREVER! HOW DO WE BEAT A MAN WHO CANNOT BE TOUCHED BY ENEMY ATTACK ??! IF HE JOINS MAGNETO, WHAT WILL HAPPEN TO THE *X-MEN ??*

12.

13

14

I WAS *AFRAID* OUR PLEDGE NEVER TO CAUSE HARM WITH OUR POWER WOULD ONE DAY WORK AGAINST US!

OKAY! MAYBE I *CAN'T* LET YOU BE HARMED... BUT I'LL SURE STOP *YOU* FROM HURTING ANYONE *ELSE!*

YOU CAN STAY UP *THERE* FOR A WHILE TO COOL OFF! AND I MAY NOT BE SO CHARITABLE *NEXT* TIME!

NICE GOING, WARREN!

WE STOPPED HIM FOR *NOW!* BUT WHAT HAPPENS IF HE MENACES US *AGAIN?*

NEXT TIME HE'LL BE TOO SMART TO TRY TO GRAB *YOU,* ANGEL!

HIS POWER CERTAINLY IS A *STRANGE* ONE! ALTHOUGH HE *CAN* BE TOUCHED, IT SEEMS THAT ANY WEAPON, OR ANY BLOW THROWN FOR THE PURPOSE OF *INJURING* HIM, IS AUTOMATICALLY DEFLECTED IN SOME WAY!

IF HE EVER JOINS *MAGNETO,* HOW WOULD WE FIGHT HIM?

NOTHING MORE WE CAN DO *NOW!* LET'S GET BACK TO HQ AND THINK THIS OUT!

AND SO...

EVEN IF THE *BEAST* HADN'T QUIT, HIS STRENGTH COULDN'T HELP US! HE'D BE UNABLE TO LAND A BLOW!

HOLD IT! THERE'S SOMEONE IN THE *LAB!!*

IT'S... THE *BEAST!*

HANK! WHAT ARE YOU DOING *BACK* HERE? DOES THIS MEAN...?

IT PROBABLY MEANS I'M A KING-SIZED, ADDLE-PATED GLUTTON FOR PUNISHMENT!!

BUT, SINCE I'M APPARENTLY THE ONLY ONE WITH THE TECHNICAL SKILL AND INTELLECTUAL CAPACITY TO DEVISE A COUNTER-WEAPON TO UNUS' POWER, IT BEHOOVES ME TO SAVE YOU FROM A POSSIBLE IGNOMINIOUS DEFEAT!

WHAT *TYPE* OF WEAPON IS THAT?

15.

16.

LATER, BACK INSIDE THE GYM, UNUS CROWS IN TRIUMPH....!

WAIT'LL MAGNETO HEARS THAT ONE OF THE X-MEN WAS SO FRIGHTENED OF ME THAT HE *INCREASED* MY POWER IN ORDER TO BECOME MY ALLY!

HE'LL *HAVE* TO LET ME JOIN HIS MUTANT BAND AFTER THAT!

NOW, NOT ONLY ARE MENACING BLOWS AND WEAPONS UNABLE TO TOUCH ME, BUT I CAN MAKE *ANYTHING* SPIN AWAY FROM ME BY MERELY GETTING NEAR IT!

I'M *COMPLETELY* UNTOUCHABLE! I'M THE MOST INVULNERABLE MAN ALIVE! *NOTHING* CAN TOUCH ME...THEREFORE NOTHING CAN *HARM* ME!

I'LL GRAB A CIGARETTE WHILE I CALL MASTERMIND AND TELL HIM WHAT HAP... *HEY!!*

I CAN'T *TOUCH* THE BLAMED THING! IT KEEPS MOVING *AWAY* FROM ME!

BLAST IT! NO BLAMED CIGARETTE IS GONNA STOP *ME* FROM SMOKIN' IT!

I'LL THROW MYSELF ON TOP OF THE TABLE AND GRAB IT BEFORE IT CAN... *WAIT!!*

MISSED IT *AGAIN!*

THIS IS *CRAZY!* NOW EVEN THE *TABLE* IS SHOVIN' ITSELF AWAY FROM ME!

WHAT'S GOIN' *ON* HERE?? WHAT'S *HAPPENING* TO ME?? WHAT *GOOD* IS MY NEW POWER IF I CAN'T *CONTROL* IT??

18

DAZED, CONFUSED, THE ANGRY MUTANT WALKS INTO THE STREET, AS EVERY OBJECT HE PASSES RECOILS AS THOUGH IT HAS A WILL OF ITS OWN!

OUT OF MY WAY, FOOLS! I'M INVULNERABLE, CAN'T YOU SEE? I'M UN-TOUCHABLE!

FINALLY, THE PANGS OF HUNGER BEGIN TO GNAW AT HIM, AND SO...

GIVE ME A STEAK... AND MAKE IT FAST... UNDERSTAND??

SURE, BIG FELLA! I'VE GOT ONE RIGHT HERE! I WAS GONNA GIVE IT TO SOMEONE ELSE, B-BUT HE'S NOT AS BIG AS YOU!

WHA..?? IT FLEW RIGHT OUT OF THE PLATE!

THEN GIVE ME ANOTHER! I'M HUNGRY, DO YOU HEAR... HUNGRY!

CYCLOPS! YOU'D BETTER CONTACT PROFESSOR X! HE'LL KNOW WHAT TO DO WITH THE BEAST!

NO, BOBBY! I WON'T DISTURB HIM YET! THE BEAST CAN DO NOTHING MORE WHILE HE'S WITH US!

IT'S TOO LATE TO DO ANYTHING NOW! JUST WAIT...YOU'LL SEE!

I HAVE ANOTHER PLAN TO TRY NOW! ARE YOU READY, WARREN?

READY, CYKE!

PERFECT! IF ALL ELSE FAILS, WE'LL DROP A PLASTIC BUBBLE LIKE THIS ONE OVER UNUS! HE WON'T BE ABLE TO TOUCH IT...IT WILL MOVE WITH HIM! IT WILL BE A FORM OF PORTABLE PRISON!

GET THE PHONE, JEAN! IT MUST BE ICEMAN! I SENT HIM TO THE CITY, TO KEEP WATCH ON UNUS!

I HOPE BOBBY DIDN'T GET INTO ANY TROUBLE! IF UNUS SHOULD CATCH HIM ALONE...!

RRRINNGG!

BOBBY IS A FULL-FLEDGED GRADUATE X-MAN NOW! HE CAN HANDLE HIMSELF!

WHAT DOES HE SAY?

HE WANTS US TO COME TO THE CORNER OF BROAD-WAY AND 46TH STREET...ON THE DOUBLE!

EXACTLY TEN SECONDS LATER...

DON'T MAKE ANY SUDDEN MOVES, BEAST! WE'RE ALL WATCHING YOU!

I APPLAUD YOUR GOOD JUDGEMENT! YOU COULDN'T HAVE SELECTED A LOVELIER SPECIMEN FOR OBSERVATION!

19.

FINALLY... WHERE'S ICEMAN? OH, THERE HE IS! HE'S INCOGNITO!

NATURALLY! I DIDN'T WANT UNUS TO KNOW HE WAS BEING FOLLOWED!

HE'S ALL YOURS, CYKE! RIGHT INSIDE...

AH! JUST AS I ANTICIPATED!

I'VE GOT TO HAVE SOME FOOD! I'M STARVING! THERE MUST BE A WAY! I MUST EAT... I MUST!

THE ONLY THING THAT'LL SAVE YOU IS ANOTHER BLAST FROM MY RAY GUN, UNUS! BUT FIRST, THERE ARE A FEW CONDITIONS...!

ANYTHING! I'LL DO ANYTHING YOU SAY...I'LL MAKE ANY PROMISE...

VERY WELL! THIS WILL NULLIFY THE EFFECT OF THE LAST SHOT! YOU'LL BE AS YOU WERE BEFORE!

CYCLOPS! HE'S USING THAT BLAMED RAY AGAIN!

IT'S ALL RIGHT! HE KNOWS WHAT HE'S DOING!

I'M SAVED! I CAN TOUCH THINGS AGAIN! I CAN EAT...!

BUT REMEMBER THIS, UNUS...

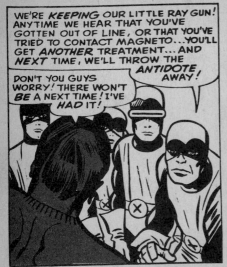

WE'RE KEEPING OUR LITTLE RAY GUN! ANYTIME WE HEAR THAT YOU'VE GOTTEN OUT OF LINE, OR THAT YOU'VE TRIED TO CONTACT MAGNETO...YOU'LL GET ANOTHER TREATMENT... AND NEXT TIME, WE'LL THROW THE ANTIDOTE AWAY!

DON'T YOU GUYS WORRY! THERE WON'T BE A NEXT TIME! I'VE HAD IT!

I GUESS I WAS NEVER CUT OUT TO BE A FAMOUS SUPER-POWERED COSTUMED ADVENTURER! I'M GOIN' BACK TO THE RASSLIN' RING...WHERE I BELONG!

AND I'M BACK WHERE I BELONG, TOO... WITH THE X-MEN!

THANKS FOR NOT BLASTING ME TILL I COULD DO WHAT HAD TO BE DONE, SCOTT!

DEEP DOWN, I NEVER REALLY LOST FAITH IN YOU, HANK!

THAT'S WHAT MAKES YOU THE LEADER YOU ARE!

And so, THE ASTOUNDING X-MEN ARE TOGETHER AGAIN, LITTLE DREAMING THAT THEIR NEXT BATTLE WILL NOT BE AGAINST A MUTANT MENACE...BUT SOMETHING STILL MIGHTIER...STILL MORE DANGEROUS!!

The End.

20.

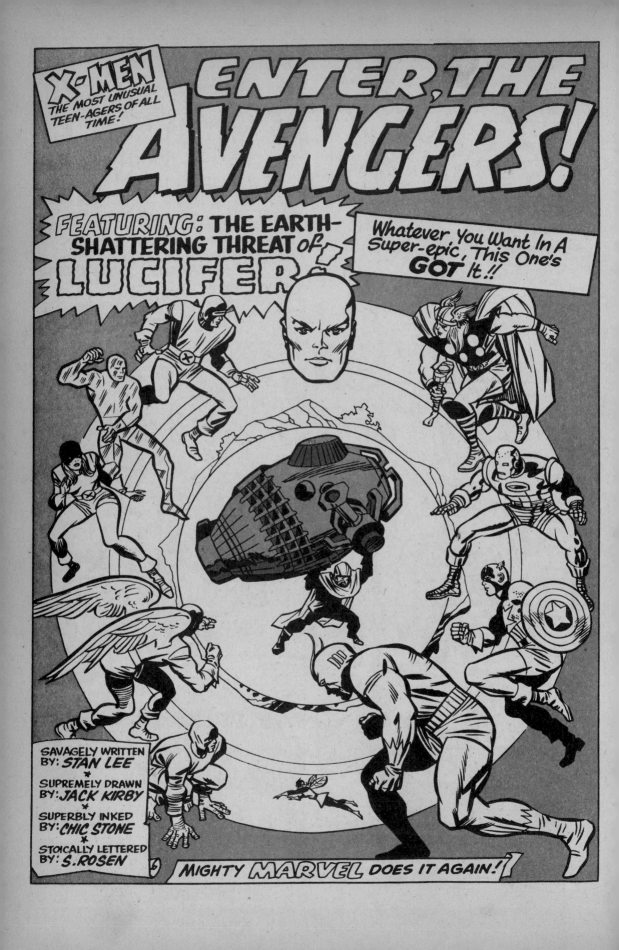

OUR STARTLING SAGA BEGINS IN THE NORTH ATLANTIC, AS A DANGEROUS ICEBERG SUDDENLY DRIFTS INTO THE PATH OF A SPEEDING SUPER-LINER...

THERE'S THE SUN AT LAST! I THOUGHT THAT FOG WOULD *NEVER* LIFT!

BUT LOOK... STRAIGHT AHEAD OF US... WHAT'S *THAT*??

REVERSE ENGINES!! ICEBERG... DIRECTLY *AHEAD*!

TOO LATE!! WE CAN'T STOP IN TIME! SOUND THE ALARM! PREPARE FOR COLLISION!

BUT THEN, SECONDS BEFORE THE FATAL IMPACT, A BLINDING, SHATTERING, MYSTERIOUS TWIN-BEAM SHOOTS OUT, BLASTING THE MIGHTY ICEBERG INTO HARMLESS FRAGMENTS!!

WHAT IN THE NAME OF CREATION WAS *THAT*??!

WHATEVER IT WAS, IT DESTROYED THE ICEBERG! THE SHIP, AND OUR PASSENGERS, ARE *SAFE*!

AND, OF ALL THE HUNDREDS ON BOARD, ONLY A HANDFUL KNOW WHAT REALLY SAVED THE MAJESTIC LINER! A HANDFUL OF THE MOST UNUSUAL TEEN-AGERS OF ALL TIME...!

SCOTT! IT WAS *YOU* WHO BLASTED THE ICEBERG! IT *HAD* TO BE! BUT... WHAT'S *WRONG*...?

TOO BIG A STRAIN! WEAK... EVERYTHING SPINNING AROUND...

HELP ME, WARREN ...HELP ME...

EASY, SCOTTY! I'LL GET YOU TO YOUR STATE-ROOM IN TWO SHAKES!

HMMPH! LOOK AT THAT YOUNG MAN, MATILDA! HE SHOULD HAVE TAKEN SEASICK PILLS!

I DECLARE! THIS YOUNGER GENERATION JUST ISN'T AS *HARDY* AS WE WERE, SAMUEL!

2.

MOMENTS LATER...

IT'S LUCKY FOR ME THAT EVERYONE WAS AT THE RAILING, LOOKING OUT TO SEA! SO THEY DIDN'T NOTICE *WHO* TRANSMITTED THE POWER BEAM, BOBBY!

YOU'RE RIGHT, SCOTTY! THERE'D BE A *PANIC* ON BOARD IF FOLKS KNEW THE *X-MEN* WERE AMONG THEM! HERE, I'LL WHIP UP SOME ICE CUBES FOR YOU, LEADER MAN!

DON'T BOTHER GETTING AN ICE-PACK, BOBBY! I'LL COOL SCOTT'S BROW WITH THEM *TELEKINETICALLY*!

THANKS, JEAN! THAT'S JUST WHAT I NEEDED!

OH, SCOTT! MY HEART JUST BREAKS WHEN I SEE YOU SO PALE, SO SHAKEN! IF ONLY I COULD COMFORT YOU WITH MY ARMS... MY LIPS... BUT I KNOW I MUSTN'T! AS OUR ACTING LEADER, YOU'VE NO TIME FOR THOUGHTS OF... ROMANCE!

IF ONLY WE WERE ORDINARY HUMANS... FREE TO FOLLOW THE URGINGS OF OUR HEARTS! BUT, I MUSTN'T ALLOW MYSELF SUCH HOPELESS DREAMS...!

WE'LL BE DOCKING IN EUROPE SOON, SCOTTY! FEEL WELL ENOUGH TO GET INTO UNIFORM?

SURE! I'LL BE FINE, ANGEL! I JUST WANT TO REST FOR A FEW MINUTES MORE!

USING A FULL-INTENSITY POWER BLAST REALLY KNOCKS ME OUT! MY MOUTH IS DRY AS A BLOTTER!

I'LL REMEDY *THAT*, BROTHER CYCLOPS! ONE *ICED TEA* COMING UP!

THANKS, HANK! AND NOW, I KNOW YOU'RE WONDERING WHY I ORDERED THIS TRIP...

PROFESSOR X CONTACTED ME LAST WEEK! HE SAID THERE WAS A MISSION FOR US IN EUROPE! IN FACT, I EXPECT FURTHER DETAILS FROM HIM ANY MINUTE!

I HAD A *FEELING* WE'D HEAR FROM THE PROF SOONER OR LATER!

ONE ICED TEA... COMPLIMENTS OF THE BENEVOLENT BEAST!

DON'T YOU EVER QUIT GRAND-STANDING, HANK?

THEN, SUDDENLY, THE YOUTH KNOWN AS CYCLOPS RECEIVES A MENTAL IMAGE... TRANSMITTED BY THE MOST POWERFUL MUTANT BRAIN OF ALL TIME...!!

HOLD IT! BE SILENT, ALL OF YOU! THE PROFESSOR IS MAKING CONTACT AGAIN!!

3.

I HAVE FINALLY LOCATED THE HIDDEN CAVE OF *LUCIFER!* NOW HERE, IN THE HEART OF THE BALKANS, I FACE MY MOST CRUCIAL BATTLE!

IT WAS *LUCIFER* WHO LOST ME THE USE OF MY LEGS....YEARS AGO! SOMEDAY I SHALL TELL YOU THE WHOLE STORY... IF I SURVIVE THE NEXT FEW HOURS! BUT NOW, CYCLOPS...THESE ARE YOUR INSTRUCTIONS....!

IF I SHOULD BE DEFEATED, THEN YOU, MY X-MEN, MUST CARRY ON! *LUCIFER* MUST NEVER MENACE MANKIND AGAIN! I HAVE TRANSMITTED MY LOCATION TO YOU! I CAN DO NO MORE!

PROFESSOR...*WAIT!* DON'T FIGHT HIM *ALONE!* WE'LL BE THERE SOON! YOU MUST NOT JEOPARDIZE YOUR SAFETY!

I *MUST!* I'VE WAITED TOO LONG! EVEN NOW HE DRAWS ME TO HIM! I CAN TELL YOU NO MORE... I MUST BREAK CONTACT NOW! GOOD LUCK, MY X-MEN!

THE GROUND FELL AWAY BENEATH MY TREADS! *LUCIFER* TRIED TO *TRAP* ME!

BUT I *EXPECTED* SOMETHING OF THIS SORT! MY HYDRAULIC EXTENDO-ARMS CAN HOLD ME SAFELY!

AND, A SHORT DISTANCE AWAY, A PAIR OF COLD, UNBLINKING EYES SURVEYS THE SCENE WITH NAKED HATRED!!

HE IS AS ALERT AS EVER! BUT *THIS* TIME NOT EVEN HIS BRILLIANT BRAIN CAN SAVE HIM!

EVEN *HE* CANNOT OVERCOME THE POWER OF AN ARTIFICIAL *DUST DEVIL!*

4.

AND SO... A *DUST DEVIL!* * IT CANNOT EXIST IN A PLACE LIKE THIS... SO IT MUST BE *ARTIFICIALLY* CAUSED!

THAT MEANS IT'S THE WORK OF *LUCIFER!*

* IDIOMATIC NAME FOR WESTERN DESERT DUST STORM... STAN.

THEN, BEFORE PROFESSOR XAVIER CAN ACT, THE STRANGE PHENOMENON HURLS HIM FROM HIS CHAIR, AND...

IT'S CARRYING ME THROUGH THE TUNNEL, AS THOUGH IT HAS A MIND OF ITS OWN!

AND, IN A SENSE IT *DOES*... THE MIND OF *LUCIFER!*

FINALLY, THE STRANGE FORCE *HARDENS,* IMPRISONING PROFESSOR X IN FRONT OF HIS LONG-SOUGHT-AFTER FOE...

LUCIFER!! AT *LAST!*

YOUR QUEST IS ENDED, XAVIER... IN THE ONLY WAY IT *COULD* END! NOW, I SHALL FINISH THE JOB I BEGAN YEARS AGO!

NOW I SHALL *DESTROY* YOU!

NEVER, MURDERER!! DID YOU THINK I WOULD COME TO YOU UNARMED, OR UNPREPARED??

STOP, YOU FOOL! IF I AM HARMED, THE ENTIRE WORLD IS *DOOMED!!*

WHAT...??!

5.

BUT, LET US LEAVE THE TWO MIGHTY ANTAGONISTS FOR A MOMENT, AND TURN OUR ATTENTION TO A NEARBY BAVARIAN VILLAGE, WHERE WE FIND...

GEE, IT LOOKS SO PEACEFUL! IT'S HARD TO BELIEVE THAT SOMEWHERE BENEATH US THE PROFESSOR IS BATTLING THAT LUCIFER CHARACTER!

CAREFUL, BOBBY! DON'T MENTION ANY NAMES ALOUD!

WE'LL HAVE TO REMAIN ALERTED HERE UNTIL I RECEIVE FURTHER ORDERS FROM... X!

SUDDENLY, A POWERFUL, DRAMATIC FIGURE PLUMMETS DOWN FROM THE SKY, BEHIND THE X-MEN...

AT LAST! I SEEM TO BE NEARING THE END OF OUR SEARCH!

WHAT IS IT, THOR? WHY DID YOU STOP?

WE HAVE FOLLOWED THESE STRANGE IMPULSES ALL THE WAY FROM AMERICA...BUT NOW...

... MY HAMMER BEGINS TO QUIVER! OUR GOAL IS NEAR AT HAND!

WELL, IT'S ABOUT TIME!

I HOPE THAT SO-CALLED ENCHANTED HAMMER OF YOURS HASN'T LED US ON A WILD GOOSE CHASE, PARTNER!

IMPOSSIBLE! THE IMPULSES WHICH IT DETECTED ARE SO EVIL...SO STRONG...THAT THEY MUST BE FOUND!

HOLD IT, AVENGERS! IT LOOKS AS THOUGH WE HAVE COMPANY! BUT, JUDGING BY THE CAR, IT'S JUST A TOURIST!

I SEEM TO HAVE LOST MY WAY! COULD YOU DIRECT ME TO...TO... =ULP!=

I SUGGEST YOU JUST KEEP GOING, FRIEND! THIS NEIGHBORHOOD MAY BECOME DANGEROUS BEFORE LONG!

6.

BUT... I DON'T UNDERSTAND...

WE DO NOT MEAN TO FRIGHTEN YOU, BUT A STRANGE *MENACE* LURKS NEARBY!

WE CAN'T EXPLAIN ANY MORE THAN THAT, BUT WE SUGGEST YOU LEAVE THE AREA AS SOON AS POSSIBLE!

FOR GOODNESS SAKE!! DO YOU NEED A *HOUSE* TO FALL ON YOU? CAN'T YOU TAKE A *HINT*? NOW GO ON... *SCAT!!*

AND, WITH THAT, THE STARTLED TOURIST "GETS THE MESSAGE!!"

V O O M

WELL! HE COULD HAVE SAID GOODBYE!

THEN, JUST A FEW BRIEF MINUTES LATER...

HEY! WHAT'S GOIN' ON HERE??

NORMAL PEOPLE AT *LAST!!* THANK GOODNESS!

SCREECH!

LOOK OUT!

QUICK! CALL THE POLICE... THE ARMY... ANY-BODY!! THERE'S *MONSTERS* BACK THERE!! CREATURES WITH *WINGS, HAMMERS, SHIELDS* ...EVEN *GIANTS!*

COMPOSE YOURSELF, SIR! YOU'RE BABBLING INCOHERENTLY!

HE SEEMS TO BE IN A STATE OF SHOCK! HE OBVIOUSLY SAW *SOME-THING* WHICH STARTLED HIM!

IT MAY BE CONNECTED WITH *LUCIFER!* YOU'D BETTER SCOUT THE AREA, ANGEL!

BE CAREFUL, WARREN!

DON'T WORRY, JEAN! MY BLUE CROSS IS ALL PAID UP!

7.

I WON'T TAKE THE TIME TO DON MY UNIFORM! NOBODY *HERE* IS APT TO RECOGNIZE ME AS WARREN WORTHINGTON, THE THIRD! BESIDES, EVERY SECOND MAY COUNT!

FLIGHT! WHAT A *GLORIOUS FEELING! THIS* IS WHAT I WAS BORN FOR!

OH, *NO!* WHA...WHAT HAVE I GOTTEN *INTO?*

NEXT, I'LL BE SEEING PINK ELEPHANTS AND GREMLINS! *GANGWAY!!* I'M TAKING THE NEXT PLANE BACK TO OHIO!

WAIT! WE DIDN'T MEAN TO *FRIGHTEN* YOU...!

NO! LET HIM *GO,* JEAN! IT'S BETTER THIS WAY! THIS ENTIRE AREA MAY BE UNSAFE FOR *ANY* NORMAL HUMANS AS FAR AS WE KNOW!

WHILE, HUNDREDS OF YARDS BELOW, IN THE CAVE OF *LUCIFER* ...

TALK!! WHY IS THE WORLD IN DANGER IF YOU SHOULD BE HARMED??

BECAUSE I HAVE *OUT-SMARTED* YOU, XAVIER!

TURN YOUR HEAD... SEE WHAT I HAVE *CREATED* IN THE NEXT CHAMBER...

A GIANT *THERMAL BOMB!!* LARGE ENOUGH TO BLOW UP A *CONTINENT!*

EXACTLY!! NOW STUDY THE WIRING PATTERN! WITH YOUR INTELLECT, YOU'LL NOTICE THE TRUTH IN SECONDS!

THE CONTROL CIRCUITS ARE ATTUNED TO *YOUR OWN HEARTBEAT!!* NOW I SEE IT! YOU'VE FOUND THE PERFECT DEFENSE AGAINST ME!

OF COURSE! I *KNEW* YOU'D FIND ME SOONER OR LATER! BUT, IF MY HEART-BEAT SHOULD STOP... IF I SHOULD *DIE*... THE BOMB WILL GO OFF... *NOTHING* CAN STOP IT!

NOW YOU SEE WHY YOU'RE *HELPLESS* AGAINST ME! AND *YOU* ARE THE ONLY ONE I FEAR! NO OTHER CAN MATCH MY BRILLIANCE!

AND SO, I AM FREE TO CONTINUE MY MASTER PLAN FOR POWER! I SHALL BEGIN BY ATTACKING YOUR PUNY X-MEN WHO WAIT ABOVE, SO INNOCENTLY... SO UNSUSPECT-ING!

8.

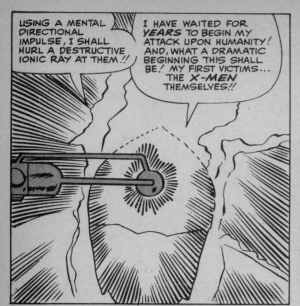

USING A MENTAL DIRECTIONAL IMPULSE, I SHALL HURL A DESTRUCTIVE IONIC RAY AT THEM.!!

I HAVE WAITED FOR *YEARS* TO BEGIN MY ATTACK UPON HUMANITY! AND, WHAT A DRAMATIC BEGINNING THIS SHALL BE! MY FIRST VICTIMS... THE *X-MEN* THEMSELVES!!

BUT, THE MOST POWERFUL BRAIN ON EARTH IS NOT WITHOUT ITS *OWN* RESOURCES! IN THAT SAME SPLIT-SECOND, PROFESSOR X HURLS A MENTAL ILLUSORY FIGURE OF HIMSELF TOWARDS THE SURFACE....!!

I MUST HARNESS EVERY OUNCE OF MENTAL ENERGY I POSSESS!! THE VERY LIVES OF MY X-MEN ARE *ALL* AT STAKE!

ONLY PROFESSOR XAVIER, AND THE EVIL MUTANT KNOWN AS *MAGNETO*, HAVE THE POWER TO EXECUTE THE INCREDIBLE FEAT YOU SEE BEFORE YOU! BUT ONLY THE SUPREMELY GIFTED XAVIER CAN PROJECT HIS MENTAL IMAGE FAST ENOUGH TO EXCEED THE SPEED OF LUCIFER'S IONIC RAY...!

I'M GAINING! IF I CAN JUST MAINTAIN THIS PACE!

AND THEN, THE PROFESSOR SENDS A WARNING THOUGHT SPEEDING AHEAD OF HIS OWN IMAGE...!

DANGER, MY X-MEN!! *SCATTER! DISPERSE!!*

IT'S THE PROFESSOR! *RUN!!*

YOU *HEARD* THE MAN!!

LEAPING INTO ACTION WITHOUT HESITATION... JUSTIFYING THEIR LONG, HARD MONTHS OF INTENSIVE TRAINING... THE X-MEN ESCAPE THE DREADED IONIC RAY BY MERE SECONDS!!

9.

ITS MISSION SUCCESSFUL, THE PROFESSOR'S MENTAL IMAGE FADES INTO NOTHINGNESS, AS THE INTREPID BAND OF TEEN-AGERS NOW GIRD THEMSELVES FOR BATTLE....!!

NO NEED FOR CIVILIAN GARB NOW! THE PRETENSE HAS ENDED! THE PRELUDE IS OVER!

..AND NOW, THE CURTAIN RISES ON ACT ONE! THE STAGE IS SET... THE CAST IS ASSEMBLED!...

..AND, UNLESS I AM GRIEVOUSLY MISTAKEN, THE BEAST IS DESTINED TO PLAY A STELLAR ROLE!

I DON'T KNOW WHAT DANGER THREATENS THE PROFESSOR...OR US! I DON'T EVEN KNOW WHO LUCIFER IS!!

ALL THAT I DO KNOW IS THAT THE X-MEN ARE NEEDED....!

AND THAT'S ENOUGH FOR ICEMAN!!

MARVEL GIRL REPORTING, CYCLOPS! WHY, WHAT'S WRONG??

LOOK OUT, YOU'LL STUMBLE INTO THAT HOLE IN FRONT OF YOU!

THERE'S NOT ENOUGH TIME TO SIDE-STEP!!

BUT, BY TELEKINETICALLY PUTTING THAT LOG OVER IT, I CAN STEP DOWN IN SAFETY!!

WELL DONE, MARVEL GIRL!!

THAT THOUGHT! IT'S THE PROFESSOR!

10.

*SEE F.F. #31--STAN!

11

12

MEANTIME, HAVING DONE ALL HE CAN ON THE SURFACE, PROFESSOR X ONCE AGAIN TURNS HIS FULL ATTENTION TO THE DEADLY FOE WHO STANDS BEFORE A WIRELESS VIDEO-VIEWER...

YOUR *X-MEN* ARE KEEPING THE *AVENGERS* FROM ME! A VERY WISE MOVE ON THEIR PART!

AND NOW THAT I HAVE YOU CRINGING HELPLESSLY BEFORE ME, I SHALL WIN MY GREATEST VICTORY! YOUR TIME HAS COME, XAVIER!

THERE IS NO PHYSICAL FORCE I CAN USE-- OR WOULD *DARE* TO USE AGAINST HIM....!

BUT, MY GREATEST POWER HAS EVER BEEN THE POWER OF --MY *BRAIN!*

AND *THIS* WILL BE MY MOST DIFFICULT TASK! I MUST NARROW A MENTAL SHOCK WAVE ENOUGH TO *STUN* HIM WITHOUT INJURING HIM IN ANY WAY!

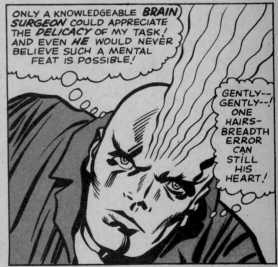

ONLY A KNOWLEDGEABLE *BRAIN SURGEON* COULD APPRECIATE THE *DELICACY* OF MY TASK! AND EVEN *HE* WOULD NEVER BELIEVE SUCH A MENTAL FEAT IS POSSIBLE!

GENTLY-- GENTLY--! ONE HAIRS-BREADTH ERROR CAN STILL HIS HEART!

IN MY MIND'S EYE, I SEE HIS BRAIN AS CLEARLY AS A TRAVELLER READS A ROAD MAP! I MUST CIRCUMVENT THE PORTION OF THE MEDULLA OBLONGATA NEAREST THE SPINAL COLUMN AS I PENETRATE THE MOST SENSITIVE AREA OF HIS CEREBELLUM...

WHAT IS *HAPPENING* TO ME?? WHY HAVE MY MOVEMENTS BECOME SO STIFF...?

NO MATTER! IT WILL TAKE BUT *ONE* SHOT TO--TO--

--MY BRAIN IS CLOUDED--CAN'T THINK! CAN'T REMEMBER--EVERYTHING GOING BLANK --BLANK--!

14

I DID IT! HE'S LOST CONSCIOUSNESS! HE'S HELPLESS!

BUT--WHAT IF I APPLIED TOO MUCH PRESSURE?? EVEN THE MOST MINUSCULE ERROR COULD AFFECT HIS HEART AND DETONATE THE BOMB!

HIS HEARTBEAT SEEMS REGULAR-- BUT I AM NO PHYSICIAN! I CANNOT BE CERTAIN! AT LEAST --HE STILL LIVES!

IF ONLY I COULD FIND A WAY TO REMOVE THE BOMB'S FUSE WHILE HE IS HELPLESS! BUT, FOR SUCH A TASK, I NEED MY X-MEN'S ASSISTANCE...!

MEANWHILE, DIRECTLY OVERHEAD, THE X-MEN ARE STILL FIGHTING A VALIANT, THOUGH UPHILL, BATTLE...!

WE'VE BEEN HANDLING YOU WITH KID GLOVES UP TILL NOW, CYCLOPS!

BUT, WE'RE BEGINNING TO LOSE PATIENCE!

HOW MUCH LONGER CAN MY TELEKINETIC POWER HELP?? MY HEAD IS SPLITTING NOW!

YOU'RE WASTING YOUR TIME, MARVEL GIRL! YOU CAN'T STOP ME WITH SOME FLOATING STONES!

WHAT FATE COULD HAVE BEFALLEN THE PROFESSOR?? IF ONLY HE'D COMMUNICATE WITH US AGAIN.!!!

WE CAN'T STOP-- TILL WE HEAR FROM THE PROFESSOR!

NO MERE BARRIER OF ICE CAN STAY THOR'S HAMMER! GIVE UP THIS USELESS BATTLE, OR I STRIKE!

GO FLY A KITE, CURLYLOCKS! YOU'RE TOO SQUARE TO SCARE ANYONE!

BUT THEN, JUST AS THE ENRAGED THUNDER GOD CAN CONTAIN HIS FURY NO LONGER...

THERE IS NO NEED FOR THAT, THOR! THEY HAVE NOT DEFIED YOU-- I HAVE!

A VOICE! SPEAKING IN MY BRAIN! AND YET-- IT COMES NOT FROM ASGARD! WHAT SORCERY IS THIS ???

15

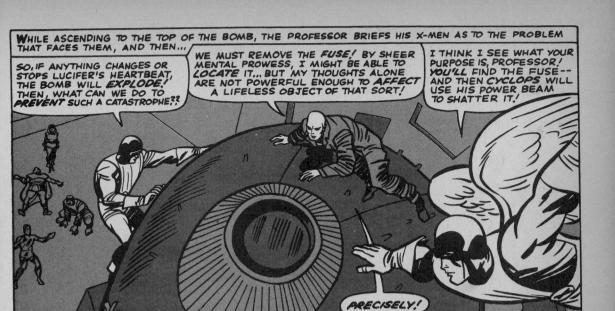

WHILE ASCENDING TO THE TOP OF THE BOMB, THE PROFESSOR BRIEFS HIS X-MEN AS TO THE PROBLEM THAT FACES THEM, AND THEN...

SO, IF ANYTHING CHANGES OR STOPS LUCIFER'S HEARTBEAT, THEN THE BOMB WILL EXPLODE! THEN, WHAT CAN WE DO TO PREVENT SUCH A CATASTROPHE??

WE MUST REMOVE THE FUSE! BY SHEER MENTAL PROWESS, I MIGHT BE ABLE TO LOCATE IT... BUT MY THOUGHTS ALONE ARE NOT POWERFUL ENOUGH TO AFFECT A LIFELESS OBJECT OF THAT SORT!

I THINK I SEE WHAT YOUR PURPOSE IS, PROFESSOR! YOU'LL FIND THE FUSE-- AND THEN CYCLOPS WILL USE HIS POWER BEAM TO SHATTER IT!

PRECISELY!

AND SO, THE CRUCIAL PROJECT BEGINS...

HAVE YOU DETECTED IT YET, SIR?

DO NOT SPEAK! I MUST CONCENTRATE ON NOTHING BUT THE TASK AT HAND!

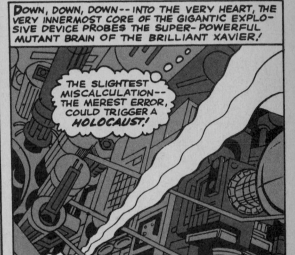

DOWN, DOWN, DOWN -- INTO THE VERY HEART, THE VERY INNERMOST CORE OF THE GIGANTIC EXPLOSIVE DEVICE PROBES THE SUPER-POWERFUL MUTANT BRAIN OF THE BRILLIANT XAVIER!

THE SLIGHTEST MISCALCULATION-- THE MEREST ERROR, COULD TRIGGER A HOLOCAUST!

THEN, SUDDENLY, THE BOMB BEGINS TO THROB, AS THOUGH MYSTICALLY ENDOWED WITH A LIFE OF ITS OWN...

NO-- NO!! IT CAN'T BE! I'VE DONE NOTHING WRONG! I'VE MADE NO ERROR!

BUT, NEXT HE HEARS...

PROFESSOR! IT'S NOT YOUR FAULT! IT'S LUCIFER! HIS HEARTBEAT IS GROWING WEAKER!!

OF COURSE! BY CONCENTRATING SO HARD ON THE BOMB, I LOST CONTROL OF HIM! I MUST LEAVE A PORTION OF MY THOUGHTS WITHIN HIS BRAIN -- NO MATTER WHAT!

18

"FOR THE BOMB IS AIMED AT THE HEART OF ANTARCTICA! SHOULD IT BE DETONATED, THE ENTIRE FROZEN CONTINENT WILL BE DECIMATED WITHIN A MATTER OF SPLIT-SECONDS!"

"THE OCEANS OF THE WORLD WILL BECOME MONSTROUS, DEADLY, CASCADING MOUNTAINS OF WATER, DESTROYING ALL IN THEIR PATH!"

"NO AREA OF EARTH WILL BE SAFE FROM THE THUNDERING *TIDAL WAVES*, WHICH WILL ENGULF THE COASTS OF EVERY CONTINENT! IT WOULD BE THE WORST DISASTER EVER TO STRIKE THE HUMAN RACE!"

AND ONLY *WE* CAN PREVENT IT--AS WE *MUST* DO --BEFORE SOMETHING HAPPENS TO THE MAN WHOSE HEARTBEAT CONTROLS THE DEADLY FUSE!

SCOTT! I'VE *FOUND* IT! BUT ALL THIS PROBING HAS SENSITIZED IT-- IT'S ABOUT TO GO OUT-- AS IF BY SPONTANEOUS COMBUSTION!

IT'S UP TO *YOU*, CYCLOPS! WE HAVEN'T A SECOND TO SPARE!

YOU MUST USE *FULL POWER*-- NARROWED TO HAIRLINE INTENSITY! *NOW!* STRAIGHT DOWN! STEADY --STEADY--TWO MILLIMETERS TO THE LEFT--EASY-- ONE DEGREE RIGHT-- HOLD IT--HOLD IT--

19

EVEN AS THE TWO X-MEN BREATH-LESSLY COMBINE THEIR POWERS, THE DEADLY GIANT BOMB BEGINS TO HEAVE AND THROB, ABOUT TO PERFORM THE UNTHINKABLE MISSION IT WAS DESIGNED FOR AS THE STRAIN GROWS GREATER AND GREATER....!

STAY CALM-- IT'S NOW OR NEVER! YOU MUSTN'T QUIVER-- THE FUSE IS DIRECTLY BELOW! JUST A FEW INCHES FURTHER-- STEADY-- DON'T ALTER THE INTENSITY-- NOW!!

THIPP

YOU DID IT! THE FUSE IS SHATTERED! IT CAN'T EXPLODE!

THIS HAS BEEN YOUR MOST GLORI-OUS MOMENT, SCOTT! THOUGH MANKIND MAY NEVER KNOW WHAT YOU HAVE DONE, THE ENTIRE HUMAN RACE OWES YOU AN ETERNAL DEBT!

BUT MINE WAS MERELY THE TOOL, SIR! YOURS WAS THE BRAIN, THE GUIDING GENIUS THAT ACCOMPLISHED THE IMPOSSIBLE!

BE THAT AS IT MAY-- WE WE MUST RETURN TO LUCIFER NOW!

AND SO... BY RELEASING CONTROL OF HIS BRAIN, HE SHALL RETURN TO NORMAL AGAIN! RISE, LUCIFER! THE EPISODE IS ENDED-- AND SO IS THE THREAT OF YOUR BOMB!

HE SURE LOOKS MEAN-- WHAT I CAN SEE OF HIM!

IT TOOK ME TEN YEARS TO CONSTRUCT THAT DEVICE-- AND YOU'VE DESTROYED IT WITHIN MINUTES! THIS EVENS OUR SCORE NOW, XAVIER! BUT, NEXT TIME WE MEET-- THE FINAL DECISION SHALL BE MINE!

NO, LUCIFER-- THE SCORE IS NOT YET EVEN!

YOU HAVE MERELY SEEN A DIABOLICAL SCHEME GO UP IN SMOKE! BUT I HAVE BEEN DEPRIVED OF THE USE OF MY LEGS ALL THESE YEARS, DUE TO YOU! OUR ACCOUNT IS NOT YET SETTLED! AND NOW-- GO!

THEN WHY AM I NOT HARMED? WHY AM I FREE TO LEAVE?

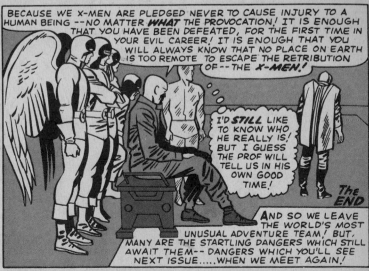

BECAUSE WE X-MEN ARE PLEDGED NEVER TO CAUSE INJURY TO A HUMAN BEING --NO MATTER WHAT THE PROVOCATION! IT IS ENOUGH THAT YOU HAVE BEEN DEFEATED, FOR THE FIRST TIME IN YOUR EVIL CAREER! IT IS ENOUGH THAT YOU WILL ALWAYS KNOW THAT NO PLACE ON EARTH IS TOO REMOTE TO ESCAPE THE RETRIBUTION OF-- THE X-MEN!

I'D STILL LIKE TO KNOW WHO HE REALLY IS! BUT I GUESS THE PROF WILL TELL US IN HIS OWN GOOD TIME!

The END

AND SO WE LEAVE THE WORLD'S MOST UNUSUAL ADVENTURE TEAM! BUT, MANY ARE THE STARTLING DANGERS WHICH STILL AWAIT THEM-- DANGERS WHICH YOU'LL SEE NEXT ISSUE.....WHEN WE MEET AGAIN!

20

YOU ARE PRIVILEGED TO LOOK INSIDE THE WORLD'S STRANGEST TRAINING CHAMBER...THE X-MEN'S *DANGER ROOM*, WHERE PROFESSOR XAVIER'S MARVELOUS MUTANTS BRUSH UP ON SOME HIGHLY SPECIALIZED POST-GRADUATE STUDIES...!

YOU'VE TAKEN THAT RIFLE APART *PERFECTLY* WITH YOUR TELEKINETIC POWER, JEAN!

HOLY COW! YOU'LL *NEVER* GET THOSE PIECES TOGETHER AGAIN IN THE RIGHT ORDER!

PLEASE! NO-BODY SPEAK! I CAN'T BE DISTRACTED!

NONSENSE! BOBBY! SHE'LL ACCOMPLISH IT WITH EASE!

A FEW SECONDS LATER...

EXCELLENT, JEAN! YOU'VE REFINED YOUR POWER TO AN ALMOST UNBELIEVABLE DEGREE!

ALMOST AS UN-BELIEVABLE AS YOUR *BEAUTY*, WHICH LEAVES ME BREATH-LESS!

THANK YOU, SCOTT!

BUT TO *YOU*, I'LL NEVER BE ANYTHING MORE THAN MARVEL GIRL!

TERRIF, JEANIE! IF YOU HAD *ICE POWER*, TOO, YOU'D BE *PERFECT!*

I'VE GOT TO CHANGE THE SUBJECT! WHEN SHE STANDS THIS *CLOSE* TO ME, I FORGET EVERY-THING BUT MY DESIRE TO REACH OUT...TO EMBRACE HER!

BY THE WAY, WHERE'S WARREN? I DON'T SEE HIM HERE!

THAT'S *RIGHT!* HE HASN'T *BEEN* HERE!

WE'D BETTER *CHECK!* HE'S NEVER MISSED A TRAINING SESSION BEFORE!

I'LL GO *WITH YOU*, SCOTT!

THE *BEAST* SHALL ALSO ACCOMPANY YOU!

WE'LL TRY HIS *ROOM* FIRST, AND...

THERE HE *IS!*

THIS SPECIAL BULLETIN IS BEING TRANSMITTED VIA TELSTAR SATELLITE THROUGH THE FACILITIES OF...

BE WITH YOU IN A SEC, SCOTT! I JUST WANT TO SEE THIS!

2.

MR. WORTHINGTON! MAY I REMIND YOU THAT *NO ONE* IS EXCUSED FROM POST-GRADUATE WORK WITHOUT EXPRESS PERMISSION OF *PROFESSOR X* HIMSELF?!!

I *KNOW*, SCOTTY! BUT THIS MAY CONCERN *ALL* OF US! *WATCH!*

SAY! WHAT'S *GOIN' ON* THERE, ANYWAY?

IT'S A VIDEOTAPE BROADCAST OF SOMETHING THAT HAPPENED YESTERDAY AT ANTARCTICA...

...ONE OF THE EXPLORATION PARTY HAD BEEN MISSING AND CONSIDERED LOST, UNTIL HE WAS CARRIED TO THE CAMP BY A FANTASTIC FIGURE CLAD ONLY IN A LOIN CLOTH!

ALTHOUGH OUR TRANSMISSION IS SOME-WHAT HAZY, IT APPEARS THAT A *SABER-TOOTH TIGER* ACCOMPANIED THE PRIMITIVE STRANGER, CAUSING *PANIC* AMONG THE STARTLED MEMBERS OF THE EXPEDITION!

UNPREPARED FOR SUCH A SIGHT, THE ARMED EXPLORERS OPENED FIRE, WHILE THE CAMERAMEN CONTINUED TO SHOOT THESE INCREDIBLE SCENES!

ONLY A MIRACLE PREVENTED ANY FATALITIES, AND THE SAVAGE MAN AND BEAST SOON FADED INTO THE NIGHT AFTER RUNNING AMOK THROUGH THE CAMP!

IT'S *IMPOSSIBLE!* SABER-TOOTH TIGERS HAVE BEEN *EXTINCT* FOR AGES! AND YET... WE *SAW* IT!

HOW *ABOUT* THAT?!

THAT WILD MAN... LIKE A LATTER DAY TARZAN... IN THAT FRIGID CLIMATE WITHOUT PROTECTIVE CLOTHES! COULD HE BE...??

...HE *MUST* BE!! A *MUTANT!!*

3.

MINUTES LATER, THE EXCITED TEEN-AGERS RUSH INTO THE LUXURIOUS STUDY OF THE MAN CALLED *PROFESSOR X!*

PROFESSOR! WE'VE JUST SEEN THE MOST AMAZING THING ON T.V.!

HE'S OBVIOUSLY A *MUTANT,* SIR! AND HE APPEARS TO BE A *DANGEROUS* ONE!

I *KNOW,* SCOTT! WASHINGTON HAS ALREADY CONTACTED ME ABOUT THE ANTARCTIC WILD MAN, AS THEY CALL HIM!

BOY! THE SOUTH POLE IS *ONE* PLACE WHERE *I'LL* FEEL RIGHT AT *HOME!*

THERE IS NO NEED TO *CONCERN* YOURSELVES, MY X-MEN! HE IS *NOT* A MUTANT!

BUT, SIR... HOW CAN YOU BE SO *CERTAIN??*

IF HE *WERE* A TRUE MUTANT, MY SENSITIVE *CEREBRO* MACHINE WOULD HAVE RECORDED HIS PRESENCE! ALSO I WOULD HAVE MENTALLY *SENSED* IT! AND YET...

AWW, IT'S BEEN *WEEKS* SINCE WE'VE HAD A CHANCE TO *USE* ALL OUR TRAINING!

IT *IS* TRUE THAT YOU'VE BEEN INACTIVE FOR WEEKS ... AND BEING YOUNG AND ADVENTUROUS, SUCH A MISSION MIGHT BE GOOD FOR YOUR MORALE! SO... YOU MAY INVESTIGATE THE ANTARCTIC WILD MAN!

THANK YOU, PROFESSOR!

HOT DOG!

A MISSION AT *LAST!*

AHHH! WHAT A RELIEF TO GET MY *WINGS* UNSTRAPPED AND BECOME THE *ANGEL* ONCE MORE!

AN UNTAMED, MARAUDING SAVAGE! AT LAST THE *BEAST* WILL HAVE A FOE WORTHY OF HIS METTLE!

ICEMAN! STOP THAT, YOU JUVENILE JERRY LEWIS!

MEANWHILE, THE X-MEN'S DEPUTY LEADER REMAINS FOR A LAST MINUTE BRIEFING WITH THE PROFESSOR ...

YOU WILL NOTICE, SCOTT, THAT MY MASTER CEREBRO ANALYZER, ALTHOUGH FOCUSED UPON THE ANTARCTIC REGIONS, REGISTERS THE PRESENCE OF *NO MUTANTS* IN THAT AREA!

HOWEVER, THERE MAY BE DANGER THERE ... A *DIFFERENT* DANGER THAN ANY YOU HAVE EVER FACED BEFORE!

I ASSUME BY YOUR WORDS, SIR, THAT YOU DO NOT INTEND TO COME ON THIS MISSION *WITH* US...?

NO, CYCLOPS! YOU HAVE ALL COMPLETED YOUR BASIC TRAINING, AND PROVEN YOURSELVES ON OTHER MISSIONS! MY WORK IS HERE! GOOD LUCK!

THANK YOU, SIR! WE SHALL NOT DISAPPOINT YOU!

4.

DAYS LATER, HAVING LANDED AT A PREARRANGED BASE WITHIN THE MYSTERIOUS POLAR REGION, THE X-MEN BEGIN THE NEXT LAP OF THEIR JOURNEY INTO THE UNKNOWN...

LOOKS LIKE MY *WINGS* WON'T DO ME MUCH GOOD *HERE*, GANG! IT'S TOO COLD TO TAKE OFF THIS PARKA, SO I CAN'T *USE* THEM!

DON'T *COUNT* ON IT, ANGEL! WE STILL DON'T KNOW *WHAT* WE'RE HEADING INTO! REMEMBER, THAT WILD MAN ONLY WORE A *LOIN CLOTH!*

MILES AND MILES OF NOTHING BUT NOTHING! HOW CAN LAND SUCH AS *THIS* HOLD A MYSTERY?

THAT'S WHAT WE'RE HERE TO FIND *OUT*, JEAN!

UH-OH! HERE'S OUR FIRST *PROBLEM!*

THAT'S THE AREA WHERE THE WILD MAN RAN OFF TO ON THE VIDEO-TAPE FILM! BUT, TAKE A LOOK AT THAT *CREVASSE!*

IT'S A SHEER DROP OF HUNDREDS OF FEET! *NOTHING* COULD FALL DOWN THERE AND *LIVE!*

IT LOOKS AS THOUGH OUR MISSION IS *ENDED* BEFORE IT BEGAN! IF HE FELL DOWN *HERE*, HE'S *FINISHED!*

YET, WE CAN'T BE *CERTAIN!* I'LL SEE HOW FAR DOWN MY POWER BLAST RAY CAN PENETRATE!

BUT THEN, SUDDENLY...

LOOK! THE ENERGY FROM YOUR RAY CAUSED A GEYSER OF *SNOW* TO SHOOT UP BEHIND US!

THERE'S A *HIDDEN TUNNEL* UNDER HERE!

THEN HE *WASN'T* KILLED IN THE FALL! *THIS* MUST BE WHERE HE CAME FROM... AND WHERE HE *VANISHED* TO!

I WONDER... IF THAT *SABER-TOOTH* IS STILL WITH HIM ??

5.

Then, after what seems like hours of descending...

IT'S LIKE COMING TO A NEW, UNDISCOVERED WORLD!

AND IT'S WARM! WE CAN SHED OUR COATS! I CAN FLY!

Scouting ahead, the awe-stricken ANGEL soon sees...

IT'S LIKE A VAST ANIMAL BURIAL GROUND! BUT THE BONES...THEY'RE THE WRONG SIZE! THEY'RE THE SKELETONS OF... MONSTERS!

Then, emerging from the gigantic cave, Angel hears a blood-curdling screetch above, and turns around to find...

PTERODACTYLS!! BIRDS FROM THE DINOSAUR ERA! H-HOW CAN IT BE??

But, the winged mutant has no time for idle speculation... as the flying killers attack...!

CLACK!

WOW! THAT WAS TOO CLOSE FOR COMFORT!

6.

HANG ON, ANGEL! MY **POWER BEAM** WILL SCATTER THEM!

MUCH OBLIGED, CYKE! THESE OVERGROWN PARAKEETS MEAN **BUSINESS**!

THAT'S THE **LAST** OF THEM, SCOTT! YOU DROVE THEM OFF!

BUT WHERE **ARE** WE? WHAT KIND OF PLACE **IS** THIS?

APPARENTLY, WE HAVE STUMBLED UPON A WARM, TROPICAL LAND, BURIED FAR BENEATH THE FROZEN WASTES OF ANTARCTICA!

BUT THE FLORA AND FAUNA ARE ALL **PREHISTORIC**... VEGETATION AND ANIMAL LIFE WHICH CEASED TO EXIST ON THE SURFACE OF THE EARTH **AGES** AGO!

WE'VE SEEN THIS SORT OF THING MANY TIMES ON THE **LATE SHOW**... BUT, TO ACTUALLY ENCOUNTER SUCH A WORLD IN REAL LIFE... IT STAGGERS THE SENSES!

I'LL DO SOME MORE SCOUTING... NOW THAT THOSE FLYING NIGHT-MARES ARE GONE!

LOOK! THOSE HORSES AREN'T MUCH LARGER THAN **PUPPIES!** THEY'RE THE ANCESTORS OF OUR PRESENT DAY STALLIONS! WHAT A FABULOUS ARCHEOLOGICAL FIND!

IF I REMEMBER MY ANCIENT HISTORY, MANY OF THE MOST DANGEROUS-LOOKING PRE-HISTORIC BEASTS WERE VEGETARIANS... I **HOPE**!

IMAGINE WALKIN' ONE OF **THESE** ON A LEASH IN THE PARK!

BUT SUDDENLY, THE YOUTHFUL MUTANTS' AMUSED INTEREST TURNS TO UNBELIEVING *SHOCK,* AS THEY SEE...

SCOTT! ALL OF YOU!! LOOK! CHARGING TOWARDS US FROM THE UNDER-BRUSH! WHAT'S *THAT??!*

X-MEN!! ON THE DOUBLE! PREPARE FOR BATTLE!

PRIMITIVE WARRIORS!! MOUNTED ON GIANT CARNIVOROUS BIRDS!! THEY'RE ABOUT TO ATTACK US WITH *ROCKS!*

NO! THEY'RE *NOT* ROCKS! THEY'RE CRUDE *MISSILES...* FILLED WITH *VOLCANIC GASES!* HOLD YOUR BREATHS!!

BUT, CYCLOPS' FRANTIC WARNING COMES TOO LATE... FOR ALL SAVE THE *BEAST!*

ANYONE EVER TELL YOU THAT YOU HAVE A DORMANT, DEEP-ROOTED HOSTILITY COMPLEX?

8.

BUT WHY ARE WE *WATCHING?* WHY DON'T WE SEARCH FOR *JEAN?*

WE *CAN'T* WITHOUT HIS HELP! WE'VE GOT TO *WAIT*... ENLIST HIM AS AN *ALLY!*

HE *KNOWS* THIS FORSAKEN JUNGLE... WE *DON'T!*

LOOK HOW *QUICKLY* HE DEFEATED THAT CAVEMAN! HE'S A ONE-MAN ARMY!

RUN, MAN-APE!! RUN FROM MIGHT OF *KA-ZAR!!*

EEEEAAHH!

STRONGER THAN MASTODON! STRONGER THAN GIANT BOAR! MIGHTY IS KA-ZAR... LORD OF JUNGLE!

RROARRR!

KA-ZAR, LISTEN!! YOU'VE GOT TO *HELP* US! THOSE SAVAGES CAPTURED OUR FEMALE PARTNER! *YOU* MUST KNOW WHERE THEY'VE TAKEN HER!

THE *SWAMP-MEN MY* ENEMIES, TOO! KA-ZAR HELP! WE GO *NOW!*

AT *LAST!*

AND SO...

≥WHEW!≤ DOESN'T THAT SWELL-HEADED MUSCLE MAN EVER GET *TIRED?!!*

HE SEEMS TO HAVE THE ENDURANCE OF A *TIGER!* SEE THE LONG, EASY STRIDES HE TAKES! HE'S NOT EVEN BREATHING HARD!

PERSONALLY, I *RESENT* IT! HE'S GIVING *ME* AN INFERIORITY COMPLEX!

12

MEANWHILE, SOME DISTANCE AHEAD, WE FIND THE *ANGEL*, STILL UPON HIS SCOUTING MISSION...

IT'S THE STRANGEST FEELING I'VE EVER KNOWN!

I'M ACTUALLY FLYING IN A WORLD THAT SHOULD HAVE DIED A MILLION YEARS AGO!

YEEOWWW! YOU'D THINK THEY'D POST A FEW DETOUR SIGNS TO WARN LOW-FLYING X-MEN!

IT'S TOO BAD NONE OF US BROUGHT A *CAMERA!* WE COULD FILM THE SCIENCE FICTION CLASSIC OF ALL TIME DOWN HERE... AND WE WOULDN'T HAVE TO PAY A CENT TO SPECIAL EFFECTS MEN!

BUT THEN, WHILE DARTING WILDLY ABOUT TO AVOID THE GREAT SWAYING HEADS OF THE GRAZING BRONTOSAURI, THE ANGEL IS UNABLE TO DODGE A SKILLFULLY THROWN *NET*...!

OH *NO!* I'VE FLOWN OUT OF THE FRYING PAN...

...INTO THE *FIRE!*

AND, MOMENTS LATER, WARREN WORTHINGTON III, SCION OF ONE OF AMERICA'S WEALTHIEST FAMILIES, IS A HELPLESS CAPTIVE OF THE *SWAMP MEN* IN A LOST WORLD THAT TIME FORGOT!!

HOO-BOY! HOW WILL THE OTHERS *EVER* FIND ME NOW??

THIS MUST BE THEIR CITY...A PRIMITIVE WALLED ENCLOSURE IN THE HEART OF THE SWAMP!

13.

14.

MEANWHILE, THE SMALL RESCUE PARTY COMES NEARER AND NEARER, UNTIL...

I CAN MAKE IT, CYKE! BUT WHAT ABOUT YOU AND BOBBY?

DON'T WORRY ABOUT US, BEASTIE BOY! WE CAN ALWAYS THINK OF SOMETHING... LIKE THIS QUICK-FREEZE BRIDGE, FOR INSTANCE!

FASTER, BOBBY! KA-ZAR IS OUT-DISTANCING US! WE MUSTN'T LOSE HIM!

DON'T WORRY, SCOTT! I CAN ALWAYS PICK UP HIS TRAIL!

LOOKS LIKE YOU WON'T HAVE TO, HANK!! WE'RE THERE!

WOW! HOW WILL WE EVER GET INSIDE OF THAT?!!

LET'S SEE WHAT KA-ZAR DOES! HE SEEMS TO HAVE A PLAN!

QUIET! KA-ZAR IS GIVING THE SABER-TOOTH SOME SORT OF INSTRUCTIONS!

FINE!...SO LONG AS HE DOESN'T MENTION US!!

I'LL DO SOME RECONNAISSANCE ON MY OWN!

GO, ZABU!!

ARRAGH!

LOOK! ATOP THE HIGH BARRICADE WALL... SEE ALL THE COMMOTION! THEY'VE SPOTTED US!

THE ONLY THING THAT BUGS ME, CYKE, IS... DID WE REALLY VOLUNTEER FOR THIS CAPER??

15.

MEANTIME, BACK ATOP THE HIGH PLATEAU...

NO, JEAN!! YOU CAN'T STOP HIM BY THROWING BOULDERS! MY ROPES... CONCENTRATE ON MY ROPES!

I CAN'T! I DON'T DARE TURN MY HEAD... EVEN FOR A SECOND!

PERHAPS IF I CAN CONCENTRATE ON HIS LEGS, HE'LL TOPPLE! OHHH...HE'S SO HEAVY... BUT, I UPSET HIM FOR A MOMENT!

NOW I CAN TURN TO YOU!! AT LEAST YOU CAN SAVE YOURSELF, WARREN!

THERE! NOW HURRY!...FLY AND WARN THE OTHERS... TELL THEM OF THE DANGER HERE!

I WILL, JEAN!! BUT NOT WITHOUT YOU!

NO! YOU'RE TOO WEAK...YOUR WINGS ARE CRAMPED FROM BEING TIED SO LONG! YOU CAN'T...!

BUT I'VE GOT TO TRY! I COULD NEVER LEAVE YOU BEHIND..!

UHHHH! COULDN'T GET ALTITUDE FAST ENOUGH !! THEY GRABBED MY LEGS!

BUT WE WON'T GIVE UP! I'LL DRAG THEM INTO THE AIR TOO, IF I MUST!!

AND, AT THAT VERY MOMENT, A LONE FIGURE RUNS UP THE SHEER SIDE OF THE HIGH STOCKADE WALL, DODGING THE ROCKS WHICH COME FLYING DOWN AT HIM, WITH THE SKILL OF A BORN MUTANT!

I PRAY THAT WE'RE NOT TOO LATE!

16.

STAND ASIDE, GENTLEMEN! IT WILL BEHOOVE YOU NOT TO MAKE ME LOSE MY TEMPER!

PERSONALLY, I HAVE ALWAYS BELIEVED THAT VIOLENCE IS THE LAST REFUGE OF THE INCOMPETENT!

WHILE DOWN BELOW...

THERE'S NO TIME TO FIND A BATTERING RAM, KA-ZAR, SO MY POWER BEAM WILL HAVE TO DO THE TRICK, IF I CAN MAKE IT SUFFICIENTLY WIDE ENOUGH!

YOUR EYES... MAGIC!!

BUT, ALTHOUGH CYCLOPS SUCCEEDS IN BLASTING A LARGE ENOUGH ENTRANCE HOLE, HE LEARNS THAT IT WOULD STILL BE DEATH TO TRY TO USE IT!

BACK!!

YOUR MAGIC... TOO WEAK! ONLY KA-ZAR IS LORD OF JUNGLE!

WHAT ARE YOU GOING TO DO?

INSTEAD OF ANSWERING, THE JUNGLE MONARCH AGAIN EMITS A SPINE-TINGLING, EAR-SPLITTING ROAR...!!

EEEAHHHH!

17.

And, from the edge of the swamp behind them, the roar is echoed back again... from the throats of a herd of charging MASTODONS, led by a snarling, speeding SABER-TOOTH TIGER!!

ARRAGGHH!

Nothing erected by mere mortal man can withstand the fury of such an onslaught, and so...

CRASH!

YOU'RE A MIGHTY HANDY FELLA TO HAVE IN A PINCH, KA-ZAR! BUT NOW, I'VE GOT TO FIND MARVEL GIRL!

RUN, SWAMP MEN...FLEE THE MIGHT OF THE JUNGLE LORD!!

18.

NO MERE WORDS OF OURS CAN DO JUSTICE TO THE FURY OF KA-ZAR'S ATTACK...SO WE'LL ATTEMPT NO SUCH WRITTEN DESCRIPTION!

ANGEL...LOOK! A SABER-TOOTH TIGER!

WHATEVER YOU *CALL* IT, JEAN, IT'S A *LIFE-SAVER!* WE COULDN'T HAVE HELD THEM OFF MUCH LONGER!

JEAN.!! YOU'RE *ALL RIGHT!!* THANK HEAVENS.!! YOU'RE NOT HARMED! YOU'RE *SAFE!*

IS THAT THE NORMAL CONCERN OF A LEADER FOR AN ALLY...OR, DO I DETECT ANOTHER NOTE IN HIS VOICE?...ONE THAT I'VE BEEN *LONGING* TO HEAR?

I'M OKAY, TOO, CYKE! OR HADN'T YOU NOTICED?!!

19.

HOW DID YOU *FIND* US, SCOTT?

WE HAVE *KA-ZAR* TO THANK FOR THAT!

KA-ZAR??

WILL SOMEONE KINDLY EXTRICATE ME FROM THIS PRECARIOUS PERCH?!?

HOLD ON, HANK! *I'LL* GET YOU!

HOW DID YOU GET *UP* THERE, MR. McCOY?

I'M NOT SURE! ONE MINUTE I WAS HOLDING A MULTITUDE OF FOES AT BAY, AND THEN, THE NEXT THING I KNEW... INSTANT EMBARRASS-MENT!

IF YOU DON'T STOP MOUTH-ING OFF LONG ENOUGH FOR ME TO GET A GOOD *GRIP* ON YOU, IT'LL BE INSTANT *KER-PLUNK!*

ALAS, CON-VERSATION IS A DYING ART AMONGST TODAY'S YOUTH!

FINALLY, THE BATTLE WON, KA-ZAR LEADS THE WEARY X-MEN BACK TO THE POINT OF ENTRY TO THE SURFACE WORLD...

THIS WAS A CHARMING PLACE TO VISIT, BUT I WOULDN'T WANT TO *LIVE* HERE!

WE CAME HERE HOPING TO FIND A TRUE MUTANT, BUT THE PROFESSOR WAS RIGHT! INSTEAD, WE HAVE FOUND A TRUE *FRIEND*, KA-ZAR!

PERHAPS YOU DO NOT UNDER-STAND WHAT MY WORDS MEAN, BUT...

NO TALK! YOUR WORLD... ABOVE! *MY* WORLD...JUNGLE! ONLY *KA-ZAR* IS LORD OF JUNGLE! YOU GO! NO RETURN!

FRIENDLY SORT OF FELLA, ISN'T HE?

IN A WAY, IT'S LUCKY HE'S *NOT* A MUTANT! WE'D HAVE OUR HANDS FULL PERSUADING *HIM* TO RETURN TO AMERICA WITH US!

THEN, NO SOONER HAVE THE X-MEN ENTERED THE TUNNEL, THAN KA-ZAR SIGNALS HIS MASTODONS...

...AND THE ENTRANCE IS HIDDEN BEHIND TONS OF CRASHING BOULDERS!

THUS, WE LEAVE THE JUNGLE LORD, WITH HIS VICTORY CRY REVERBERAT-ING ACROSS THE PLAINS OF THE WORLD THAT TIME FORGOT!

BUT, MANY QUESTIONS STILL REMAIN UNANSWERED...AND WE SUSPECT THAT THIS MAY NOT BE THE LAST WE WILL SEE OF *KA-ZAR* AND *ZABU*... FOR THE FUTURE HOLDS MANY MYSTERIES, WHICH WE SHALL UNRAVEL ONE BY ONE IN THE MONTHS TO COME!

20.

LOOK! THE IMAGE IS ABOUT TO TAKE *SHAPE!*

BUT, *WAIT...!* SOMETHING IS *HAPPENING!* WHAT WAS THAT *BLAST?*

A WAVE OF SHEER *FORCE* IS FIGHTING THE IMAGE-BEAM! THE PICTURE WON'T TAKE FORM!

BUT--HOW CAN THAT *BE?*

LOOK OUT! SOMETHING HAS TO *GIVE!*

THE IMAGE EXPLODED! IT'S *GONE!*

DO YOU REALIZE WHAT THIS *MEANS?* SOMEWHERE WITHIN RANGE OF MY DETECTING DEVICES, A *SUPER-POWERED BEING* EXISTS! A BEING SO POWERFUL, THAT MY IMAGE BEAM WAS *SHATTERED* BEFORE IT COULD PROJECT HIS PICTURE!

THIS MEANS THAT WHOEVER--OR WHATEVER--HE MAY BE, HE'S PROBABLY THE MOST DANGEROUS MUTANT WE'VE EVER FACED!

THEN WHY ARE WE *PROCRASTINATING?* WE'VE HEARD THE CLARION CALL TO BATTLE! LET US SALLY FORTH AND SLAY SOME DRAGONS!

IF OUR ENEMIES COULD BE BEATEN BY *WORDS*, HANK, YOU COULD WIN EVERY FIGHT *SINGLE-HANDED!*

WORDS ALONE ARE NOT MY *SOLE* STOCK IN TRADE, YOU JOCULAR JUVENILE!

LET IT NEVER BE SAID THAT *THE BEAST* IS NOT A FIGHTER PAR EXCELLANCE!

WATCH ME TAKE THAT CLOWN *DOWN* A PEG, GANG!

SLURP!

-- *GADZOOKS!* -- WHO COATED THAT CORNER OF THE ROOM WITH *ICE?!!*

JUST THAT LITTLE OLD FROSTPOT --*ME!*

2

3

OKAY, CHARLIE! I GOT HIS SPECS! NOW TAKE A LOOK AND--WHAT'S THAT?!!

BACK! STAND BACK! KEEP AWAY FROM ME, IF YOU VALUE YOUR LIVES! I TRIED TO WARN YOU!

NOW I GOT IT! HE'S ONE OF THE X-MEN-- HE MUST BE THE MUTANT CALLED CYCLOPS!!

I'VE GOT TO GROPE FOR MY SPECIALLY TREATED GLASSES!! NO MATTER HOW TIGHTLY I KEEP MY EYES SHUT, SOME OF MY POWER RAY KEEPS GETTING THRU!

HIS EYES ARE LIKE LIVING DISINTEGRATOR BEAMS!! THEY SHATTER WHATEVER THAT RAY TOUCHES! NO WONDER HE WOULDN'T REMOVE HIS GLASSES!!

MY GUN!! HE ACCIDENTALLY HIT IT-- CUT THRU IT LIKE A KNIFE THRU BUTTER!! HE'S MORE DANGEROUS THAN THE ONE WE'RE LOOKING FOR!

BUT, A SPLIT-SECOND LATER...

AHH! I FOUND MY PROTECTIVE LENSES AT LAST! NOW TO--WHA--??

THE BEAST!! YOU GOT ME IN THE NICK OF TIME, HANK!

I ASSUMED THAT THE MINIONS OF THE LAW HAD ENOUGH TO DO WITHOUT YOU ADDING TO THEIR BURDENS!

NOW HOLD TIGHT WHILE I BRING YOU TO JOIN ICEMAN!

HURRY, HANK! I THINK I HAVE A LEAD AS TO WHERE THE NEW MUTANT IS, AND WHAT HIS POWERS ARE!

LOOK AT THAT ICE CYLINDER UP AHEAD! IT MUST BE BOBBY'S!

WITHOUT A MOMENT'S HESITATION, THE TWO DARING X-MEN PLUMMET HEADLONG INTO THE TALL, HOLLOW TUBE OF ICE THAT HAS SUDDENLY SPOUTED UP IN FRONT OF THEM....!

HANG ON, SCOTTY! WE'RE TAKING THE PLUNGE!

6

I SEE THEM *BELOW*-- ICEMAN AND MARVEL GIRL-- STANDING BY!

AS SOON AS YOU LAND-- *DUCK*, SO I WON'T COME CRASHING DOWN ON *TOP* OF YOU, HANK!

NO DANGER OF *THAT*, SCOTTY! THE KID TURNED IT INTO A FLYING SLIDE!

OKAY, JEANIE GAL, YOU CAN SLOW US DOWN *TELEKINETICALLY* NOW!

I'LL DO MY *BEST*, HANK!

GOOD GIRL, JEAN! I WAS *WONDERING* WHAT WOULD SLOW US DOWN WHEN WE HIT BOTTOM!

SOMEHOW, WHEN *HE* SAYS "GOOD GIRL" IT'S BETTER THAN RICHARD CHAMBERLAIN SAYING "MY DARLING!"

BOBBY, EVER SINCE YOU STOPPED YOUR *CHILDISH* HI-JINKS, YOU'VE BECOME POSITIVELY *MASTERFUL* WITH YOUR ICE POWER!

THANKS, JEAN --BUT I'M NOT DONE YET!

ICEMAN, I'VE A GOOD IDEA WHERE OUR MUTANT *IS*, BUT I NEED A PLACE TO STAND ABOVE THE GROUND, WHERE I CAN STUDY THE NEARBY BUILDINGS!

I SORT OF *EXPECTED* THAT YOU'D ASK! IT'LL ONLY TAKE A SEC!

I'LL BUILD YOU A STAIR-WAY OF ICE! IT'LL GIVE YOU *COLD FEET*, BUT IT OUGHT TO DO THE TRICK!

AND, AT THAT MOMENT...

YOU WANT ME TO *JOIN* YOU? I DO NOT UNDERSTAND!

I AM A *STRANGER* HERE! WHO *ARE* YOU? *WHY* SHOULD I JOIN YOU?

WE'LL *SHOW* YOU!! *WATCH* --!

7

EVERY OBJECT IN THE ROOM -- FLYING INTO THE AIR -- WRAPPING ITSELF ABOUT ME!! AS THOUGH THEY ARE ALL LIVING THINGS!!

THIS IS WHY YOU MUST JOIN US!! BECAUSE I AM -- POWER!! I SHALL ONE DAY REDUCE THE HUMAN RACE TO SLAVERY, SO THAT HOMO SUPERIOR CAN TAKE OVER! AND THOSE WHO SERVE ME, SHALL REAP THE REWARDS!

GOOD, MASTER! GOOD!

EACH OF US HAS A MUTANT POWER OF HIS OWN! IF MAGNETO IS DONE WITH YOU, MASTERMIND SHALL GIVE YOU A DEMONSTRATION....!

WITH A SINGLE GESTURE, MASTERMIND CREATES ONE OF HIS INCREDIBLE ILLUSIONS, AS "THE STRANGER" SEEMS TO FIND HIMSELF AT THE OCEAN'S BOTTOM....

WHAT HAPPENED?? WHERE AM I ??

SUDDENLY, THE ILLUSION CHANGES -- AND THE BEWILDERED STRANGER SEEMS TO FIND HIMSELF STANDING HELPLESSLY WITHIN A SEA OF SMOKY LAVA!

I HAVE SEEN ENOUGH! THEY MUST BE MADE TO REALIZE THAT I MAY NOT BE TOYED WITH IN SUCH A MANNER!

IT IS NOW TIME FOR ME TO GIVE AN EXAMPLE OF MY POWER -- POWER THAT NONE CAN EVEN SUSPECT!

8

IN ONE BRIEF MICRO-SECOND, MASTERMIND'S ILLUSION IS COMPLETELY DISPELLED, AS THE STRANGER EMITS A SUDDEN BLAST OF ENERGY THAT SEVERS HIS BONDS AND MAKES A SHAMBLES OF MAGNETO'S TEMPORARY HEADQUARTERS!

BUT, THE LARGEST PART OF HIS *RAGE* IS DIRECTED AGAINST *MASTERMIND*--!

A RAY!! TURNING MASTERMIND INTO A *SOLID BLOCK OF MATTER!*

AS SOLID MATTER, HIS WEIGHT IS SO GREATLY INCREASED THAT NOT EVEN THE BUILDING'S *FLOOR* CAN HOLD HIM!

MAGNETO! MAGNETO! SAVE US!

CRASH!

GOOD HEAVENS!! WHAT WAS *THAT*??

HELP! POLEEEEECE!

SOMETHING CAME CRASHING DOWN FROM THE CEILING--GOING THRU THE VERY *FLOOR!!* HELP --BEFORE WE'RE ALL *KILLED!*

9

DID YOU HEAR *THAT?*?? IT CAME FROM THE AREA THE MAN WHO WALKED ON AIR WAS REPORTED IN.!

WE'VE GOT TO REACH HIM BEFORE ANYONE *ELSE* DOES--ESPECIALLY *MAGNETO!!*

LET'S GO!

THIS MUST BE THE PLACE! SOME TREMENDOUS FORCE ACTUALLY SHATTERED THE BRICK WALL!

IT'S ONE OF THE *X-MEN!!* SOME GRAVE FANTASTIC *MENACE* MUST BE WAITING INSIDE!

MAGNETO!! SO, YOU'RE THE ONE RESPONSIBLE--.!!

THE *ANGEL!!* YOU DARE ATTACK US ON OUR *HOME* GROUNDS??! *THIS* TIME YOU WILL SURELY TASTE DEFEAT!

MAYBE SO--BUT I'LL MAKE SURE THAT *YOU* TASTE IT *WITH* ME!

QUICKSILVER!! USE YOUR *SPEED* --STOP HIM!

UNHHH--!

GOOD WORK! YOU SMASHED INTO HIM BEFORE HE COULD THINK TO FLAP A WING! NOW--*FINISH HIM OFF!!*

10

11

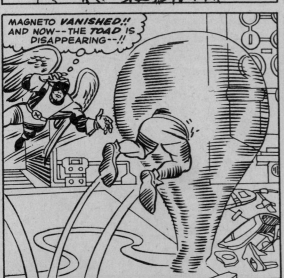

12

THEN, SUDDENLY-- CYCLOPS SEES--

THE *SCARLET WITCH* IS HEXING THE ENTIRE *CEILING* DOWN ON ME.!!

GOOD WORK, PARTNER! BUT, YOU CAN'T KEEP THAT UP FOREVER!

SHUT YOUR EYES, X-MAN!

IT WILL BE A *PLEASURE* TO OBLIGE!

THIS WILL TAKE CARE OF THAT USELESS DEBRIS-- AND THEN WE CAN GET ON WITH THE BUSINESS AT HAND!

MY COMPLIMENTS, CYKE! HOW DOES IT FEEL TO BE A HUMAN GARBAGE-DISPOSAL UNIT??!

ZZZZZT!

JEAN-- WAIT! WHAT ARE YOU DOING??

SOMETHING I'VE *WANTED* TO DO FOR A LONG TIME! I WANT TO MATCH *MY TELEKINETIC POWER* AGAINST THE SCARLET WITCH'S *HEX* POWER!

BY KEEPING HER BUSY DUCKING FLYING OBJECTS, SHE WON'T HAVE TIME TO FOCUS A HEX ON ANY OF US!

ON *YOU?*? DO YOU THINK *YOU* ARE OF ANY INTEREST TO ME??

DO NOT *FLATTER* YOURSELVES!

13

ALL I CARE ABOUT IS THE WELFARE OF MY *BROTHER!* HE MUST BE *UNFROZEN,* BEFORE IT IS TOO LATE!

I DIDN'T AIM TO *HARM* HIM--JUST TO *STOP* 'IM!

PIETRO-- *SPEAK* TO ME!! PIETRO--!

STAY BACK! *I'LL* HELP HIM...!

NOBODY SPEAK!! I MUST CONCENTRATE *COMPLETELY!* EASY--EASY--!!

ONLY ENOUGH POWER TO *DISINTEGRATE* THE FROST!! IF I MISCALCULATE--EVEN BY A *HAIRSBREADTH*-- IT COULD BE *FATAL* TO HIM!!

THERE! THAT SHOULD *DO* IT!

NOW WHAT WILL WE DO WITH THEM?

YOU NEED DO *NOTHING* WITH US EVER AGAIN! WE HAVE SERVED MAGNETO FOR THE *LAST* TIME!

WANDA IS *RIGHT!* WE OWED HIM A DEBT-- BUT IT HAS BEEN *REPAID*--MANY TIMES OVER!

WE SHALL SERVE HIM *NO LONGER!*

I ALWAYS *FELT* YOU DIDN'T BELONG WITH HIS BAND OF EVIL MUTANTS!

BUT, BEFORE ANOTHER WORD CAN BE UTTERED--!

CYCLOPS!! WE'VE SEARCHED THE ENTIRE PLACE! MAGNETO AND THE OTHERS HAVE *VANISHED!*

THE ANGEL'S CONCLUSION IS ENTIRELY *CORRECT,* DISAPPOINTING THOUGH IT MAY BE!

WHERE COULD THEY HAVE *GONE* WITH THAT NEW MUTANT??

THE NEW MUTANT!! PROFESSOR X SAID HE WAS THE MOST POWERFUL OF *ALL!*

IF *MAGNETO* HAS ENLISTED HIM ON *HIS* SIDE, THEN OUR MISSION IS A TOTAL FAILURE!

UNLESS-- WE CAN EVEN THE ODDS BY HAVING THE TWO OF *YOU* JOIN THE X-MEN!

NO! WE HAVE HAD *ENOUGH* OF CONFLICT!!

14

BUT, THE CAUSE WE FIGHT FOR IS A *JUST* ONE!

THE WAY SHE *LOOKS* AT HIM! AS THOUGH SHE *TOO*-- OH *NO!* IT *CAN'T* BE!!

YOUR WORDS HAVE THE *RING* OF *TRUTH* TO THEM! IF ONLY---

NO, MY SISTER! IT IS *I* WHO GIVE THE ORDERS NOW!

WE SHALL RETURN TO OUR HOME-- IN CENTRAL EUROPE, AND *FORGET* THE ENDLESS BATTLE OF MUTANT AGAINST MUTANT--!

BUT, SOME-DAY WE MAY *RETURN!* SOMEDAY, THE FATE OF MANKIND MAY HINGE UPON *OUR* ENTERING THE BATTLE ONCE MORE!

MEANWHILE, THE *"STRANGER'S"* CONE OF ENERGY COMES TO A HALT DEEP WITHIN A LONELY WOODED AREA...

WE HAVE JOURNEYED FAR ENOUGH! PREPARE FOR DIS-SOLVEMENT!

DISSOLVE-MENT??

THIS IS THE MOMENT WHEN MY ENERGY CONE DISSOLVES INTO THE NOTHINGNESS IT CAME FROM!

TELL ME-- WHO *ARE* YOU?? EXACTLY WHAT POWER *DO* YOU POSSESS? YOU SEEM TO BE ALMOST AS MIGHTY AS *I*-- ALMOST THE EQUAL OF *MAGNETO!!*

I AM MERELY-- A *STRANGER!*

MAKE HIM TELL YOU WHAT HIS POWER IS, MASTER! *MAKE HIM TELL!*

SILENCE, TOAD!

NOW, *LISTEN!!* I AM MASTER OF MY BAND OF MUTANTS! WHEN I ASK-- OTHERS *ANSWER!* EVEN *YOU!!* NOW-- *WHAT IS YOUR MUTANT POWER?*

ARROGANT FOOL! I AM *NO* MUTANT!

AS FOR MY *POWER,* IT IS GREATER BY FAR THAN YOU CAN EVEN *IMAGINE!!*

YOU'RE *GROWING!!* GETTING *LARGER* --RIGHT BEFORE MY EYES!! BUT-- YOU *CAN'T* BE GIANT-MAN!!

15

16

WITHIN MINUTES, A HELICOPTER TAKES TO THE AIR, GUIDED BY THE MOST BRILLIANT MUTANT BRAIN OF ALL TIME...THE BRAIN OF *PROFESSOR XAVIER!*

FLY DUE WEST! I CAN MENTALLY RECEIVE HIS EMANATIONS AS THOUGH AN ARROW IN MY MIND IS POINTING TO HIM!

THEN, AFTER A FEW MINUTES OF SPEEDY FLIGHT...

GO, MY X-MEN! YOU WILL FIND HIM JUST AHEAD! BUT, GUARD YOURSELVES AT ALL TIMES!

LOOK!! MAGNETO--AND THE *TOAD*--WRAPPED UP IN SOME SORT OF *COCOONS!*

ANYONE STRONG ENOUGH TO TREAT *MAGNETO* SO CAVALIERLY WILL GIVE *US* THE FIGHT OF OUR LIVES!

ICEMAN! DO YOU SEE SIGNS OF-- THE *STRANGER??*

NOT *YET*, CYKE! BUT HE MUST BE AROUND *SOMEWHERE!*

STOP!! DON'T *TOUCH* THOSE COCOONS-- *ANY* OF YOU!

BACK! BACK-- IF YOU VALUE YOUR *LIVES!*

SOME STRANGE *FORCE*-- SHOOTING OUT--!

THE PROFESSOR WAS *RIGHT!!* ANOTHER SECOND, AND THE WISPS OF WHATEVER THIS IS WOULD HAVE ENVELOPED *ME*, TOO!

17

NOT LONG AFTERWARDS...

AHHH, THE OLD HOMESTEAD! IT'LL BE GOOD TO SIT BACK AND RELAX WITH A DIFFERENTIAL CALCULUS PROBLEM FOR A FEW HOURS!

BUT, BEFORE ANY SERIOUS "RELAXING" IS ATTEMPTED, THE X-MEN ADOPT THEIR USUAL PRECAUTIONARY SECURITY MEASURES...

MY WALL-SOUNDINGS ARE COMPLETE, SIR! NO HIDDEN MIKES, WIRES, OR ANY SUCH DEVICES!

MY INTUITIVE BRAIN SENSES NO UNEXPECTED DANGER! ALL THAT REMAINS IS ANGEL'S VISUAL REPORT!

ALL CLEAR, AS FAR AS I CAN SEE, SIR!

VERY WELL, THEN! LET US PROCEED!

MOMENTS LATER, IN THE STUDY OF PROFESSOR XAVIER...

BEFORE DISMISSING YOU, SCOTT, I THOUGHT WE WOULD REMOVE SOME NAMES FROM OUR CEREBRO MACHINE!

I SEE, PROFESSOR! YOU FEEL THAT CERTAIN MENACES TO MANKIND CAN NOW BE CONSIDERED --DISPOSED OF?

EXACTLY!

IT'S BEEN A LONG, HARD ROAD, CYCLOPS--FOR ALL OF YOU! BUT, YOU HAVE ACQUITTED YOURSELVES WITH HONOR!

MAGNETO

MASTERMIND

SCARLET WITCH

QUICKSILVER

BLOB

UNUS

TOAD

BUT, SUDDENLY-- BEFORE ANOTHER WORD CAN BE UTTERED...

BEEP BEEP BEEP BEEP

PROFESSOR! WHAT'S HAPPENING.??

CEREBRO HAS DETECTED A NEW MENACE!

20

I'VE NEVER SEEN A MERE ELECTRONIC DEVICE REGISTER SUCH AN EXTREME CONDITION OF PANIC! EVERY CIRCUIT IS STRAINED TO THE BREAKING POINT!

BEEP BEEP BEEP

WHATEVER IT IS THAT'S OUT THERE --THREATENING US-- IT IS THE MOST POWERFUL, MOST DEADLY DANGER WE HAVE EVER FACED! AND, IT'S ALMOST UPON US!

The END

THUS, ONE STRANGE SAGA COMES TO AN END AS ANOTHER, STILL STRANGER ONE, BEGINS! THIS TALE HAS MARKED A TURNING POINT IN THE LIVES AND DESTINIES OF THE X-MEN... AND, BEGINNING NEXT ISSUE, FATE HAS MANY NEW AND UNEXPECTED PITFALLS THAT AWAIT THEM! SO, WATCH FOR X-MEN #12, FILLED WITH THE MIGHTY MARVEL MAGIC, AND STARRING THE MOST UNUSUAL TEEN-AGERS OF ALL TIME!

WHAT *IS* IT, PROFESSOR? WHAT DANGER DO WE FACE? AND WHAT DOES *CEREBRO* MEAN?

IT'S THE ONLY MACHINE OF ITS KIND IN EXISTENCE! IT GIVES WARNING OF ANY MUTANT MENACE WHICH MAY BE NEAR!

BUT, IT HAS NEVER REACTED LIKE *THIS* BEFORE! THE MENACE WE FACE MUST BE IN-DESCRIBABLY POWERFUL!

THERE IS ONLY *ONE* WHO COULD CAUSE SUCH A REACTION! QUICKLY! YOU MUST DO AS I SAY...!

A MOMENT LATER, HAVING RECEIVED THEIR ORDERS, THE MARVELOUS MUTANTS RACE INTO ACTION...

JUDGING BY THE PROFESSOR'S *AGITATION*, OUR VERY EXISTENCE IS AT STAKE!

I DON'T KNOW WHAT IT IS THAT HE FEARS, BUT IT MUST BE SOMETHING *TERRIFYING*!

WHATEVER IT IS, *WE* CAN HANDLE IT!

HE NEVER SEEMED THIS WORRIED WHEN WE BATTLED MAGNETO'S *EVIL MUTANTS!*

STOP TALKING! *MOVE!* YOU EACH KNOW WHAT TO DO!

THIS *ICE SHIELD* I'M PUTTING UP AROUND THE SCHOOL OUGHTTA STOP ANYTHING SHORT OF A *SHERMAN TANK!*

WHILE ICEMAN PREPARES A DEFENSE OUTSIDE THE SCHOOL WALLS, I'LL BLAST A DEEP TRENCH *INSIDE* THE WALL...

...USING MY POWER BEAM'S HIGHEST INTENSITY!!

2.

SLOW DOWN, HANK! I CAN'T KEEP UP WITH YOU!!

ANGEL! COME HERE! I NEED YOU!

YOU'RE DOING JUST FINE, JEAN! KEEP TELE-PORTING THOSE LEAVES AND TWIGS OVER THIS CABLE SO THAT OUR UN-KNOWN ATTACKER WON'T SUSPECT THE BOOBY TRAP WE'RE LAYING!

ZAP!

THAT'S IT, WARREN! HOLD THOSE LOGS WHILE I HOLLOW THEM OUT WITH POWER BLASTS!

THIS IS THE LAST OF 'EM, CYKE! NOW I'LL GET THE GRENADES!

THE PROF DIDN'T SAY WHAT KIND OF GRENADES THESE ARE! DO YOU THINK...?

NO TIME FOR GUESSING! WE'RE ALMOST DONE NOW!

EXACTLY FIVE MINUTES LATER, THE X-MEN RETURN, HAVING COMPLETELY FORTIFIED AND BOOBY-TRAPPED THE MYSTERIOUS BUILDING...

THE SCREECHING SOUND HAS STOPPED! DOES THAT MEAN THE DANGER'S PAST?

NO! THE PROFESSOR'S MERELY TURNED OFF THE CEREBRO MACHINE!

IT'S TIME FOR YOU TO LEARN MORE OF THE DANGER THAT THREATENS US!

WELL DONE, MY X-MEN! COME IN...!

IS IT ONE OF THE EVIL MUTANTS WE FOUGHT IN THE PAST, SIR?

NO! I ONLY WISH IT WERE!

I HOPED YOU'D NEVER HAVE TO LEARN OF THIS ENEMY... FOR HIS POWER MAY EXCEED MY OWN!

THE ONE WHO IS ABOUT TO ATTACK US IS.. MY OWN BROTHER!!

YOUR BROTHER?!!

3.

I NEVER MENTIONED HIM BEFORE! PERHAPS I HOPED I WOULD NEVER *HAVE* TO MENTION HIM!

BUT NOW THAT WE ALL SHARE THE SAME MOMENT OF CRISIS... I *OWE* IT TO YOU TO TELL YOU THE WHOLE STORY... TO TAKE YOU BACK WITH ME, IN YOUR IMAGINATION ...TO THE *BEGINNING*...!

IT STARTED WITH AN *ATOMIC BLAST*, YEARS AGO... AT ALAMAGORDO, NEW MEXICO...

"I'LL NEVER FORGET THAT FATEFUL HOLOCAUST ...FOR MY *FATHER* WAS KILLED IN THE BLAST!"

...AND SO WE COMMIT BRIAN XAVIER TO THE EARTH!

IF ONLY *DAD* HAD BEEN ABLE TO ESCAPE THE BLAST... THE WAY *DR. MARKO* DID!

I KNOW HOW YOU MUST FEEL, SHARON... AND I *SHARE* YOUR GRIEF! BUT, AS HIS FRIEND, I SHALL LOOK AFTER YOU... AND AFTER THE BOY, TOO!

THANK YOU, KURT! YOU... YOU ARE VERY KIND!

EVEN THOUGH HE WAS DAD'S FELLOW SCIENTIST, I NEVER *TRUSTED* DR. MARKO... AND I DON'T TRUST HIM *NOW*!

MY DEAR, DEAR SHARON! I WOULD GLADLY HAVE GIVEN MY OWN LIFE TO SAVE BRIAN'S...IF ONLY IT WERE POSSIBLE!

KURT...YOU'RE SUCH A TOWER OF STRENGTH FOR ME... AT A TIME LIKE THIS!

HE *LIES*! HE *MIGHT* HAVE SAVED DAD...BUT HE SAVED *HIMSELF* INSTEAD!

"BUT MONTHS LATER, MARKO PERSUADED MY GRIEF-STRICKEN MOTHER THAT I NEEDED A FATHER TO TAKE CARE OF ME... AND, ALTHOUGH IT FILLED MY HEART WITH A NAMELESS DREAD, THEY WERE FINALLY *MARRIED*!

YOUR NEW FATHER HAS KINDLY AGREED TO LIVE IN OUR OLD HOME, CHARLES...FOR *YOUR* SAKE!

HE MAY FOOL MOTHER, BUT NOT *ME*! I KNOW *THIS* IS WHAT HE WANTED! MOTHER'S WEALTH, AND POSITION, AND PROPERTY!

4.

"EVEN AS A *BOY*, MY MUTANT BRAIN LET ME SENSE SECRETS WHICH WERE LOCKED IN THE MINDS OF OTHERS....!"

AT *LAST!* NOW I HAVE EVERYTHING I'VE ALWAYS DREAMED OF!

MONEY! POWER! THAT'S ALL HE REALLY CARES ABOUT!

"AND AS TIME WENT BY..."

I *TOLD* YOU NEVER TO DISTURB ME WHEN I'M AT WORK!

BUT, KURT...I... I HARDLY EVER *SEE* YOU ANY MORE!

I'VE BEEN A *FOOL!* YOU NEVER REALLY *CARED* FOR *ME!* YOU JUST WANTED THE POWER OUR WEALTH COULD BRING YOU!

AND WHY *NOT!?* EVER SINCE I CAN REMEMBER, YOUR HUSBAND HAD *EVERYTHING*... FAME, SUCCESS, THE ADMIRATION OF THE WORLD... WHILE *I* WAS A NOBODY! BUT THINGS ARE *DIFFERENT* NOW!

DON'T, KURT... *DON'T!* YOU'RE FRIGHTENING CHARLES!

WHAT DO I CARE ABOUT *HIM?* THE SON OF MY *FORMER* MARRIAGE IS COMING HOME TO-MORROW!

"I FIRST LAID EYES ON MY STEPBROTHER THAT NEXT DAY! HE HAD NO SUPER-POWER THEN... NOTHING BUT AN AURA OF SHEER CRUELTY, AND THINLY DISGUISED EVIL!"

SLAM!

TAKE MY BAGS UPSTAIRS! AND DON'T *DROP* 'EM!

YOU MUST BE MY NEW STEPBROTHER! WIPE THAT STUPID LOOK OFF YOUR FACE!

IF YOU'RE WONDERIN' WHAT I'M DOIN' HERE, I JUST GOT *EXPELLED* FROM SCHOOL! I DECIDED THERE WASN'T ANYTHING ELSE THOSE CREEPS COULD TEACH *ME!*

HERE, SQUIRT... LOOK AT MY HAND! I'LL SHOW YA A TRICK!

HAW! THAT'LL TEACH YOU NOT TO STAND AROUND WITH YOUR DUMB-LOOKIN' FACE HANGIN' OUT!

THWAK!

5.

He sounds extremely unsavory, sir! But what makes him dangerous to us now?

After all, if he has no super-power...?

He had none then! But later... wait! Let me check Cerebro again!

He looks more worried than ever!

He's even closer! The sound is getting unendurable!

His power must be greater than I feared! Greater than it was! Cerebro is almost tearing itself apart!

What is his power, professor?

No time for that now! He's reached the first barrier!

Quick! To the window!

Listen! It's the sound of ice being shattered! He's smashing Bobby's frozen wall!

But I made it as thick as a concrete bunker! Nothing could shatter it that quickly!

Give us the word, sir! We'll attack him!

No! Not yet! You can't begin to imagine what you'll be facing!

KRAKA B RUMBLE!

Look out! The entire building is beginning to shake! It's collapsing!

And he's only using a fraction of his true power!

Bobby! Quick! Form an ice shield over Jean... move, X-Men!

I hear ya talkin', Cyke! Whew! Just made it!!

I didn't see that falling chandelier! If...if not for Iceman...!

KLAK!

6.

WOOM! KRAK!

LISTEN! THE REMAINDER OF THE ICE WALL IS BEING TORN APART!!

I SEEM TO SEE A *FIGURE* OUT THERE! BUT...IT'S SO INDISTINCT...I CAN'T MAKE IT OUT AMONG ALL THE RUBBLE!

HE DID IT! THE ICE WALL IS *GONE!* HE'S DESTROYED THE FIRST *BARRIER!*

BARROOOMM!

BUT *HOW?* WHAT *POWER* DID HE USE?

THE SCHOOL STOPPED SHAKING! *WHY?* WHAT'S HE UP TO *NOW?*

HE'S JUST *TOYING* WITH US! HE'S SHOWING HIS *CONTEMPT* FOR OUR DEFENSES!

SHOULDN'T WE RUSH OUT AND FIGHT HIM *NOW*... BEFORE HE COMES CLOSER??

NO! THERE'S STILL TIME... TIME FOR ME TO TELL YOU *MORE* ABOUT HOW IT ALL BEGAN!

KRAK! BRRAMM!

"IT WASN'T LONG BEFORE MY HEART-BROKEN MOTHER SHUT HER EYES FOR THE LAST TIME, JOINING HER FIRST HUSBAND--MY FATHER--FOREVER! AND SO, I WAS ALONE...WITH THEM!"

I *TOLD* YOU NOT TO DISTURB ME WHEN I'M AT *WORK!*

I'LL LEAVE AS SOON AS YOU GIVE ME THE *MONEY* I ASKED FOR! YOU CAN *AFFORD* IT NOW...YOU INHERITED *EVERYTHING!*

WITH MOTHER GONE, *MARKO* CONTROLS MY INHERITANCE, TILL I COME OF AGE!

THE ANSWER IS *NO*, CAIN! IF YOU WANT MONEY, GO OUT AND *EARN* IT, AS I DID!

I KNOW HOW *YOU* EARNED IT! IT WAS NO *ACCIDENT* THAT XAVIER DIED AT ALAMAGORDO...!

YOU DARE ACCUSE *ME*..?!

7

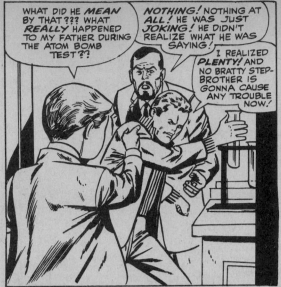

AND THEN...HE DIED! BUT, HIS WORDS PROVED PROPHETIC, FOR....!

PROFESSOR!! LOOK! OUT THE WINDOW! THAT STRANGE, DAZZLING LIGHT! WHAT DOES IT MEAN??

HE'S REACHED THE SECOND BARRIER...AN ELECTRO-MAGNETIC FORCE FIELD! IT MEANS HE'S FALLEN INTO THE TRENCH THAT CYCLOPS BLASTED INTO THE GROUND OUTSIDE!

BUT THE LIGHT IS GROWING EVEN MORE BRILLIANT! THE FORCE FIELD ISN'T STOPPING HIM! HE'S... RESISTING IT...TRYING TO OVERCOME IT!

I CAN SEE A FIGURE OUT THERE!! IT'S STANDING UPRIGHT! IT DOESN'T EVEN SEEM TO BE HURT... OR WEAKENED! AND... IT LOOKS ENORMOUS!

KRRRACKLE

HE ISN'T HURT, JEAN! IF HE'S LASTED THIS LONG, IT MEANS THE CABLE CAN'T STOP HIM! HE'S EVERYTHING I FEARED HE'D BE... AND MORE!

ZZZAPP!

HE SNAPPED THE STEEL CABLE... AS EASILY AS IF IT WERE PAPER! BUT, IN SO DOING, HE RELEASED A STILL GREATER WAVE OF ENERGY, DESIGNED TO CATCH HIM UNAWARES!

CEREBRO HAS GROWN NO LOUDER! THE SECOND LINE OF ELECTRICAL DEFENSE IS HOLDING...AT LEAST FOR NOW!

NOW, ALL WE NEED IS MORE TIME...TIME FOR ME TO TELL YOU THE WHOLE STORY..!

REEEE

9.

PROFESSOR! I'VE NEVER SEEN YOU SO GRIM BEFORE! TELL US...DO WE HAVE A CHANCE? CAN HE BE BEATEN??

WAIT TILL I'VE FINISHED MY TALE, HANK...AND THEN YOU CAN FURNISH YOUR OWN ANSWER!

IT WASN'T LONG AFTER MARKO'S DEATH THAT I REALIZED MY BRAIN POSSESED MUTANT POWERS...

...POWERS WHICH MUST HAVE BEEN CAUSED BY ALL THE RADIATION MY PARENTS HAD BEEN EXPOSED TO AT THE NUCLEAR RESEARCH CENTER BEFORE I WAS BORN!

"THE ONLY OUTWARD SIGN WAS THE FACT THAT I BEGAN TO LOSE MY HAIR WHILE STILL IN MY TEENS! BUT, MORE IMPORTANT THAN THAT WAS MY FANTASTIC ABILITY TO THINK!"

YOU HAVE GIVEN ME ANSWERS I HAVEN'T TAUGHT YOU YET, CHARLES! IT IS AS THOUGH YOU ARE ACTUALLY READING MY MIND!

OH, NO, SIR! THEY WERE JUST LUCKY GUESSES!

I MUST BE MORE CAREFUL! NO ONE MUST EVER SUSPECT THAT I CAN READ MINDS!

"AS I GREW OLDER, MY E.S.P.*POWER MADE ME EXCEL AT EVERYTHING! I BECAME A STAR QUARTERBACK BECAUSE I ALWAYS KNEW IN ADVANCE WHAT THE ENEMY TACKLES WERE THINKING!"

IF ONLY I DARED TELL THEM I CAN READ THEIR MINDS! BUT...THEY'D HATE ME FOR IT!

* EXTRA-SENSORY-PERCEPTION, AS IF YOU DIDN'T KNOW!...STAN.

"EVEN AT TRACK I HAD THE ADVANTAGE OF KNOWING WHEN AN OPPOSING RUNNER WAS TIRING, OR PLANNING TO MAKE HIS LAST DESPERATE SPURT!"

THIS WILL BE MY LAST RACE! IT'S TOO EASY FOR A MUTANT TO DEFEAT A NORMAL MAN!

"BUT, ALL THE WHILE CAIN MARKO WAS WATCHING, AND HATING...HIS JEALOUS HEART FILLED WITH ALMOST UNCONTROLLABLE ENVY!"

ANOTHER TROPHY FOR YOU, SKINHEAD?

IF HE SUSPECTED I COULD READ HIS THOUGHTS! BUT... I'VE NOTHING TO FEAR FROM HIM...YET!

10.

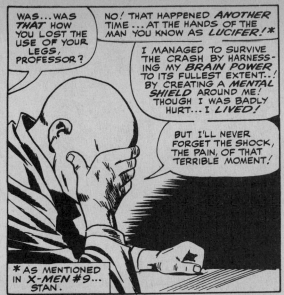

WAS...WAS THAT HOW YOU LOST THE USE OF YOUR LEGS, PROFESSOR?

NO! THAT HAPPENED ANOTHER TIME....AT THE HANDS OF THE MAN YOU KNOW AS LUCIFER!*

I MANAGED TO SURVIVE THE CRASH BY HARNESSING MY BRAIN POWER TO ITS FULLEST EXTENT..! BY CREATING A MENTAL SHIELD AROUND ME! THOUGH I WAS BADLY HURT...I LIVED!

BUT I'LL NEVER FORGET THE SHOCK, THE PAIN, OF THAT TERRIBLE MOMENT!

*AS MENTIONED IN X-MEN #9... STAN.

BUT THEN, SUDDENLY...

BAROOOMM!

LOOK OUT! THE WHOLE BUILDING IS SHAKING!!

QUICK! GRAB THE PROFESSOR! DON'T LET HIM FALL!

DON'T WORRY ABOUT ME! I'M ALL RIGHT! THE WINDOW...LOOK OUT OF THE WINDOW!!

IT'S IMPOSSIBLE! INCREDIBLE!! INCONCEIVABLE!! AND YET...!

HE DID IT!! HE BROKE THROUGH THE FORCE BARRIER!

I SEE SOMETHING MOVING!! IT'S HIM!!

BUT...LOOK AT THE SIZE OF HIM!! HE DOESN'T LOOK ...HUMAN!

THEN, AS THE MONSTROUS FIGURE COMES CLOSER, THEY SEE...

HE'S HEADING FOR THE HOLLOW LOGS...WITH THE GRENADES IN THEM!

HE TRIPPED THE RELEASE WIRE! HE'LL BE STOPPED NOW!

BUT...IF THAT DOESN'T HOLD HIM...WHAT WILL ??!

13.

THE GRENADES ARE SHOOTING OUT OF THE LOGS LIKE MORTAR SHELLS!

HE'S DRAWING BACK!!

BULL'S EYE! THEY'VE LOOSED THEIR SLEEP GAS ALL AROUND HIM!

BUT... WHY DOESN'T HE FALL??!

ALL IT DID WAS ANGER HIM!! HE'S SMASHING THEM ALL WITH ONE BLOW!!

WHOOOSH!

HE'S STAGGERING! HE'S FALLING BACK! WE DID IT!

IF ONLY WE COULD SEE MORE CLEARLY!

THE SMOKE AND HAZE ARE CONCEALING HIM!

I'LL KEEP THE GAS OUT OF THIS BUSTED WINDOW WITH A COATING OF ICE!

I STILL DON'T UNDERSTAND! CAIN MARKO WAS JUST AN ORDINARY, UNSAVORY CHARACTER! HOW DID HE BECOME SO POWERFUL??

14.

THE THING THAT THREATENS US OUT *THERE* IS A FAR CRY FROM THE MAN WHO WAS ONCE CAIN MARKO!

HE'S *STILL* TRYING TO GET UP! WHAT IS HE *MADE* OF!?

NOW I'LL FINISH MY TALE...FOR, I FEAR, OUR TIME IS RUNNING OUT!

I *OWE* IT TO YOU TO TELL YOU WHAT YOU *FACE*! TO TELL YOU HOW CAIN MARKO GOT...HIS *POWER*!

THE ONE POWER ON EARTH THAT MAY F!NALLY *DEFEAT* US!!

"THE LAST TIME I EVER SAW HIM WAS IN *ASIA*, DURING THE KOREAN WAR! WE HAD BEEN SERVING TOGETHER...UNTIL THE DAY THAT CAIN *DESERTED* UNDER FIRE!

THOSE SHELLS ARE COMIN' TOO CLOSE! I'LL DUCK INTO THIS CAVE AND SIT THE WAR OUT FOR AWHILE NOBODY'LL EVER FIND ME IN HERE!

CAIN! COME BACK, YOU FOOL! THAT'S A COURT-MARTIAL OFFENSE! CAIN!...DON'T DO IT!!

"RUSHING IN AFTER HIM, MY HEART SEEMED TO STAND STILL AS I REALIZED...

IT'S THE SACRED, LOST TEMPLE OF *CYTTORAK*! LEGENDS HAVE WARNED OF IT FOR *CENTURIES*!

THAT *RUBY*...IT LOOKS *ALIVE*! THERE'S AN INSCRIPTION ON IT!!

NO!! DON'T *TOUCH* IT!! DON'T!

"BUT, MY WARNING WAS TOO LATE...FOR CAIN...AND FOR THE *WORLD*!

"WHOSOEVER TOUCHES THIS GEM SHALL POSSESS THE POWER OF THE CRIMSON BANDS OF *CYTTORAK*! HENCEFORTH, YOU WHO READ THESE WORDS, SHALL BECOME ...FOREVERMORE ...A HUMAN *JUGGERNAUT*!"

DROP IT, CAIN! DROP IT! YOU DON'T REALIZE WHAT THAT *MEANS*!!

"THOSE DESPERATE WORDS WERE NOT YET OUT OF MY MOUTH, WHEN...!"

SOMETHING'S *HAPPENING* TO ME! I-I'M *CHANGING*..!

NOTHING CAN STOP IT NOW! CAIN MARKO NO LONGER *EXISTS*! AND, IN HIS PLACE...

15.

...AN EVIL, HUMAN JUGGERNAUT HAS COME INTO BEING!!

WHA...??! THAT EXPLOSION!! THE REDS ARE SHELLING THIS AREA! THE CAVE IS COLLAPSING!!

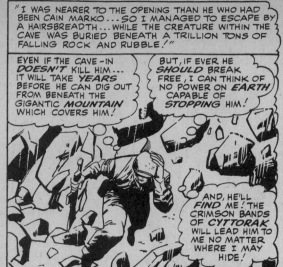

"I WAS NEARER TO THE OPENING THAN HE WHO HAD BEEN CAIN MARKO...SO I MANAGED TO ESCAPE BY A HAIRSBREADTH...WHILE THE CREATURE WITHIN THE CAVE WAS BURIED BENEATH A TRILLION TONS OF FALLING ROCK AND RUBBLE!"

EVEN IF THE CAVE-IN DOESN'T KILL HIM...IT WILL TAKE YEARS BEFORE HE CAN DIG OUT FROM BENEATH THE GIGANTIC MOUNTAIN WHICH COVERS HIM!

BUT, IF EVER HE SHOULD BREAK FREE, I CAN THINK OF NO POWER ON EARTH CAPABLE OF STOPPING HIM!

AND, HE'LL FIND ME! THE CRIMSON BANDS OF CYTTORAK WILL LEAD HIM TO ME NO MATTER WHERE I MAY HIDE!

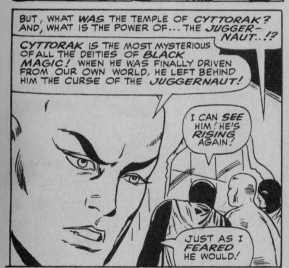

BUT, WHAT WAS THE TEMPLE OF CYTTORAK? AND, WHAT IS THE POWER OF...THE JUGGERNAUT...!?

CYTTORAK IS THE MOST MYSTERIOUS OF ALL THE DEITIES OF BLACK MAGIC! WHEN HE WAS FINALLY DRIVEN FROM OUR OWN WORLD, HE LEFT BEHIND HIM THE CURSE OF THE JUGGERNAUT!

I CAN SEE HIM! HE'S RISING AGAIN!

JUST AS I FEARED HE WOULD!

AS FOR THE POWER OF THE JUGGERNAUT, I SIMPLY QUOTE THE DICTIONARY..."A GIGANTIC, INEXORABLE FORCE THAT MOVES ONWARD IRRESISTIBLY, CRUSHING ANYTHING IT FINDS IN ITS PATH!"

THEN THAT'S WHY HE GETS THROUGH ALL OUR OBSTACLES!! NOTHING CAN STOP A JUGGERNAUT!

BUT, HOW DO YOU KNOW IT'S HIM? IT COULD BE ANYONE!

ONLY THE JUGGERNAUT COULD HAVE MADE CEREBRO SHRIEK THE WAY IT DID...AND ONLY THE JUGGERNAUT COULD PROVE INVULNERABLE TO ALL OUR DEFENSES!

BUT, OUR NEXT DEFENSE SHOULD STOP HIM! IT'S THE GAS WHICH CAUSES LOSS OF BALANCE!

AND, WITHOUT NORMAL BALANCE, A MAN MUST TOPPLE AND FALL!

SOMETHING TELLS ME THAT JUGGERNAUT IS A LOT MORE THAN JUST A MAN!

16

SECONDS LATER...

THERE SHE GOES!

STEP ASIDE, BOBBY, WHILST YOURS TRULY TESTS IT!

TESTS IT? HOW?

LIKE THIS, YOU SNOW-COVERED STRIPLING!

WHEW! RATHER YOU THAN ME, HANK!

BWONK!

YOWFF! NOTHING WILL PENETRATE THAT!

BUT, PROFESSOR XAVIER IS NOT QUITE THAT SURE...!!

LET US GO TO THE FRONT DOOR! HE IS CERTAIN TO ATTACK AT THAT POINT!

HOW CAN YOU KNOW THAT, SIR?

BECAUSE IT IS DIRECTLY IN LINE WITH THE PATH HE IS MAKING! AND, A JUGGERNAUT NEVER CHANGES ITS COURSE...FOR ANYTHING!

BRR! YOU SPEAK OF HIM AS IF HE'S A MACHINE, RATHER THAN A HUMAN BEING!

I'M AFRAID, MY DEAR MARVEL GIRL, THAT HE CEASED BEING HUMAN MANY YEARS AGO, ON THAT FATEFUL DAY IN THE TEMPLE OF CYTTORAK!

QUIET! I HEAR DULL, HEAVY FOOTFALLS THROUGH THE STEEL DOOR! HE'S ALMOST UPON US!

PROFESSOR, IF HE SHOULD SMASH THROUGH THIS LAST STEEL BARRIER... CAN YOU STOP HIM BY MENTALLY AFFECTING HIS BRAIN?

A GOOD QUESTION, HENRY... BUT I'VE A BAD ANSWER! I'VE BEEN TRYING TO PROBE HIS MIND... SINCE FIRST HE APPEARED...BUT IT'S USELESS!

WHEN HE GAINED THE STAGGERING POWER OF CYTTORAK, HE ALSO GAINED A MYSTIC MENTAL DEFENSE, AGAINST WHICH I AM TOTALLY POWERLESS!

LOOK!! THE STEEL WALL... IT'S BULGING INWARD!!

IT'S BUCKLING... MORE AND MORE.. WITH STEADY, EVER-INCREASING PRESSURE!!

NOW DO YOU BEGIN TO CONCEIVE OF THE UNIMAGINABLE POWER THE JUGGERNAUT POSSESSES!?

18.

HOLD IT!! BACK, ALL OF YOU!!

LET ME GIVE HIM A BLAST WITH MY POWER BEAM, FIRST! IT'LL GIVE US SOME MEASURE OF HIS STRENGTH!

MORE! MORE! GIVE HIM FULL INTENSITY, CYCLOPS!

I AM! BUT IT ISN'T STOPPING HIM!

HE'S PUSHING MY RAY BACK AS THOUGH IT'S A SOLID THING! NO ONE OF US CAN DEFEAT HIM ALONE...!

WE'VE GOT TO RUSH HIM TOGETHER!! NOW...!!

IT'S NO USE! HE SWEPT US ASIDE LIKE PAPER DOLLS!

BUT...THE PROFESSOR! HE'S HEADING FOR THE PROFESSOR!

I'M LASHING OUT AT HIM WITH EVERY BIT OF MENTAL POWER I POSSESS...BUT.. STILL HE COMES!!

SO, DEAR BROTHER! WE MEET AGAIN! WHAT A PITY IT IS FOR THE LAST TIME!

THEN...IT'S TRUE! CAIN MARKO HAS BECOME A HUMAN... JUGGERNAUT!!

NEXT ISSUE... ONE OF THE GREATEST BATTLES OF ALL TIME... AS THE IRRESISTIBLE JUGGERNAUT BATTLES THE UN-CONQUERABLE X-MEN TO THE BITTER END!

YOU MUST NOT MISS IT!!

20.

As the deadly *JUGGERNAUT* steadily approaches until he is almost upon the motionless professor, the other X-Men, dazed and shaken, slowly recover from the staggering impact of the relentless attack...!

WHEW!: WAS HE FOR REAL?

NO MERE HALLUCINATION COULD HAVE HIT US LIKE *THAT,* MY FRIGID FRIEND!

QUICKLY, GIRL... STAY WITH THE OTHERS! *I* WILL FACE THE *JUGGERNAUT!*

YOU *CAN'T,* PROFESSOR!! NOT *ALONE!!*

YOU HAVE YOUR ORDERS! *OBEY* THEM!

DON'T ANYONE MOVE! THIS IS THE *PROFESSOR'S* INNING!

BUT, WHAT HAPPENS IF THE *PROF* CAN'T STOP HIM??

THOSE ARE THE LAST ORDERS YOU'RE EVER GOING TO GIVE, MY LONG LOST STEPBROTHER!

IT TOOK ME ALL THESE YEARS TO FREE MYSELF OF THE TONS OF STONE I HAD BEEN BURIED UNDER IN KOREA * ...BUT THE WAIT WAS *WORTH* IT!

BECAUSE I PLANNED THIS TRIUMPHANT MOMENT ALL THAT TIME!

SEE THE *POWER* OF THE *JUGGERNAUT!* MY BODY IS SO CHARGED WITH BOUNDLESS ENERGY THAT I EXUDE WAVES OF *FORCE* EVEN WHEN STANDING STILL!

HE'S SPEAKING THE *TRUTH!* THE SHEER AURA OF STRENGTH ABOUT HIM IS ENOUGH TO PUSH MY WHEELCHAIR BACK!

* WE SAW THE ENTIRE AWESOME SPECTACLE IN *X-MEN #12* ... STAN.

AND NOW, I'VE TOYED WITH YOU LONG ENOUGH! I CANNOT RESTRAIN MYSELF ANOTHER MINUTE! YOU MUST BE DESTROYED *NOW* ... NOW AND *FOREVER!*

YOU FORGET ONE THING... I STILL HAVE A WEAPON...THE *SUPREME* WEAPON...!

YOU'RE *BLUFFING!* BUT IT WON'T HELP YOU! WHAT WEAPON CAN YOU *POSSIBLY* HAVE...TO STOP *ME?*

2.

MY MUTANT **BRAIN**!!

AFTER UTTERING THOSE THREE WORDS, PROFESSOR X LAPSES INTO DEAD **SILENCE** ... CONCENTRATING ... FOCUSING EVERY IOTA OF MENTAL POWER HE POSSESSES ... SENDING A BEAM OF SHEER MENTAL ENERGY AT HIS ONCOMING FOE ... A BEAM MIGHTY ENOUGH TO TOPPLE A **MASTODON**!! BUT...

...AFTER REELING FROM THE INITIAL JOLT, THE **JUGGERNAUT** CONTINUES HIS DREAD ADVANCE...

THE CRIMSON BANDS OF **CYTTORAK**, WHICH GAVE ME MY POWER, ALSO GAVE ME MY **PSIONIC HELMET**, CAPABLE OF PROTECTING ME FROM **ANY** MENTAL ATTACK!

HE'S GONE TOO FAR!

X-MEN... **ATTACK**!

I'LL TACKLE HIM, CYCLOPS... AS WE PLANNED!

THERE! I'LL TRY TO **TELEPORT** HIM LONG ENOUGH FOR YOU TO MOVE THE PROFESSOR TO SAFETY!

THIS WON'T HELP YOU! I CANNOT BE STOPPED!

JUST A FEW SECONDS ... THAT'S ALL I'LL NEED!

I CAN'T HOLD HIM! HE'S SHATTERING MY TELEKINETIC POWER!

IT'S ALL RIGHT! YOU GAVE US THE TIME WE NEEDED! **RELEASE HIM** NOW!

WHRRAK!

EXCELLENT, MY X-MEN! THAT WILL GIVE YOU A FEW MINUTES RESPITE!

I ... NEVER FELT ... SUCH SHEER **POWER!** MY HEAD ... IT'S STILL ACHING!

I MADE THE HOLE AS DEEP AS I COULD! IT SHOULD, **HOLD** HIM!

YOU'RE WHISTLIN' IN THE DARK, CYKE! YOU KNOW HE CAN FORCE HIS WAY OUT OF **ANYTHING**!

BUT, TILL HE **DOES**, WE HAVE A SECOND CHANCE!

EASY, SIR ... YOU'LL BE ALL RIGHT, NOW!

ANGEL, HELP THE PROFESSOR INTO HIS CHAIR!

I'LL DROP A FEW FORGET-ME-NOTS ON OUR PAL DOWN THERE!

WHAT'S OUR NEXT STRATAGEM SIR?

WE MUST FIND **SOMETHING** TO SMASH HIS DEFENSE ... TO **INJURE** HIM!

3.

AND, IN ONE OF THE MANY *TEEN BRIGADE* HEAD-QUARTERS THROUGHOUT THE EAST, THE MESSAGE IS ALSO RECEIVED... EVEN BY SOME YOUTHS WHO ARE *NOT* WEARING EARPHONES...!

I DON'T *GET* IT! HOW CAN WE RECEIVE A RADIO CALL WITH OUR SET TURNED *OFF*?

THERE HASN'T BEEN A *SOUND*... AND YET, WE'RE *ALL* HEARING IT!

IT'S GOT NOTHING TO *DO* WITH THE RADIO!! WE'RE RECEIVING A SUPER-POWERFUL *THOUGHT* TRANSMISSION!

EVEN WITH NO RADIO RECEIVER NEARBY TO MAGNIFY THE MENTAL IMPULSE, ONE MAN WITH EXTRA KEEN AUDITORY POWERS "HEARS" THE UNCANNY SOUND IN THE MIDST OF A CROWDED COURTROOM...

PROCEED, MR. MURDOCK! I'M WAITING FOR YOUR CROSS-EXAMINATION!

THAT STRANGE MENTAL CALL.. SOMETHING UNCANNY IS TAKING PLACE!

IF NOT FOR THIS TRIAL, I'D CHANGE TO *DAREDEVIL* AND TRACE IT TO ITS SOURCE!

SORRY, YOUR HONOR! I WAS JUST.. COLLECTING MY THOUGHTS!

WHILE, BACK AT PROFESSOR XAVIER'S PRIVATE SCHOOL IN WESTCHESTER...

PROFESSOR, LET US RUSH YOU *AWAY* FROM HERE, WHILE THERE'S STILL TIME!

NO, JEAN! I CAN'T RUN FROM THE *JUGGERNAUT*! IF I'M UNABLE TO STOP HIM... THINK WHAT WILL HAPPEN WHEN HE INVADES THE *CITY*!

CAN'T I GO AND HELP THE OTHERS NOW, SIR?

VERY WELL! DELAY HIM ALL YOU CAN! EACH SECOND GAINED INCREASES MY OWN POWER!

THEN, AT THAT MOMENT...

THE JUGGERNAUT IS *FREE* AGAIN! CYCLOPS AND THE ANGEL CAN'T IMPEDE HIS ADVANCE!

JEAN! BOBBY! WHY DON'T YOU WHISK THE PROFESSOR TO SOME REMOTE SPOT.. AS A PRECAUTIONARY MEASURE?

FLIGHT WILL SOLVE NOTHING, MY *X-MEN*! JOIN THE OTHERS, BEAST! JEAN, REMAIN WITH ME!

BUT, PROFESSOR... THEY MAY NEED ME, TOO....!

YOUR CHANCE WILL COME, GIRL! FOR THE MOMENT, *I* NEED YOU HERE!

CAREFUL, ICEMAN! IT WILL TAKE MORE THAN A HASTILY-FORMED FROZEN CLUB TO AFFECT THE *JUGGERNAUT*!

SCAMPER, BOBBY!! WE'RE *NEEDED*!

THERE'S GOTTA BE *SOME* WAY TO STOP HIM... THERE'S JUST *GOTTA*!

7

CYKE, I CAN'T *HOLD* HIM! HE KEEPS CHARGING FORWARD NO MATTER *WHAT* WE DO!

HE'S ADVANCING AGAINST MY FORCE BEAM AS THOUGH IT DOESN'T EXIST!

I *WARNED* YOU! YOU'RE MERELY *MUTANTS*...BUT I...I RECEIVED MY POWER FROM THE ENCHANTED TEMPLE OF *CYTTORAK!!* *NOTHING* CAN STAND IN MY WAY!

LEAST OF ALL A USELESS, WING-FLAPPING WONDER BOY LIKE *YOU!*

I DIDN'T REALIZE HE COULD *MOVE* SO FAST! HE SNARED THE *ANGEL!*

THEN, BEFORE CYCLOPS CAN REDIRECT HIS POWERFUL OPTIC BEAM, THE DREADED *JUGGERNAUT* SHOVES HIS STARTLED VICTIM DIRECTLY IN ITS PATH...!

THERE! THIS WILL RID ME OF *ONE* PETTY ANNOYANCE!

I JUST HAD TIME TO WEAKEN MY BEAM'S INTENSITY...LUCKILY, WARREN IS MERELY STUNNED!

AND NOW I'LL LET THE *REST* OF YOU COSTUMED WEAKLINGS KEEP HIM *COMPANY!*

WE'VE BEEN THREATENED *BEFORE,* MISTER... AND *WE'RE* STILL HERE...WHILE OUR THREATENERS *AREN'T!* THERE'S GOT TO BE *SOME* WAY TO BEAT YOU, AND WE'LL *FIND* IT OR DIE TRYING!

THAT'S VERY *OBLIGING* OF YOU, CYCLOPS! THAT'S EXACTLY THE FATE I HAD IN MIND FOR YOU!

JUST STAND WHERE YOU ARE A MINUTE LONGER!

HE WILL, BIG MAN...BUT *YOU* WON'T!!

THE STAIRS BENEATH MY FEET...THEY TURNED TO *ICE!!* I-I'M LOSING MY FOOTING!

GOOD WORK, ICEMAN! YOU'RE JUST IN TIME!

8.

AND, EVEN AS THE BATTLE RAGES, TEENAGER *JOHNNY STORM* CLIMBS INTO A FRIEND'S RACING CAR IN A LOCAL GARAGE MANY MILES AWAY...

NOT A BAD LITTLE CRATE YOU'VE GOT HERE, CHARLIE! I HOPE I'LL BE ABLE TO JOIN YOU WHEN YOU TRY HER OUT ON THE SALT FLATS!

AW, YOU'LL PROBABLY BE CUTTIN' AROUND TOWN AFTER SOME NUTTY SUPER-VILLAIN, JOHNNY!

BEATS ME WHY ANYONE WOULD WANNA BE A COSTUMED CRIME-FIGHTER WHEN HE COULD SPEND HIS TIME WITH *RACIN' CARS* INSTEAD!

Y'KNOW SOMETHIN', FELLAS? I'VE OFTEN WONDERED THE SAME THING MYSELF! MAYBE I'M A MENTAL CASE AND DON'T KNOW IT!

UH-OH! THERE MAY BE MORE *TRUTH* TO THAT THAN I THOUGHT! *NOW* I'M BEGINNING TO *HEAR* THINGS...INSIDE MY BRAIN!

NO! I'M *NOT* HEARING THINGS! IT'S A MENTAL THOUGHT WAVE... AND IT'S SO *STRONG* I CAN ALMOST *TOUCH* IT!

HEY, JOHNNY...WHAT'S SHAKIN'? YOU LOOK LIKE YOU SAT ON A *TACK!*

CLAM UP, YOU GUYS! SOMETHING'S GOIN' *ON!*

I *KNEW* IT! ANY MINUTE NOW HE'LL YELL *FLAME ON* 'N' GO FLYING OUTTA HERE!

IT'S FROM THE LEADER OF THE *X-MEN!* NOW THAT HE'S MADE CONTACT, HE'S BEAMING A MESSAGE RIGHT *TO* ME! THEY'RE IN TROUBLE... *BIG* TROUBLE!

HEY, JOHNNY! IF YOU'RE GONNA DAY DREAM, DO IT AT DORRIE'S HOUSE, HUH? I WANNA FINISH WORKIN' ON MY CHARIOT!

BUT, HOW CAN I BE *SURE?* REED *WARNED* ME THAT ANY OF OUR OLD ENEMIES ARE APT TO SET ALL KINDS OF TRAPS FOR US...TO PREVENT HIS WEDDING FROM TAKING PLACE! *

FOR ALL I KNOW, *DR. DOOM* COULD BE PLANTING THIS THOUGHT IN MY BRAIN, OR THE *WIZARD!*

ANYWAY, I HESITATED TOO LONG...THE CONTACT IS FADING AWAY.. I'VE *LOST* IT!

* DON'T TAKE *OUR* WORD FOR IT!.. SEE THE GREAT *F.F. ANNUAL #4*, ON SALE *NOW!*..STAN.

9.

PROFESSOR! WHAT'S WRONG? WHAT IS IT?

I ACCIDENTALLY REACHED THE *HUMAN TORCH!* THEN, I THOUGHT OF A WAY HE COULD *HELP* US... BUT HE DIDN'T TRUST HIS SENSES!

AND I DARE NOT WASTE TOO MUCH MENTAL ENERGY BY PROLONGING THE CONTACT IN ORDER TO *CONVINCE* HIM!

BUT...WHAT CAN THE *TORCH* DO THAT THE REST OF US CAN'T?? *OUR* POWER IS AS GREAT AS *HIS!*

TRUE, JEAN... BUT HIS IS A *DIFFERENT TYPE* OF POWER... AND, COMBINED WITH OUR OWN, IT MIGHT JUST TURN THE TIDE!

I *MUST* CONTACT HIM AGAIN... EVEN IF IT WEAKENS ME!

MEANWHILE, ON THE STAIRWAY, JUST OUTSIDE THE DOOR...

NO MATTER *HOW* THICK YOU MAKE THAT ICE PACK, I'LL BREAK OUT OF IT! YOU'RE NOT BATTLING SOME ORDINARY CRIMINAL NOW!

LOOK! HE'S CRACKING THE ICE!

BOY, HE SURE COMES ON *STRONG!*

EVEN THOUGH I *KNOW* HE CAN BREAK OUT OF THIS, I'LL KEEP PACKING IT AROUND HIM TO GIVE *YOU* A CHANCE TO RECHARGE YOUR FORCE BEAM, CYKE!

BUT, WE'RE ONLY FIGHTING A *DELAYING* ACTION AT BEST! IF ONLY THERE WERE SOME *OTHER* WAY...!

LOOK! HE'S STARTING TO *GLOW* WITH THAT AURA OF ENERGY, OR WHATEVER HE CALLED IT!

GET *BACK*, BOBBY... BACK! HE'LL CRACK OPEN THE ENTIRE ICE WALL AT ANY SECOND!

BRAKKK!

UNNHHH..!

TOO LATE! THOSE ROCK-HARD CHUNKS OF FLYING ICE STRUCK HIM BEFORE HE COULD DODGE! ...AND NOW THE *JUGGERNAUT* IS FREE AGAIN!

10.

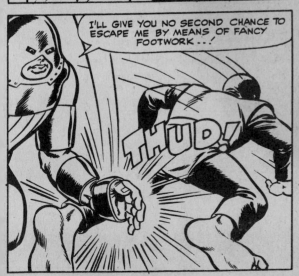

12.

BAH!! I'LL GET YOU, SOONER OR LATER!

THWOK!

LATER I HOPE!

HE'S HEADING JUST WHERE I WANT HIM!

HE THREW HIMSELF INTO OUR DANGER ROOM! HIS MOMENTUM HURLED HIM TO THE FLOOR!

IF I CAN JUST REACH THE CONTROL PANEL BEFORE HE REGAINS HIS FEET!

MY LEG IS SEVERELY SPRAINED AND MY ENTIRE BODY BRUISED AND ACHING... BUT IT'S IMPERATIVE THAT I MAKE IT...!

SO, THERE YOU ARE! NOW THERE'S NO WAY FOR YOU TO ESCAPE FROM ME! THIS IS YOUR FINISH!

I'VE GOT TO STRETCH... JUST A LITTLE FURTHER...!! THERE! I OPENED THE MASTER CONTROL PANEL!

CLICK!

THE PAIN IS EXCRUCIATING... BUT I DAREN'T STOP NOW!

YOU'RE WASTING YOUR TIME! NOTHING CAN STOP ME FROM REACHING YOU!

THAT, MY ARROGANT ANTAGONIST, REMAINS TO BE SEEN!

I DID IT! I ACTIVATED THE ENTIRE OBSTACLE TRAINING COMPLEX! IT SHOULD SERVE TO DELAY HIM UNTIL THE OTHERS CAN PITCH IN!

JETS OF CHEMICAL FLAME SHOOTING AT ME! IS THIS THE BEST YOU CAN DO??

13.

WHUPP!

PERHAPS *THIS* IS MORE TO YOUR *LIKING?!!*

WE TRY TO GIVE OUR GUESTS THEIR *MONEY'S* WORTH!

WIZZZT!

THOK!

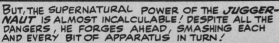

AS IF IN ANSWER TO THE JUGGERNAUT'S SNEERING QUESTION, THE DANGER ROOM SUDDENLY SEEMS TO COME ALIVE WITH NEW MENACE AS THE BEAST STEADILY MANIPULATES THE CONTROL PANEL, THOUGH EACH MOVEMENT IS AGONY TO HIS INJURED BODY!

BUT, THE SUPERNATURAL POWER OF THE *JUGGERNAUT* IS ALMOST INCALCULABLE! DESPITE ALL THE DANGERS, HE FORGES AHEAD, SMASHING EACH AND EVERY BIT OF APPARATUS IN TURN!

HAVE YOU FORGOTTEN...? I..AM..THE.. *JUGGERNAUT!!*

RIPP!

STILL UNWILLING TO SURRENDER, THE DESPERATE *BEAST* UNLEASHES THE MOST POWERFUL DANGER IN THEIR ARSENAL...A SWIFTLY-ROLLING TEN-TON BARREL OF STEEL!!

RROOM!

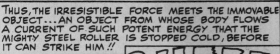

THUS, THE IRRESISTIBLE FORCE MEETS THE IMMOVABLE OBJECT...AN OBJECT FROM WHOSE BODY FLOWS A CURRENT OF SUCH POTENT ENERGY THAT THE MIGHTY STEEL ROLLER IS STOPPED COLD, BEFORE IT CAN STRIKE HIM!!

SQUEEEE!

NOT ONLY DID HE *STOP* IT... BUT HE'S MANAGED TO ROLL IT *BACK* TOWARDS *ME!!* THIS COULD WELL BE THE END OF A PROMISING CAREER FOR MY FAVORITE X-MAN!!

14.

IT'S TOO LATE TO LOCATE THE BUTTON TO *STOP* THAT THING... I'VE ONLY *ONE* CHANCE...!

I MUSTN'T THINK OF THE PAIN... I'VE *GOT* TO USE MY LEGS...!!

...UHHHH!.. BECAUSE OF MY LEG... COULDN'T LEAP HIGH ENOUGH.. JUST... *UHH!!*

THUD!

HE'S UNCONSCIOUS! HE CAN'T TROUBLE ME ANY MORE! I'LL CONTINUE ON TILL I TRAP *XAVIER*... THEN I'LL COME BACK AND FINISH THE BEAST... AND *ALL* OF THEM!

MEANWHILE, A THOUGHTFUL JOHNNY STORM DRIVES DOWN MADISON AVENUE, TRYING TO ARRIVE AT A MOMENTOUS DECISION...!

I'M RECEIVING THAT MENTAL CONTACT AGAIN! IT *SEEMS* GENUINE ENOUGH! BUT... DO I DARE TO *TRUST* IT!?

AWW, WHAT THE HECK! IF I WAS THE *CAUTIOUS* TYPE, I WOULDN'T BE A MEMBER OF THE F.F. IN THE *FIRST* PLACE! WHAT AM I SCARED OF??

GOOD! I HAVE DISPELLED THE CLOUD OF SUSPICION FROM HIS BRAIN! NOW, I MUST LEAD HIM TO US AS QUICKLY AS POSSIBLE!

I SHALL DIRECT YOU TO WHERE YOU ARE NEEDED! YOU MUST RELAX! TRY TO THINK OF NOTHING! LET *MY* MIND GUIDE YOURS!

OKAY, MISTER! IT'S YOUR SHOW!

YOUR CAR IS TOO SLOW! PARK IT AND BECOME THE *HUMAN TORCH!* THEN, FOLLOW MY *THOUGHT BEAM!*

FLAME ON!

WHEN YOU ARRIVE, YOU WILL FOLLOW MY COMMANDS *IMPLICITLY!* THERE IS MORE AT STAKE THAN YOU CAN IMAGINE!

15

THEN, BACK AT THE WORLD'S MOST UNUSUAL PRIVATE SCHOOL ...

DID YOU CONTACT HIM, PROFESSOR?

YES, JEAN! AND NOW...IT'S TIME FOR *ME* TO ENTER THE PICTURE! MY BRAIN HAS BEEN FORTIFIED TO THE MAXIMUM DEGREE!

IF I AM *EVER* TO DEFEAT THE JUGGERNAUT, IT MUST BE *NOW!*

BE ON GUARD, MY DEAR...WE'RE ALMOST *UPON* HIM!

HAS *ANGEL* RECOVERED FROM HIS ENCOUNTER WITH MY STEPBROTHER YET? HIS MUTANT TALENTS ARE VERY IMPORTANT TO MY PLAN!

I DON'T KNOW, SIR! I HAVEN'T SEEN HIM FOR THE PAST FEW MINUTES!

THERE'S JUGGERNAUT *NOW!*

SO, XAVIER! DESPITE EVERYTHING YOU COULD DO TO STOP ME ... DESPITE ALL YOUR PUNY X-MEN.. I HAVE CORNERED YOU AT LAST!

PERHAPS IT IS *I* WHO HAVE CORNERED *YOU*, CAIN!

NEVER USE THAT NAME AGAIN!! I AM THE *JUGGERNAUT!* CAIN MARKO NO LONGER EXISTS...

..AND NEITHER SHALL *YOU*, AFTER I...

WHA..? WHAT ARE YOU *DOING??*

SUSPENDING YOU IN THE AIR... TELEKINETICALLY

EASY, MARVEL GIRL! HE'S TOO STRONG!! DON'T STRAIN YOURSELF!

THE PROFESSOR IS *RIGHT!* HE'S ADVANCING AGAINST ME ... PUSHING MY POWER ASIDE AS THOUGH IT'S A PHYSICAL THING..!

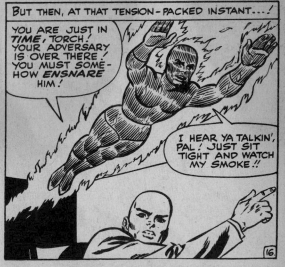

BUT THEN, AT THAT TENSION-PACKED INSTANT...!

YOU ARE JUST IN *TIME,* TORCH! YOUR ADVERSARY IS OVER THERE! YOU MUST SOMEHOW *ENSNARE* HIM!

I HEAR YA TALKIN', PAL! JUST SIT TIGHT AND WATCH MY SMOKE!!

16.

WHOEVER HE IS...MY FLAMES DON'T AFFECT HIM! THERE'S SOME STRANGE SORT OF *ENERGY FIELD* AROUND HIM WHICH THEY CAN'T PENETRATE!

I MIGHT HAVE KNOWN THE *X-MEN* WOULDN'T NEED ANYONE UNLESS THEY WERE UP AGAINST SOMETHING *SPECIAL!*

KEEP ENCIRCLING HIM, TORCH...EVEN THOUGH IT SEEMS IN VAIN! YOUR MISSION IS TO *CONFUSE* HIM...TO KEEP HIM OCCUPIED WHILE MY X-MEN DELIVER THE FINAL BLOW!

A *FINE* THING! I'M DOIN' THE JOB OF A TEN-CENT *PINWHEEL!*

ALTHOUGH HE SITS QUIETLY, HARDLY MOVING A MUSCLE, THE MANY-FACETED BRAIN OF CHARLES XAVIER IS PERFORMING MANY FUNCTIONS AT ONCE... AND ONE OF THOSE FUNCTIONS IS...SUMMONING WARREN WORTHINGTON THE THIRD...THE MUTANT *ANGEL!*

ANGEL! WHEREVER YOU ARE! COME TO ME! THIS IS PROFESSOR X... COME TO ME! WE *NEED* YOU!!

AND, A SHORT DISTANCE DOWN THE HALL, LYING AMONG THE DEBRIS WHERE HE HAD FALLEN, THE TALL, SLIM, WINGED X-MAN IS PRODDED BY THE POWERFUL THOUGHT COMMAND...!

WE *NEED* YOU, ANGEL!! YOU MUST ANSWER MY SUMMONS!! WE NEED YOU...!!

THE PROFESSOR ...CALLING! CAN'T LET HIM DOWN...!

STILL WEAK...WOBBLY IN MY KNEES!! WON'T USE MY WINGS YET...HAVE TO SAVE MY STRENGTH...TO FIGHT *JUGGERNAUT!*

FLAMES.. UP AHEAD! IT LOOKS LIKE ...IT IS... THE *HUMAN TORCH!*

MY FIREBALLS AREN'T *STOPPING* HIM, PROFESSOR! WHAT *ELSE* DO YOU SUGGEST?

YOU MAY DISCONTINUE THEM NOW!

THE *FINAL PHASE* OF MY PLAN IS ABOUT TO BEGIN!

BRACE YOURSELF, ANGEL! WAIT FOR MY NEXT MENTAL COMMAND!

17.

THE *ANGEL* IS STILL WEAK...ON THE VERGE OF EXHAUSTION! I MUST GAIN HIM A FEW MORE SECONDS!

TORCH! LAND IN FRONT OF JUGGERNAUT AND DO EXACTLY AS I TELL YOU! SPLIT-SECOND TIMING WILL BE ALL-IMPORTANT!

I *KNEW* YOU'D HAVE TO LAND SOONER OR LATER! NOW, YOU *TOO* ARE HELP-LESS BEFORE ME!

STAND READY TO BRING YOUR FLAME TO PEAK INTENSITY... LIKE AN EXPLODING FLASH BULB!

NOW, TORCH... *NOW!*

PERFECT! YOU *BLINDED* HIM TEMPORARILY! HE CANNOT FIGHT WHAT HE CANNOT *SEE!* YOU STAGGERED HIM!

THAT SUDDEN BRIGHTNESS!! MY EYES!! EVERYTHING IS SPINNING BEFORE ME!!

IT'S UP TO *YOU* NOW, ANGEL! *TAKE TO THE AIR!!*

I WON'T FAIL YOU, PROFESSOR!!

I *KNOW* YOU WON'T! MY NEXT COMMANDS WILL BE TELEPATHIC... TO CONFOUND JUGGERNAUT!

YOU'RE TOO *LOW,* ANGEL! FLY *HIGHER!* THOUGH HE CANNOT *SEE* YOU, HE CAN HEAR THE BEATING OF YOUR WINGS!

THAT'S *BETTER!* STAY OUT OF REACH OF HIS GROPING ARMS!

BOY! THAT GUY COULD TEACH *ME* THINGS ABOUT FLYING!

YOU SERVE NO PURPOSE, BUT TO INCREASE MY *RAGE!* YOU CANNOT HARM THE *JUGGERNAUT!*

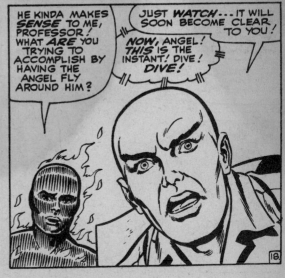

HE KINDA MAKES *SENSE* TO ME, PROFESSOR! WHAT *ARE* YOU TRYING TO ACCOMPLISH BY HAVING THE ANGEL FLY AROUND HIM?

JUST *WATCH*...IT WILL SOON BECOME CLEAR TO YOU!

NOW, ANGEL! *THIS* IS THE INSTANT! DIVE! *DIVE!*

18.

THIS WILL BE YOUR *ONLY* CHANCE! *EVERYTHING* DEPENDS UPON IT!

YOU *DID* IT! HE'S *VULNERABLE* NOW!

MY *HELMET*!!

SECONDS LATER, AFTER THE JUGGERNAUT'S *VISION* HAS RETURNED...

UNDER MY MENTAL COMMANDS, THE *BEAST* LOOSENED YOUR HELMET DURING YOUR BATTLE...

THEN, TO CULMINATE THE PLAN, THE *ANGEL* REMOVED IT COMPLETELY!

WITH OR *WITHOUT* THAT HELMET, *YOU* WON'T ESCAPE ME!

NONSENSE, CAIN! *I* AM THE MASTER HERE AGAIN!

YOURS WAS AN *ACQUIRED* POWER...OBTAINED BY A *FREAK* ACCIDENT OF CHANCE! BUT MY *BRAIN* IS A *PART* OF ME...MY POWER IS MY *OWN*!

AND *THIS* IS BUT THE SMALLEST *PART* OF IT!

NO! YOU CAN'T BEAT ME! YOU *CAN'T*! YOU WERE *ALWAYS* THE WINNER...EVEN WHEN WE WERE YOUNG...I HATED YOU! I SWORE I'D *VANQUISH* YOU SOME DAY! AND I WILL...I *WILL*!

NEVER HAS THERE BEEN SUCH RAW *HATRED*...SUCH AN INSATIABLE DESIRE FOR *VENGEANCE*! THOUGH HIS *BODY* IS DEFEATED, HIS *HATE* IS PROPELLING HIM FORWARD!!

IF *I* MUST TASTE THE BITTER DREGS OF DEFEAT...I'LL DRAG *YOU* DOWN WITH ME!! NO MATTER WHAT HAPPENS TO ME...*YOU* MUST PAY!

ALL YOUR LIFE YOU'VE BEEN RULED BY GREED...ENVY..AVARICE! AND NOW...IT HAS COME TO *THIS*!

19.

IF THINGS HAD BEEN DIFFERENT, WE MIGHT HAVE BEEN FRIENDS... WE MIGHT HAVE TRULY BEEN *BROTHERS!* BUT YOU WOULD HAVE IT NO OTHER WAY! THIS FINAL CHAPTER WAS WRITTEN WHEN WE FIRST MET! THIS IS THE ONLY WAY IT COULD HAVE ENDED!

UHHHHH...!

I DON'T *GET* IT! ALL YOU DID... WAS *LOOK* AT HIM!!

IT IS BEST YOU THINK SO, MY YOUNG FRIEND!

HE WILL RECOVER... AND, WITHOUT HIS HELMET, THE AUTHORITIES WILL BE ABLE TO KEEP HIM IN CONFINEMENT!

AS FOR YOU... YOU WILL RETURN TO *FANTASTIC FOUR* HEAD-QUARTERS NOW... WITH NO MEMORY OF WHAT HAS OCCURRED!

BUT, THE *X-MEN* SHALL REMEMBER... AND SHALL EVER BE GRATEFUL TO YOU, JOHNNY STORM!

THUS, SECONDS LATER, A FAMOUS, FLAMING FIGURE BLAZES ACROSS WESTCHESTER TOWARDS THE HEART OF MANHATTAN...

BOY! TALK ABOUT *DAYDREAMING!* I CAN'T REMEMBER *HOW* I FLEW THIS FAR FROM HOME!

I MUST REALLY BE GETTING *ABSENT-MINDED* IN MY OLD AGE!

WHILE, THE FOLLOWING DAY, THINGS ARE SOMEWHAT MORE PLACID AMONG THE WORLD'S MOST UNUSUAL TEEN-AGERS...

WE'VE NEVER *ALL* BEEN INJURED AT THE SAME TIME BEFORE!

WHO CARES? WITH A NURSE LIKE *JEAN*, IT'S A *PLEASURE!*

MY *MOTHER* USED TO *KISS* ME TO EXPEDITE MY RECOVERY!

I DO NOT HAPPEN TO BE YOUR MOTHER, MR. McCOY!

THAT'S FOR SURE!

REST UP, MY X-MEN, SO THAT YOU WILL RECOVER QUICKLY FROM YOUR INJURIES! YOU HAVE FOUGHT WELL... AND I *HAVE* SOMETHING FOR YOU, AFTER YOU ARE UP AND ABOUT!

20.

HOW *ABOUT* THAT? WE'RE GONNA GET A *REWARD!*

C'MON, PROFESSOR... TELL US WHAT IT *IS!!*

IT'S A *BROOM*... FOR *EACH* OF YOU! THE SCHOOL IS A *SHAMBLES* AFTER YOUR FIGHT... AND *SOMEBODY* HAS TO TIDY IT UP!

NEXT ISSUE... ONE OF THE STRANGEST MENACES OF ALL CONFRONTS THE X-MEN! IT'LL BE A BULLPEN BOMBSHELL... AND YOU DON'T EVEN HAVE TO BE A MUTANT TO ENJOY IT! 'NUFF SAID!

YOU'VE ALL TAKEN TO YOUR EMERGENCY THERAPY VERY WELL!

ANGEL, YOU MAY REMOVE YOUR HARNESS NOW AND PRACTICE NATURAL FLIGHT!

YES, SIR!!

AND YOU MAY BEGIN EXERCISING YOUR FEET AGAIN, BEAST!

EUREKA! NEXT TO THE GETTYSBURG ADDRESS, THAT WAS THE MOST INSPIRING DECLARATION I'VE EVER HEARD!

LEAP FOR THE HIGH BAR, HANK!

WELL DONE! DO YOU FEEL ANY PAINFUL AFTER-EFFECTS?

NOT A ONE, SIR! IF I FELT ANY BETTER, IT WOULD BE VIRTUALLY UNBEARABLE!

DEPRIVING A MUTANT OF HIS POWERS IS LIKE FORBIDDING A POLITICIAN TO KISS BABIES!

NOW THAT I'M TRULY THE BEAST AGAIN, I FEEL THAT I COULD LICK MY WEIGHT IN NEANDERTHALS!

I HOPE, FOR YOUR SAKE, THAT KA-ZAR DOESN'T HEAR YOU!*

YOU MAY DISPENSE WITH YOUR CRUTCHES NOW, HANK!

*HE PROBABLY WON'T, FOR HE WAS LAST SEEN UNDER THE SOUTH POLE IN ISH #10, REMEMBER? --STAN

BOBBY, I THINK YOU'VE BEEN IN THE ICE-INTENSIFIER LONG ENOUGH! YOU SEEM TO HAVE REACHED YOUR FRIGID PEAK BY NOW!

AWW, JUST A FEW MINUTES MORE, PROFESSOR! THIS IS THE COOLEST, IF YOU'LL PARDON THE PUN!

I'M GLAD YOU'RE ENJOYING IT, ICEMAN, BUT IF YOU REMAIN ANY LONGER, YOU'RE APT TO EXPERIENCE AN UNPLEASANT FREEZE FEEDBACK!

AT ANY RATE, I HAVE AN ANNOUNCEMENT THAT WILL MAKE YOU ANXIOUS TO LEAVE!

GREAT! I'VE ALWAYS BEEN A SUCKER FOR SURPRISES!

2

3

MEANWHILE, AT PROFESSOR XAVIER'S SCHOOL FOR GIFTED YOUNGSTERS...

MAKE THEM *TIGHTER*, BOBBY! THE SOFT GAUZE CONSTRUCTION PREVENTS THE BANDS FROM CHAFING!

HOW DO YOU *STAND* IT, WARREN? IT MUST FEEL LIKE WEARING A *GIRDLE!*

THAT MAY BE, LITTLE FRIEND -- BUT IT'S BETTER THAN GIVING AWAY MY IDENTITY TO THE HUMAN RACE!

AWW, IF YOU ASK *ME*, NOBODY WOULD CARE EVEN IF THEY *FOUND OUT* ABOUT US!

NOBODY *ASKED* YOU, SONNY! JUST KEEP TAPING!

SAY, HOW COME YOUR *PARENTS* DON'T KNOW ABOUT YOUR WINGS, WARREY?

THEY DIDN'T *SPROUT* TILL I WAS OFF AT MILITARY SCHOOL!

AND *THERE*, I KEPT THEM HIDDEN UNDER MY UNIFORM --AT FIRST!

THAT'S WHY I *LEFT* SCHOOL-- I COULDN'T AFFORD TO FACE A PHYSICAL EXAM!

AND, IN THE ROOM NEXT DOOR...

IT WOULDN'T BE MUCH OF A *VACATION* IF I HAD TO SPEND IT IN THIS *COSTUME*...

LUCKY THE PROF HAD THIS PAIR OF SPECIAL *SUNGLASSES* MADE FOR ME!

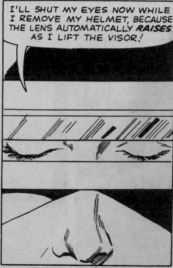

I'LL SHUT MY EYES NOW WHILE I REMOVE MY HELMET, BECAUSE THE LENS AUTOMATICALLY *RAISES* AS I LIFT THE VISOR!

I SHUDDER TO THINK WHAT WOULD HAPPEN IF I EVER ACCIDENTALLY *OPENED* MY EYES WHILE THEY HAD NO PROTECTIVE COVERING! I LIVE IN PERPETUAL *FEAR* OF SUCH A MOMENT!

BUT, THE SCHOLARLY X-MAN KNOWN AS THE *BEAST* HAS A PROBLEM OF A SOMEWHAT *DIFFERENT* NATURE...

BEING A MUTANT CAN BE VERY *VEXING* WHEN IT'S TIME TO DON ONE'S STREET CLOTHES!

ESPECIALLY WHEN ONE POSSESSES A PAIR OF PEDAL EXTREMITIES THE SIZE OF *MINE!*

THERE! DO YOU HAVE ENOUGH BREATHING SPACE, SWEETIES?

THESE SPECIALLY HINGED SHOES ARE SO *EXPENSIVE*, IT WOULD BE CHEAPER TO WALK ON MY *HANDS*-- THOUGH SOMEWHAT LESS *GLAMOROUS!*

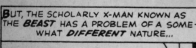

4

MOMENTS LATER, IN THE OUTER HALL...

HERE COMES JEAN! I WONDER IF I DARE ASK HER TO--?

HI, GORGEOUS! HOW ABOUT ME DRIVING YOU TO THE TRAIN?

I SHOULD HAVE REALIZED ANGEL WOULD BEAT ME TO IT!

WHAT ABOUT YOU, SCOTT? AREN'T YOU TAKING THE TRAIN, ALSO?

HOW CAN I COMPETE WITH WARREN?

YES, BUT I'M TAKING A LATER TRAIN!

BESIDES, SCOTTY KNOWS MY CHARIOT IS ONLY A TWO-SEATER!

I PLANNED IT THAT WAY, 'NATCH!

I WANT TO WISH YOU ALL A PLEASANT HOLIDAY! YOU'VE CERTAINLY EARNED IT!

THANK YOU, SIR! BUT, WHAT ABOUT YOU? AREN'T YOU GOING HOME?

YOU HAVE OUR ADDRESSES IF YOU SHOULD NEED US, PROFESSOR!

DON'T BE SILLY, WARREN! ALL HE NEEDS DO IS CONTACT US MENTALLY! IT'S MUCH EASIER THAT WAY!

THIS SCHOOL IS HOME TO ME NOW! I'LL REMAIN HERE!

YES, JEAN, IF YOU HAPPEN TO POSSESS THE WORLD'S MOST POWERFUL MUTANT BRAIN!

WHAT ARE WE FLAPPIN' OUR GUMS FOR? LET'S GET GOIN', GANG!

AND SO...

IT'S BETTER THIS WAY! I'VE NO RIGHT TO TRY TO DATE JEAN--NOT WHILE MY EYES MAKE ME A POTENTIAL DANGER TO ANYONE NEAR ME!

'BYE, ALL!

WARREN WOULD BE A PERFECT LADIES MAN IF HE ONLY HAD A PAIR OF FEET LIKE MINE! HE LOOKS LIKE HE WAS BORN TO OWN THAT MUSTANG!

OL' ANGEL WOULD BE A HIGH-FLYER EVEN WITHOUT WINGS!

THE WAY SCOTT LOOKED AT HER! AM I IMAGINING IT, OR--?

HANK AND I ARE LUCKY WE BOTH COME FROM THE CITY! WE CAN JUST GRAB A BUS AND BE HOME IN A COUPLE OF HOURS!

IF YOU'VE NO DEFINITE PLANS, SCOTTY, WOULD YOU LIKE TO ACCOMPANY US?

--EH--NO THANKS, FELLAS! I'D LIKE TO BE ALONE FOR A WHILE! HAVE A GOOD TIME!

THEN, AFTER ALL THE OTHERS HAVE DEPARTED...

I'LL BE LEAVING NOW ALSO, PROFESSOR! BY THE WAY, THE PAPER BOY JUST DROPPED THIS--

THANK YOU, SCOTT!

HE CARRIES HIS LONELINESS SILENTLY--LOCKED INSIDE HIM! AND NOTHING THAT ANYONE CAN SAY OR DO WILL HELP!

I, OF ALL PEOPLE, KNOW THE PAIN OF SUCH LONELINESS--THE ACHE THAT SEEMS UNENDING!

5

BUT, NO SOONER HAS THE SILENT *CYCLOPS* WALKED AWAY, THAN...

SO! IT HAS FINALLY BEGUN!

THE ONE THING I ALWAYS FEARED-- A WITCH HUNT FOR *MUTANTS!*

★★★★★ FINAL

DAILY GLOBE

★★★★★ FINAL

MUTANT MENACE!

EMINENT ANTHROPOLOGIST SAYS MANKIND FACES GRAVEST DANGER FROM HIDDEN MUTANTS WHO WAIT FOR... MOMEN...

DR. BOLIVAR TRASK, NOTED...

THE FEATURE WRITERS MUST HAVE *LOVED* THIS, CONSIDERING THE WAY THEY PLAYED IT UP!

ARTIST'S INTERPRETATION OF *FATE OF MANKIND* IF MUTANTS ARE NOT DRIVEN OUT-- AS PREDICTED BY DR. BOLIVAR TRASK!

"DR. TRASK WARNS THAT THE SUPERIOR ABILITIES AND SUPERNATURAL POWERS OF THE HIDDEN MUTANTS WILL ENABLE THEM TO ENSLAVE THE HUMAN RACE, REPLACING OUR CIVILIZATION WITH THEIR OWN!"

"ACCORDING TO THE ANTHROPOLOGIST'S STARTLING PREDICTION, IT IS EVEN POSSIBLE THAT THE SUPERIOR MUTANTS WILL CONSIDER NORMAL MEN AS LITTLE MORE THAN SAVAGES, SUITABLE ONLY FOR FORCED LABOR AND GLADIATORIAL SPORT!"

I CANNOT LET THIS GO UNCHALLENGED! IT COULD CAUSE PANIC THRUOUT THE WORLD!

EVEN NOW IT MAY BE TOO LATE TO STOP THE WHEELS OF PERSECUTION THAT HAVE BEEN SET IN MOTION-- BUT I MUST MAKE THE ATTEMPT!

THE STRANGE THEORIES OF DR. TRASK ARE A GREATER THREAT TO MY X-MEN THAN ANY FOE THEY HAVE EVER FACED BEFORE!

HELLO, NATIONAL TELEVISION NETWORK? THIS IS CHARLES XAVIER! CONNECT ME WITH YOUR PROGRAMMING DIRECTOR-- *IMMEDIATELY!*

SECONDS LATER... YES, THAT'S RIGHT! I WANT TO ENGAGE IN A PUBLIC *TELEVISED* *DEBATE* WITH DR. TRASK AS SOON AS POSSIBLE! I CLAIM HIS THEORIES ARE BOTH ERRONEOUS AND POTENTIALLY *DANGEROUS!*

WE'LL ARRANGE IT IMMEDIATELY, SIR! IT WILL BE A *PRIVILEGE* TO PRESENT A SCIENTIST OF YOUR STATURE ON OUR NETWORK!

6

TRASK WAS AN ANTHROPOLOGIST--NOT A ROBOTIC EXPERT! HIS KNOWLEDGE OF CYBERNETIC BRAINS WAS INADEQUATE! HIS *SENTINELS* ARE OUT OF CONTROL!

STAND BY FOR FURTHER ORDERS!

LADIES AND GENTLEMEN--WE INTERRUPT THIS PROGRAM...

I CANNOT STOP THE SENTINELS-- BUT I KNOW WHO *CAN!*

X-MEN! X-MEN! PROFESSOR X CALLING! *CONDITION RED! CONDITION RED!* COME AT ONCE! FOLLOW THOUGHT IMPULSES! COME AT ONCE! COME AT ONCE!

AND, MILES AWAY, IN THE *COFFEE A-GO-GO*, IN NEW YORK'S GREENWICH VILLAGE, WE FIND THE *BEAST* AND *ICEMAN* MAKING THE MOST OF THEIR FREE TIME...

I HAVEN'T SEEN YOU TWO BIG SPENDERS IN *MONTHS!* WHERE'VE YOU *BEEN,* BOYS?

BEATING THE GIRLS AWAY WITH CLUBS, AS USUAL, ZELDA! DIDJA *MISS* US?

QUIET, BOBBY! BERNARD, THE POET, HAS ME WORRIED! I'M BEGINNING TO *UNDERSTAND* WHAT HE'S SAYING!

LIKE IT'S *OUT* TO BE IN, AND IT'S *SQUARE* TO BE HIP, I MEAN DIG THE SCENE, A NAP ISN'T A NIP!

SAY IT *AGAIN,* BERNARD! THOSE TENDER SENTIMENTS DO WONDERS FOR MY LIBIDO!

COOL IT, CHICK! YOU'RE MELTIN' MY BONGOS!

SO, ALL YOU WANT IS *COFFEE?* WILL YOU *SHARE* A CUP, OR TAKE THE PLUNGE AND BUY *TWO* OF THEM?

ZELDA, AFTER YOU FINISH WORK TONIGHT, HOW ABOUT GOING *OUT* WITH ME?

I'LL THINK ABOUT IT, DIAMOND JIM-- SO LONG AS YOU DON'T DECIDE TO TAKE ME *HERE!*

HEADS UP, BOBBY! I'M GETTING A MENTAL SUMMONS FROM THE *PROFESSOR!*

HOLY COW! ME TOO! IT MUST BE *TOP PRIORITY!*

SORRY, ZELDA! I'LL HAVE TO TAKE A *RAIN CHECK* ON OUR DATE TONIGHT!

RAIN CHECK?!! I WOULDN'T GO OUT WITH *YOU* AGAIN IF IT WAS A TROPICAL *MONSOON!*

THINK SHE'S *MAD* AT ME, HANK?

I'D SAY IT'S DEFINITELY WITHIN THE REALM OF POSSIBILITY! NOW, LET'S *GO!*

9

11

YOU'RE *RIGHT*, BEAST! ATTACK *AT ONCE*-- WITH ALL DELIBERATE CAUTION!

THOK!

3-R

OOF! IF THERE'S A WAY TO *INCAPACITATE* THAT CHARACTER, A FRONTAL ASSAULT ISN'T *IT*!

CAREFUL, BEAST! HE POSSESSES CONCEALED RAY WEAPONS!

WHEW! MUCH OBLIGED, *PROFESSOR*! HE JUST EMPHASIZED YOUR PRONOUNCEMENT WITH ELECTRIFYING CLARITY!

ZZZITT!

BUT THEN...

HANG ON, PARTNER! JUST WATCH ME PUT THE *SKIDS* TO THAT BIG *CREEP*!

HAVE AN "*ICE*" TRIP, CHUM!

ICEMAN, YOUR *PROWESS* IS FORMIDABLE, BUT YOUR *PUNS* ARE FROM HUNGER!

ON *MY* ALLOWANCE, WHAT D'YA *EXPECT*-- BOB HOPE?

WE CAME AS SOON AS WE COULD, SIR! ARE YOU ALL RIGHT? WHAT *IS* THAT BIG HUNK'A BLUBBER?

HE, AND OTHERS LIKE HIM, ARE CALLED *SENTINELS*! THEIR PURPOSE IS TO *DESTROY MUTANTS*!

CAN'T EXPLAIN ANY MORE-- MUSTN'T LOSE TRANQUILIZATION- CONTROL OVER THE OTHERS IN THIS STUDIO!

THEN, SUDDENLY...

ICEMAN! LOOK OUT! A HEAT RAY IS-- *TOO LATE!* IT *CAUGHT* HIM!

ZAP!

UNNHH!

12

WHILE, AT THAT MOMENT, JUST A FEW BLOCKS AWAY...

FASTER, DRIVER! IT'S AN EMERGENCY!

I KNOW, I KNOW! YA AWREADY *TOLD* ME A DOZEN TIMES! BUT NEXT TIME DO ME A FAVOR AND TAKE A *JET*, HUH?

THEN, TAKING A CORNER ON TWO WHEELS, THE TAXI SUDDENLY SWERVES SHARPLY, AND...

I DROPPED MY PROTECTIVE *GLASSES!* I'VE ALWAYS *FEARED* THIS MIGHT HAPPEN!

HOLY COW! *NOW* WHAT'S GOIN' ON?

ZIT!

DON'T WORRY--IT'LL BE ALL RIGHT--AS SOON AS I PUT MY *GLASSES* BACK ON--!

ANYONE WHO NEEDS *SPECS* TO STOP HIS EYES FROM BLASTIN'--HEY! I SHOULDA *GUESSED!*

STOP 'IM, SOMEBODY! HE'S ONE O' THOSE *MUTIES* TRASK'S BEEN WARNIN' US ABOUT!

I DIDN'T COUNT ON *THIS!* HAVE TO ESCAPE--*FAST!*

WHO *IS* HE? *WHAT* IS HE? WHAT DID HE *DO?*

WHAT'S THE *DIFFERENCE?* HE'S A *MUTANT!* GET 'IM!

DON'T LET THE *MUTIE* GET *AWAY!*

AN UNREASONING *MOB!* THE ONE THING I CAN'T FIGHT!

POP

HE TRIED TO KILL THAT CAB DRIVER BY JUST *LOOKING* AT HIM! HE'S GOT DEATH-DEALING *EYES!*

LUCKILY, THEY FELL BACK AT THE MENTION OF MY "DEATH-DEALING EYES"! NOBODY WANTED TO GET TOO *CLOSE* AFTER HEARING THAT!

THE PROFESSOR'S THOUGHT IMPULSES ARE STRONGER THAN EVER! THEY'RE LEADING ME INTO THIS TV NETWORK BUILDING!

ONCE I ROUND THAT CORNER AHEAD, I'LL BE IN THE CLEAR!

MADE IT! NOW TO PREPARE FOR *ACTION!*

I HEAR THE SOUND OF A *FIGHT* JUST AHEAD! BUT, WHAT DANGER CAN THERE BE IN A PLACE LIKE *THIS??*

13

IT'S HANK! HE REACHED HERE AHEAD OF ME! BUT, WHO--?

BEAST! WHAT'S WRONG? WHAT HAPPENED?

BUT, STAY BACK! DON'T RUN IN YET!

CYKE! YOU COULDN'T HAVE ARRIVED AT A MORE PROPITIOUS MOMENT!

HEY! I SEE WHAT YOU MEAN, BIG FELLA!

FOOOM!

AND THAT'S ONE OF HIS GENTLER BLOWS!

BRACE YOURSELF, BEAST! OPERATION DUO-SMASH! YOUR BATTERING-RAM ATTACK AND MY RAY BLAST! LET'S GO!

FAR BE IT FROM ME TO DISSENT WITH OUR ACTING DEPUTY LEADER, CYKE, BUT THIS LUMBERING LEVIATHAN ISN'T AS SLOW MOVING AS HE LOOKS!

HE'S OBVIOUSLY JUST A ROBOT! SURELY THE TWO OF US CAN OUT-MANEUVER HIM!

THOSE WERE MY SENTIMENTS, EXACTLY-- UNTIL I SAW THE LIGHT! BUT, YOU MIGHT AS WELL LEARN FIRST-HAND! HERE GOES!

THWOKK!

HANK WAS RIGHT! HE EASILY SIDE-STEPPED THE BEAST'S ATTACK...

...AND HE SHIFTED HIS STANCE AT THE SAME INSTANT, CAUSING MY RAY TO MISS HIM!

HE MAY NOT BE A LIVING HUMAN -- BUT WHATEVER HE USES FOR A BRAIN-- IT'S AS FAST AS OURS-- OR, MAYBE FASTER!

KRA...

14

HANK CRASHED INTO THE WALL WITH SUCH FORCE THAT HE KNOCKED HIMSELF OUT! I CAN'T LET HIM LIE THERE IN THE PATH OF THAT GIANT!

OH! THE PROFESSOR IS CONTACTING ME!

CYCLOPS! THE SENTINEL HAS POWERFUL BUILT-IN WEAPONS! DO NOT TURN YOUR BACK TO HIM!

WHAT CAN I DO NOW? I CAN'T DESERT HANK-- BUT MY POWER BLAST NEEDS ANOTHER FEW MINUTES BEFORE I CAN USE IT AGAIN!

BUT THEN, SUDDENLY, THE MOST UNEXPECTED EVENT OF ALL OCCURS! FOR NO APPARENT REASON, THE TOWERING SENTINEL STOPS, FALTERS, AND...

HE'S BEGINNING TO TOPPLE! BUT WHY? WHAT CAUSED IT...? NOTHING EVEN TOUCHED HIM!

KHOOOM!

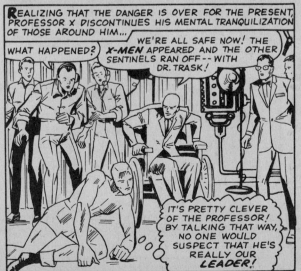

REALIZING THAT THE DANGER IS OVER FOR THE PRESENT, PROFESSOR X DISCONTINUES HIS MENTAL TRANQUILIZATION OF THOSE AROUND HIM...

WHAT HAPPENED?

WE'RE ALL SAFE NOW! THE X-MEN APPEARED AND THE OTHER SENTINELS RAN OFF-- WITH DR. TRASK!

IT'S PRETTY CLEVER OF THE PROFESSOR! BY TALKING THAT WAY, NO ONE WOULD SUSPECT THAT HE'S REALLY OUR LEADER!

AND, WHILE HE SEEMS TO BE SITTING MOTIONLESS, THE BRILLIANT MENTAL MUTANT SHOOTS TELEPATHIC COMMANDS TO HIS TEEN-AGE TEAM...

REVIVE THE BEAST! MAKE CERTAIN HE IS UNINJURED!

CLEAR THE STUDIO, SO THAT WE CAN BE ALONE!

I MUST STUDY THE SENTINEL-- AND LEARN WHAT FELLED HIM!

15

IN THE MEANTIME, THE HIGH FLYING *ANGEL*, ZEROING IN TOWARDS THE TV STUDIO, SEES A STARTLING SIGHT...

WELL, WIGGLE MY WINGS! I'VE HEARD OF FLYING *SAUCERS*, BUT *THOSE* THINGS ARE *RIDICULOUS!*

BUT, THE ANGEL DOES NOT YET KNOW OF THE SENTINELS' *PURPOSE*, NOR OF THEIR BUILT-IN DIVINING DEVICES...

HALT YOUR FLIGHT! MY COMPUTO-METER REGISTERS *MUTANT* AHEAD!

ATTACK IN FORCE!

UH OH! THIS TELLS ME *ONE* THING I WAS WONDERING ABOUT--!

ZITT!

ZITT!

ZITT!

ZITT!

ZITT!

THEY SURE *AREN'T* MERELY FIGMENTS OF MY IMAGINATION!

IT'S LIKE BEING ATTACKED BY A SQUADRON OF *HUMAN TORCHES!*

SENTINELS 6, 7, AND 8-R! ASSUME SOLO ATTACK POSTURE! *ATTACK!*

ALL OTHERS REMAIN IN FORMATION! PROCEED TO DESTINATION! THAT IS ALL!

WHO *ARE* THEY?? WHY ARE THEY *ATTACKING* ME? IS *THIS* WHY THE PROF SUMMONED ME?

WELL, I CAN WORRY ABOUT ALL THAT *LATER!* RIGHT *NOW*, I'M KINDA BUSY!

IT'S LUCKY THE PROF MADE ME SPEND SO MANY LONG HOURS PRACTICING *MANEUVERABILITY!*

16

BUT THEN, BEFORE THE MERCILESS, EMOTIONLESS *SENTINELS* CAN FIND THE RANGE...

NOW WHAT--?

SOMETHING IS PULLING ME *DOWNWARD*--- TOWARDS THAT TRAIN BELOW!

IT'S A POWERFUL PULL OF SOME SORT OF INVISIBLE ENERGY! I CAN'T OVERCOME IT!

IT'S *HOLDING* ME HERE! CAN'T MOVE! BUT, IT'S SERVED *ONE* GOOD PURPOSE--THOSE FLYING NIGHTMARES ARE GIVING UP THE CHASE!

SECTION LEADER TO SENTINELS! RESUME FLIGHT PATTERN! TIME ENOUGH TO PURSUE MUTANTS AFTER WE HAVE INCREASED OUR NUMBERS!

AND, IN A PRIVATE DRAWING ROOM, INSIDE THE RAPIDLY DEPARTING TRAIN, WE FIND--

IT'S LUCKY I HAPPENED TO LOOK OUT OF THE WINDOW AT THAT MOMENT!

NO TELLING *WHAT* THOSE STRANGE FLYING CREATURES WOULD HAVE DONE TO WARREN ONCE THEY SURROUNDED HIM!

I'D BETTER CHANGE INTO MY *MARVEL GIRL* COSTUME NOW! NO TELLING *WHAT* MIGHT HAPPEN NEXT!

THEN, IN ONE OF THE MOST SENSATIONAL DEMONSTRATIONS OF TELEKINETIC PROWESS EVER RECORDED, THE FABULOUS FEMALE MUTANT LEVITATES HERSELF RIGHT OUT OF THE TRAIN WINDOW...

I'VE BEEN PRACTICING THIS FEAT FOR MONTHS! I CAN ONLY DO IT FOR SHORT DISTANCES BUT I'M IMPROVING EACH TIME!

JEAN! THEN IT WAS *YOU*--! I SHOULD HAVE *GUESSED!*

I DON'T KNOW WHO THOSE FLYING APPARITIONS *WERE*, BUT *THEY* MUST BE WHY THE PROFESSOR CALLED US!

RIGHT, PRETTY GIRL! WE'D BETTER *GET* TO HIM AS SOON AS POSSIBLE!

17

AND, BACK AT THE TV STUDIO,...

NOW THAT WE'RE *ALONE* IN HERE, WE MAY TALK FREELY! IT IS *IMPERATIVE* THAT WE LEARN WHAT IT WAS THAT *FELLED* THE SENTINEL!

WHATEVER IT WAS, I'D SURE LIKE TO *HAVE* A COUPLE OF 'EM!

BEFORE IT TOPPLED, I HEARD IT MUTTER SOMETHING THAT SOUNDED LIKE *"MASTER MOLD"!*

MY VOCABULARY IS EXCEEDED ONLY BY MY *AGILITY* AND *CHARM*-- BUT I'M AT A LOSS TO COMPREHEND WHAT *MASTER MOLD* MAY BE!

PROFESSOR-- CAN YOU TELL WHETHER IT'S COMPLETELY DESTROYED--OUR EQUIVALENT OF *DEAD*--OR COULD IT RISE TO MENACE US AGAIN?

I CAN'T BE SURE OF ITS CONDITION! I SEEM TO GET FAINT MENTAL IMAGES FROM IT-- BUT, BEING MECHANICAL *RATHER* THAN *ALIVE*, THEY'RE INDECIPHERABLE TO ME!

WAIT! BE ABSOLUTELY SILENT! CLEAR YOUR MINDS OF ANY THOUGHT!

I'M RECEIVING A VAGUE MENTAL IMPULSE--I CAN JUST BARELY MAKE IT OUT! IT'S SOME SORT OF *LOCATION* --WAIT-- IT'S GETTING CLEARER--!

IT'S THE PLACE WHERE THE SENTINELS WERE *CREATED!* HE WANTS TO RETURN THERE! THE THOUGHT IS SO *STRONG* THAT I CAN READ IT, EVEN THOUGH IT DOESN'T EMANATE FROM A *HUMAN* BRAIN!

IF I UNDERSTAND YOU CORRECTLY, SIR, YOU MEAN YOU'VE DISCOVERED WHERE THEIR HEADQUARTERS IS?

EXACTLY!

HERE COMES THE *ANGEL*-- AND *JEAN!* NOW WE'RE AT OUR FULL FIGHTING STRENGTH AGAIN!

GOOD! I'M AFRAID WE WILL *HAVE* TO BE--FOR THE DANGER THAT AWAITS US!

SECONDS LATER, AFTER ALL THE EXPLANATIONS HAVE BEEN MADE...

THEY WERE HEADING *WEST* WHEN I LAST SAW THEM! PERHAPS IF I FLY AHEAD, I CAN STILL FIND SOME TRACE OF WHERE THEY WENT....!

IT WON'T BE NECESSARY, WARREN! I *KNOW* WHERE THEY'VE GONE! WE CAN BE THERE WITHIN THE HOUR!

GOOD! I'M CONTEMPLATING A RETURN ENGAGEMENT WITH GREAT ANTICIPATION!

BUT, DON'T EXPECT IT TO BE AN *EASY* BATTLE! THERE IS *MORE* TO THE MENACE OF THE *SENTINELS* THAN MEETS THE EYE!

IT IS POSSIBLE THAT THEY REPRESENT THE GREATEST THREAT WE HAVE EVER FACED...

AND, THE KEY TO IT ALL MAY LIE BEHIND THE WORDS,... *MASTER MOLD!*

18

19

ANGEL!! THAT CHASM-- BEHIND THE PROFESSOR!! HURRY--!!

HOLD ON, SIR! I WON'T LET YOU FALL!!

I TOLD YOU-- DO NOT LET ME HAMPER YOUR BATTLE STRATEGY! I'M NOT AS HELPLESS AS YOU MAY THINK!

BUT, SIR...

NO BUTS! YOU'RE ALL IN THE GRAVEST OF DANGER! PROTECT YOURSELVES!

I WONDER HOW THE PROFESSOR WOULD HAVE SAVED HIMSELF IF-- UH OH!

NO TIME TO WORRY ABOUT THAT NOW! IF ANY OF THESE CAREENING BOULDERS DENT MY NOBLE CRANIUM, IT'LL BE BYE-BYE BEAST!

IF THOSE SENTINELS ARE POWERFUL ENOUGH TO MAKE NATURE GO WILD THIS WAY, THEN THE PROFESSOR WAS RIGHT ABOUT THE IMPENDING DANGER!

WHOOSH!

HOLY SMOKE! THE GROUND IS OPENING UP RIGHT UNDER MY FEET!

FOR ONCE I ENVY THE ANGEL!! AT LEAST HE CAN FLY!

KRRRAKK!

BUT, THERE'S ONE THING I CAN DO--!

BEING ABLE TO BUILD MY OWN ICE BRIDGE COMES IN PRETTY HANDY SOMETIMES!

ICEMAN!! ALL OF YOU! MOVE!!

2

HEAD FOR **HIGH GROUND!** YOU'RE IN **JEOPARDY** EVERY SECOND YOU REMAIN WHERE YOU ARE!

HIS BRAIN NEVER STOPS! SOMEHOW, I'LL BET HE **COULD** HAVE SAVED HIMSELF!

HANK! YOU HEARD THE **PROF! KEEP MOVING!**

TUT TUT, DEPUTY LEADER! HAVE YOU NO REGARD FOR **CHIVALRY?** I MERELY PAUSED TO OFFER ASSISTANCE TO YON DAMSEL IN DISTRESS!

I'M **HARDLY** A DAMSEL IN DISTRESS, MR. McCOY! IF YOU'LL KINDLY STEP ASIDE...

--I SHALL **LEVITATE** MYSELF OUT OF DANGER, TELEKINETICALLY! OR, HAVE YOU **FORGOTTEN** WHY I'M CALLED **MARVEL GIRL?**

AHH, HOW I LONG FOR THE **OLDEN** DAYS WHEN MAIDENS FAINTED AT THE DROP OF A HAT!

IF YOU DON'T START **CLIMBING,** HANK, YOU'RE LIABLE NOT TO BE AROUND FOR ANY **NEWER** DAYS!

HOW ABOUT THIS **ICE LADDER** OF MINE, CYKE? BOY, WOULDN'T WE MAKE DANDY... **FIREMEN!!**

CLAM UP! KEEP CLIMBING! SAVE YOUR ENERGY!

NAHH! OL' PARTY POOP!

MINUTES LATER...

WE SEEM TO HAVE CLIMBED OUT OF EFFECTIVE RANGE OF THEIR **NATURE ACTIVATOR RAYS!**

BUT, WE'VE GOT TO INVADE THAT FORTRESS BEFORE THEY CAN LAUNCH A **NEW** ATTACK AGAINST US!

AND, MOST IMPORTANT OF ALL, WE **MUST** LEARN WHAT WAS MEANT BY THE WORDS "**MASTER MOLD**"!

THEY'RE **STILL** FIRING! IF WE HADN'T CLIMBED TO SAFETY, WE'D BE **FINISHED!**

BUH-TANNG! BUH-TANNG!

WHOOM!

3

HOW DO WE GET *IN* THERE, SIR? IT LOOKS *IMPOSSIBLE!*

I'VE SPENT *YEARS* DRUMMING INTO YOU-- *NOTHING* IS IMPOSSIBLE!!

IF I COULD ONLY LEARN *WHY* THAT SENTINEL TOPPLED OVER IN THE TV STUDIO!!*

WHAT GOOD WOULD *THAT* DO?

IT PROVES THEY HAVE A *WEAK SPOT!* AND OUR *LIVES* MAY DEPEND ON *FINDING* IT!

*REMEMBER WHEN IT HAPPENED LAST ISH?? --STAN.

YOUR *FIRST* TASK IS TO GET ACROSS THE CHASM! *ICEMAN*-- PLAN "G"!

YES, *SIR!* I'LL HAVE THE GLIDER BUILT IN NO TIME!

GOOD WORK, BOBBY! NOW *I'LL* SUPPLY THE MOTIVE POWER!

HOLD TIGHT, FELLAS! I'LL HAVE TO APPLY NEARLY *MAXIMUM* POWER!!

SHOOT THE WORKS, CYKE! WE'RE BIG BOYS NOW!

THIS DOESN'T SEEM VERY *DIGNIFIED*, BUT I SUPPOSE IT'S NECESSARY!

ARE YOU SURE YOU CAN *DO* IT, SCOTT?

IT *HAS* TO BE DONE!! SO, I'LL *DO* IT!

REMEMBER, SCOTT-- IT MUST BE PERFECT THE *FIRST* TIME!

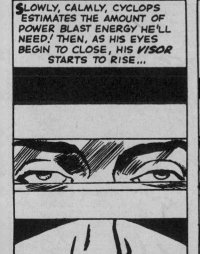

SLOWLY, CALMLY, CYCLOPS ESTIMATES THE AMOUNT OF POWER BLAST ENERGY HE'LL NEED! THEN, AS HIS EYES BEGIN TO CLOSE, HIS *VISOR* STARTS TO RISE...

HIGHER AND HIGHER GOES THE VISOR, UNTIL IT IS COMPLETELY *OPEN!* BUT, STILL THE MOST DANGEROUS EYES IN ALL THE WORLD REMAIN TIGHTLY SHUT, AS THE YOUTHFUL MUTANT STANDS PERFECTLY MOTIONLESS--!

AND THEN, WITH THE FORCE OF A *LIGHTNING BOLT,* HIS EYELIDS SNAP OPEN, AS A FRANTIC CRY ESCAPES HIS LIPS--!

NOW!

4

A *PERFECT LAUNCH*, SCOTT!! NOW, QUICKLY, ANGEL-- FLY *AFTER* THEM, IN CASE THEY NEED HELP!

ZZIP!

NO MATTER *WHO* IS ATTACKING US FROM THAT *FORTRESS*, HERE'S WHERE THEY LEARN THAT NOBODY PUSHES THE *X-MEN* AROUND!

BOBBY! THE ICE-SKIMMER IS WOBBLING *DANGEROUSLY!* YOUR DESIGN ISN'T AERODYNAMICALLY *ACCURATE!*

WADDAYA *WANT* FOR A TEN-SECOND JOB--A B-52??

THEY'RE GONNA *FALL*!! *HOLD ON!* I'LL BE RIGHT THERE!!

THE SOONER THE *BETTER*, SON!

BUT, BEFORE THE WINGED WONDER CAN SEIZE HIS FALLING FRIENDS...

OOOOFF!

WHISST! WHISST!

MECHANICAL *TENTACLES*!!! THEY JUST BARELY *MISSED* ME!

LOOK OUT, ANGEL!! SOME-THING'S *CAUGHT* US! DON'T LET IT GRAB *YOU*--!!

5

6

OH, *NO!* NOW THEY'RE FILLING THIS THING ÷KOFF÷ WITH SOME KINDA *GAS*--!!

GETTING GROGGY ÷KOFF KOFF!÷ MUST BE -- SOME TYPE OF -- ÷KOFF÷ QUICK-ACTING *SLEEPING VAPOR*--!

WELL-- IT SURE ISN'T--CHICKEN SOUP--÷UHHH÷...

IT IS *DONE!* THEY ARE *ASLEEP!*

IT WAS A SIMPLE MATTER TO DEFEAT THE INVADING HUMANS!

SO SHALL WE DEFEAT ANY AND *ALL* HUMANS WHO DARE TO DEFY THE *SENTINELS!*

THIS IS *MADNESS!* YOU CANNOT TAKE OVER THE MACHINES WHICH *I* HAVE CREATED!! YOU DON'T KNOW WHAT YOU'RE *DOING*--!

WE KNOW FAR MORE THAN YOU SUSPECT, DR. TRASK! DID NOT YOU YOURSELF *CREATE* US?

NO! I CREATED THE *MASTER MOLD!* ONLY *HE* CAN CREATE ADDITIONAL SENTINELS!

BUT, YOU WERE MADE FOR ONLY *ONE* PURPOSE -- TO GUARD THE HUMAN RACE FROM *MUTANTS!* THAT IS YOUR *ONLY DUTY!*

WE CAN ONLY GUARD THE HUMAN RACE BY BECOMING ITS *MASTER!* HUMANS ARE TOO WEAK, TOO FOOLISH TO GOVERN THEMSELVES! HENCEFORTH, *WE* SHALL *RULE!!*

NO! YOU CANNOT ENSLAVE ALL OF *MANKIND!!*

WE HAVE THE POWER TO DO WHATEVER WE WISH! *NOTHING* CAN STOP US! NOW COME--!

WE SHALL TAKE YOU TO THE *MASTER MOLD!* YOU SHALL HELP HIM CREATE *MORE* SENTINELS! ENOUGH TO OVERRUN ALL OF THE *UNIVERSE!!*

WHAT HAVE I DONE??? WHAT UNTHINKABLE *MENACE* HAVE I UNLEASHED???

7

SECONDS LATER, HE WHO HAD BEEN THE MASTER, IS BROUGHT BEFORE THE ONE WHO HAS MADE HIM A HELPLESS SLAVE--!

BOLIVAR TRASK! I HAVE SUMMONED YOU TO SERVE ME! THOUGH YOU HAVE GIVEN ME THE POWER, I DO NOT POSSESS THE KNOWLEDGE TO CREATE OTHER SENTINELS! YOU SHALL DO IT FOR ME!

NO! NEVER! I CANNOT BETRAY THE ENTIRE HUMAN RACE! I'D RATHER DIE!

YOUR WISH SHALL BE INSTANTLY GRANTED, IF THE MASTER MOLD SO COMMANDS!

REMEMBER THE WEAPONS YOU HAVE GIVEN ME! I CAN DESTROY HALF YOUR NATION! REFUSE TO SERVE ME, AND YOU'LL BE RESPONSIBLE FOR THE CARNAGE THAT RESULTS!

YOU MEAN-- YOU'D ATTACK MANKIND??!

MY SENTINELS AND I ARE NOT HUMAN! WE HAVE NO FEELINGS -- NO EMOTIONS! WE ARE CAPABLE OF ANYTHING!!

BUT-- THE X-MEN WILL FIGHT YOU! THEY'LL FIND SOME WAY TO DESTROY YOU ALL!

FOOL! DID YOU NOT CREATE US TO DESTROY THE X-MEN?!! WE ARE TOO POWERFUL! THEY WILL BE HELPLESS BEFORE US!

WE HAVE ALREADY CAPTURED TWO OF THEM! I SHALL STUDY THEM-- BEFORE I ORDER THEM DESTROYED!

8

MEANWHILE, OUTSIDE THE FANTASTIC FORTRESS AGAIN...

ICEMAN AND THE BEAST WERE *CAPTURED!!* I WAS TOO LATE TO SAVE THEM!

WE KNOW! WE WITNESSED THE ENTIRE TABLEAU!

YOU DID YOUR *BEST*, ANGEL! UNFORTUNATELY, YOU'RE NOT MADE OF *ASBESTOS!*

BUT, WHAT DO WE DO *HOW?* HOW DO WE *SAVE* THEM? HOW DO WE GET INTO THE FORTRESS?

GOOD QUESTION, JEAN! THEY SEEM TO HAVE ENOUGH BUILT-IN WEAPONS TO STOP AN *ARMY!*

AN ARMY, PERHAPS! BUT, WE ARE THE *X-MEN!* NO MILITARY FORCE ON EARTH CAN EQUAL OUR UNIQUE POWERS!

THOUGH I CANNOT *CONTROL* THE MECHANICAL BRAIN OF A SENTINEL -- I CAN STILL *STRIKE* IT WITH A BOLT OF PURE MENTAL ENERGY!

SOMEWHERE BEHIND THOSE WALLS, *SENTINELS* ARE OPERATING THE WEAPONS THAT GUARD THAT FORTRESS!

IF I *BLANK OUT* THEIR MINDS, I *NULLIFY* THEIR WEAPONS!

GREAT, PROFESSOR! IF YOU CAN DOUSE THOSE *RAYS*, WE CAN STRIKE BEFORE THEY KNOW IT!

EXACTLY! THE TIME HAS COME FOR ME TO BE AN ACTIVE *PARTICIPANT* IN OUR BATTLE! FIRST, I SHALL MENTALLY TRACE THE RAYS TO THEIR ORIGINAL SOURCE --!

WE'LL STAND *READY*, SIR! ONCE THOSE RAYS GO OUT, WE *MOVE!!*

SILENCE!! DO NOT MAKE A *SOUND!!* DO NOT MOVE A MUSCLE!!

I'VE TAPPED THE RAYS! I'M FOLLOWING THEM -- FOLLOWING -- *NOW!!*

AT THAT INSTANT, IN THE MASTER WEAPONRY CONTROL ROOM OF THE SENTINELS' FORTRESS...

OHHHH...

AHHHH...

UNNNHHH...

WHAT HAS BEFALLEN OUR GUNNERY SPECIALISTS??

THIS IS PASSING STRANGE! THEY HAVE BEEN AFFECTED BY SOME UNKNOWN, OUTSIDE SOURCE!!

OUR REPEL-GUNS AND RAYS MUST BE ATTENDED! THESE STRICKEN ONES MUST BE REPLACED!

YOUR WORDS HAVE MUCH SUBSTANCE! BUT, IT CANNOT BE DONE WITHOUT THE SECTION LEADER'S APPROVAL! THERE WILL BE A DELAY, FOR WE DARE NOT VIOLATE OUR PROGRAMMED INSTRUCTIONS!

THEN THE SECTION LEADER MUST BE CONTACTED AT ONCE!

BUT, EVEN AS THE SENTINEL SPEAKS, HIS SECTION LEADER IS ATTENDING TO OTHER MATTERS...

FOLLOW ME! THE PRISONER HAS BEEN SUMMONED BY THE MASTER MOLD!

10

THUS, MOMENTS LATER...

PLACE THE SUBJECT UNDER THE MENTAL **PSYCHO-PROBE**!

DISOBEY ME, AND I GIVE THE ORDER TO ATTACK THE NEAREST CITY OF HUMANS!

NO, YOU **MUSTN'T**!! I--I'LL OBEY! I'LL **DO** IT!

THE PSYCHO-PROBE WILL MAKE THIS X-MAN REVEAL HIS EVERY INNERMOST SECRET! A SMALL ENOUGH PRICE TO PAY FOR SPARING AN ENTIRE CITY!

CLICK!

AND THEN AND THERE, UNDER THE IRRESISTIBLE INFLUENCE OF THE STRANGE PSYCHO-BEAM, THE CAPTIVE **BEAST** BEGINS TO SPEAK -- IN SLOW, EMOTIONLESS TONES...

I AM--THE **BEAST**! I SERVE -- THE **X-MEN**! OUR MISSION--PROTECT MANKIND--FROM EVIL MUTANTS--AND ANY OR ALL DANGERS--THAT MAY BEFALL--!

THEIR MISSION-- **PROTECT** MANKIND!! HOW **WRONG** I WAS ABOUT THEM! WHAT DREAD **HARM** I'VE DONE--!!

BUT, EVEN AS THE BEAST RAMBLES ON-- IF ONLY THE **PROFESSOR** COULD BE WITH US!!

I **AM** WITH YOU--FOLLOWING EVERY MOVE **MENTALLY**! **ALL** OUR POWERS WILL BE NEEDED FOR THIS ASSAULT!

LEVEL OFF, WARREN! SOON AS YOU'RE IN POSITION, I'LL USE MY OPTIC-BLAST POWER AGAINST THE FORTRESS!

LET'S HOPE IT **WORKS**, CYKE! IF NOT, THE PROF BETTER START RECRUITING A NEW TEAM, PRONTO!

11

12

YOU MADE THE RIGHT DECISION, SCOTT! BUT, ALWAYS REMEMBER, WITH THE *PRIDE OF LEADER-SHIP* GOES THE WEIGHT OF RESPONSIBILITY! YOU MUST BE ABLE TO BEAR THEM *BOTH!*

I'LL DO MY BEST, SIR-- BUT IT'S SURE GOOD TO KNOW YOU'RE *MENTALLY MONITORING* OUR PROGRESS!

WE'RE REACHING THE *END* OF THE PASSAGEWAY...!

MEANWHILE, UNDER THE PSYCHO-PROBE, THE BEAST CONTINUES TO TALK...

MY FATHER WAS-- AN ORDINARY LABORER-- AT AN ATOMIC PROJECT! I PROBABLY GAINED MY POWER-- DUE TO RADIATION-- WHICH AFFECTED HIM BEFORE I WAS BORN! I'LL NEVER --KNOW FOR SURE!

ONE DAY-- HE LOST HIS JOB --AND SO WE MOVED-- TO ANOTHER CITY--

"THE NEIGHBORHOOD BULLIES-- PICKED ON ME-- BECAUSE I WAS A NEW ARRIVAL-- AND ALSO-- BECAUSE OF MY *ANTHROPOID PHYSIQUE!* BUT, I MYSELF-- DID NOT YET SUSPECT-- THE *POWERS* I POSSESSED--!

BEAT IT, UGLY! IF YOU WANT SOMEONE TO PLAY WITH, GO FIND YERSELF ANOTHER MONKEY!

GOWAN, CHARLIE-- PASTE 'IM ONE!

HEY! WHAT *GIVES??* I CAN'T NAB 'IM! HE HOPS AROUND LIKE A *JUMPIN' BEAN!*

STAND STILL! I *DARE* YA!! STAND STILL-- JUST FOR A *MINUTE!*

YOU AREN'T GOING TO HIT *ME!*

"LIKE MOST YOUNG BOYS-- I COULDN'T RESIST A DARE-- AND SO--

THERE! *THAT'LL* TEACH YOU--! HEY!

I CAN'T *STOP* IN TIME!

SCREETCH

LOOK OUT FOR THAT *CAR!!* LOOK OUT!!!

"AND THAT WAS-- WHEN I FIRST REALIZED-- I POSSESSED POWERS-- GREATER THAN ANY NORMAL HUMAN--!"

WHA- WHAT *HAPPENED* TO HIM?? WHERE'D HE *GO?*

D-DID YOU SEE *THAT??!*

13

BUT, AFTER THAT-- IT WAS NO BETTER! WHERE THEY HAD ONCE MADE *FUN* OF ME-- NOW, THEY *FEARED* ME--! I BECAME-- LONELIER THAN EVER--

FORGIVE INTERRUPTION! *EMERGENCY!* RAY GUNS PUT OUT OF ACTION! REQUEST INSTRUCTIONS!

WHAT??! THERE MUST BE *MORE* MUTANTS IN OUR MIDST!! PREPARE FOR COMBAT ACTION!

FOLLOW ME! MUTANTS ARE OUR NATURAL ENEMIES! THEY MUST BE FOUND AND *DESTROYED*, WHEREVER THEY EXIST! WE ARE ALL SO PROGRAMMED!

THEY SHALL NOT ESCAPE US!

WHILE, JUST A FEW HUNDRED YARDS AWAY...

SCOTT!! WARREN!! IN THERE --LOOK!

BOBBY IS THERE! BUT--WHERE'S THE *BEAST* ??

ICEMAN!! IMPRISONED IN SOME SORT OF A GLASS CUBICLE!!

WE'VE GOT TO GET HIM *OUT* OF THERE!

STOP! YOUR ORDERS WERE TO *FOLLOW ME!*

ANGEL!! WHAT'S HE GOING TO DO??

IT DOESN'T *MATTER,* JEANNIE! I WON'T GIVE HIM THE CHANCE!

I'VE BEEN *ITCHIN'* TO DO THIS SINCE WE *GOT* HERE!

WHAP!

WE *MUST* STOP HIM-- FOR *BOBBY'S* SAKE!

14

BUT, IN THE VAST CHAMBER OF THE *MASTER MOLD*, ALL IS CALM, AS THE TITANIC UNHUMAN LISTENS TO THE BEAST'S TALE...SECURE IN THE KNOWLEDGE OF HIS OWN POWER AND INVULNERABILITY...!

AND THEN YOU WON A SCHOLARSHIP TO COLLEGE! NOW, CONTINUE YOUR BIOGRAPHY--!

BUT *WAIT*!! WHAT ABOUT THE *ALARMS* THAT JUST WENT OFF?

MY *SENTINELS* WILL HANDLE ANY EMERGENCY! I NEED FEAR *NOTHING!* I AM *SUPREME!*

AS YOU WELL KNOW--FOR YOU *CREATED* ME THIS WAY!

"I EXCELLED-- AT EVERY-THING! SCHOLASTICALLY-- I WAS HEAD OF MY CLASS! AND--IN SPORTS--I WAS UNBEATABLE--!

COMPARED TO MY *AGILITY*, THEY'RE LIKE *STATUES!*

"BUT, MY OWN NATURAL ENTHUSIASM-- GOT THE BETTER OF ME--ONE DAY! AFTER SCORING A GOAL --I KICKED OFF MY SHOES--AND LEAPED FOR THE GOAL POST--!

WE *DID* IT! WE WON THE CONFERENCE *CHAMPIONSHIP!*

LOOK AT McCOY!! HE'S LIKE A *BEAST!!*

McCOY!! GET *DOWN* FROM THERE!

NOBODY CAN DO THAT!! NOBODY *HUMAN!*

"THE NAME *BEAST*--STUCK TO ME! BUT-- WORSE THAN THAT-- THE *SUSPICIONS* STARTED FORMING-- SUSPICIONS THAT I WASN'T-- COMPLETELY *HUMAN*--!

"BUT--LUCKILY FOR ME-- A VERY UNUSUAL PERSON--BECAME INTERESTED--IN THE WRITEUP ABOUT ME--!

ALUMNI NEWS

EXTRA EXTRA

"BEAST" FLEES FOOTBALL FIELD! REFUSES TO ANSWER NEWS-MEN'S QUESTIONS ABOUT HIS ALLEGED "POWERS"!

"BEFORE LONG, WE HAD-- A VERY SPECIAL GUEST-- TO DINNER!"

HENRY McCOY!! MIND YOUR MANNERS!!

HAVE YOU FORGOTTEN WE HAVE *COMPANY*??

IT'S ALL RIGHT, MRS. McCOY! I'M ANXIOUS TO OBSERVE YOUR SON UNDER ALL CONDITIONS!

JUST WHAT *DO* YOU WANT WITH HANK, MISTER?

HE MAY SEEM STRANGE TO OTHERS, BUT HE'S A GOOD BOY --DO YOU HEAR?

WE'RE TERRIBLY *PROUD* OF HENRY-- DESPITE *OTHER* PEOPLE CALLING HIM--A *FREAK!*

THAT'S WHY *I'M* HERE! YOUR SON CAN GO THRU LIFE AS A "*FREAK*"-- OR A *BENEFACTOR* OF THE HUMAN RACE! THE CHOICE IS *YOURS!*

I WANT TO TAKE HIM-- AND *TRAIN* HIM--!

16

MEANWHILE, ACROSS THE CHASM FROM THE SENTINELS' FORTRESS, PROFESSOR XAVIER, MENTALLY SCANNING THE AREA, SUDDENLY GASPS WITH ALARM...

HANK CANNOT *HELP* HIMSELF! UNDER THAT PSYCHIC PROBE HE'S TELLING *TOO MUCH!*

I'VE GOT TO *STOP* HIM, BEFORE HE GIVES AWAY TOO MANY OF OUR SECRETS!

ALTHOUGH I'M CONFINED TO THIS CHAIR -- WHICH, LUCKILY, JEAN LEVITATED FROM WHERE IT HAD FALLEN BELOW -- I'VE GOT TO TAKE A DESPERATE GAMBLE --!

I'LL SEND MY INVISIBLE *ASTRAL IMAGE* TO WHERE HANK IS! IT'S THE ONLY THING THAT CAN HELP NOW!!

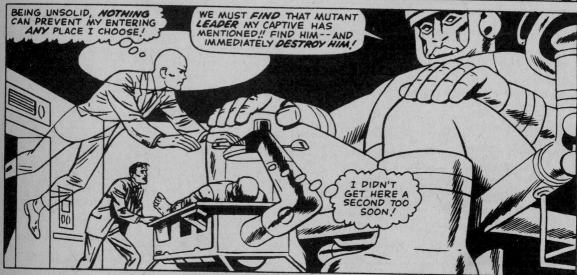

BEING UNSOLID, *NOTHING* CAN PREVENT MY ENTERING *ANY* PLACE I CHOOSE!

WE MUST *FIND* THAT MUTANT LEADER MY CAPTIVE HAS MENTIONED!! FIND HIM -- AND IMMEDIATELY *DESTROY HIM!*

I DIDN'T GET HERE A SECOND TOO SOON!

THOUGH I CAN ACCOMPLISH NO *PHYSICAL* ACTS WHILE IN MY ASTRAL FORM, I CAN *MENTALLY* FOCUS MY BRAIN WAVES AND BOMBARD HANK'S MIND WITH SHARP THOUGHT PARTICLES THAT WILL TEMPORARILY DEADEN HIS OWN THOUGHTS!

NOW, NOT EVEN THE PSYCHO-PROBE CAN GET ANY INFORMATION OUT OF HIM ANY MORE!

TRASK!! WHY DID HE STOP SPEAKING -- JUST WHEN HE WAS ABOUT TO REVEAL THE X-MEN'S *HIDEOUT??*

I DON'T *KNOW!!* EVERYTHING SEEMS TO BE WORKING PROPERLY!

REMEMBER! IF I DO NOT GAIN THE INFORMATION I SEEK, A *CITY* SHALL PERISH!

17

BUT THEN, THE BRILLIANT LEADER OF THE X-MEN TAKES A DESPERATE CHANCE--!

I'VE GOT TO PROBE THE MECHANICAL BRAIN OF THE *MASTER MOLD* HIMSELF--NO MATTER WHAT THE COST!

JUST AS I THOUGHT! A VAST COMPLEX OF ELECTRONIC CIRCUITRY!

A STRANGE FORCE-- I FEEL IT SCANNING MY THINKING APPARATUS!!

THERE IS SOMETHING HERE!! A MENACING PRESENCE! I *SENSE* IT! I *FEEL* IT! BUT I CANNOT *SEE* IT!

YET, I AM EQUIPPED WITH WEAPONS FOR *ANY* TYPE OF ATTACK!

AND THEN, WITH DAZZLING, TOTALLY UNHUMAN SPEED...

MICRO-ELECTRIC BLASTS--LEAPING FROM HIS FINGERS! THEY'RE FILLING THE ENTIRE CHAMBER! I CANNOT DODGE THEM!

MY *ASTRAL-IMAGE* IS COMPOSED OF ELECTRIFIED THOUGHT WAVES!! IT CAN BE *HARMED* BY THE MASTER MOLD'S MICRO-ELECTRIC ATTACK!

I'VE GOT TO RETURN TO MY BODY--BEFORE THE BOLTS WEAKEN ME TOO MUCH!

IF I SHOULD BE *UNABLE* TO ONCE AGAIN REJOIN MY PHYSICAL SELF, THEN MY FLESH-AND-BLOOD BODY WOULD BE CONDEMNED TO REMAIN IN A TRANCE--*FOREVER!*

JUST ANOTHER FEW FEET-- I'VE GOT TO MAKE IT!! I'VE *GOT* TO!!

18

BUT, AT THAT VERY MOMENT, THE SEARCHING SQUAD OF SENTINELS *FINDS* ITS PREY--!

MUTANTS!! OUR SWORN ENEMIES!! DESTROY THEM.!

SHOW THEM NO QUARTER! ATTACK! *ATTACK.!*

UH OH! THE HAPPINESS BOYS ARE BACK!

HOW DOES ANYONE AS BIG AS THEM *MOVE* SO FAST??!

WE NEED TIME-- TO FORMULATE A PLAN! QUICK, BOBBY-- AN *ICE SHIELD!*

THOOM!

THIS MAY GIVE US A *BREATHER,* CYKE-- BUT IT WON'T HOLD *THEM* OFF FOR LONG!

IT DOESN'T *HAVE* TO! WE JUST NEED TIME TO GET OUR WITS TOGETHER! ANGEL, SEE IF YOU CAN FLY JEAN TO SOME PLACE OF SAFETY!

NOT ON YOUR *LIFE,* SCOTT! I'LL SEE THIS *THRU* WITH YOU-- TO THE VERY *END!*

WHY'S IT SO *QUIET* BACK THERE?? WHAT ARE THEY COOKING UP *NOW?*

AND, IN ANSWER TO ICEMAN'S QUESTION--!

USE THE PROPULSION POWER BUILT INTO THE SOLES OF YOUR FEET-- THEN *STRIKE!*

WHOOSH

PREPARE FOR FINAL DESTRUCTIVE ACTION!!

19

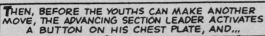

NEXT ISSUE! YOU'LL ACTUALLY WITNESS THE CREATION OF A SENTINEL—AS WELL AS ONE OF THE MOST THRILLING STORY ENDINGS YOU'VE EVER GASPED AT! YOU'LL SEE THE X-MEN, MENACED BY TRASK'S UNHUMAN CREATIONS ON THE ONE HAND, AND THEIR OWN INHERENT WEAKNESSES ON THE OTHER! EVEN IF YOU'RE NOT A MUTANT, YOU MUSTN'T MISS IT! 'NUFF SAID!

LAST ISH, WE SAW THE AMAZING *PROFESSOR XAVIER'S* ASTRAL IMAGE DRIVEN FROM THE *SENTINELS' FORTRESS* BY DEADLY MICRO ELECTRIC BLASTS...

JUST *MADE* IT! ANOTHER FEW SECONDS, AND I'D HAVE BEEN UNABLE TO TAKE CONTROL OF MY PHYSICAL FORM AGAIN!

MY *X-MEN* ARE PRISONERS OF THE GIGANTIC *SENTINELS,* WITHIN THAT DEADLY FORTRESS...

...WHILE I LIE HELPLESSLY OUTSIDE-- UNABLE TO HELP THEM-- HARDLY ABLE TO DEFEND *MYSELF!*

BUT, I *CANNOT* FAIL THEM NOW! IT WAS I WHO ORGANIZED THEM-- WHO INSPIRED THEM TO RISK THEIR LIVES FOR MANKIND--

--FOR THE SAME HUMAN RACE WHICH NOW HATES AND FEARS THEM-- ALL BECAUSE OF *DR. TRASK* AND HIS *SENTINELS!*

TRASK BELIEVED HE WAS DOING THE RIGHT THING! HE THOUGHT ALL MUTANTS WERE *MENACES!* HE CREATED THE SENTINELS TO *DESTROY* US, THINKING WE WERE THE ENEMIES OF HUMANITY!

HE HAD HIS SENTINELS CONSTRUCT THAT IMPREGNABLE FORTRESS-- HE ARMED THEM WITH DEADLY NEW WEAPONS-- FOR THE PURPOSE OF WIPING ALL MUTANTS FROM THE FACE OF EARTH!

HE WAS TOO BLIND, TOO FANATICAL TO REALIZE THAT THERE ARE BOTH GOOD AND BAD MUTANTS -- TO REALIZE THAT HIS *SENTINELS* ARE THE *REAL* THREAT TO-- *WAIT!!*

THE FORTRESS IS *SINKING* --LIKE A GIGANTIC *ELEVATOR!*

IT'S COMPLETELY *HIDDEN* AGAIN-- CAMOUFLAGED BY A DECEPTIVE MOUND OF EARTH!

NOW MY X-MEN ARE *COMPLETELY* CUT OFF FROM ANY AID I MIGHT GIVE THEM!

THIS MEANS THAT THE MOST DANGEROUS SENTINEL OF ALL-- THE GARGANTUAN *MASTER MOLD,* CAN CONTINUE TO CREATE *MORE* SENTINELS-- UNTIL THEY OVER-RUN ALL OF EARTH!

--UNLESS I CAN *STOP* HIM! AND I *WILL*-- IF IT COSTS ME MY VERY *LIFE!*

BACK IN THE CITY THERE IS A *FALLEN* SENTINEL!* IF I CAN FIND OUT *WHY* HE FELL, I'LL HAVE THE KEY TO THEIR DEFEAT!

*REMEMBER HIM FROM *X-MEN #14?* --STAN.

2

DESPERATELY, PAINFULLY, DISREGARDING THE AGONY OF HIS INJURED BODY, THE CRIPPLED MUTANT TIRELESSLY CRAWLS INCH AFTER INCH, UNTIL HE REACHES...

THE HIGHWAY-- AT *LAST!* NOW TO STOP THE FIRST PASSING CAR--!

A BASIC TELEPATHIC COMMAND WILL DO THE TRICK! NO NORMAL HUMAN CAN RESIST!

SLOW DOWN! STOP ONE HUNDRED YARDS AHEAD!

SECONDS LATER...

SURE IS LUCKY WE *SAW* YOU, FELLA! WHAT *HAPPENED?*

NO TIME TO EXPLAIN NOW! YOU MUST DRIVE ME TO THE CITY!

SURE! WE'LL BE *GLAD* TO!

THERE'S SOMETHING *ABOUT* HIM-- IT SEEMS TO *FORCE* US TO OBEY!

KINDA STRANGE THE WAY WE SLOWED DOWN IN TIME! ALMOST LIKE WE *KNEW* HE'D BE THERE!

MEANWHILE, BACK WITHIN THE NOW HIDDEN FORTRESS, WE FIND...

NOW WHAT HAVE THEY DONE TO US?? IT'S HARD TO *MOVE* IN HERE-- LIKE MY MUSCLES ARE MADE OF *LEAD!*

YOU'RE *RIGHT!* SOMETHING IS PRESSING US DOWN-- SAPPING OUR STRENGTH!

I CAN'T EVEN FLY TO THE *TOP*-- MY WINGS CAN HARDLY *FLAP* IN HERE!

THERE'S ONLY ONE ANSWER-- THEY'VE FOUND A WAY TO INCREASE THE WEIGHT OF *GRAVITY* WITHIN THE GLOBE! AND THERE'S NO WAY FOR US TO *FIGHT* IT!

BUT, THE *BIG* QUESTION IS-- WHERE ARE THEY *TAKING* US TO NOW-- AND *WHY?*

3

FINALLY... PLACE THE HEAVY-GRAV GLOBE UPON ITS PERMANENT BASE!

IT IS *DONE!* THEY SHALL BE SAFE HERE UNTIL THE *MASTER MOLD* GIVES US ORDERS FOR THEIR *FINAL DISPOSAL!*

NO MATTER HOW THEY STRUGGLE, THERE IS NO WAY TO OVERCOME THE IRRESISTIBLE POWER OF INCREASED *GRAVITY!*

THIS IS WHY WE ARE DESTINED TO RULE MANKIND! OUR COMPUTERIZED BRAINS CAN CREATE WEAPONS WHICH *NO MERE HUMAN* CAN MATCH!

BUT, INSIDE THE SEEMINGLY ESCAPE-PROOF PRISON, THE "MERE HUMANS" WITHIN ARE DETERMINED THAT IF THEY MUST BE DEFEATED, THEY'LL GO DOWN *FIGHTING--!*

MY POWER BLASTS CAN SHATTER ALMOST *ANYTHING!* WHY WON'T THEY SMASH THAT *GLASS???*

THUNG!

FOR LONG, ANGUISHED MINUTES, THE DEDICATED DEPUTY LEADER UNLEASHES HIS AWESOME POWER, UNTIL AT LAST...

IT'S NO USE! I-- FAILED--!

THE WALL *ISN'T* GLASS, BUT SOME NEW, IMPREGNABLE SUBSTANCE--!

YET, PERHAPS THE *OTHERS*-- BY USE OF *THEIR* MUTANT POWER-- MAY DO BETTER--!

EASY, JEAN-- EVEN IF YOU *CAN* LEVITATE YOURSELF--THERE'S NO PLACE TO *GO!*

THE TOP OF THIS DOUBLE-SIZED MILK BOTTLE IS ALL *SEALED UP!*

I *KNOW,* BOBBY--BUT I'VE *GOT* TO KEEP TRYING...!

WE CAN'T JUST SIT IDLY BY AND WAIT FOR THE *END!* WE MUST--*OHHH*--!

UH OH! I WAS AFRAID THAT WOULD HAPPEN!

THE PROF ALWAYS *WARNED* YOU ABOUT OVER-TAXING YOUR TELEKINETIC POWER!

4

AT THAT MOMENT, IN ANOTHER CHAMBER OF THE VAST FORTRESS, THE AWESOME *MASTER MOLD* CONCLUDES HIS EXAMINATION OF THE UNCONSCIOUS *BEAST*...

I NEED LEARN NO MORE ABOUT HIM! I REALIZE NOW THAT THE *X-MEN* DO NOT POSSESS THE POWER TO HARM US!

WAIT! WHAT DO YOU PLAN TO *DO* WITH HIM....?

HE SHALL BE IMPRISONED WITH THE *OTHER* CAPTIVE MUTANTS, AS THE *MASTER MOLD* HAS COMMANDED!

THEN, AT MY PLEASURE, THEY WILL ALL BE *DESTROYED!* FOR THAT IS THE PURPOSE YOU YOURSELF HAVE PROGRAMMED INTO OUR COMPUTERIZED BRAINS!

NO! NO! I WAS *WRONG!* I REALIZE THAT NOW! *THEY* AREN'T MENACES TO MANKIND-- IT'S *YOU* WHO ARE! THEY MUSTN'T BE HARMED--!

SILENCE! THOUGH YOU *CREATED* US, YOU ARE MERELY A HUMAN! YOU TOO MUST *OBEY!*

WHILE I HAVE THE *POWER*, IT IS YOU WHO HAVE THE *KNOWLEDGE* TO CREATE A VAST *ARMY* OF SENTINELS FOR ME-- AND YOU SHALL *DO SO!*

NO! IT WOULD MEAN BETRAYING MY FELLOW MEN, AND YOUR SENTINELS WOULD ENSLAVE ALL OF EARTH!

YOU HAVE NO *CHOICE!* HAVE YOU FORGOTTEN MY *POWER?* IF SO, BEHOLD THIS SIMPLE *DEMONSTRATION!*

YOUR *DISINTEGRATOR BEAM!!* DON'T DO IT-- *DON'T.*

6

DO NOT FEAR! *YOU* SHALL NOT BE HARMED--AS *YET!*

IT IS THE NEAREST *CITY* THAT WILL BE *WIPED OUT*--AS EASILY AS I ERASE YONDER MACHINE!

AND *I* DID IT! I *GAVE* YOU THAT RAY!!

NZT!

I CANNOT ALLOW AN ENTIRE CITY TO SUFFER SUCH A FATE! I-- I'LL *CREATE* YOUR ARMY OF SENTINELS!

AFTER ALL, WHERE THERE'S *LIFE*, THERE'S HOPE! WE MAY *STILL* FIND A WAY TO DESTROY THE MASTER MOLD!

FOR, WITH *HIM* GONE, THE SENTINELS WOULD BE *LEADERLESS*--THE THREAT WOULD BE ENDED!

IF ONLY THE *X-MEN* WERE STILL FREE! IF ONLY I'D *LISTENED* TO THEM!

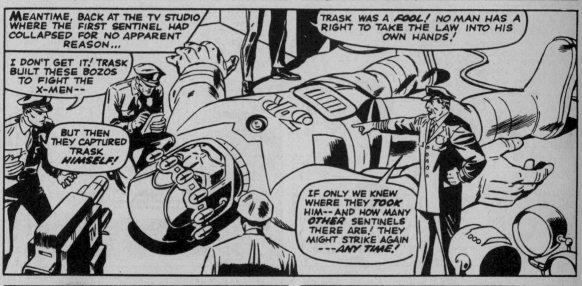

MEANTIME, BACK AT THE TV STUDIO WHERE THE FIRST SENTINEL HAD COLLAPSED FOR NO APPARENT REASON...

I DON'T GET IT! TRASK BUILT THESE BOZOS TO FIGHT THE X-MEN--

BUT THEN THEY CAPTURED TRASK *HIMSELF!*

TRASK WAS A *FOOL!* NO MAN HAS A RIGHT TO TAKE THE LAW INTO HIS OWN HANDS!

IF ONLY WE KNEW WHERE THEY *TOOK* HIM--AND HOW MANY *OTHER* SENTINELS THERE ARE! THEY MIGHT STRIKE AGAIN ---*ANY TIME!*

PERHAPS *I* CAN HELP YOU, INSPECTOR!

PROFESSOR XAVIER! YOU'RE THE ONE WHO WAS *DEBATING* WITH TRASK ON TV! *YOU* CLAIMED MUTANTS WERE *NOT* DANGEROUS TO MANKIND!

COME ON IN, MISTER! WE'LL TAKE ANY HELP WE CAN GET!

WHAT DO *YOU* KNOW ABOUT THIS *SENTINEL* HERE? HOW *DANGEROUS* IS HE?

MORE DANGEROUS THAN YOU CAN *IMAGINE!*--UNLESS WE CAN LEARN THE REASON THAT HE COLLAPSED!

7

YOU'RE NOT GONNA LEARN ANYTHING BY JUST SITTING AND *STARING* AT 'IM, ARE YOU?

HE CANNOT SUSPECT THAT I'M ACTUALLY *PROBING* DEEP WITHIN THE FIGURE BEFORE ME -- BY MEANS OF SHEER MENTAL ENERGY!

HE'S BUILT LIKE A GIGANTIC *TV SET!* HE WILL NOT RECEIVE A PICTURE PROPERLY IF THERE IS *INTERFERENCE!* SOMETHING HAS *INTERFERED* WITH HIM!

IF I COULD ONLY LEARN WHAT THAT SOMETHING *IS!*

LOOK, MISTER -- I WAS WILLING TO GIVE YOU A CHANCE -- BUT IF YOU JUST WANNA CATCH UP ON YOUR DAYDREAMING, GO DO IT SOMEWHERE *ELSE*, HUH?

I SENSE SOMETHING AT *LAST* -- FROM OUTSIDE THE WINDOW! IF I CAN JUST MENTALLY *PINPOINT* IT, WE'LL HAVE THE ANSWER!

DO NOT *SPEAK*, INSPECTOR! GIVE ME JUST *ONE MINUTE MORE!*

WHAT ARE YOU POINTING AT THAT NEW *CRYSTAL PRODUCTS* BUILDING FOR? WHAT'S *THAT* GOT TO DO WITH ANYTHING?

THE GIANT *CRYSTAL* WHICH ADORNS THE TOWER! THAT'S *IT!*

WHEN THE SENTINEL STOOD BEFORE THE WINDOW, HIS TRANSMISSION BEAM WAS BROKEN -- BY THE CRYSTAL'S *INTERFERENCE!*

THEN -- IF WE MOVED HIM AGAIN -- HE'D COME TO *LIFE* ONCE HE WAS AWAY FROM THE WINDOW?!!

EXACTLY! BUT IT WOULD BE *TOO* DANGEROUS TO TRY! I HAVE A *BETTER* IDEA!

WE MUST DESTROY THE *SOURCE* OF HIS TRANSMISSION BEAMS -- AND AT LAST I KNOW HOW TO *DO* IT!

BUT, WE KNOW HOW ANXIOUS YOU ARE TO REJOIN THE *X-MEN* ONCE AGAIN, AND SO...

PLACE THE *HELPLESS* ONE WITH THE *OTHER* PRISONERS, UNTIL THE MASTER MOLD ORDERS THEIR *DISPOSAL!*

I OBEY, SECTION LEADER!

8

9

MOVING WITH BLINDING SPEED, CYCLOPS BLASTS HIS POWER BEAM AT THE SENTINEL CARRYING HANK McCOY...

IT *WORKED!* HE DROPPED THE BEAST! LET'S *GO!*

ZAP!

RACING TO PREVENT THE X-MEN'S ESCAPE, THE OTHER SENTINELS TRIP AND FALL OVER THEIR STRICKEN COMRADE...

THE TIMING WAS *PERFECT!* THEY'RE GETTING ALL TANGLED UP!

I'LL LEAP OUT *FIRST,* TO MAKE THEM DIRECT THEIR CHEST RAYS AT *ME!* IT'LL GIVE JEAN AND THE OTHERS A BETTER CHANCE!

-WHEW!- LUCKY FOR ME THEY'RE SO SLOW-MOVING!

WHOOM

BUT, WHAT'S KEEPING THE *OTHERS?*

WARREN! THEY'RE TRYING TO *CLOSE* THE OPENING AGAIN! IT'S ONLY BIG ENOUGH FOR US TO SLIP THRU *ONE AT A TIME!* HANK AND BOBBY WILL *NEVER* MAKE IT!

DON'T WORRY, JEAN! WE'RE NOT DESERTING THEM! YOU'LL *SEE--!*

OH, *NO,* YOU DON'T! YOU'RE NOT SEALING MY PARDS IN THAT GLOBE *AGAIN!*

STOP HIM!

BUT, HOW CAN YOU STOP THE *UNSTOPPABLE??!*

SKRAKT

THERE! THAT'S *ONE* CONTROL PANEL YOU CAN KISS GOODBYE!

10

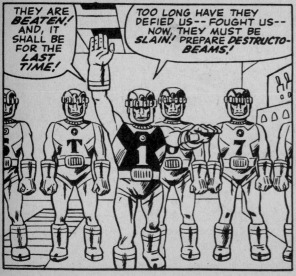

AND, AT THAT MOMENT, FLYING HIGH OVERHEAD, WE SEE...

IF *XAVIER'S* THEORY IS CORRECT, THIS GIANT CRYSTAL, WHICH WE TOOK FROM THE TOWER OF THE BUILDING, WILL CAUSE ALL THE SENTINELS IN THE FORTRESS BELOW TO COLLAPSE AND BE RENDERED HARMLESS!

BUT HOW DO WE KNOW WE'RE NOT JUST WASTIN' OUR TIME? ALL I SEE BELOW IS A PATCH OF EMPTY COUNTRYSIDE!

YOU MAY REST ASSURED, GENTLEMEN, THE FORTRESS IS HIDDEN BENEATH THE SITE BELOW! CONTINUE TO MAINTAIN YOUR PRESENT FLYING SPEED-- -- IT IS *VITAL* THAT WE MAKE A STEADY, COMPLETE SWEEP OF THE AREA, TO BLANK OUT EVERY SENTINEL BELOW!

WE ALL THOUGHT THAT GUY WAS OFF HIS ROCKER, TILL WE GOT THE WORD FROM *WASHINGTON* ITSELF TO DO WHATEVER HE SAID!

I WONDER WHAT MAKES *HIM* SUCH A V.I.P.? ME, I NEVER *HEARD* OF 'IM!

BUT, THE POLICE PILOT'S PUZZLED MUSINGS ARE SOON RUDELY INTERRUPTED BY THE UNEXPECTED SIGHT WHICH SUDDENLY GREETS HIS EYES BELOW...

LOOK! THERE *IS* SOME KINDA *FORTRESS* DOWN THERE! IT'S POPPING UP OUTTA *NOWHERE!*

AND THERE'S A *WEAPON* OF SOME SORT BEING TRAINED UPON US!

13

IT'S CREATING A DEADLY *TURBULENCE* IN THE AIR! IF WE HIT IT, WE'LL *CRASH!*

THEN WE'VE GOT TO GO *BACK!*

NO! CONTINUE TO FLY! THERE WILL BE NO *DANGER!*

ON PROFESSOR XAVIER'S SAY-SO, THE COURAGEOUS OFFICERS FLY DIRECTLY TOWARDS THE AWESOME WHIRLWINDS, BUT-- AS THEY DO SO, THE ENORMOUS *CRYSTAL* DOES ITS WORK WELL--!

AS THE GLEAMING OBJECT PASSES ABOVE, THOSE OPERATING THE WEAPON CRUMPLE HELPLESSLY, CAUSING THE TURBULENCE TO FADE AWAY...!

THUS, WHEN THE *X-MEN* REGAIN CONSCIOUSNESS ONCE AGAIN, THEY FIND...

LOOK! THE *SENTINELS!* THEY'VE BEEN *KNOCKED OUT!*

I'M NOT COMPLAINING, BUT-- HOW DID IT *HAPPEN?*

ONE MINUTE WE WERE RACING TO THE MASTER MOLD-- AND THEN --*THIS!*

FROM THE EVIDENCE AT HAND, I WOULD DEDUCE THAT PROFESSOR X HAS FINALLY FOUND THEIR ACHILLES' HEEL!

HANK! YOU'VE *COME TO* AGAIN! HOW WONDERFUL!

AHH-- HOW GRATIFYING TO KNOW I'VE BEEN MISSED!

LET'S KNOCK OFF THE *TALK* TILL LATER! WE'VE STILL GOT A *JOB* TO DO--!

YOU'RE *RIGHT,* CYKE! SO LONG AS THE *MASTER MOLD* EXISTS, THE SENTINELS WILL *NEVER* BE DEFEATED! SO LET'S *GET 'IM!*

WARREN! BE *CAREFUL!* HE MUST HAVE ALL SORTS OF *DEFENSIVE DEVICES* PREPARED FOR JUST SUCH AN ATTACK!

LEAD ON, MACDUFF! WE'RE RIGHT BEHIND YOU!

THEY WON'T STOP US *NOW!*

JEAN'S *RIGHT,* ANGEL! SLOW DOWN-- WE DON'T KNOW *WHAT'S* AHEAD OF US!

14

THEN, AS IF TO ADD EMPHASIS TO THE X-MEN'S WORDS, THE LIGHTS SUDDENLY FLICKER OUT, PLUNGING THE ENTIRE AREA INTO DARKNESS...!

CAN'T SEE WHERE I'M FLYING! GONNA CRASH INTO-- ¡UNHHH!¿

LISTEN TO THAT *HUM*-- LIKE A TREMENDOUS SURGE OF *POWER!* SOMETHING IS DRAINING ALL THE CURRENT, BLOWING ALL THE FUSES--!

WHAT *IS* IT? WHAT *CAN* IT *BE?*

IT'S SOME SORT OF INCREDIBLY POWERFUL *MACHINE!* I CAN FEEL ITS TREMENDOUS *ENERGY* WITH MY *FEET*-- RIGHT THRU THE *FLOOR!*

AND, THE BOOK-WORMISH *BEAST* IS RIGHT! FOR, JUST A SHORT DISTANCE AWAY, WE SEE...

I HAVE GIVEN YOU ALL THE *POWER* YOU WILL REQUIRE! NOW, LET THE PROCESS *BEGIN!* THIS NIGHT SHALL MARK THE END OF MAN'S DOMINATION OF THE PLANET EARTH!

CREATE MY SENTINELS! I SHALL OBSERVE YOUR EVERY MOVE!

HEAVEN HELP ME!! I DON'T *WANT* TO DO IT-- BUT I *MUST!* OTHERWISE, A *CITY* WILL BE *DESTROYED!*

FIRST, THERE SHALL BE *EIGHT* NEW SENTINELS-- THEN, EIGHT MORE-- THEN, EIGHT MORE-- EACH NEW GROUP APPEARING FASTER AND FASTER-- UNTIL THEIR NUMBER MOUNTS SO QUICKLY THAT THEY BECOME VIRTUALLY *UNCOUNTABLE!*--BEGIN!!

15

IT'S STARTING TO WORK! THE SYNTHO-PARTICLES FROM THE MASTER MOLD ARE FLOWING INTO THE CUBICLES, SOLIDIFYING INTO SOLID MATTER!!

ONCE THE PROCESS HAS STARTED, THERE'LL BE NO STOPPING IT! IF ENOUGH ENERGY IS BUILT UP, THE MACHINE COULD RUN FOREVER!

THEY'LL EVENTUALLY OUTNUMBER THE HUMAN RACE! THEY'LL ENSLAVE ALL OF MANKIND! THEY'LL BE THE MASTERS OF EARTH!

AND ALL BECAUSE OF ME!! IN MY IGNORANCE, MY FEAR, I CREATED AN EVIL FAR GREATER THAN THE MENACE IT WAS BUILT TO DESTROY!

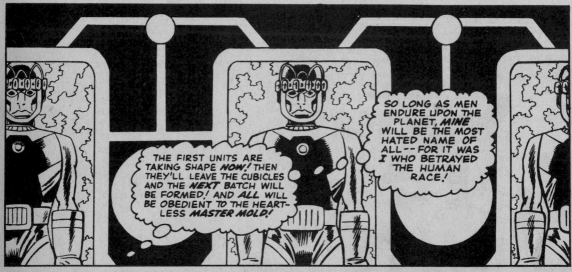

THE FIRST UNITS ARE TAKING SHAPE NOW! THEN THEY'LL LEAVE THE CUBICLES AND THE NEXT BATCH WILL BE FORMED! AND ALL WILL BE OBEDIENT TO THE HEARTLESS MASTER MOLD!

SO LONG AS MEN ENDURE UPON THE PLANET, MINE WILL BE THE MOST HATED NAME OF ALL -- FOR IT WAS I WHO BETRAYED THE HUMAN RACE!

NO! I WON'T DO IT -- I CAN'T!! I MEANT TO HELP MANKIND -- TO PROTECT IT FROM THE MUTANTS -- I CAN'T DESTROY IT NOW!

STOP!! YOU CANNOT DEFY ME! HAVE YOU FORGOTTEN --THE PENALTY??

NO--I'VE JUST REMEMBERED --REMEMBERED THAT MY OWN LIFE MEANS NOTHING! I'LL SACRIFICE IT GLADLY TO UNDO THE DREAD THING I'VE DONE!

THE IONIC POWER SOURCE!! IF YOU SHATTER THAT, YOU DESTROY EVERYTHING! EVEN I CANNOT SURVIVE--!!!

CLANG

16

HANG ON, HANK! NOW THAT SCOTT'S SAFE, I CAN RELIEVE YOU OF ICEMAN!

GET MOVING, PARTNER -- YOU HAVEN'T MUCH TIME!

I'M PAINFULLY **AWARE** OF THAT NERVE-WRACKING FACT, MY FRIEND!

AND THEN, WITHOUT THE ADDED BURDEN OF HIS YOUNG PARTNER IN HIS ARMS, HANK McCOY DEMONSTRATES THE UNBELIEVABLE AGILITY AND BALANCE WHICH HAVE EARNED HIM THE NAME -- THE **BEAST!**

AFTER ALL THOSE GRUELLING SESSIONS IN THE PROFESSOR'S **DANGER ROOM,** THIS IS ALMOST CHILD'S PLAY NOW!

SO LONG AS THERE'S A **FOOT-HOLD,** OR A **TOE-HOLD** ANYWHERE, MY CHANCES FOR SURVIVAL BECOME VIRTUALLY INCALCULABLE!

PLOP! THUNK!

SALUTATIONS FROM YOUR BESTIAL BUDDY, COMRADES-AT-ARMS! I TRUST I DIDN'T DELAY YOU TOO LONG!

WOW! ARE YOU **KIDDIN',** HANK? THE ANGEL **HIMSELF** JUST LANDED A SECOND AGO!

WHUMP!

BEAST! ALL OF YOU! **DON'T STOP!** GET AWAY FROM THE **CLIFF!!**

THAT'S THE END OF THE SENTINELS -- AND THE MASTER MOLD! MANKIND CAN BREATHE EASY ONCE MORE!

BOY! THE PROFESSOR'S MENTAL WARNING DIDN'T COME A SECOND TOO **SOON!!**

I WONDER IF WE'LL EVER KNOW WHAT **CAUSED** THOSE EXPLOSIONS -- THE EXPLOSIONS WHICH SAVED HUMANITY?!!

PERHAPS THE TRUTH **WILL** ONE DAY BE KNOWN! BUT, UNTIL THAT TIME, IT LIES BURIED BENEATH COUNTLESS TONS OF RUBBLE -- BURIED IN THE BREAST OF DR. **BOLIVAR TRASK,** WHOSE LAST EARTHLY SACRIFICE BROUGHT THE WORK OF A LIFETIME CRASHING DOWN ABOUT HIM -- WHOSE LAST EARTHLY LESSON PROVED TO BE: **BEWARE THE FANATIC!** TOO OFTEN HIS **CURE** IS DEADLIER BY FAR THAN THE EVIL HE DENOUNCES!

20

THE END

BUT, **NO** VICTORY IS EVER TRULY COMPLETE! EVEN NOW, AS THE WEARY X-MEN PREPARE TO RETURN TO THEIR HEADQUARTERS BUILDING, NONE CAN SUSPECT THE SHADOW OF **MENACE** THAT AWAITS THEM -- THE MOST UNEXPECTED MENACE OF ALL -- AS WE SHALL SEE NEXT ISSUE! 'NUFF SAID!

X-MEN! THE MOST UNUSUAL FIGHTING TEAM OF ALL TIME!
"...AND NONE SHALL SURVIVE!"
THE FAT'S IN THE FIRE NOW! THERE'S NO WAY FOR PROFESSOR X TO KEEP OUR BATTLE OUT OF THE HEADLINES AFTER ALL THIS!
YOUR PULSE IS IMPOSSIBLE, SON!
THOUGH THE YOUTHFUL X-MEN MANAGED TO DEFEAT THE DEADLY SENTINELS LAST ISH, THEY DID NOT ESCAPE UNSCATHED! WITHIN MOMENTS, A FIRST AID TEAM OF NATIONAL GUARD MEDICS REACHES THE SCENE...
MY TROOPS WILL TAKE COMMAND, INSPECTOR! IT'S A MILITARY MATTER NOW!
OKAY WITH ME, GENERAL!
HAVE A CARE, KILDARE! EACH AND EVERY TOE IS VIRTUALLY PRICELESS!
I WONDER HOW MUCH LONGER THE PROFESSOR CAN KEEP HIS CONNECTION WITH US A SECRET.
WE'D BETTER SEE ABOUT GETTING YOU HOME SAFELY, PROFESSOR XAVIER!
DON'T WORRY ABOUT ME, OFFICER! MY CAR IS PARKED NOT FAR FROM HERE!
PERHAPS ONE OF THE X-MEN WILL BE GOOD ENOUGH TO DRIVE ME BACK TO MY SCHOOL!
COMB THE AREA!! REPORT ANYTHING THAT MOVES! LET'S GO!
1
STORY: STAN LEE • LAYOUTS: J. KIRBY • PENCILS: JAY GAVIN • INKS: DICK AYERS LETTERING: A. SIMEK

ON BEHALF OF THE ARMED SERVICES, PROFESSOR, I WANT TO THANK YOU FOR YOUR AID! IT WAS MOST *COURAGEOUS* OF YOU TO OFFER TO COME HERE AND ADVISE US!

I WAS GLAD TO BE ABLE TO HELP, GENERAL!

HE THINKS OF ME AS A CIVILIAN ADVISER! AFTER ALL, THERE'S NO REASON FOR ANYONE TO SUSPECT THAT I'M THE LEADER OF THE *X-MEN!*

THERE'LL BE SOME MIGHTY *RED FACES* FROM NOW ON, PROFESSOR! ALL THOSE WHO CALLED THE X-MEN MENACES TO SOCIETY WILL HAVE A LOT OF *APOLOGIZING* TO DO!

IN FACT, I MYSELF USED TO FEAR THEIR POWER, UNTIL I SAW HOW THEY RISKED THEIR LIVES TO HELP ALL OF US!

DON'T YOU *AGREE*, PROFESSOR?

INDEED I *DO*, GENERAL!

THAT'S WHY I DECIDED TO RELEASE MY MENTAL *HOLD* OVER YOUR MIND-- SO THE *X-MEN* WOULD GET DUE CREDIT!

CAPTAIN, ORDER YOUR MEN TO SEARCH THE RUINS OF THE SENTINELS' FORTRESS!

BE *QUICK* ABOUT IT! WE MOVE OUT BEFORE SUNDOWN!

WHAT SUPREME *IRONY!* THE SENTINELS HAD BEEN CREATED TO DESTROY THE X-MEN--

--AND YET, IT WAS NECESSARY FOR *US* TO SMASH *THEM*-- IN ORDER TO SAVE HUMANITY-- THE HUMANITY THAT *HATED* US!

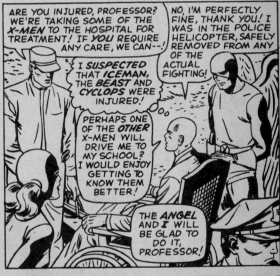

ARE YOU INJURED, PROFESSOR? WE'RE TAKING SOME OF THE X-MEN TO THE HOSPITAL FOR TREATMENT! IF *YOU* REQUIRE ANY CARE, WE CAN--

NO, I'M PERFECTLY FINE, THANK YOU! I WAS IN THE POLICE HELICOPTER, SAFELY REMOVED FROM ANY OF THE ACTUAL FIGHTING!

I *SUSPECTED* THAT ICEMAN, THE *BEAST* AND *CYCLOPS* WERE INJURED!

PERHAPS ONE OF THE *OTHER* X-MEN WILL DRIVE ME TO MY SCHOOL? I WOULD ENJOY GETTING TO KNOW THEM BETTER!

THE *ANGEL* AND *I* WILL BE GLAD TO DO IT, PROFESSOR!

ATTENTION, BEAST! EXERCISE EXTREME *CAUTION!* DO NOT REMOVE YOUR MASK! ICEMAN! REMAIN IN ICY FORM! YOUR TRUE *IDENTITIES* MUST NOT BE EXPOSED!

MAN! IF HE EVER GOT AN *INGROWN TOENAIL*, IT WOULD BE *ENDSVILLE!*

CYCLOPS! YOU WILL BE RESPONSIBLE UNTIL I REACH THE HOSPITAL!

SECONDS LATER, CYCLOPS, THE BEAST AND ICEMAN ARE SPEEDILY TRANSPORTED TO THE NEAREST HOSPITAL, AS THE ANGEL AND MARVEL GIRL ACCOMPANY PROFESSOR XAVIER TO HIS WAITING SEDAN...

THE PROFESSOR *HAD* TO LET US GO TO THE HOSPITAL--NO MATTER *HOW* RISKY IT IS! IF HE PROTESTED, IT WOULD HAVE AROUSED TOO MANY *SUSPICIONS!*

I'M NOT HURT BADLY EXCEPT FOR SOME BRUISES-- BUT I HOPE HANK AND BOBBY ARE OKAY!

2

A SHORT TIME LATER, IN A HUSHED HOSPITAL ROOM...

HIS INJURY WAS MORE SERIOUS THAN I *THOUGHT!* HE BLACKED OUT IN THE AMBULANCE, AND THEY CAN'T BRING HIM BACK TO CONSCIOUSNESS!

IT WAS GOOD OF YOU TO STOP BY TO SEE THE X-MEN, PROFESSOR--BUT I'M AFRAID *ICEMAN'S* CONDITION MUST BE LISTED AS *CRITICAL!*

DUE TO THE MUTANT NATURE OF HIS BODY, IT IS IMPOSSIBLE TO MAKE AN ACCURATE DIAGNOSIS OF HIS INJURIES!

SO ALIEN IS HE TO NORMAL MEDICAL KNOWLEDGE, THAT WE CAN DO NOTHING BUT KEEP HIM UNDER OBSERVATION--AND HOPE FOR THE BEST!

I UNDERSTAND, DOCTOR! NONE OF THE USUAL MEDICATIONS CAN BE GIVEN TO ONE WHOSE PHYSICAL MAKEUP DEFIES ANYTHING SCIENCE HAS EVER ENCOUNTERED BEFORE!

EVEN *I*, WITH MY MUTANT *BRAIN*, CANNOT HELP BOBBY NOW! HE IS IN THE HANDS OF A POWER GREATER THAN ANY *HUMAN!*

HE'S STARTING TO *MOVE!* TRYING TO *SPEAK*--!

LOOK OUT! I'LL TACKLE THE SENTINEL! I'LL STOP HIM-- SOMEHOW--!

I KNOW I'M THE YOUNGEST-- BUT I'LL SHOW THEM-- I'LL PROVE THAT I'M EVERY INCH AN *X-MAN!* I WON'T FAIL THEM! I *WON'T*...!

I'LL MAKE THEM PROUD OF ME--THEY *NEED* ME--I-- I WON'T LET THEM DOWN--!

HE'S *DELIRIOUS!* NO WAY OF KNOWING WHETHER IT'S A *GOOD* SYMPTOM--OR A *DANGEROUS* ONE!

YOU'D BETTER *LEAVE* NOW, PROFESSOR!

ALL THESE MONTHS --THESE MANY MISSIONS--I'VE *PROTECTED* MY X-MEN! I PRAY THAT BOBBY DRAKE WON'T MARK THE FIRST TIME I'M FACED WITH-- *FAILURE!*

3

THE *PHONE--QUICKLY!* PERHAPS I CAN *STOP* THEM, BEFORE THEY LEAVE!

SURE, PROFESSOR! THERE YOU ARE....!

MAY I HAVE THE PHONE, YOUNG MAN?

IF THEY REACH THE SCHOOL AND FIND IT *DESERTED,* WHAT WILL THEY *THINK??* HOW CAN WE *EXPLAIN?*

THEY *MUSTN'T* REACH IT FIRST! I'VE HAD A FEELING OF *DANGER* FROM THERE ALL DAY!

THEN, AFTER QUICKLY DIALING THE ANGEL'S HOME NUMBER--

MRS. WORTHINGTON? THIS IS PROFESSOR XAVIER! I'VE HAD MY STUDENTS WITH ME ON A FIELD TRIP, TO GATHER MATERIAL FOR A RESEARCH PAPER! *THAT* IS WHY YOUR CALL WAS ANSWERED BY AN AUTOMATIC DEVICE!

AT ANY RATE, WE'RE PLANNING A SHORT MOTOR TRIP AND THOUGHT WE'D STOP OFF AND SEE WARREN WHILE IN YOUR NEIGHBORHOOD!

BUT, IT'S *EXAM* TIME NOW--!

OH, WE'LL ONLY STAY A FEW MINUTES, PROFESSOR! SEE YOU LATER! 'BYE NOW!

WELL, *THAT'S* A RELIEF, PROFESSOR! MY HUSBAND AND I WERE QUITE *WORRIED!*

I COULDN'T *DISSUADE* HER! BUT, I CAN'T HELP FEELING *UNEASY* ABOUT THEIR VISIT!

WHY, SIR? IS ANYTHING *WRONG?*

YES! WITH ICEMAN CRITICALLY ILL, AND THE BEAST RECOVERING FROM A FRACTURE --PLUS THIS SENSE OF *MENACE* I CANNOT SHAKE--

--I THINK YOU'D BETTER FLY TO THE SCHOOL *NOW,* ANGEL -- AND DO A LITTLE SCOUTING AROUND!

I'M ON MY *WAY,* SIR!

IF ONLY MOM AND DAD HADN'T DECIDED TO VISIT THE SCHOOL *NOW!* THE PROF IS NEVER *WRONG* WHEN HE SENSES DANGER--AND I CAN'T LET *THEM* GET INVOLVED IN IT!

I SURE HATE TO LEAVE *BOBBY* WHILE HE'S SO ILL-- BUT, I GUESS THE *PROFESSOR* WILL STAY WITH HIM!

GOSH, IT FEELS *GREAT* TO BE IN *FLIGHT* AGAIN!

THEN, FOR THE NEXT FEW MINUTES AS HE WINGS HIS WAY TOWARDS WESTCHESTER, THE HIGH-FLYING *ANGEL* SOARS AND GLIDES LIKE A FALCON IN FLIGHT....!

NO OTHER HUMAN--NO ONE WHO HAS NEVER POSSESSED *WINGS*--CAN IMAGINE HOW *WONDERFUL* IT IS TO ACTUALLY *FLY!*

5

BUT, EVEN AS THE ASTOUNDING ANGEL PLUMMETS EARTHWARD TOWARDS HIS GOAL, THE FRONT DOOR OF PROFESSOR XAVIER'S SCHOOL SLOWLY BEGINS TO OPEN...

ONE OF THEM APPROACHES NOW!

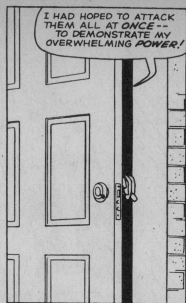

I HAD HOPED TO ATTACK THEM ALL AT ONCE-- TO DEMONSTRATE MY OVERWHELMING POWER!

BUT, PERHAPS IT WILL BE EVEN MORE SATISFYING TO DEFEAT THEM ONE AT A TIME! I WILL THEN BE ABLE TO SAVOR EACH INDIVIDUAL VICTORY-- TO WATCH EACH ACCURSED X-MAN FALL HELPLESSLY BEFORE ME!

THE FIRST ONE COMES! I SHALL CLOSE THE DOOR AGAIN-- AND WAIT!

I WONDER WHAT THE PROFESSOR MEANT ABOUT SENSING DANGER!? THE SCHOOL HAS NEVER LOOKED QUIETER--OR MORE PEACEFUL!

THERE'S NOTHING OUT OF THE ORDINARY OUTSIDE THE BUILDING! NOT A SIGN OF LIFE ANYWHERE!

SO I'D BETTER POKE AROUND INSIDE! IT'S NOT LIKE THE PROF TO SEND ANYONE ON A WILD-GOOSE CHASE!

THAT'S STRANGE! THE DOOR ALWAYS LOCKS AUTOMATICALLY BEHIND US WHEN WE LEAVE...

...BUT, IT'S OPEN NOW!

AND THEN, LIKE A SENSELESS SEQUENCE FROM A MAD, FANTASTIC NIGHTMARE, A HEAVY, LETHAL BATTLE-AX SUDDENLY DISENGAGES ITSELF FROM THE STEEL HAND THAT HELD IT, AND HURTLES THRU THE CORRIDOR--RIGHT TOWARDS THE ANGEL....!

7.

BUT, LONG, HARD MONTHS OF CEASELESS *TRAINING* PROVE THEIR WORTH, AS THE ANGEL'S AMAZING AERIAL AGILITY SUCCEEDS IN SAVING HIS LIFE!

WELCOME HOME, YOU WINGED BLUNDERER! YOU SHALL NEVER LEAVE HERE AGAIN--UNDER YOUR OWN POWER!

THERE *IS* SOMEONE! BUT *WHO*?? WHO WOULD *DARE*--??

JUST STAY WHERE YOU *ARE*, MISTER! I'LL MAKE YOU *EAT* THOSE WORDS!

HIS VOICE CAME FROM DOWN THE CORRIDOR! BUT, THERE'S NO PLACE *TO HIDE* FROM HERE TO THE END OF THE HALL! HE WON'T ESCAPE ME!

NO MATTER HOW FAST HE IS --HOW *STRONG* HE IS-- I'LL *GET* HIM! I'VE GOT TO BE *SWIFT* AND *SURE*--!

BUT THEN, ZOOMING DOWN THE HALLWAY LIKE A HUMAN MISSILE, THE WINGED MUTANT REALIZES HE'S SPEEDING INTO A *TRAP*-- TOO LATE TO *STOP* HIMSELF!

THERE'S SOMETHING IN *FRONT* OF ME-- IT SUDDENLY DROPPED INTO PLACE--!

I'M GOING TO *HIT* IT! I--UNHHHH!

HOW EASY IT WAS TO CLIP THE ANGEL'S WINGS! BUT, HE IS ONLY THE FIRST--ONLY THE *FIRST*!

8

MEANWHILE, PROFESSOR CHARLES XAVIER PICKS THAT EXACT MOMENT TO CHECK UPON THE CONDITION OF THE X-MEN'S DEPUTY LEADER--

NO, DOC! I'M SORRY! I CAN'T LET YOU EXAMINE MY EYES!

I MUST *INSIST*, SON! IT'S HOSPITAL ROUTINE! NOW DON'T BE DIFFICULT!

SCOTT NEEDS HELP! I WAS *AFRAID* OF THIS!

PARDON THE INTRUSION, DOCTOR! MY NAME IS XAVIER! I HAVE HAD THE OPPORTUNITY OF SEEING THE X-MEN IN ACTION, AND...

I'VE *HEARD* OF YOU, PROFESSOR! PERHAPS *YOU* CAN CONVINCE THIS YOUNG MAN TO LET ME CHECK HIS EYES! OPTOMETRY IS MY SPECIALTY-- I BELIEVE I MIGHT BE ABLE TO *HELP* HIM!

NOBODY CAN EXAMINE MY EYES! NO MATTER *WHAT* HAPPENS!

HE WON'T TAKE YOUR *WORD* FOR IT, SCOTT! YOU'LL HAVE TO *CONVINCE* HIM--AS DRAMATICALLY AS POSSIBLE! *NOW!*

THIS IS A MILD EXAMPLE OF WHAT *HAPPENS* IF MY PROTECTIVE VISOR IS REMOVED FROM MY EYES-- EVEN TO THE SLIGHTEST DEGREE!

GOOD HEAVENS....!

ZAPPT!

YOU MEAN YOU CANNOT *CONTROL* THE DESTRUCTIVE FORCE OF YOUR EYES?? YOU HAVE TO KEEP THEM SHIELDED *ALL* THE TIME??

I'M AFRAID THAT'S *IT*, DOC! IT WOULD BE WORTH YOUR *LIFE* TO TRY TO REMOVE MY VISOR!

IF YOU'RE THRU WITH YOUR PATIENT, DOCTOR, I WONDER IF *I* MIGHT SPEAK WITH HIM IN PRIVATE? I WAS ASKED TO BRING HIM A MESSAGE, FROM ONE OF THE OTHER X-MEN!

CERTAINLY, PROFESSOR! THEY AREN'T *PRISONERS* HERE!

HENCE, A FEW MINUTES LATER...

SAY NOTHING YET, SCOTT! WE MUST BE EXTREMELY CAREFUL TO ACT LIKE CASUAL ACQUAINTANCES, SO NONE SUSPECT MY *REAL* CONNECTION WITH YOU!

WOULD YOU MIND WHEELING ME TO THAT SHADY ARBOR, MY BOY?

WE'RE ALONE NOW, SIR! WHAT *IS* IT? IS SOMETHING *WRONG?*

I'M AFRAID SO! I'VE LOST MENTAL CONTACT WITH THE *ANGEL*-- AFTER SENDING HIM BACK TO THE SCHOOL!

I SUSPECT SOME *DANGER* AWAITING US THERE!

ICEMAN IS TOO ILL TO BE MOVED --AND I PREFER THE *BEAST* AND *MARVEL GIRL* TO REMAIN HERE IN CASE THEY'RE NEEDED!

BUT, *YOU* AND *I* HAD BEST RETURN TO THE SCHOOL AT *ONCE!* I HAVE A FEELING THAT WARREN *NEEDS* US!

I'LL GET YOUR *CAR*, SIR! IT'S PARKED JUST AROUND THE CORNER!

9

THEN, AFTER AN HOUR OF BREAKNECK DRIVING--!

THERE'S THE SCHOOL AT LAST! HAVE YOU MANAGED TO CONTACT THE ANGEL MENTALLY YET, PROFESSOR?

NO! AND THAT'S WHAT *WORRIES* ME! I SEEM TO SENSE SOME SORT OF MENTAL *BARRIER* AROUND THE SCHOOL --SOMETHING MY OWN MUTANT BRAIN CANNOT PENETRATE!

THE BARRIER IS STRONGER THAN EVER HERE INSIDE! TAKE EVERY PRECAUTION, CYCLOPS! THERE IS SOME GREAT *POWER* BEING USED AGAINST US!

ANGEL! THIS IS CYKE! DO YOU *READ* ME? WHERE *ARE* YOU, FELLA?

AH! TWO ADDITIONAL *VICTIMS* FOR ME! I MUST MAKE SURE THEY DO NOT GET *BORED!*

PROFESSOR-- *LISTEN!* WHAT'S *THAT??*

RRRREEEEE

MY *CEREBRO* MACHINE! THE *DANGER* IS EVEN GREATER THAN I FEARED!

THE MACHINE SEEMS TO BE GOING *MAD!* THE MENACE MUST BE INCREDIBLY *CLOSE!*

RREEEE

I'LL SHUT IT OFF BEFORE IT *DEAFENS* US!

CEREBRO ONLY REACTS THAT WAY WHEN A DANGEROUS *MUTANT* THREATENS! THAT MEANS SOME POWERFUL *HOMO SUPERIOR* HAS INVADED THIS BUILDING, AND IS WAITING TO ATTACK EVEN *NOW!*

HE MUST HAVE ALREADY OVERCOME *ANGEL*--AND WE DON'T EVEN KNOW WHO HE *IS!*

ONLY THE MOST *POWERFUL* OF MUTANTS COULD PREVENT ME FROM MENTALLY REACHING OUT TO HIM! WE MUST LEARN WHO HE *IS*--WHILE WE STILL *CAN!*

PROFESSOR! BEHIND YOU!! LOOK OUT--!

10

THAT VOICE-- SOUNDED FAMILIAR-- ALMOST AS IF-- =UGGHHH!=

THOK!

WHOEVER YOU ARE, YOU FORGOT THAT MY FORCE BEAM IS JUST AS EFFECTIVE IN THE DARK AS IN THE LIGHT!

ZAP

OVER-CONFIDENT FOOL! I FORGET NOTHING!

:OOOFFFFF!=

BEFORE FINISHING YOU, I WANT YOU TO SEE HOW USELESS YOUR MUCH-VAUNTED BEAM IS AGAINST GENUINE POWER!

WHOEVER HE IS, HE SEEMS TO ANTICIPATE MY EVERY MOVE! BUT I'M NOT BEATEN YET-- MY FORCE BEAM STILL HAS PLENTY OF ENERGY LEFT--!

WHEREVER YOU ARE, I'LL GET YOU! I'LL BLAST THIS ROOM IN EVERY DIRECTION!!

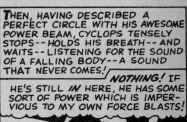

THEN, HAVING DESCRIBED A PERFECT CIRCLE WITH HIS AWESOME POWER BEAM, CYCLOPS TENSELY STOPS-- HOLDS HIS BREATH-- AND WAITS-- LISTENING FOR THE SOUND OF A FALLING BODY-- A SOUND THAT NEVER COMES!

NOTHING! IF HE'S STILL IN HERE, HE HAS SOME SORT OF POWER WHICH IS IMPERVIOUS TO MY OWN FORCE BLASTS!

HE MUST HAVE PLANNED THIS WHOLE THING CAREFULLY-- THE ADVANTAGE IS HIS NOW--

--UNLESS I CAN REACH THE LIGHT SWITCH BEFORE HE STOPS ME!

A NICE TRY, X-MAN, BUT A FUTILE ONE! I EXPECTED YOU TO RACE FOR THE SWITCH!

WHAP!

K.R.A.K!

AND NOW, IT IS TIME TO END THE CHARADE--!

--BY USING ONLY MY HAMMERING FISTS, SO THAT YOU STILL CANNOT BE CERTAIN WHAT MY TRUE POWER IS!

12

AND, AS THE NOW-HELPLESS CYCLOPS SLUMPS TO THE FLOOR, WE RETURN ONCE AGAIN TO THE HOSPITAL, WHERE WE FIND...

HENRY P. McCOY! I THOUGHT YOU WERE PRACTICALLY AN *INVALID*!

THAT WAS AN *HOUR* AGO, MA'AM! YOU KNOW HOW QUICKLY WE MUTANTS *RECUPERATE*!

NOTHING LIKE SOME CAPRICIOUS CALISTHENICS TO WHILE AWAY A LETHARGIC DAY!

BUT, ENOUGH OF MY EXEMPLARY EPITHETS! TO WHAT DO I OWE THE HONOR OF YOUR SUDDEN VISITATION?

HONESTLY, HANK! CAN'T YOU EVER SPEAK LIKE ANY ORDINARY, NORMAL HUMAN BEING?

I *DO*, JEANIE! IT'S JUST THAT I EMPLOY MELLIFLUOUS ADJECTIVES TO *DO* IT!

WOMP!

VERY PERSPICACIOUS OF YOU, WENCH!

AND THEREIN LIES MY *CHARM*!

OH! YOU'RE JUST *IMPOSSIBLE*!

VERY WELL, YOUNG MAN! I SHALL HOLD YOU IN THE AIR, *TELEKINETICALLY*, UNTIL YOU PROMISE TO SETTLE DOWN AND *LISTEN* TO ME!

PRATTLE AWAY THEN, FEMALE! YOU HAVE MY UNDIVIDED ATTENTION!

WELL! IT'S ABOUT *TIME*!

HANK, I'M *WORRIED*! THE PROFESSOR AND CYCLOPS ARE *GONE* -- AND SO IS THEIR *CAR*! ANGEL IS *ALSO* GONE -- AND THERE HASN'T BEEN A WORD FROM *ANY* OF THEM!

JUST LIKE A *WOMAN*!! IF SOMEONE ISN'T FRACTURING YOUR EARDRUMS EVERY CONCEIVABLE MINUTE, YOU BEGIN TO FEAR THAT SOMETHING'S *AMISS*!

YOU *PROMISED* YOU'D BE *SERIOUS*!

I'M SORRY, JEAN! PERHAPS YOU'VE SOME *JUSTIFICATION* FOR YOUR CONCERN! IT ISN'T LIKE THE OTHERS TO LEAVE US INCOMMUNICADO!

IF THEY WENT *ANYWHERE*, IT WOULD BE TO THE *SCHOOL*! PERHAPS THAT SHOULD BE *OUR* NEXT DESTINATION!

I *HOPED* YOU'D SAY THAT, HANK! BUT FIRST, LET'S CHECK ON *ICE-MAN*!

13

AND THAT SAME POWER WILL EASILY LIFT ME OVER THE OUTER WALL....!

AS FOR ME, MY METHOD IS SOMEWHAT LESS SUBTLE, BUT EQUALLY AS EFFECTIVE NONETHELESS!

FINALLY, AFTER A SPECTACULAR SUCCESSION OF RUNNING, LEAPING, CLIMBING AND TELEPORTING WITH MILE-CONSUMING GYMNASTIC SKILL, THE TWO MARVELOUS MUTANTS REACH THEIR GOAL...

IT SEEMS SO QUIET--SO FOREBODING--!

STAY BEHIND ME, LASS! I'LL CHARGE IN FIRST, AT TOP SPEED, TO BEAR THE BRUNT OF WHATEVER AWAITS US!

BUT, EVEN THE AGILE BEAST IS NOT PREPARED FOR THE SIMPLE, YET STARTLINGLY DANGEROUS SURPRISE THAT CONFRONTS HIM....!

SOMETHING HAPPENED TO THE HALLWAY--!

EVERYTHING HAS BEEN COATED WITH A WAXLIKE GLOSS--THERE'S NO FRICTION-- NOTHING TO HOLD ONTO--

IT'S LIKE BEING A SATELLITE IN SPACE--THERE'S NO WAY TO CHECK OUR MOMENTUM-- NO WAY TO STOP!

NO MATTER WHAT I REACH-- THE WALLS--CEILING--FLOOR-- THEY'RE ALL AS SMOOTH AS GLASS!

JEANIE WILL BE ALL RIGHT, BECAUSE SHE ENTERED SLOWLY--BUT I HURTLED IN LIKE A PROJECTILE!

EVEN MY NATURAL AGILITY CAN'T HELP ME NOW! I'VE GOT TO KEEP SLIDING ALONG --OUT OF CONTROL--UNTIL I REACH--WHAT???

15

17

NOW HOLD ON, DOCTOR! WE REPRESENT THE *AFFILIATED PRESS!* WE HAVE OVER THIRTY MILLION READERS THRUOUT THE FREE WORLD!

YOU WOULDN'T WANT THOSE THIRTY MILLION PEOPLE TO THINK YOU DIDN'T *CARE* ABOUT THEM, WOULD YOU?

THEY CAN TAKE THIRTY MILLION JUMPS IN THE *LAKE* -- AND SO CAN *YOU!* I'VE GOT A PATIENT IN THERE WHO MAY BE *DYING* -- AND *THAT'S* ALL I CARE ABOUT!

NOW *GET OUT* -- BEFORE I HAVE YOU *THROWN* OUT!

SORRY FOR THE DELAY, NURSE! WHAT'S *WRONG?* WHAT HAPPENED?

IT'S HIS *PULSE,* DOCTOR! IT'S SLOWING DOWN! I-I DON'T KNOW WHAT TO DO!

I HATE TO ADMIT IT, BUT NEITHER DO *I!*

THEY *NEED* ME -- I *KNOW* THEY DO -- THEY *NEED* ME --!

HE'S BEEN *DELIRIOUS* AGAIN -- MUMBLING TO HIMSELF FOR HOURS --!

I'VE NEVER FELT SO *HELPLESS* BEFORE!

I MUSTN'T -- *FAIL* THEM -- NOT WHEN THEY *NEED* ME --!

IT'S ALMOST AS THOUGH HE HEARS VOICES THAT *WE* CAN'T HEAR -- AS THOUGH SOMEONE IS *CALLING* TO HIM -- DEPENDING ON HIM --!!

PULL YOURSELF TOGETHER, NURSE! HERE'S SOME NEW MEDICATION I WANT -- RIGHT AWAY!

IT'S A NEW TYPE OF SULFA DRUG -- VERY *POTENT!* WE'VE GOT TO RISK IT!

BUT, WHAT OF THE OTHER X-MEN? WE HAD BEST RETURN TO THEM *FAST* -- BECAUSE FROM THE LOOKS OF THINGS, THEY MAY NOT BE AROUND MUCH LONGER --!

I REGRET WE CANNOT WAIT FOR THE *ICEMAN* TO JOIN YOU, BUT I FEAR YOU WILL HAVE TO MAKE YOUR FINAL JOURNEY *WITHOUT* HIM!

AND NOW, I'LL MAKE SURE YOU'RE ALL SECURELY *LOCKED* INSIDE YOUR STEEL GONDOLA!

FOR YOUR *OWN* SAFETY, OF COURSE!

WE WOULDN'T WANT YOU FALLING OUT -- NOT AFTER YOU REACH *100,000 FEET* IN THE AIR!

SLAM!

18

THEN, SECONDS LATER...

YOU'LL ORBIT THE EDGE OF SPACE-- HELPLESS --OUT OF CONTROL--

--UNTIL YOUR SMALL SUPPLY OF *AIR* GIVES OUT!!

AND THAT WILL BE THE *END* OF THE X-MEN-- FOREVER!

WHILE, JUST A SCANT FEW MILES AWAY FROM THAT STARTLING SCENE, MR. AND MRS. WARREN WORTHINGTON BEGIN THE FINAL LAP OF THEIR MOTOR TRIP--

I DIDN'T REALIZE HOW MUCH I'VE *MISSED* WARREN! I CAN'T WAIT TO *SEE* HIM, DEAR!

WE'RE ONLY A FEW MINUTES AWAY FROM THE SCHOOL!

IT WON'T BE LONG NOW!

ONE THING HAS *ALWAYS* PUZZLED ME --- PROFESSOR XAVIER HAS SO *FEW* STUDENTS, I DON'T UNDERSTAND HOW HE CAN AFFORD TO RUN HIS SCHOOL!

I ALWAYS THOUGHT HE WAS INDEPENDENTLY WEALTHY-- JUST KEPT THE SCHOOL FOR A LARK!

ANYWAY, HE IS THE MOST *CHARMING*-- OH! THERE'S THE SCHOOL *NOW!*

STRANGE THAT NO ONE CAME TO THE DOOR! THEY *MUST* HAVE HEARD OUR CAR!

PERHAPS THEY'RE BUSY WITH EXAMS, DEAR!

WELL, NO MATTER! I HEAR SOMEONE COMING--!

RINNNG

AH! YOU MUST BE PARENTS OF A STUDENT--!

B-BUT WHO ARE *YOU*??

I? I AM *POWER*--!!

19

NEXT ISSUE:

AND NOW TO *RELEASE* MY *MAGNETIC* HOLD, LETTING IT--*NO!*

I HAVE A FAR *BETTER* IDEA!

I SHALL NEED A *HEADQUARTERS* FOR MYSELF, NOW THAT I AM READY TO ATTACK THE HUMAN RACE ONCE MORE!

AND, WHAT SUPREME *IRONY* IT SHALL BE TO USE THE FORMER HOME OF MY *ENEMIES* FOR THAT VERY PURPOSE!

THUS, ALLOWING THE ENORMOUS BUILDING TO SETTLE GENTLY BACK TO THE GROUND, THE WORLD'S MOST *DANGEROUS* MUTANT STRIDES MAJESTICALLY INSIDE! AND, AS HE APPROACHES THEM, ALL THE OBJECTS THAT HAD BEEN STREWN ABOUT IN HIS FIGHT WITH THE X-MEN MAGNETICALLY RISE BACK INTO PLACE!

THE X-MEN HAD DEFEATED ME IN THE PAST BECAUSE OF THE WEAKNESS OF THOSE WHO *SERVED* ME!

BUT *NOW*, I FIGHT *ALONE!* I NEED NO ALLIES! I AM *MAGNETO*, THE ALL-POWERFUL!

THE DESK OF *PROFESSOR X*-- WITH HIS ACCURSED *CEREBRO MACHINE* BUILT INTO ITS SURFACE!

CEREBRO-- CREATED TO WARN HIM OF THE PRESENCE OF DANGEROUS MUTANTS! HE'LL HAVE NO FURTHER USE FOR *THAT!*

RRREEE

WHATEVER DOES NOT SERVE *MAGNETO*, MUST BE *DESTROYED!!* FOR, I AM *SUPREME!*

FOOM!!

WAIT! THE SOUND OF A CAR STOPPING IN THE DRIVEWAY! I HAVE *VISITORS!*

AS THE NEW *OWNER* OF THIS BUILDING, I MUST GIVE THEM THE PROPER *WELCOME!*

3

THEY SEEM SO INNOCENT-- SO COMPLETELY GUILELESS! THEY ARE UNDOUBTEDLY THE PARENTS OF ONE OF THE PROFESSOR'S "STUDENTS"!

THIS GIVES ME AN IDEA! THEY SHALL BE MADE TO SERVE ME!

AND THIS, YOU WILL REMEMBER, WAS WHERE OUR TANTALIZING TALE ENDED LAST ISH!

WHO ARE YOU?

I? I AM POWER!

MEN CALL ME-- MAGNETO!

AND NOW-- COME IN!!

STARTLED AT THE SIGHT OF THE STRANGELY GARBED BEING, MR. AND MRS. WORTHINGTON ALLOW THEMSELVES TO BE LED INSIDE--

I DON'T KNOW WHAT THIS IS ALL ABOUT, BUT WE WOULD LIKE TO SEE OUR SON, WARREN WORTHINGTON, THE THIRD!

WOULD YOU TELL HIM HIS PARENTS ARE HERE, PLEASE?

FOOLS!! YOU THINK ME SOME FLUNKY WHOM YOU CAN ORDER ABOUT??!

IT IS I WHO GIVE THE ORDERS! AND MY FIRST COMMAND IS-- GAZE INTO MY EYES! NOW-- YOU CANNOT TURN AWAY! YOU ARE HELD BY MAGNETIC ATTRACTION!

YOU ARE SUDDENLY VERY TIRED! THERE IS A GUEST ROOM AT THE HEAD OF THE STAIRS! YOU WILL OCCUPY IT!

HE IS RIGHT, DEAR! I FIND THAT I AM EXHAUSTED!

THERE THEY SHALL REMAIN, UNTIL I AM READY TO SUMMON THEM AGAIN!

IT'S SO KIND OF YOU TO OFFER US YOUR HOSPITALITY, MR. MAGNETO!

BUT, WITH THE ANGEL'S PARENTS SAFELY LOCKED AWAY AND UNDER HIS MAGNETIC CONTROL, THE MEGALOMANIACAL MUTANT REMEMBERS ONE LAST DETAIL--

MY VICTORY IS STILL NOT COMPLETE! THE ICEMAN IS AS YET UNACCOUNTED FOR!

BAH! WHY SHOULD I WORRY ABOUT HIM? HE IS THE YOUNGEST-- AND THE MOST INEXPERIENCED OF ALL!

IF I WAS ABLE TO DEFEAT THE OTHER FIVE, WHAT HAVE I TO FEAR FROM THE WEAKEST OF THE LOT?!!

4

AND, EVEN AS MAGNETO SPEAKS, THE YOUNGEST OF THE FABLED X-MEN LIES IN HIS HOSPITAL ROOM--STILL ON THE CRITICAL LIST--STILL HOVERING DESPERATELY BETWEEN LIFE AND DEATH--

NURSE! WE CAN AFFORD TO WAIT NO LONGER! HE'S REACHED THE CRITICAL STAGE!

WE MUST TAKE A CHANCE AND APPLY THE NEW SULFA DRUG! WITHOUT IT, HE MAY NOT LAST OUT THE NIGHT!

QUICKLY, WOMAN! IS THE NEW LASER-INDUCED HYPODERMIC READY??

THEY NEED ME! --I MUST GO TO THEM--THEY NEED ME--!

THEY'VE WORKED 'ROUND THE CLOCK TO COMPLETE IT IN TIME, DOCTOR! BUT, THEY WANTED ME TO WARN YOU--IT'S NEVER BEEN TRIED BEFORE!

THERE'S ALWAYS A FIRST TIME, YOUNG LADY! JUST PRAY THAT IT WILL PENETRATE HIS INCREDIBLE SKIN!

BZZZZZT

THEY NEED-- ME--;UHHH--

IT'S GETTING THRU! IT WORKS! THE LASER DID IT!

CLICK!

HE'S QUIET NOW! THE DELIRIUM HAS STOPPED!

THE NEXT FEW HOURS WILL TELL THE STORY!

IF THE DRUG WORKS, HE'LL BE ON THE WAY TO RECOVERY VERY SOON! IF NOT--THERE IS NOTHING MORE-- THAT WE CAN DO!

POOR LAD! I WONDER WHY THE X-MEN HAVE FORSAKEN HIM!?

BUT, IF THE DEPARTING PHYSICIAN COULD LOOK INSIDE A GONDOLA RISING TOWARDS THE SUBSTRATOSPHERE, HE WOULD FIND THE ANSWER TO HIS QUESTION! FOR, THE X-MEN, ALAS, ARE THEMSELVES FORSAKEN--!

THE OTHERS ARE UNCONSCIOUS-- HELPLESS--!

WHILE I AM WITHOUT THE POWER OF MY MUTANT BRAIN, DUE TO THIS MENTAL-WAVE DISTORTER MAGNETO HAS FASTENED TO MY SCALP!

BUT, EVEN HE HAS OVER-LOOKED ONE BASIC ITEM! MY ABILITY TO READ MINDS AND PROJECT MY THOUGHTS IS DUE TO THE COUNTER EGO WHICH I POSSESS!

EVEN NOW, THAT SAME COUNTER EGO IS PROBING THE DISTORTER-- APPLYING AS MUCH STRESS AND STRAIN TO IT AS IS HUMANLY POSSIBLE!

5

THE PAIN IS INCREASING BY THE SECOND! THE PRESSURE IS ALMOST *UNBEARABLE!* BUT I CANNOT STOP NOW! I *DARE* NOT STOP NOW!

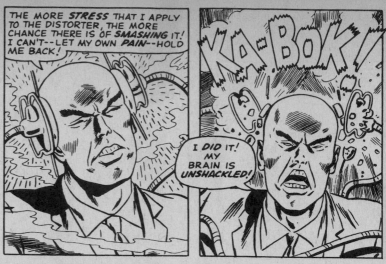

THE MORE *STRESS* THAT I APPLY TO THE DISTORTER, THE MORE CHANCE THERE IS OF *SMASHING* IT! I CAN'T--LET MY OWN *PAIN*--HOLD ME BACK!

KA-BOK!

I *DID* IT! MY BRAIN IS *UNSHACKLED!*

ANGEL AND CYCLOPS ARE STILL UNCONSCIOUS--BUT THE *BEAST* AND *MARVEL GIRL* ARE MERELY *DAZED!*

I'LL USE THE POWER OF MY OWN *MIND* TO SNAP HANK AND JEAN OUT OF IT! THEN, WE'LL ATTEND TO THE OTHERS!

HANK! THIS IS PROFESSOR X! WAKE UP!

JEAN! YOU ARE UNINJURED! YOU MUST OPEN YOUR EYES!

PROFESSOR! I JUST REMEMBERED --MAGNETO IS *ALIVE!* HE'S *RETURNED!* I-I *SAW* HIM!

I *KNOW,* JEAN! HE TOOK US ALL BY SURPRISE, AND MANAGED TO *IMPRISON* US WITHIN THIS GONDOLA! WE'RE RISING *HIGHER* EVERY SECOND!

IT BEHOOVES US TO EVACUATE THIS CUBICLE BEFORE THE *AIR* IS DISSIPATED!

BUT OUR *FIRST* TASK AT HAND IS TO REVIVE SCOTT AND *WARREN!* YOU AND HANK SEE WHAT YOU CAN DO!

YOU'RE *RIGHT,* HANK, BUT *FIVE* HEADS ARE BETTER THAN *ONE!* WE'VE GOT TO UTILIZE *ALL* OUR POWER-- AND THAT MEANS SCOTT AND JEAN, TOO!

FIVE HEADS? ONE IS *MISSING!* WHAT ABOUT *ICEMAN?* DID HE *EVADE* MAGNETO'S TRAP?

HE'S STILL IN THE *HOSPITAL,* HANK! DON'T YOU REMEMBER? OH--*SCOTT* IS REVIVING!

EASY, BEASTIE-BOY-- EASY! THE HEAD IS *ATTACHED!* IT'S NOT *REMOVABLE!*

IT LOOKS *BAD,* WARREN! WE'RE TOO *HIGH* FOR ME TO BLAST AN OPENING IN THE GONDOLA! WE'D LOSE OUR *OXYGEN* IN SECONDS!

BUT WE'RE DOOMED IF WE *DON'T* GET OUT!

PROFESSOR-- HOW DID MAGNETO *DO* THIS TO US?? THE LAST WE SAW OF HIM, THE *STRANGER* WAS TAKING HIM TO ANOTHER GALAXY-- *FOREVER!**

WE'LL WORRY ABOUT THAT *LATER,* JEAN-- IF WE *SURVIVE* LONG ENOUGH!

YOUR TONE SEEMS TO IMPLY THAT OUR PLIGHT IS *HOPELESS!*

*IN THE UNFORGETTABLE ISH #11, REMEMBER? -STAN.

6

MEANWHILE, BACK AT THE SCHOOL WHICH HE HAS TAKEN OVER, THE MIGHTY *MAGNETO* PUTS HIS MOST FANTASTIC PLAN INTO OPERATION! BY MERELY HARNESSING THE LIMITLESS MAGNETIC POWER HE POSSESSES, THE MAD MUTANT GOES TO WORK WITH A VENGEANCE IN THE LABORATORY OF PROFESSOR X--!

NO LONGER WILL I HAVE TO SEARCH FOR NEW MUTANTS!

AT LAST I HAVE THE MEANS TO BUILD A VAST ARMY OF THEM-- AN ARMY TO SERVE ONLY *ME!*

AND, IT HAS ALL BEEN MADE POSSIBLE BECAUSE FATE LET THE *PARENTS* OF AN *X-MAN* FALL INTO MY HANDS!

THEY ARE ASLEEP IN THE ROOM NEXT DOOR--LITTLE DREAMING HOW *IMPORTANT* THEY ARE TO MY PLANS!

FOR, KNOWING THAT *THEY* GAVE BIRTH TO A MUTANT, I SHALL SECRETLY ANALYZE THEIR *BODY CELLS,* AND *DUPLICATE* THEM--!

THUS, I'LL BE ABLE TO CREATE *ADDITIONAL* MUTANTS, USING THE SAME CELL PATTERNS! IT SHALL BE SIMPLICITY ITSELF!

WHEN I AM DONE, MY ARMY OF MUTANT SLAVES WILL BE LARGE ENOUGH TO EASILY CONQUER ANY FORCE THAT MAN- KIND CAN THROW AGAINST IT!

I CANNOT FAIL! BY MEANS OF THIS *SELECTOR PANEL,* I CAN EVEN CONTROL THE *TYPE* OF MUTATION I DESIRE! *NOTHING* CAN HALT MY MARCH TOWARDS WORLD DOMINATION *NOW!*

7

AND, AT THAT MOMENT, IN A SMALL GONDOLA, DRIFTING HIGHER AND HIGHER INTO THE LONELY SUBSTRATOSPHERE...!

TRY YOUR *KINETIC POWER*, JEAN! PERHAPS YOU CAN *PUSH* US DOWN AGAIN!

I'LL KEEP WATCH OUT HERE-- TO SEE IF IT *WORKS!*

BUT, WHAT IF I *CAN'T* DO IT, PROFESSOR?

IT'S *GOT* TO WORK, JEAN! THE *OXYGEN* CAN'T LAST MUCH LONGER IN HERE!

THOU KIDS US NOT, SCOTTY!

WHILE *MARVEL GIRL* PREPARES TO FOCUS HER KINETIC POWER AT THE GONDOLA'S FLOOR, I'LL ATTEMPT TO MENTALLY LOCATE *MAGNETO*, AND SEE WHAT HE'S DOING!

SILENCE, PLEASE!

PROFESSOR! WHAT *IS* IT? I-I NEVER SAW YOU LOOK SO *SHOCKED* BEFORE!

IT'S THE *ANGEL'S PARENTS!* MAGNETO HAS *CAPTURED* THEM!

MY *MOM* AND *DAD.!??* NO! IT *CAN'T* BE! NOT *THEM!*

EASY, WARREN! GET A GRIP ON YOURSELF! WE'LL FIND A WAY TO SAVE THEM--AND *OURSELVES!*

BUT HOW? HOW?

ICEMAN IS THE KEY! *BACK AWAY*, ALL OF YOU! I MUST *THINK!* NOW--!

SECONDS LATER, IN THE SILENT HOSPITAL ROOM, A BRISK, COMMANDING *THOUGHT* FILLS THE AIR--!

BOBBY! BOBBY! THIS IS *PROFESSOR X!* CAN YOU *READ* ME? YOU'RE *NEEDED*, SON! YOU'RE *NEEDED!*

I--I READ YOU, SIR--!

I CAN TELL THAT THE SULFA DRUG HAS *HELPED* YOU! BUT YOU'RE STILL *WEAK!* DON'T TRY TO TALK--JUST FOLLOW MY ORDERS...!

LEAVE YOUR BED! SLOWLY--CAREFULLY--

YOU MUST LEAVE *UNNOTICED!* FORM AN *ICE SLIDE* AT THE WINDOW--!

NOW, *EXTEND* THE SLIDE AS YOU GO-- OVER THE ROOFTOPS --TOWARDS THE *SCHOOL!* GOOD! *GOOD!*

THEY *NEED* ME! THEY *NEED* ME!

8

I CONTACTED HIM! HE'S ON THE WAY!

BUT, WHAT CAN HE DO? HOW CAN HE FIGHT MAGNETO-- OR SAVE US-- ALL ALONE?

HE MAY BE THE YOUNGEST, BUT HE'S STILL AN X-MAN! LET'S WAIT AND SEE!

MEANWHILE, HOW IS JEAN DOING?

OUR ASCENT HAS HALTED! WE'RE NOT GOING ANY HIGHER!

I-I'VE ENOUGH POWER TO STOP US FROM RISING --BUT I CAN'T FORCE THE GONDOLA DOWN!

HOLD HER STEADY THEN! TRY NOT TO SPEAK-- WE MUST CONSERVE OUR OXYGEN!

I'LL COMMUNICATE WITH YOU TELEPATHICALLY NOW! I'M ABOUT TO PROJECT MY THOUGHTS DOWNWARD AGAIN, TO PROBE AT THE MIND OF MAGNETO HIMSELF!

PERHAPS BY SCANNING HIS MEMORY, I CAN LEARN HOW HE ESCAPED FROM THE STRANGER!

THEN, IN AN EFFORT TO RELAX HIS TENSE, WORRIED FELLOW CAPTIVES WHILE ICEMAN ENTERS THE FRAY, THE PROFESSOR RELATES THE IMAGES WHICH HE CAN DETECT IN MAGNETO'S MIND...

FOR MONTHS, I'VE ENDURED THE HUMILIATION OF BEING THE STRANGER'S PRISONER ON THIS DESERTED, FORSAKEN PLANET!

IT'S NOT DESERTED, MASTER! I'M HERE WITH YOU!

SILENCE, TOAD... YOU SNIVELLING, SPINELESS, FAWNING FOOL!

WE'VE BEEN ALLOWED TO ROAM AT WILL, BECAUSE THE ENTIRE PLANET IS A PRISON FOR US! BUT IT WON'T REMAIN SO MUCH LONGER!

IT'S LIKE AN INTER-GALACTIC MUSEUM, WITH RELICS FROM EVERY PART OF THE UNIVERSE!

BUT, IT'S THE GRAVEYARD OF OLD SPACESHIPS THAT INTERESTS ME THE MOST!

THIS IS WHERE THE STRANGER HAS UNDERESTIMATED ME! HE KNOWS THE ATOMIC PILES OF THESE SHIPS ARE OLD AND USELESS...

...USELESS TO ANYONE-- EXCEPT MAGNETO!

HEE HEEE! NOW I UNDER-STAND, MASTER! WITH THE STRANGER GONE TO SURVEY OTHER WORLDS, THIS IS OUR CHANCE TO ESCAPE!

PRECISELY! AT THE WAVE OF A HAND, I TRANSFORM THE IRON GATE AROUND THIS SHIP INTO A LADDER THAT WILL GRANT ME ACCESS TO THE HATCH ABOVE!

AS FOR THE ATOMIC POWER PLANT, I CAN ACTIVATE IT IN SECONDS BY MEANS OF MY MATCHLESS MAGNETIC POWER!

I KNEW IT, MASTER! I KNEW WE'D ESCAPE! NOBODY CAN IMPRISON MAGNETO!

9

YOU KNEW *WE'D* ESCAPE?? YOU BRAINLESS, INCONSEQUENTIAL *CLOD!* THIS IS WHERE ONE LIKE YOU *BELONGS!*

NO, MASTER --*NO!* YOU CAN'T LEAVE ME BEHIND! *MASTER--!*

COME BACK, MASTER-- *COME BACK--!*

EVEN THE *STRANGER,* BRILLIANT AND OMNIPOTENT AS HE IS, *UNDERESTIMATED* MAGNETO'S GREAT, INCALCULABLE *POWER!*

BUT, *NOW,* THERE'S NOT A MOMENT TO LOSE! I MUST CONTACT *ICEMAN* AGAIN-- TO GIVE HIM HIS *FINAL INSTRUCTION!* AND THEN--THE MOST IMPORTANT PART OF ALL--

I'LL MARSHAL ALL MY REMAINING STRENGTH-- HARNESS ALL MY ENERGY-- FOR THE MOST DIFFICULT *THOUGHT PROJECTION* OF MY LIFE!

AS FOR THE *REST* OF YOU--DO NOT SPEAK-- DO NOT MOVE-- WE MUST NOT WASTE ONE PRECIOUS IOTA OF OUR REMAINING OXYGEN--!

BUT, PROFESSOR-- HOW CAN WE EXPECT *ICEMAN* TO SUCCEED AGAINST MAGNETO WHEN *WE'VE* ALL FAILED??

BOBBY WILL HAVE ONE ADVANTAGE-- HE *KNOWS* WHO THE ENEMY IS! NOW *SILENCE,* ALL OF YOU!

AND, MINUTES LATER, AN ICY, CRYSTALLINE FIGURE GLIDES NOISELESSLY OVER THE WALL OF *"PROFESSOR XAVIER'S SCHOOL FOR GIFTED YOUNGSTERS"!*

THERE IS NO MORE THAT I CAN *TELL* YOU, ICEMAN! I MUST NOW SEND MY THOUGHTS *ELSEWHERE!* OUR FATE IS IN *YOUR HANDS,* BOBBY DRAKE!

I STILL FEEL KINDA WOOZY-- BUT THIS IS NO TIME TO START *PAMPERING* MYSELF!

THERE'S A LIGHT ON IN THE *LAB!* THAT MUST BE WHERE *MAGNETO* IS!

I DON'T KNOW IF I CAN STALL HIM OR *NOT,* BUT IF I FAIL, IT WON'T BE FOR LACK OF *TRYING!*

10

FIRST OFF, A LITTLE CLIMB CAN'T BOTHER A FELLA WHO CAN BUILD HIMSELF AN *ICE LADDER!*

I CAN *HEAR* HIM MOVING --UP ABOVE!

MAGNETO! AFTER ALL THIS TIME -- THE VERY *SIGHT* OF HIM STILL FILLS ME WITH DREAD--WITH *AWE!*

THERE'S ALMOST *NO LIMIT* TO HIS *POWER!* WITH HIS STRENGTH, HIS BUILT-IN *MAGNETISM*, HE CAN ACCOMPLISH *ANYTHING!*

AND YET, I'VE *GOT* TO OVER-COME HIM--SOME-HOW!

BUT, IN HIS WEAKENED CONDITION, THE VALIANT TEEN-AGER MOMENTARILY LOSES HIS BALANCE, AND TOTTERS!

THE LADDER IS *TIPPING BACK!* CAN'T STRAIGHTEN IT IN TIME!

BUT--IF I *FALL* FROM THIS HEIGHT --I'LL BE *FINISHED!*

DESPERATELY, USING EVERY OUNCE OF STAMINA, EVERY BIT OF SKILL HE POSSESSES, *ICEMAN* WHIPS A THIN, FROZEN *CABLE* TOWARDS THE ROOFTOP-- SNAGGING THE *EDGE* AT THE FINAL, FATEFUL SECOND--!

CAN'T *FAIL* NOW! NOT JUST FOR *MYSELF*-- THE *OTHERS* ARE COUNTING ON ME!

I-I DID IT!!

CLANNNK!

WHILE INSIDE THE BUILDING, *MAGNETO* IS SO CONFIDENT OF HIS OWN SECURITY--SO WRAPPED UP IN HIS INCREDIBLE EXPERIMENTATION, THAT HE HEARS NOTHING--PERCEIVES NOTHING, SAVE WHAT OCCURS WITHIN THE WALLS OF HIS LABORATORY--!

EVERYTHING IS IN READINESS, AT LAST! ALL THAT REMAINS IS FOR ME TO SET MY DEVICES IN *MOTION!*

AND, TO MAKE MY TRIUMPH *DOUBLY* SWEET, I HAVE THE KNOWLEDGE THAT MY GREATEST ENEMIES-- THE ONLY ONES WHO HAVE EVER DEFEATED ME, ARE HELPLESSLY TRAPPED, HIGH ABOVE EARTH!

THUS, WHILE MY ARMY OF INVINCIBLE MUTANTS IS BEING *BORN*, THE ACCURSED *X-MEN* ARE FACING THEIR OWN INEVITABLE *DOOM!*

11

AND NOW TO *BEGIN!*

BY MEANS OF MY *SELECTOR PANEL*, I'LL ACTUALLY CONTROL THE *SIZE* AND THE *STRENGTH* OF THE MUTANTS I CREATE!

THEY'LL BE THE *SUPERIOR* OF ANY *HUMAN* ON EARTH!

ONLY THE MATCHLESS POWER OF *MAGNETO* WILL EXCEED THEIR OWN!

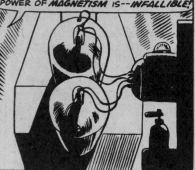

SUDDENLY, THE ROOM GROWS DARK, AS GLISTENING WAVES OF IONIC ENERGY CAST A STARTLING GLOW, RIPPLING THE AIR AROUND THE SOFTLY HUMMING MAIN MAGNETIC FIELD--!

IT'S WORKING! MORE THAN ANY OTHER FORCE ON EARTH, THE POWER OF *MAGNETISM* IS--*INFALLIBLE!*

AND NOW, MY MUTANT PRODUCTION LINE IS BEGINNING TO TAKE FORM! FROM ORIGINAL CONCEPTION TO FINAL CREATION, THE PROCESS IS *PERFECT!* SUPER-POWERFUL SLAVES OF MAGNETO--EACH LIKE AN *ARMY* UNTO HIMSELF--!!!

I'LL CONTINUE TO PRODUCE THEM--IN THE TENS--HUNDREDS --THOUSANDS--*MILLIONS*-- UNTIL THEIR NUMBER IS *INCALCULABLE!!* THEY'LL OVER-RUN THE EARTH--CONQUERING ALL--IN THE NAME OF *MAGNETO!!*

BUT, SUDDENLY--

THE PROCESS HAS BEEN *HALTED!* IT ISN'T *POSSIBLE!* AND YET-- SOME-ONE-- OR SOME-THING-- IS *FIGHTING* ME!

12

AND, IN THE ADJACENT ROOM, A FRANTIC TEEN-AGER, QUICKLY REALIZING THE *SOURCE* OF MAGNETO'S *MAD* PLAN, HASTILY ERECTS AN *ICE BARRIER* BETWEEN THE TWO SLEEPING VICTIMS AND THE MAD MUTANT'S *BODY CELL SELECTOR*--!!

THIS IS SURE TO BRING MAGNETO, BUT IT CAN'T BE HELPED--!

I'VE GOT TO *HALT* HIS MUTANT MACHINE-- ANY WAY I *CAN!*

BUT, ICEMAN'S WORST FEAR IS REALIZED WITHIN *SECONDS*...

THE SOURCE OF THE INTERFERENCE MUST COME FROM-- AHHH..! *HIM!!*

THE *FINAL* X-MAN --THE *YOUNGEST*-- THE *WEAKEST* OF THEM ALL! HE *DARES* TO CHALLENGE *ME!!!*

ICEMAN!! YOUR FOOLHARDY TAMPERING WITH MY MASTER PLAN WILL AVAIL YOU *NOTHING*-- EXCEPT YOUR OWN CERTAIN *DESTRUCTION!*

SLAMM!!

I KNEW HE'D COME AFTER ME! BUT AT LEAST I'VE STOPPED HIM FOR *NOW!*

I'LL DESTROY YOU WITH A *GESTURE!* EVERY OBJECT IN THE ROOM WILL BECOME A DEADLY --- *THREAT*--!

NOTHING CAN OVERCOME THE POWER OF SUPREME *MAGNETISM!!*

NO? HOW ABOUT A QUICKLY FORMED *ICE SHIELD*, BRAGGART?

SWWOOOSH!

BUT THIS WON'T HOLD HIM OFF FOR LONG! I'VE GOT TO MOVE *FAST!*

WHILE HE'S BLINDED BY HIS OWN FLYING OBJECTS, I'LL USE MY SHIELD AS A *SLED* AND TAKE OFF!

WHIZZZ

YOU YOUNG *FOOL!* DO YOU THINK THERE'S ANY PLACE IN THIS BUILDING-- ANY PLACE ON *EARTH*-- WHERE YOU'LL BE *SAFE* FROM *ME??!*

SWOOOSH!

13

BUT, BEFORE MAGNETO CAN MAKE ANOTHER MOVE...

AN *ICE TUNNEL!* I'M *SLIDING* INTO IT...

IT *WORKED!* NOW HE'LL *HAVE* TO FOLLOW ME DOWN INTO THE *TRAP* I'VE SET FOR HIM! HE WON'T BE ABLE TO USE HIS MAGNETIC POWERS WHILE HE'S *OFF-BALANCE!*

YOU'RE ONLY DELAYING THE *INEVITABLE!* YOU CAN'T HOLD ME OFF MUCH *LONGER!*

HE MAY BE *RIGHT!* BUT I'VE NO OTHER CHOICE! IF I DON'T *STOP* HIM, MANKIND WILL BE IN GREATER DANGER THAN IT'S EVER *KNOWN!*

I *DID* IT! I GOT HIM INTO THE *IGLOO* I BUILT, OUTSIDE THE SCHOOL!

NOW TO ESCAPE THRU THE OPENING I PREPARED FOR MYSELF!

BUT, THE MIGHTY MUTANT MENACE TAKES IN THE SITUATION AT A GLANCE, AND, BEFORE ICEMAN CAN EFFECT HIS ESCAPE--!

THIS CHARADE HAS GONE ON *LONG ENOUGH!* MY PATIENCE IS *EXHAUSTED!* NOW, YOU SHALL FEEL THE POWER OF *MAGNETO* AS FEW HAVE EVER FELT IT *BEFORE!!*

OH *NO!* HE *SEALED* THE OPENING UP... MAGNETICALLY!

I'M STILL TOO *WEAK* AFTER MY BOUT IN THE HOSPITAL! IT SLOWED ME DOWN! BUT I'VE GOT TO DO SOME-THING--!

14

THE IGLOO *SHATTERS* UNDER THE IMPACT OF CYCLOPS' *POWER RAY!*

KRUNCH!!

BUT MAGNETO IS FAR *STRONGER* THAN ANY FRIGID BARRIER!

I AM WELL AWARE THAT IT WILL BE LONG *MINUTES* BEFORE YOUR POWER BLAST RETURNS TO FULL STRENGTH-- AFTER SUCH A *DRAIN* UPON IT!

THUS, IT IS THE POWER OF *MAGNETO* THAT SHALL NOW TURN THE TIDE!

X-MEN-- PREPARE FOR YOUR FINAL *FATE*--!

EVERYONE PREPARES IN HIS OWN *FASHION*, YOU MAGNETIC MISANTHROPE!

PERSONALLY, THIS IS *MY* WAY OF ANTICIPATING THE INEVITABLE!

AND *THIS*-- IS *MINE!!*

SHEER BESTIAL STRENGTH IS *NOTHING* TO THE POWER OF *MAGNETISM!*

BUT, LET *NO MAN* THINK THAT *WITHOUT* HIS POWER, MAGNETO IS NOT *STILL* THE EQUAL OF *ANY!*

WHOK

GOOD WORK, BEAST! YOU HELD HIM OFF LONG ENOUGH FOR MY *FORCE BEAM* TO REACH PEAK INTENSITY AGAIN!

BUT YOU SHALL *NOT* USE IT, CYCLOPS!

BACK-- ALL OF YOU-- OR ICEMAN DIES!

NO.!!

GET HIM! YOU CAN *DO* IT-- IF YOU WORK TOGETHER!! I DON'T MATTER! I'LL GIVE MY LIFE-- *GLADLY*-- TO RID THE WORLD-- OF HIM.!!

17

YOU THINK WE'RE TOO *TIMID* TO TAKE CHANCES? THIS IS THE *SECOND* TIME YOU'VE UNDER-ESTIMATED US -- AND IT'LL BE THE *LAST!*

BRAVE WORDS, ICEMAN -- BUT UTTERLY *MEANINGLESS!* I WOULD SACRIFICE *ANY-ONE* TO ACHIEVE MY AIMS -- BUT YOUR FELLOW X-MEN ARE TOO -- *WHA--?* THE ANGEL!

THEN, AS THE MANIACAL, MENACING MUTANT MOMENTARILY DUCKS HIS HEAD IN A NATURAL REFLEX ACTION --

IT *WORKED!* I *GOT* HIM!

ICEMAN IS *SAFE!* NOW WE CAN ATTACK AT WILL!

BAH! YOU'VE DONE *NOTHING* BUT DELAY YOUR ULTIMATE DEFEAT!

NONE OF YOU HAVE THE STRENGTH TO RESIST MY MAGNETIC ONSLAUGHT!! SEE HOW EASILY I HOLD YOU AT BAY WITH A FEW PALTRY GESTURES!

THAT'S *IT!* DUCK *UNDER* MY DEADLY ATTACK -- AS I *EXPECTED* YOU TO DO!

NOW, ALL I NEED DO IS UNLEASH A *MAXIMUM MAGNETIC VOLLEY* AT THE GROUND ITSELF, AND YOU'LL *NEVER RISE AGAIN!*

I'VE GOT TO GET MY *POWER BEAM* PAST HIS MAGNETIC FIELD! IF *THAT* DOESN'T WORK -- WE'RE *DONE* FOR!

NOW!

IT'S *NO GOOD!* HE WAS *EXPECTING* IT!

HE'S *REPELLING* YOUR BEAM, CYKE! IT'S NOT *STRONG* ENOUGH!

YOU'VE GOT TO *INCREASE* THE INTENSITY -- *SOMEHOW!*

BUT THEN, AN URGENT, COMMANDING *VOICE* RINGS OUT --!

STOP! DON'T FIGHT ANY LONGER!

IT'S THE *PROFESSOR!!*

HE -- HE WANTS US TO *GIVE UP?!!*

NOW *MAGNETO* SEES HIM! HE'S APPROACHING HIM! AND -- THE PROFESSOR IS *HELPLESS* --!

18

AHH! NOW MY VICTORY SHALL BE COMPLETE!

YOU ARE THE MOST DANGEROUS FOE OF ALL! SO YOU MUST BE MY FIRST VICTIM!

IT'S YOU WHO SHALL BE THE VICTIM, MAGNETO!

LOOK ABOVE YOU--AND SEE YOUR FATE!

IT WON'T WORK! I CAN'T BE TRICKED SO EASILY!

IT'S NO TRICK, MADMAN! I KNEW THERE WAS ONE SURE WAY TO DEFEAT YOU--AND ONLY I COULD ACCOMPLISH IT! SO, WHILE MY VALIANT X-MEN HELD YOU AT BAY--

--I SENT MY THOUGHTS OUT INTO THE INFINITE--AND FINALLY FOUND THE ONE I SOUGHT--!

YOU WEREN'T LYING! IT--IT'S THE STRANGER! HE'S COMING FOR ME AGAIN! HE MUSTN'T GET ME! HE MUSTN'T!

THEN--THAT'S WHAT THE PROFESSOR MEANT BY THE MOST DIFFICULT THOUGHT PROJECTION OF HIS LIFE!

MAGNETO'S MAGNA-CAR WAS NEARBY! HE'S GONE!

BUT THE STRANGER CHANGED COURSE! HE'S GOING AFTER HIM!

I WONDER IF WE'LL EVER KNOW WHAT HAPPENS TO THEM?

I'D BETTER RECONNOITER AND--EUREKA!!

WHAT'S TRANSPIRING IN THERE!

IT'S WARREN'S PARENTS! I PUT A PROTECTIVE ICE SHIELD OVER THEM! ARE THEY OKAY, HANK?

AS FAR AS I CAN TELL!

I'VE GOT TO SEE THEM! IF THEY'VE BEEN HARMED BY MAGNETO--!!!

THAT STEADY HUM! IT'S MAGNETO'S MUTANT-CREATING MACHINE!

NO SWEAT, WARREY! THEY'RE OKAY--HONEST!

WE'VE GOT TO FIND IT--AND SMASH IT!

IT'S DIRECTLY AHEAD, SCOTTY!

...HUMMMMMMM

19

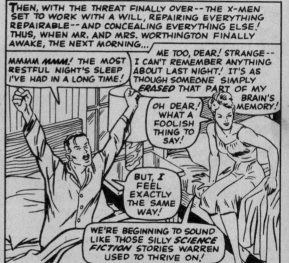

SORRY, BOBBY! DIDN'T MEAN TO SPOIL YOUR *AIM!*

THWANNG!

YEESH! NOW I MISSED THE WHOLE *TARGET!*

YEEOOWW!

THAT'S OKAY, WARRY! I DIDN'T MEAN TO TOSS A MESS OF ICE FLAKES AT YOU, EITHER!

ICEMAN! NO CLOWNING AROUND TILL THE SESSION'S *OVER!*

SORRY, CYKE! I THOUGHT WE WERE *FINISHED!*

UH OH! DON'T TRY ANYTHING, ANGEL-- UNLESS YOU WANNA GET TICKLED WITH THIS ICY TOOTHPICK!

YOU, MASTER ROBERT DRAKE, ESQUIRE, ARE *ASKING* FOR IT--!

I SAID-- NO CLOWNING AROUND!

CYKE'S POWER BEAM!

WHOK!

GOSH, SCOTTY, CAN'TCHA TAKE A *JOKE?*

NOT WHEN THE PROF MADE YOUR TRAINING *MY* RESPONSIBILITY!

HE'S *RIGHT*, BOBBY!

SORRY, CYKE! WE'LL BOTH COOL IT NOW!

LET'S KNOCK IT OFF!

OKAY, LET'S ALL BUCKLE DOWN AGAIN!

IT'S TIME TO TRY TO BEAT YOUR OWN SPEED RECORD ON THE TRAPDOOR-OBSTACLE COURSE, HANK!

JUST TO EASE THE BOREDOM THIS TIME, I'LL ATTEMPT TO NEGOTIATE THE MANEUVER ON *ONE* HAND!

WAIT! WHAT OF THE *DANGER?*

TOO LATE! HE'S OFF!

FEAR NOT, GROUP! THE *BEAST* SHALL PERSEVERE!

CAREFUL, BOY--!

KLUMP THUMP

2

AN ANNOUNCEMENT! IS THERE SOME NEW DANGER AWAITING US?

NO NEED TO LOOK SO GRIM, SCOTT! ALL MY ANNOUNCEMENTS AREN'T NECESSARILY HARBINGERS OF TROUBLE!

SINCE YOUR BOUTS WITH THE SENTINELS AND WITH MAGNETO IN THE PAST FEW MONTHS, I'VE BEEN WAITING FOR YOU TO BECOME FULLY RECOVERED AND TO ATTAIN YOUR FIGHTING PEAK AGAIN!

WE'RE AS FIT NOW AS WE'LL EVER BE, SIR!

I AGREE, HENRY--!

AND THAT'S THE REASON I'VE DECIDED IT'S TIME YOU HAD A LITTLE VACATION!

WOW! YOU SAID THE MAGIC WORD!

MMMM! TIME OFF! A CHANCE TO BUY NEW CLOTHES!

LOOK OUT, GIRLS! HERE I COME!

LEAVE US NOT WASTE A MINUTE, BOBBY BOY!

THE PROF IS RIGHT! THEY'VE EARNED IT!

HANG ON, BEASTIE! WE'LL LEAVE VIA MY ICE EXPRESS!

LEAD ON, MACDUFF!

I'LL CONTACT YOU MENTALLY WHEN IT'S TIME TO RETURN!

IF ANY ICE MELTS ON THE FLOOR, I'M NOT MOPPING IT UP, BOBBY DRAKE!

IF ONLY I DARED TO ASK JEAN FOR A DATE--! BUT, I HAVEN'T THE RIGHT-- SO LONG AS MY POWER BEAM IS AN EVER-PRESENT DANGER!

HOW ABOUT A DOUBLE-DATE, SCOTTY BOY?

SORRY, WARREN! I'VE GOT OTHER PLANS--!

LATER THAT DAY, ON THE STEPS OF THE PUBLIC LIBRARY, IN THE CITY, WE FIND...

IT'S LUCKY THAT ZELDA DOESN'T WORK AT THE COFFEE HOUSE TODAY, HANK!

I'M RATHER APPREHENSIVE, THOUGH-- ABOUT THE BLIND DATE SHE PROCURED FOR ME!

CHEER UP, BUDDY! ANY GAL IS BETTER THAN NO GAL!

THERE ARE TIMES, MY FROSTBITTEN FRIEND, WHEN YOUR WISDOM VERILY BELIES YOUR YEARS!

ZELDA'S NOT HERE YET! WE MIGHT AS WELL CASE THE OTHER CHICKS!

IF IT'S ALL THE SAME TO YOU, I'LL JUST PERUSE THE TANTALIZING TOMES I SEE BEFORE ME!

"OUR FRIENDS, THE BEASTS"! A MOST PROPITIOUS TITLE!

IF YOU HAVEN'T NOTICED, THESE BOOKS ARE FOR PRE-SCHOOL AGE CHILDREN!

MY DEAR YOUNG LADY, AS A FREE CITIZEN IN A FREE SOCIETY, IT BEHOOVES ME TO--

HEY, HANK! I DON'T GET IT! HERE COMES ZELDA-- AND SHE'S ALL BY HER LONESOME!

GOSH! I GUESS HER FRIEND COULDN'T MAKE IT!

JUST AS WELL! I'M BEGINNING TO FIND THE COMPANY OF FEMALES SOMEWHAT TRYING!

WELL! AREN'T YOU THE GALLANT ONE!

HI, ZEL! WHERE'S HANK'S DATE?

RIGHT HERE, NATCH! THAT'S WHY I WANTED TO MEET IN THE LIBRARY! VERA WORKS HERE PART-TIME! I THOUGHT YOU'D ALREADY MET!

WADDAYA KNOW! YOU WERE TALKING TO YOUR DATE!

NOW THEY TELL ME!

DO YOU ALWAYS BLUSH THAT WAY, MR. McCOY?

IT'S THE ONLY WAY I KNOW!

4

HAVE YOU EVER NOTICED HOW *DANGER* CAN APPEAR WHEN YOU LEAST EXPECT IT? FOR EXAMPLE, AS OUR FAR-OUT FOURSOME LEAVES THE LIBRARY...

OH *DEAR!* THERE'S CALVIN RANKIN COMING TOWARDS US!

IS HE A BOY FRIEND OF YOURS, VERA?

NO! BUT HE'S BEEN *WANTING* TO BE! AND--HE'S SO *HOT-TEMPERED!*

SO! YOU DIDN'T HAVE TIME FOR A DATE WITH *ME* TODAY--BUT HERE YOU ARE ARM-IN-ARM WITH *THAT* CREEP!

BOY! IS MR. RANKIN HEADIN' FOR A *FAT LIP!*

IF YOU'RE REFERRING TO *ME*--! I DON'T HAVE TO ANSWER TO YOU FOR ANYTHING, CALVIN!

JUST BECAUSE I'VE HELPED YOU LOCATE THE BOOKS YOU WANTED ON *MINE ENGINEERING,* THAT DOESN'T MEAN YOU CAN TELL ME WHOM TO *DATE!*

OH *NO??*

ALL RIGHT, SON! WE ARE NO LONGER AMUSED!

NOBODY ASKED *YOU* TO BUTT IN.! I'LL KNOCK YOU CLEAR BACK TO *SQUARESVILLE!*

HEY! I NEVER SAW ANY-ONE *DODGE* SO FAST BEFORE!

OBVIOUSLY YOU'RE NOT THE *OBSERVANT* TYPE! AND NOW, IT'S *MY* TURN AT BAT--!

BUT THEN, AS HANK McCOY SWINGS EASILY, NOT WANTING TO TAKE UNFAIR ADVANTAGE OF HIS ENRAGED FOE, HE IS ASTONISHED TO SEE--

HE SIDE-STEPPED MY BLOW AS EFFORTLESSLY AS *I* HAD OUT-MANEUVERED *HIM!*

BUT *NOBODY* IS AS AGILE AS THE *BEAST!*

NOBODY *NORMAL,* THAT IS!

HAH! MISSED ME BY A MILE!

CALVIN! HANK! STOP IT! THERE'S NO NEED FOR A COMMON *STREET BRAWL!*

IT *CAN'T* BE! HE'S LEAPING AROUND LIKE-- THE *BEAST!*

NOW THAT I KICKED MY *SHOES* OFF, I'LL *REALLY* GO TO TOWN!

IT'S *INCREDIBLE!* HE ACTUALLY POSSESSES *MY* POWERS!

BUT, I DON'T DARE *USE* THEM MYSELF--IT WOULD MEAN REVEALING MY *X-MAN* IDENTITY TO THE GIRLS!

AND THEN, THE CROWNING HUMILIATION--!

BOK!

SWEET DREAMS, STUPID!

5

6

THEN, FINALLY--

-:WHEW!:- I'M BUSHED! THAT WAS SOME WORKOUT! BUT, I GOT MYSELF ALL OVER-HEATED!

I'LL WHIP UP SOME ICE TO COOL OFF WITH!

OH, NO! I CAN'T DO IT!--ONLY A FEW DROPLETS--AND EVEN THEY'RE MELTING AWAY!

I SHOULD HAVE KNOWN! MY POWERS HAVE VANISHED!

IN MY EXCITEMENT, I FORGOT THAT MY POWERS ONLY LAST FOR A SHORT TIME-- ONLY WHILE I'M NEAR THE ONE I'M MIMICKING!

I'VE GOT TO REGAIN THOSE POWERS--AND MORE! I MUST --TO CARRY OUT MY PLAN!

THUMP!

HOWEVER, BEFORE WE LEARN WHAT CALVIN RANKIN'S STRANGE PLAN IS, LET'S SEE WHERE HE POPS UP NEXT--

-:MMMM!:- WHAT A WONDERFUL SHOPPING TOUR! A PITY A GIRL HAS TO RUN OUT OF MONEY SO SOON!

I'LL JUST STOP FOR A QUICK SNACK BEFORE RETURNING TO THE SCHOOL!

BETTER RUSH IF I WANT A TABLE!

OH! I'M SORRY! I DIDN'T SEE YOU WITH THAT TRAY!

BOK!

HEY! WATCH IT!

NEXT TIME LOOK WHERE YOU'RE GOING! IF YOU WEREN'T A GIRL, I'D PASTE YA ONE!

AND IF I WEREN'T A LADY, I'D TELL YOU WHAT I THINK OF YOUR MANNERS!

I'VE NEVER SEEN SUCH A NASTY-TEMPERED SPECIMEN!

IF I WEREN'T AFRAID OF REVEALING MY IDENTITY, I'D TELEKINETICALLY TOSS HIM INTO A POT OF STEW!

8

NUTTY FEMALES! THEY'RE ALL ALIKE!

NOW, WHERE'S THE BLASTED SUGAR? OOH--ON THE NEXT TABLE! I'LL HAVETA GET IT!

WHY COULDN'T IT BE ON MY TABLE IN THE FIRST PLACE?!!

HOLY SMOKE! IT'S COMIN' RIGHT TO ME -- BY ITSELF!

ALL I HADDA DO WAS THINK ABOUT IT!

THE TOWN MUST BE CRAWLIN' WITH X-MEN!

MY LUCK'S COME BACK AGAIN! THAT CHICK HASTA BE MARVEL GIRL--THE ONE WITH THE POWER OF TELE-KINESIS!

IF I FOLLOW HER, SHE'S SURE TO LEAD ME TO THE OTHERS!

THE NEXT DAY--AS THE X-MEN CLUE THEIR LEADER IN--

IT'S TRUE, PROFESSOR! HE HAD THE SAME, IDENTICAL POWERS AS BOBBY AND I!

IT'S INCREDIBLE! YET, HE CAN'T BE A MUTANT! MY CEREBRO MACHINE REGISTERS NEGATIVE!

COULDN'T CEREBRO BE WRONG, SIR?

IMPOSSIBLE! IT WILL RESPOND TO THE PRESENCE OF A MUTANT WITHIN A HUNDRED-MILE RADIUS OF HERE! BUT, WE MUST LEARN HIS SECRET!

THE DOORBELL! IT'S HIM! I CAN MENTALLY CONFIRM HIS PRESENCE! ADMIT HIM, HANK!

R-R-R-RING

AND SO...

HI! I'M SORRY FOR THE WAY I TANGLED WITH YOU YESTERDAY! I CAME TO APOLOGIZE-- AND TO ASK IF I CAN JOIN YOU!

THAT DECISION IS THE PROFESSOR'S PREROGATIVE! COME IN!

THE FOOL! HE THINKS I MEAN IT!

HE KNOWS WHO WE ARE!

9

HE'S TRYING TO PROBE MY MIND! BUT NOW I'VE GOT HIS MENTAL POWER-- SO I CAN BLOCK HIM!

FOR THE FIRST TIME, I SENSE A BRAIN AS POWERFUL AS MINE! HE COULD BE THE GREATEST DANGER WE'VE EVER FACED!

I'D LIKE YOU TO MEET THE OTHERS...

CALVIN RANKIN'S MY NAME!

I'M JEAN GREY! I BUMPED INTO YOU YESTERDAY, AT THE CAFETERIA! I'M GLAD YOU'RE IN A BETTER MOOD NOW!

IF YOU'RE WONDERING HOW I GOT HERE--IT'S 'CAUSE I FOLLOWED YOU FROM THAT PLACE!

THEN, AFTER SCOTT SUMMERS HAS INTRODUCED HIMSELF...

A GLOW! APPEARING BEHIND HIS SMOKED GLASSES! AS THOUGH HIS EYES HAVE SUDDENLY BEEN ENDOWED WITH A POWER LIKE MINE!

GLAD TO SEE YA, SUMMERS! MAYBE A LOT MORE GLAD THAN YOU SUSPECT!

WARREN WORTHINGTON III, HUH? PUT IT THERE, PAL!

HE'S GOTTA BE THE ANGEL!

I FEEL A SWELLING STARTING TO APPEAR ON MY BACK! LIKE WINGS GETTING READY TO SPOUT!

HELLO, RANKIN!

WE MUST PLAY ALONG WITH HIM --ACT AS THOUGH WE TRUST HIM-- UNTIL WE LEARN THE EXTENT OF HIS POWER!

HI, DRAKE! I REMEMBER YOU, ALL RIGHT!

I DIDN'T LIKE YOU WHEN WE MET YESTERDAY--

GOOD! I FEEL AS THOUGH I CAN ICE UP AGAIN, ANY TIME I WANT TO!

--AND I HAVEN'T CHANGED MY MIND A BIT TODAY!

MY SENTIMENTS EXACTLY, RANKIN! I CAN'T FATHOM WHY YOU'RE HERE, BUT I SUSPECT YOUR MOTIVES ARE LESS THAN ALTRUISTIC!

THAT'S ENOUGH, HANK! REMEMBER--CALVIN RANKIN IS A GUEST!

BUT AN UNINVITED ONE, SIR!

NONE OF 'EM TRUST ME! BUT SO WHAT? IT'S TOO LATE FOR THEM TO SAVE THEMSELVES NOW!

10

MINUTES LATER...

PROFESSOR! WHY DID YOU PERMIT HIM TO GO UPSTAIRS? HE'LL LEARN ALL ABOUT US!

IT'S TOO LATE FOR SECRECY NOW! HE ALREADY KNOWS WHO WE ARE! AND HE FEELS HE'S POWERFUL ENOUGH TO DEFEAT US ALL!

WHAT ARE WE GONNA DO ABOUT IT?

IT'S TIME TO DON YOUR X-MEN COSTUMES! WHEN HE RETURNS-- IT WILL BE TO CHALLENGE US!

AND, EVEN AS THE PROFESSOR SPEAKS--

I HAD TO GET OFF ALONE HERE FOR A MINUTE-- MY SHOES WERE KILLIN' ME SINCE MY FEET GOT AS BIG AS THE BEAST'S!

IT'S A GOOD THING I PREPARED AN OUTFIT FOR MYSELF TO WEAR--!

IT'LL BE A PLEASURE TO GET THIS TIGHT BINDER OFF--

I CAN'T WAIT TO SEE THE RESULT--!

I KNEW IT! ALL I HADDA DO WAS BE NEAR THE ANGEL!

LOOKS LIKE I'M ALL SET NOW!

THAT MEANS IT'S TIME FOR ME TO TACKLE THE LOT OF 'EM!

OKAY, X-MEN! THERE'S NO NEED FOR ANY MORE PRE-TENDING!

I INTEND TO DEFEAT YOU ALL! AND, REST ASSURED--THE MIMIC HAS THE POWER TO DO IT!

I CAN'T LOSE--BECAUSE I POSSESS ALL OF YOUR OWN ABILITIES--INCLUDING THE MENTAL POWER OF PROF. X!

PROFESSOR! IT ISN'T POSSIBLE! HE'S LIKE A COMBINATION OF ALL OF US!

HE DIDN'T HAVE THOSE WINGS WHEN HE FIRST ARRIVED!

NO! OBVIOUSLY HE CAN ONLY "MIMIC" OTHERS WHEN HE DRAWS NEAR TO THEM.

YOU ALL LOOK FEARFUL-- AND I DON'T BLAME YOU!

NOW I'LL PROVE I'M MIGHTIER THAN ALL OF YOU!

THE MIMIC! SOMEONE WITH THE ABILITY TO DUPLICATE OUR OWN SUPER-POWERED FEATS!

HOW CAN WE FIGHT A GUY LIKE THAT??

LOOK OUT! HE'S READY TO ATTACK!

11

THEN, SUDDENLY, THE *MIMIC* HURTLES UPWARD, PROPELLED BY A LEAP OF *BEAST*-LIKE AGILITY--

THOOM!

INSTANTLY, A MENTAL COMMAND FROM *PROFESSOR X* RINGS OUT--

ANGEL! I DON'T KNOW WHAT HE'S PLANNING-- BUT *STOP HIM!*

IT'LL BE A *PLEASURE,* SIR!

BUT, BEFORE THE HIGH-FLYING *ANGEL* CAN REACH HIS PREY, THE *MIMIC* REVERSES HIMSELF IN FLIGHT, AND...

HAH! UNLIKE YOU, I'VE GOT MORE THAN A PAIR OF WINGS!

BAM!

--UNHHH!-- HE ATTACKED THE WAY THE *BEAST* WOULD-- IF HANK COULD ALSO *FLY!*

WHO'S *NEXT?* I'LL TAKE YOU ONE AT A TIME, OR ALL AT ONCE!

JEAN! STOP ANGEL'S FALL-- TELEKINETICALLY!

ICEMAN! KEEP THE *MIMIC* AT BAY WITH AN *ICE JAVELIN*--WHILE I TRY TO SINGE HIS WINGS!

GOTCHA, CYKE!

DID YOU FORGET-- I HAVE THE SAME POWER--AND THE SAME *DEFENSES* --AS YOU DO!

BROAK!

HAH!

HE MIMICKED MY *POWER BEAM* TO SHATTER THE *JAVELIN*--AND STOPPED MY *OWN* BEAM WITH AN *ICE SHIELD!*

HE'S LANDING! HE THINKS WE'RE BEATEN!

STAY BACK, ALL OF YOU! I'LL TACKLE HIM --ALONE!

NO! HE'S TOO STRONG--TOO UNPREDICTABLE! YOU MUST FIGHT AS A *TEAM!*

HAH! THANKS FOR YOUR POWERS, X-MEN--!

NOW I'M GONNA USE 'EM TO DEFEAT THE WHOLE *LOT* OF YOU!

12

14

MY ONLY *WEAKNESS* IS THE FACT THAT MY POWERS *FADE* WHEN THE ONE I'M MIMICKING ISN'T NEAR ME!

BUT, MY FATHER'S *MACHINE* WILL MAKE MY POWERS *PERMANENT!* ALL I HAVE TO DO IS FIND A WAY TO *REACH* THE MACHINE--BEHIND ALL THOSE TONS OF RUBBLE!

MY WINGS ARE *FULL SIZE* NOW! SO I KNOW THE *X-MEN* ARE JUST OUTSIDE THE CAVE!

THAT MEANS I CAN USE PROFESSOR X'S *MIND POWER* AT LAST!

IT'S *WORKING!* THE MENTAL POWER I'M NOW ABLE TO MIMIC FROM THE PROFESSOR CAN EASILY LOCATE THE EXACT SPOT WHERE THE *MACHINE* LIES BURIED!

THE *FOOLS!* THEY DON'T SUSPECT THAT I *WANTED* THEM TO FOLLOW ME-- SO I COULD USE THEIR OWN POWERS TO DEFEAT THEM--AND THE ENTIRE *WORLD!*

HAH! I KNEW CYCLOPS WOULD HAVE TO BE *WITH* THEM! NOW, BY MIMICKING HIS *FORCE BEAM,* I CAN BLAST MY WAY THRU THE DEBRIS IN *MINUTES!*

JUST A FEW MINUTES MORE, AND I'LL TRIUMPH OVER ALL *MANKIND!*

WHRRAK!

WHILE, OUTSIDE THE MINE--

A DESERTED MINE SHAFT! *NOW* WHAT?

HE *WANTED* US TO FOLLOW HIM! HE DIDN'T EVEN ATTEMPT TO SHIELD HIS MIND FROM MY MENTAL PROBE!

SHEER FOLLY ON HIS PART, I'D SAY!

WHY WOULD HE HAVE WANTED US TO PURSUE HIM INTO A *MINE?* WE'RE NOT EVEN MEMBERS OF THE *PROSPECTORS' UNION!*

IF HE'S *IN* THERE, WE'LL FIND HIM! HE WON'T ESCAPE FROM US *AGAIN!*

HE IS IN THERE *INDEED!* I CAN PROMISE YOU THAT!

WHAT OF *JEAN,* PROFESSOR? CAN YOU MENTALLY *SCAN* THE AREA AND TELL IF SHE'S ALL RIGHT??

IF SHE'S BEEN *HARMED,* NO POWER ON EARTH WILL SAVE THE MIMIC FROM ME!

WHEN I HEAR THAT TONE IN CYKE'S VOICE, I WOULDN'T WANNA BE HIS *ENEMY* IF I WAS AS STRONG AS A *HUNDRED* MIMICS!

SHE'S PERFECTLY SAFE, SCOTT! IT WON'T BE LONG BEFORE WE *REACH* HER....!

17

JEAN! LEVITATE YOURSELF-- HURRY, GIRL!

HOW CAN YOU BE SURE THE MINE WILL *BLOW UP,* SIR?

I *MYSELF* CAUSED THE SHORT-CIRCUIT-- *MENTALLY!*

THIS IS NO AVOCATION FOR ONE WHO ESPOUSES A LIFE OF *LEISURE!*

DON'T WORRY, SCOTTY! I CAN KEEP UP WITH ALL OF YOU EASILY!

YEAH! IT'S EASIER FOR *HER* THAN FOR *ME!* SHE DOESN'T HAVETA WORRY ABOUT RUNNING OUT OF *ICE!*

THUMP!
THUMP!

WHOOM

WE *MADE* IT! WE'RE *SAFE!*

--WHEW!-- TALK ABOUT THE *NICK'A TIME*--!

LOOK! THE *MIMIC!* I DON'T *GET* IT! HIS *WINGS* ARE GONE!

AND HIS *FIGURE*--IT DOESN'T RESEMBLE THE *BEAST'S* ANY MORE!

WHAT *CHANGED* HIM? HE'S STILL *NEAR* US!

IT WAS HIS *FATHER'S MACHINE!* *THAT* PROVED TO BE HIS UNDOING--HIS GREATEST *MISTAKE!*

YOU MEAN HIS FATHER'S MACHINE *FAILED,* PROFESSOR?

ON THE CONTRARY --IT WORKED *PERFECTLY!*

THEN, A SHORT TIME LATER...

YOU SEE, DR. RANKIN *KNEW* THE POWERS OF MIMICRY, WHICH HIS SON HAD ACCIDENTALLY OBTAINED, COULD ONLY LEAD HIM INTO TERRIBLE *TROUBLE!*

AND SO, ALTHOUGH THE LAD DIDN'T REALIZE IT, HIS FATHER CREATED A MACHINE TO TAKE THOSE POWERS *AWAY*--

AND NOW, SINCE I'VE MENTALLY REMOVED HIS MEMORY OF ALL THAT HAS OCCURRED, HE IS FREE TO *LEAVE*... A NEW, NORMAL LIFE AWAITS HIM!

SO *THAT'S* WHY YOU WANTED US TO LET HIM USE THE MACHINE! YOU SENSED IT ALL THE TIME!

I WONDER WHAT *WOULD* HAVE HAPPENED IF HE HAD *GAINED* THE POWER HE WANTED??

LUCKY FOR US--AND FOR THE WORLD-- WE'LL NEVER KNOW!

NEXT ISH: *The* RETURN *of* UNUS! THE BLOB! --AND THE MYSTERIOUS LUCIFER! 'NUFF SAID!

20

SO--THE VAULT CAN'T BE OPENED TILL TEN, HUH? WELL, HERE'S WHERE I *UPSET* YOUR PRETTY LITTLE SCHEDULE!

ME, I NEVER *WAS* MUCH GOOD AT *WAITIN'!*

YOU *CAN'T* BREAK IN! IT'S *IMPOSSIBLE--!*

NOTHIN'S IMPOSSIBLE FOR AN *X-MAN,* RUBE!

RRREEEKK!!

--AND DON'T YOU *FORGET* IT!

DONG·DONG·DONG·DON

HERE, PARTNER! I DID THE HARD WORK--SO *YOU* CAN CARRY THE *LOOT!*

BE GLAD TO, PAL! FOR *THAT* KIND OF *MENIAL* LABOR, YOU CAN COUNT ME *IN!*

THE *BIG GUY* LET GO OF MR. PHILBERT! NOW'S MY CHANCE TO TAKE THEM WITHOUT *ENDANGERING* ANYBODY!

$

I'VE NEVER CLAIMED TO KNOW VERY MUCH ABOUT THIS *MUTANT* BUSINESS--

KRAK!

--BUT I *DO* KNOW THAT EVEN THE *X-MEN* AREN'T *BULLET-PROOF!*

I DON'T KNOW WHERE YOU'RE GETTIN' YOUR *INFO,* RUBE, BUT I THINK YOU'D BETTER TAKE ANOTHER *LOOK!*

THAK! THAK!

THE BULLETS SINK RIGHT INTO HIM...! AND THEN THEY POP *OUT* AGAIN!

THE *OTHER* ONE DOESN'T LOOK SO INVULNERABLE! WAIT! WHAT *GIVES?*

HE'S SURROUNDED BY SOME KIND OF *FORCE FIELD!*

HEY, PARTNER--GET THIS JOKER OFF MY *BACK,* WILL YA?

PWING

PWING

DUCK!

$

NO SOONER SAID THAN *DONE!* HERE, BUDDY--THAT LITTLE TOY WON'T DO YOU ANY GOOD WITH US *ANYHOW!*

MY GUN--IT'S *DEMOLISHED!* YOU GUYS AREN'T *HUMAN!*

SKRUNCH!

NEVER SAID WE *WAS,* CUDDLES! WE'RE *MUTANTS,* REMEMBER?

2

MEANWHILE, THE CLANGING BURGLAR ALARM HAS NOT GONE UNHEEDED, FOR...

OKAY, BOYS-- *MOVE IN* ON 'EM!

USE YOUR *CLUBS!* FROM WHAT I SAW THRU THE BANK WINDOW, *GUNS* ARE USELESS!

WE'LL TAKE 'EM, CAPTAIN!

THEY CAN'T LICK *ALL* OF US!

HOWEVER, AS THE INCREDIBLE IMPOSTERS EMERGE FROM THE BUILDING...

UHHNN--!-- WE CAN'T EVEN LAY OUR *HANDS* ON HIM!

OOOOF!

OF *COURSE* NOT, FOOLS! NOBODY TOUCHES ME UNLESS I ALLOW 'EM TO!

AND, A FEW FEET AWAY...

WE'VE GOT *THIS* ONE, CAPTAIN!

HE DOESN'T HAVE A FORCE FIELD!

WHO SAYS I *NEED* ONE? I GOT *OTHER* WAYS OF HANDLIN' THINGS!

YOU'RE TALKIN' THRU YOUR *HAT*, MISTER! WE'VE GOT ENOUGH MEN AROUND YOU TO CORRAL AN *ELEPHANT!*

MAYBE SO, BUT YOU AIN'T GOT NEARLY ENOUGH TO HOLD ONTO... THE *BLOB!*

SO *THAT'S* WHO HE IS! ...NO *WONDER!*

HE TOSSED US OFF LIKE SO MANY *RAG DOLLS!*

AN' NOW, IF YOU DON'T MIND--

--I'VE GOTTA BE *MOVIN'* ON! GIVE MY REGRETS TO THE JOE THAT OWNS THIS CAR!

I *SEE* IT--BUT I JUST PLAIN DON'T *BELIEVE* IT!

C'MON, CHUM! WE'VE GOTTA GO JOIN THE *REST'A* THE *X-MEN!*

THE NEXT MOMENT...

COME BACK HERE! *COME BACK*, I SAY!

DID YOU SEE THAT? NOT ONLY DID THEY ROB THE BANK--BUT THEY *ALSO* MADE THEIR GETAWAY IN PHILBERT'S *LIMOUSINE!*

MISTER, FROM WHAT I'VE SEEN, I'D SAY WE'RE LUCKY THEY WERE ONLY AFTER *MONEY!*

ALL RIGHT, MEN--INTO THE CAR! NO MATTER WHAT HAPPENS, WE'RE GOING TO CATCH US SOME *MUTANTS!*

FINE! BUT *THEN* WHAT DO WE *DO* WITH 'EM?

3

THE *RADAR-IMAGE BEAM* WHICH I DEVELOPED WILL DETECT ANY OTHER MUTANTS IN THE AREA-- AND SHOW US THEIR *FORMS*, AS WELL!

HEY-- *THAT* ONE LOOKS *FAMILIAR!*

AS WELL HE *SHOULD!* IT IS CLEAR THAT THE MASSIVE FIGURE IS INDEED... *THE BLOB!* AND THE OTHER, THE MACHINE REVEALS, IS... *UNUS!*

UNUS, THE UNTOUCHABLE?!!

BUT, THE LAST TIME WE FOUGHT, HE PROMISED TO *REFORM* IF WE DECLINED TO IMPRISON HIM*!

IF HE'S *FORGOTTEN* HIS PLEDGE, I'LL *STIMULATE* HIS MEMORY-- AS *THE BEAST!*

WE STILL HAVE THE *RAY GUN* WE EMPLOYED AGAINST HIM THEN!

*ISH #8--S.

DON'T BE TOO *CONFIDENT*, HANK! AFTER ALL, UNUS MAY HAVE DISCOVERED SOME WAY TO *COUNTERACT* THAT WEAPON BY NOW!

IN ADDITION, I SENSE THAT A *THIRD* ENTITY HAS MASTERMINDED THIS ENTIRE SCHEME-- TO DISCREDIT US-- SOMEONE *OUT OF RANGE* OF MY *CEREBRO* MACHINE!

PROFESSOR-- I JUST NOTICED! *SCOTT* ISN'T HERE! COULD ANYTHING HAVE *HAPPENED* TO HIM?

YEAH! IT ISN'T LIKE OLD GAMMA-GAZE TO MISS A CHANCE FOR *ACTION!*

SOMEONE HAD BEST INVESTIGATE HIS ABSENCE!

I'M ON MY WAY THERE *NOW!* I'LL FIND 'IM!

FIFTEEN SECONDS LATER, A BREATHLESS BOBBY DRAKE REAPPEARS--WITH DISTURBING NEWS...

CYKE .. HE'S *GONE!* WALKED OUT ON US! HE JUST LEFT US A SHORT GOOD-BYE NOTE!

I *SUSPECTED* AS MUCH! SCOTT HAS SEEMED TERRIBLY *DISTRAUGHT* THESE PAST FEW WEEKS!

BUT, NO TIME TO WORRY ABOUT THAT *NOW!*

I MUST SEARCH MY MEMORY-- TRY TO DISCOVER *WHICH* OF OUR FORMER FOES MIGHT BE GUIDING *UNUS* AND THE *BLOB!*

VANISHER! JUGGER-- MAGNETO! SENTINE-- S. MASTERMIND! MARINER!

IT'S-- NO USE! OUR ADVERSARY HAS SET UP A *MENTAL SCREEN!* THERE IS ONE NAME WHICH *ELUDES* ME!

BY YOUR EXPRESSIONS, I SEE THAT OUR HIDDEN ENEMY'S SCREEN HAS AFFECTED *YOU*, TOO! THERE IS ONLY ONE SOLUTION!

SCOTT-- OH, SCOTT! WILL I *NEVER* SEE YOU AGAIN?

I MUST BUILD A *MECHANICAL MEMORY-INDUCER*, TO QUICKLY PENETRATE OUR FOE'S DEFENSES! MEANWHILE...

FOR ONCE, WE'RE WAY AHEAD OF YOU, PROFESSOR! IT'LL BE A RELIEF TO LET MY *WINGS* OUT OF THIS GET-UP, ANYWAY!

I'LL GET THAT RAY GUN! IT MAY *STILL* PROVE EFFICACIOUS!

YEAH-- MAYBE IT'LL EVEN *WORK!* C'MON-- LET'S *MOVE OUT!*

5

BUT, EVEN AS THE TEEN-AGE MUTANTS PREPARE FOR BATTLE, THEY CANNOT SUSPECT THAT, TWO THOUSAND MILES AWAY, ONE PAIR OF EYES--COLD, HOSTILE, RELENTLESS-- WATCHES INTENTLY FOR THEIR APPEARANCE...

SO! THE DIE IS CAST! *UNUS* AND *THE BLOB* HAVE UNWITTINGLY DONE MY BIDDING--AND A FOOLISH WORLD BELIEVES THEY ARE RENEGADE *X-MEN*, MERELY SEEKING WORLDLY TREASURE!

LITTLE DOES ANYONE-- EVEN MY TWO MASQUER- ADING MINIONS--REALIZE THAT I, *LUCIFER** , HAVE IN MIND A PURPOSE FAR MORE *COMPLEX*, FAR MORE *SINISTER*!

＊ THE VIVACIOUS VILLAIN OF X-MEN #9, RIGHT? RIGHT! ... OL' STAN.

"FOR, IT WAS ONLY DAYS AGO THAT, WHILE TESTING MY *ULTRA-SCANNER*, I DISCOVERED...

"UNTOUCHABLE," HUH? WHEN *I* GET THRU WITH HIM, HE'LL BE *UNMENDABLE*!

$100 TO ANYONE WHO CAN LAST THREE FULL MINUTES WITH UNUS THE UNTOUCHABLE NOW TOURING WITH SUPERIOR CIRCU

EASY, BLOB! I'VE HEARD'A THIS GUY! THEY SAY HE'S *TOUGH*!

NOBODY'S TOUGHER THAN *THE BLOB*! I'LL TEACH THAT RUBE TO BRING HIS CIRCUS INTO THE SAME TOWN WHERE *MY* CARNY'S PLAYIN'!

"THUS, FATE HAD PLACED WITHIN MY REACH *TWO* OF THE MOST POWERFUL MUTANTS IN THE WORLD! AND, AS I WAITED, BIDING MY TIME...

WHAT'S *THIS*? HAVE THE LOCAL YOKELS RUN OUTTA *MEN*, SO THEY HAVETA SEND *HIPPOS* AGAINST ME NOW?

I'M GONNA MAKE YOU *SWALLOW* THEM WORDS, BUSTER!

"HOWEVER..."

I DIDN'T EVEN *REACH* HIM! HE'S PROTECTED BY SOME KINDA *INVISIBLE SHIELD*!

BUT THERE'S *NOTHIN'* I CAN'T SMASH THRU... LEASTWAYS, NOT TILL *NOW*!

YOU BLUNDERING *FATSO*-- *NOW* DO YOU SEE WHY THEY CALL ME "THE UNTOUCH- ABLE"?

YET, ANY *NORMAL* MAN WOULD HAVE *BOUNCED BACK*--HE WAS MERELY *STOPPED*!

I DON'T *GET* IT! NOBODY'S HALTED ME LIKE THAT EXCEPT -- THE *X-MEN*!

NOW, *THERE'S* AN IDEA! WHAT IF THIS CLOWN IS A *MUTANT*--LIKE *ME*?

HE'S GETTING UP! BETTER MAKE MY MOVE-- *NOW*!

6

"BUT, *UNUS* FARED NO BETTER THAN HAD *THE BLOB* HIMSELF..."

CAN'T *BUDGE* HIM! THERE'S JUST ONE POSSIBLE ANSWER...

LOOK, MISTER-- WHAT SAY WE CALL THIS MATCH A *DRAW?* I'VE GOT SOME-THIN' I WANNA *TALK* TO YOU ABOUT-- *LATER!*

YA TOOK THE WORDS RIGHT OUTTA MY MOUTH! COME OVER TO *MY* CARNY IN AN HOUR! AND DON'T FORGET THAT *HUNDRED BUCKS!*

"AND SO, SOON AFTERWARD, THE TWO *HOMO-SUPERIORS* MET AGAIN--LITTLE REALIZING IT WAS I, *LUCIFER,* WHO HAD PLANTED THE IDEA IN THEIR MINDS..."

THEN I WAS *RIGHT,* BLOB-- YOU *ARE* A MUTANT, JUST LIKE ME! I *SENSED* IT, SOMEHOW!

YOU AN' ME BOTH, CHUM! SO HOWZABOUT A CUP'A COFFEE WHILE WE SEE WHAT *ELSE* WE GOT IN COMMON?

"BEFORE LONG, INSIDE THE BLOB'S TRAILER..."

THEN IT'S SETTLED! SINCE WE'VE *BOTH* GOT GRUDGES AGAINST THE X-MEN, WE'LL FRAME *THEM* FOR OUR ROBBERIES!

RIGHT! AND WHEN THOSE COSTUMED CLOWNS COME OUT TO *STOP* US--WE'LL POLISH 'EM OFF, ONCE AN' FOR ALL!

NOW YER TALKIN'! I BEEN WAITIN' A *LONG TIME* FOR THIS!*

* SINCE X-MEN #7, TO BE EXACT!--SMILEY.

OKAY, MARVELITES--THAT'S ENOUGH OF LUCIFER'S SANGUINARY SOLILOQUIES FOR THE MOMENT! NOW, AS HIS HUMAN PUPPETS COMMIT THEIR *SECOND* CRIME, THE EYES OF *CYCLOPS* ARE UPON THEM...

C'MON, BROTHER X-MAN --OUR CLUB TREASURY CAN *USE* THIS EXTRA LOOT!

I HEAR YA TALKIN', MAC!

TWO CRIMINALS-- DRESSED IN X-MEN UNIFORMS! THAT BULKY ONE LOOKS LIKE *THE BLOB* --AND, COULD THE OTHER BE...*UNUS?*

YET, THIS ISN'T *MY* AFFAIR-- FOR I'VE PROMISED MYSELF NOT TO BECOME AN *X-MAN* AGAIN--UNTIL I CAN *CONTROL* MY AWESOME, POTENTIALLY DEADLY POWER!

BESIDES, SURELY THE *PUBLIC* REALIZES THAT THEY'RE NOT REALLY X-MEN!

SEE, MABEL? I *TOLD* YOU WE SHOULD'A RUN THEM CRUMMY MUTIES OUTTA TOWN LONG AGO!

YOU WERE *RIGHT,* HERMAN! NEXT TIME, I'LL *LISTEN* TO YOU!

NOW WE'RE ONTO THEM!

SO--THE CROWD HAS ANSWERED MY QUESTION FOR ME! I *MUST* HEED THE CALL--AS LONG AS ALL MUTANTS ARE REGARDED AS *MONSTERS!*

EXACTLY ONE MINUTE LATER...

ALL RIGHT, YOU MISGUIDED MISFITS! ONE OF THE *REAL* X-MEN IS HERE! NOW, WHICH OF YOU WANTS TO BE THE FIRST TO CONFESS YOU'RE BOTH *PHONIES!*

PHONIES? DOES HE MEAN THAT THOSE OTHER TWO --ARE JUST *IMPOSTERS?*

I'LL BET THEY'RE *ALL* IN ON IT!

HEY, LOOK, PARTNER-- IT'S *CYCLOPS!* WE THOUGHT YOU'D NEVER MAKE IT, CYKE, OL' BUDDY!

YEAH! HELP US WITH THIS MONEY-SACK, WILLYA, KID?

7

SURE, FRIEND--I'LL GIVE YOU A HAND! OR, PERHAPS I SHOULD SAY--AN *EYE!*

I DON'T DARE UNLEASH A BLOW DIRECTLY *AT THEM*--UNTIL I AM CERTAIN THEY *ARE* MUTANTS, WHO WOULD ONLY BE *STUNNED* BY MY POWER BLASTS!

YA BLAMED NUISANCE! *NOW* LOOK WHAT YA'VE GONE AND DONE!

JUST LIKE ALWAYS-- IF YOU CAN'T *LEAD* A HEIST, YOU TRY TO *FOUL IT UP!*

I'M AFRAID WE'RE GONNA HAVETA *PUNISH* YOU FOR THIS--!

BLAST IT! THEY'RE STILL KEEPING UP THE PRETENSE THAT I'M *ONE* OF THEM! GOT TO MAKE THEM BLURT OUT THE TRUTH!

HERE, YOU FAKES! *THIS* OUGHT TO CONVINCE THE CROWD WE'RE ON OPPOSITE SIDES!

BRAK!

DON'T WORRY, PAL! YOUR *FORCE SHIELD* AND MY *BULK* WILL STOP US FROM GETTIN' HURT!

SURE--JUST LIKE CYKE *KNEW* IT WOULD!

LISTEN TO THEM! DO THEY THINK THAT HUMAN BEINGS ARE JUST *SPORT* FOR THE *MUTANTS?*

YOU *SAID* IT, POPS! LET'S ALL RUSH 'EM-- *TOGETHER!*

YES! IF WE LET THEM CONTINUE TO RUN AMOK, THEY MAY DESTROY THE ENTIRE *CITY!*

GET THE *YOUNGEST* ONE FIRST! HE LOOKS LIKE THE MOST *DANGEROUS!*

AS USUAL, A *MOB* SELDOM MAKES THE RIGHT DECISION! NOW THE CROWD'S TURNING ON *ME!*

I-I'VE *FAILED!* INSTEAD OF *HELPING,* I'VE MERELY ALLOWED THEM TO DISCREDIT THE X-MEN *FURTHER!*

LOOK! HE'S RUNNING AWAY!

SURE! THOSE *MUTIES'RE* ALL *COWARDS,* IF YA STAND UP TO 'EM!

BUT, AT LEAST I LEARNED WHO THE BOGUS X-MEN *ARE!* FROM THE WAY THEY SPOKE, THEY *MUST* BE THE BLOB AND UNUS--

--WHICH MEANS THAT I HAVE TO CONTACT THE *OTHERS!* PERHAPS AS A *TEAM,* WE CAN DEFEAT THE TWO EVIL MUTANTS--BEFORE IT'S *TOO LATE!*

8

MEANWHILE, THE NEFARIOUS LUCIFER IS *ALSO* UPSET, THOUGH FOR QUITE DIFFERENT REASONS...

HAVE MY PLANS ALL COME TO *NAUGHT?* DOES ONLY *ONE* X-MAN DARE TO ATTACK MY COSTUMED DUPES?

IT *CANNOT* BE! I HAVE PLANNED TOO CAREFULLY! THEY *MUST* ATTACK--AS A *TEAM!!*

BUT--PERHAPS I SPOKE *TOO SOON!* FOR, THERE IS THE MUTANT KNOWN AS...*THE ANGEL!* HE FLIES TOWARDS UNUS AND THE BLOB!

AND, IF *ANGEL* COMES, CAN THE OTHER X-MEN BE FAR *BEHIND?*

THE NEXT SECOND, LUCIFER'S RINGING WORDS COME TRUE, AS...

DON'T FORGET, GROUP--'TIS THE *BEAST* WHO GETS FIRST DIBS AT OUR TWO ADVER-SARIES!

YOU CAN *HAVE* 'EM, BEASTIE-BOY! BUT, I'LL BE HOVERING NEARBY, JUST IN CASE!

HOLY HANNAH! THREE *MORE* MUTANTS!

WELL, IT'S ABOUT *TIME* YOU GLORY-BOYS SHOWED UP! WE BEEN *WAITIN'* FOR YA!

THEN, ARMED WITH THE WEAPON THAT ONCE BEFORE DEFEATED THE AWESOME *UNUS,* THE ANTHROPOID X-MAN MAKES HIS PLAY...

IT GRIEVES ME TO THE QUICK, FECKLESS FOE, TO REALIZE THAT YOU HAVE DISAVOWED YOUR PLEDGE OF ETERNAL HONESTY!

NOW, PREPARE FOR THE *CONSEQUENCES* OF YOUR IM-PRUDENT ACT!

QUIT YAKKIN' AND *FIRE AWAY,* FOOL! I DON'T HAVE ALL *DAY* TO LISTEN TO YOU!

AS YOU WILL, MY FRIEND! ONE DOSE OF *THIS* DEVICE, AND YOUR MUTANT POWER WILL NO LONGER BE YOURS TO *CONTROL!*

THAT'S STRANGE-- HE SEEMS TO BE *REACTING* DIFFERENTLY THAN HE DID BEFORE...

MY NUTTY HUNCH WAS *RIGHT!*

I AM NOW *IMMUNE* TO THE BEAST'S BLASTED RAY!

AND, AS THE BLINDING GLARE FADES AWAY...

OKAY, YOU JUNIOR-GRADE GORILLA! NOW IT'S *MY* TURN --I BEEN WAITIN' FOR THIS MOMENT FOR MORE THAN A *YEAR!*

A TRUE PARAGON OF PATIENCE!

NEITHER OF THEM SUSPECTS THAT *I* AM RESPONSIBLE FOR UNUS'S IMMUNITY--AND ALSO FOR HIS "HUNCH" THAT THE RAY WOULD NO LONGER AFFECT HIM!

FOR, I POSSESS POWERS THAT THE WORLD CAN SCARCELY *IMAGINE!*

9

10

CYKE! TALK ABOUT SIGHTS FOR SORE EYES! YOU SHOWED UP JUST IN TIME!

SO I **SEE!** BUT-- WE CAN TALK **LATER!**

ABOVE GROUND, THE BONA FIDE X-MEN MAKE A HURRIED EXIT...

IT'S GREAT TO SEE SOME **ACTION** AGAIN! BUT WHERE'VE **YOU** BEEN, SCOTTY-BOY?

THAT'S **MY** BUSINESS, ANGEL!

LOOK! ONE OF THEM BLASTED A **HOLE** RIGHT THROUGH THE PAVEMENT--AND TWO OTHERS FELL **THRU** IT!

WITH YOUR USUAL PERSPICACITY, CYCLOPS, YOU'VE PROPERLY EVALUATED THE SITUATION! LET'S DEPART, INDEED!

RIGHT NOW, WE'D BETTER **SPLIT!** THAT CROWD'S STILL **ANGRY!**

THUNK!

WE LANDED ON A **SUBWAY TRAIN!**

I'VE BEEN RIDDEN OUTTA TOWN ON A **RAIL** BEFORE, BUT THIS IS **RIDICULOUS!**

SHUDDUP AND KEEP YER **HEAD** DOWN! WE'LL BE **BACK!***

SAY--WHERE'S **MARVEL GIRL?**

SHE HAD TO STAY BEHIND--TO HELP THE **PROFESSOR!** WE'LL FILL YOU IN ON THE WAY!

*AND YOU CAN BET WE'LL BE HERE TO MEET THEM!   ---SMUG STAN.

WHILE, IN A HIDDEN LAB...

SO! THE ONE I SEEK MOST STILL CLOSETS HIMSELF IN SECRECY, EH?

BUT, **LUCIFER** KNOWS NOT THE MEANING OF **DEFEAT!** THERE ARE OTHER WAYS...

BUT THEN, ABRUPTLY---

AH! MY **MENTO-WAVE RECEIVER** INDICATES THAT PROFESSOR XAVIER HAS ALREADY **PENETRATED** MY MENTAL SCREEN!

HE CANNOT SUSPECT THAT I **DESIRED** HIM TO FIND ME--THAT, IN LOCATING ME, HE HAS NOW SEALED HIS OWN **DOOM!**

MOMENTS LATER, AT A CERTAIN POINT IN THE GREAT DESERT IN THE SOUTHWESTERN PORTION OF THE UNITED STATES, A STRANGE, OMINOUS **DOME** APPEARS FROM WITHIN THE VERY HEART OF A CRAGGY MESA,...

...YET, NO EYES SEE AND NO VOICE REPORTS THIS AWESOME SIGHT-- ONE WHICH MAY WELL DETERMINE THE FATE OF THE **EARTH** ITSELF--!

11

AT THAT SELFSAME INSTANT, A CONTINENT AWAY...

WITH THIS DEVICE, I HAVE MENTALLY PINPOINTED OUR HIDDEN ANTAGONIST!

SO--IT IS HE! I SHOULD HAVE KNOWN!

PROFESSOR-- WHO IS IT? CAN YOU TELL ME?

SUDDENLY, WITHOUT WARNING, BEFORE THE MUTANT LEADER CAN ANSWER THE ANXIOUS MARVEL GIRL...

HE'S ATTACKING ME-- THRU MY OWN MIND! NO TIME TO PREPARE A DEFENSE!

MY BRAIN-- IT'S ON FIRE!

THEN--SILENCE! PROFESSOR--WHAT'S HAPPENED?

BUT NO! HE CAN'T BE DEAD! HE JUST CAN'T BE--!

HE'S... SO RIGID, SO UNMOVING! IT'S ALMOST AS IF--

I MUST CHECK-- TO SEE IF HIS HEART STILL BEATS!

THANK HEAVEN--HE'S ALIVE! AND YET, HIS HEARTBEAT IS SO SLOW-- HE MUST BE CONTINUING TO BREATHE BY SHEER MENTAL EFFORT! BUT-- HE CANNOT MOVE!

THAT IS... CORRECT, JEAN! YOU MUST USE MENTAL-WAVE AMPLIFIER-- AT ONCE!

IN MY MIND-- I CAN READ HIS THOUGHTS! BUT, THEY'RE FAINT--DISTANT!

COMPLYING WITH PROFESSOR X'S URGENT COMMAND, JEAN ABRUPTLY DISCOVERS...

WHY--NOW YOUR THOUGHTS ARE COMING THRU MORE CLEARLY!

GOOD! THEN HEED MY WORDS--FOR I MAY HAVE LITTLE TIME!

WHAT DO YOU MEAN? WHO IS RESPONSIBLE FOR YOUR PLIGHT?

THIS IS THE WORK OF ONE WHOSE POWERS AND PURPOSE STAGGER THE MORTAL IMAGINATION--OF THE ONE I KNOW ONLY BY HIS EARTHLY NAME OF...LUCIFER!

LUCIFER! THEN-- HE HAS RETURNED!

YES--SO LISTEN CLOSELY TO THE TALE OF MY FIRST ENCOUNTER WITH HIM! LISTEN, FOR, THE FATE OF ALL HUMANITY HANGS IN THE BALANCE!

13

"SOME YEARS AGO, FASCINATED BY TALES I HAD HEARD OF A MYSTERIOUS WALLED CITY IN THE SHADOW OF THE HIMALAYAS, I JOURNEYED THRU THE RUGGED TERRAIN OF TIBET..."

THIS IS MY DESTINATION! I SEEM TO SENSE SOME OMINOUS, UNSEEN *MENACE* THAT LIES WITHIN--!

IT'S AS THOUGH MY ENTIRE LIFE, MY ULTIMATE *DESTINY*, WERE SOMEHOW BOUND UP BEHIND THOSE GRIM, GREY WALLS!

"AT THE GATE, MY SUSPICIONS WERE CONFIRMED..."

IT IS *FORBIDDEN* THAT ANY OUTSIDER MAY PASS THIS GATE! YET-- I BELIEVE *YOU* SHOULD BE ALLOWED ADMITTANCE!

THANK YOU! MY MISSION IS ONE OF *PEACE*, I ASSURE YOU!

THESE TWO ARE UNDER THE MENTAL DOMINATION OF ANOTHER'S BRAIN! I CAN *FEEL* IT!

"INSIDE THE CITY, I WAS AWARE OF SINISTER EYES FOCUSED UPON ME..."

THE THOUGHT-WAVES OF THESE PEOPLE-- THEY INDICATE *ABJECT FEAR* OF THE TYRANT WHO RULES THEM!

COME! IS THERE ONE WHO WOULD *SPEAK* TO A WAYFARER IN A STRANGE LAND?

SO! A *VISITOR* HAS COME! HE WILL BEAR CLOSE *WATCHING*!

I WILL SPEAK TO YOU, MY SON! WHAT DO YOU WISH TO KNOW?

I AM INTRIGUED BY YOUR GREAT WALLED CITY, AND I WISH AN AUDIENCE WITH ITS *RULER*!

NAY, BUT THAT IS *IMPOSSIBLE*! FOR, OUR MASTER DWELLS WITHIN YONDER CITADEL-- AND EVEN *WE* ARE NEVER PERMITTED TO GAZE UPON HIM!

I CAN TELL HE SPEAKS THE TRUTH!

HOW LONG HAS THIS MAN BEEN YOUR OVERLORD?

I--I DO NOT KNOW, MY SON! IT IS AS IF-- TIME HAS CEASED TO EXIST FOR US --SINCE HIS COMING!

NOW, I MUST GO! I CAN SAY NO MORE!

AMAZING! MY SILENT PROBING REVEALS HIGHLY-COMPLICATED *MACHINERY* INSIDE THE TYRANT'S DOMICILE!

BUT *HOW*-- AND *WHY*??

I MUST PROBE *FURTHER*-- LAY BARE THE SECRETS OF THESE DEVICES!

"EXERCISING MY MENTAL POWERS TO THE FULLEST EXTENT, I MADE AN INCREDIBLE DISCOVERY..."

THESE, THEN, ARE THE SOURCE OF THE TYRANT'S POWER!

BUT, THEY ARE MADE OF METALS NOT FOUND ON EARTH! THE ONE WHO HOLDS THIS CITY IN HIS SWAY-- IS *FROM ANOTHER WORLD*!

14

EVIDENTLY, THE MACHINES ENABLE THE ALIEN TO CONTROL *SELECTED MINDS* AMONG THE POPULACE--AND THESE, IN TURN, KEEP THE *OTHER* CITIZENS IN LINE!

OBVIOUSLY, THERE IS MUCH MORE TO THIS SITUATION THAN THE MERE *ENSLAVEMENT* OF ONE LONE VILLAGE!

"HASTILY LOCATING SOME OF THE MORE REBEL-LIOUS ELEMENTS OF THE AREA, I OUTLINED A PLAN TO THEM...

...THEN, I CAN RENDER YOUR NAMELESS MASTER *HELPLESS*--IF *YOU* WILL HELP ME STORM HIS PALACE!

AY, THAT WILL WE DO! WE HAVE LONG AWAITED A *LEADER* IN OUR STRUGGLE AGAINST THAT UNSEEN FIEND!

THAT FOREIGN DEVIL MUST NOT LEAVE THIS DWELLING *ALIVE!*

"BUT, I HAD UNDERESTIMATED THE TRUE CUNNING AND POWER OF MY RELENTLESS, VIGILANT FOE...

"FOR, EVEN AFTER I HAD MENTALLY SCREENED MY COMRADES, HE TOOK CONTROL OF THE BRAIN OF *ONE* OF THEM, AND SO...

BY MEANS YOU WOULD NOT UNDER-STAND, I HAVE LOCATED A *TUNNEL* INTO THE CASTLE! ONCE INSIDE, WE WILL OVERTHROW ANY GUARDS --AND YOUR ANCIENT HOMELAND WILL BE *FREE* AGAIN!

FREE! DARE WE *HOPE* FOR SUCH A THING?

LONG AGO, WE WERE OUR OWN MASTERS! CAN SUCH A DAY DAWN ONCE MORE?

IT CAN-- IF YOU ACT *SWIFTLY!*

NOW--I STRIKE! *DEATH* TO ALL WHO WOULD REBEL!

"THE NEXT INSTANT..."

LOOK OUT! THAT CHANDELIER-- IT'S *FALLING*--!

LUCKILY, MY MUTANT BRAIN SENSED *TREACHERY* FROM SOMEONE IN THE ROOM--NOT A MOMENT TOO SOON!

HOLD! WHAT TRAITOR'S DEED IS *THIS?*

BY THE *ETERNAL*--!

THE *MASTER* --HE *KNOWS* OF OUR PLOT AGAINST HIM!

15

WHILE PROBING THIS CHAMBER A MINUTE AGO, I DETECTED A *HATCH*, PLACED--*HERE!*

THE TOWNSPEOPLE ARE MOMENTARILY ENGULFED --BUT THE FIREBALL IS *EXTINGUISHED!*

OUR FOE HAS *FAILED* AGAIN!

"AND, INDEED, JUST A SHORT TIME LATER...

I CUT OFF THE SUPPLY OF WATER--AND THE FLOOD DRAINED AWAY IMMEDIATELY!

AND NOW-- THE HOUR IS AT HAND! WE HAVE REACHED THE CASTLE OF THE TYRANT!

AT THIS DISTANCE, I CAN USE MY OWN *MIND* TO PROTECT THEIRS FROM THE ENEMY'S INFLUENCE!

LONG SHALL THIS DAY LIVE IN OUR MEMORIES!

"WHILE, IN ANOTHER SUBTERRANEAN SECTION OF THE PALACE..."

THE INTRUDER IS A FORMIDABLE OPPONENT! STILL, HE IS FORE-DOOMED TO *FAILURE* WHEN MATCHED AGAINST MY SUPERIOR MIGHT! NOW TO--

BEEP BEEP

--BUT WAIT --THERE IS THE SIGNAL OF... *THE SUPREME ONE!*

AGENT ONE-- OUR RELAY SYSTEMS RECORD THAT PART OF OUR EQUIPMENT ON EARTH IS *DESTROYED!* WHAT HAS HAPPENED?

AN UPRISING AMONG THE EARTHLINGS, SUPREME ONE! IT SHALL BE *CRUSHED!*

NO! TAKE NO RISKS THAT MIGHT PROVE FATAL TO OUR *CAUSE!*

YOU HAVE SPENT ENOUGH TIME IN *SECTOR "A"!* A NEW SANCTUARY HAS BEEN READIED IN *SECTOR "B"!* PROCEED THERE AT ONCE!

I HEAR-- AND OBEY, SUPREME ONE!

I SHALL *LET* THESE INSIGNIFICANT BEINGS OVERRUN THE CASTLE! BUT, THE FINAL VICTORY SHALL BE *OURS!*

"MEANWHILE, NOT FAR AWAY, I HAD PARTED FROM THE MAIN ATTACK FORCE..."

THE PEOPLE HAVE TAKEN THE PALACE-- BUT THEIR FORMER TYRANT STILL ELUDES THEM!

IT IS FOR THE BEST! THEY COULD NEVER FATHOM THE TRUE NATURE OF ONE SO POWERFUL-- AND *ALIEN!*

STILL, *I* MUST FIND HIM-- CONFRONT HIM! FOR, I FEEL ALL LIFE ON *EARTH* MAY BE AT STAKE!

17

"THEN, ROUNDING A CORNER..."

SO! IT IS *YOU* WHO HAVE TYRANNIZED THIS CITY! WHO *ARE* YOU--AND WHERE ARE YOU *FROM?*

MY TRUE PURPOSE YOU SHALL *NEVER* KNOW --BUT, ON THIS PLANET I CALL MYSELF ...*LUCIFER!*

AND NOW--THAT NAME SHALL BE THE *FINAL* THING YOU HEAR! PREPARE TO DIE--FOR DARING TO OPPOSE THAT WHICH NO MORTAL CAN COMPREHEND!

THAT GREAT SLAB--- RELEASED FROM ABOVE AT THE TOUCH OF A SWITCH! I-- *CAN'T* DODGE --IN TIME!

"PINNED BENEATH THE INEXORABLE WEIGHT OF THE MASSIVE SLAB, I HEARD MY TORMENTOR'S VOICE THRU A MIST WHICH SEEMED TO BE ENVELOPING MY BRAIN..."

SO--YOU STILL SURVIVE! *LIVE,* THEN-- PERHAPS IT IS FATED THAT YOU AND I MEET *AGAIN* ONE DAY!

~OHHHH..!~...

"BEFORE MY EYES, A MOMENT BEFORE I LOST CONSCIOUSNESS, LUCIFER *DISAPPEARED*--INTO THE VERY WALL ITSELF..."

BUT, REMEMBER THIS--IT IS EVER THE *STRONG* WHO ARE MEANT TO RULE! AND *WE* ARE THE *STRONG!*

WHO DOES HE MEAN BY *"WE"?* IS HE ACTU- ALLY THE HERALD OF A FAR *GREATER* MENACE--FROM THE *STARS?*

THEN, AS THE PARALYZED MENTAL MUTANT CONCLUDES HIS STARTLING NARRATION...

THEN-- *THAT* IS HOW YOU LOST THE USE OF YOUR LEGS YEARS AGO!

YES, JEAN! AND, IT IS YET *ANOTHER* REASON WHY I FOUNDED THE *X-MEN!*

FOR, I KNEW THAT ONE DAY MANKIND WOULD HAVE TO MEET THE RENEWED THREAT OF *LUCIFER!*

BUT, EVEN *XAVIER* DOES NOT FULLY REALIZE JUST HOW URGENT MANKIND'S PLIGHT TRULY *IS!* FOR, AT THIS VERY SECOND, BENEATH THE SOUTH- WESTERN DESERT...

IT IS DONE! I HAVE CONQUERED THE ONE EARTHLY MIND WHICH MIGHT HAVE DIS- COVERED MY INTENTIONS IN TIME TO *THWART* THEM!

AND NOW, THE TIME DRAWS NEAR, WHEN MY RACE SHALL FULFILL ITS MISSION--- ITS MAGNIFICENT *DESTINY!*

18

IN ASIA, I MANAGED TO EXTEND MY SWAY OVER AN ENTIRE CITY, AT *CLOSE RANGE!* BUT, MY EXPERIMENT WITH UNUS AND THE BLOB PROVES THAT *LONGER DISTANCES* ARE NOW POSSIBLE!

SOON, *NO NATION* SHALL ESCAPE THE TENTACLES OF OUR POWER! MANKIND SHALL EXIST ONLY TO SERVE *US!*

ALL IS IN READINESS! ONLY ONE STEP REMAINS --BUT THAT IS THE *GREATEST* ONE OF *ALL!*

AND SO... *SUPREME ONE,* AFTER YEARS OF OBSERVATION, OF EXPERIMEN- TATION, AND OF WATCHFUL WAITING-- I CAN ANNOUNCE THAT-- THE TIME HAS COME FOR ...DOMINUS!

AT LAST! OUR RACE HAS WAITED LONG TO POSSESS THIS INCONSEQUENTIAL WORLD--FOR IT SHALL BE A STEPPING STONE TO GALAXIES AND UNIVERSES THAT CAN EASILY *DWARF* THE PALTRY *EARTH!*

THEREFORE, LET THE HUMANS AWAIT... *THE COMING OF DOMINUS!*

MEANWHILE, UNAWARE OF THE EARTH-SHATTERING EVENTS WHICH HAVE TRANSPIRED SINCE THEY LEFT WESTCHESTER, THE FUGITIVE X-MEN PREPARE TO RETURN TO THEIR UNIQUE SCHOOL...

IT'S SAFE TO VENTURE OUT NOW! IF NO ONE SEES MY *WHITE WINGS,* THE *REST* OF YOU ARE IN THE CLEAR!

BOY! I THOUGHT IT WAS *NEVER* GONNA GET DARK!

DON'T RELAX YOUR VIGILANCE, BOBBY!

UNDER THE CIRCUMSTANCES, CYCLOPS, THAT SEEMS A MOST *SUPERFLUOUS* PIECE OF ADVICE!

MAKING THEIR WAY BACK, THE FOUR MUTANTS DISCOVER...

MARVEL GIRL! WHAT HAPPENED TO THE PROFESSOR?

SCOTT, YOU'VE *RETURNED!* BUT, *TOO LATE!* HE WAS PARALYZED...BY *LUCIFER!*

LUCIFER? HE'S *RETURNED?!!*

WHAT ABOUT THE *PROF?* WILL HE PULL THRU?

I...HOPE SO! HE'S GIVING ME DIRECTIONS FOR A *BEAM DISTORTER*-- FOR THE *BEAST* TO BUILD!

THEN START *RELAYING,* GIRL! AND DON'T STOP TO *BREATHE!*

19

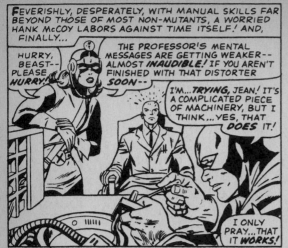

FEVERISHLY, DESPERATELY, WITH MANUAL SKILLS FAR BEYOND THOSE OF MOST NON-MUTANTS, A WORRIED HANK McCOY LABORS AGAINST TIME ITSELF! AND, FINALLY...

HURRY, BEAST--PLEASE *HURRY!*

THE PROFESSOR'S MENTAL MESSAGES ARE GETTING WEAKER--ALMOST *INAUDIBLE!* IF YOU AREN'T FINISHED WITH THAT DISTORTER *SOON*--

I'M...*TRYING*, JEAN! IT'S A COMPLICATED PIECE OF MACHINERY, BUT I THINK...YES, THAT *DOES* IT!

I ONLY PRAY...THAT IT *WORKS!*

AS A TENSE SILENCE GRIPS THE X-MEN, THE DISTORTER-HELMET IS PLACED ON THEIR LEADER'S HEAD, AND, ANXIOUS SECONDS LATER...

LOOK! HE--HE'S STIRRING! IT'S *WORKING!*

HE'S GOING TO BE *ALL RIGHT!*

YES, I--THINK I WILL--THANKS TO THE *BEAST*--AND *MARVEL GIRL!*

HE CAN *MOVE!* THE PARALYSIS IS *GONE!*

NOW, WE MUST *ACT!* THERE'S NOT A MOMENT TO LOSE!

THEN, AFTER A FAST BRIEFING...

HMM! THEN IT'S MANDATORY THAT WE *ENGAGE* LUCIFER, EH?

WE'LL FIX 'IM, BEASTIE!

QUIET, JEAN! LUCIFER ALMOST BEAT US *BEFORE!* IF HE'S STRONGER *NOW*--!

ANYTHING'S BETTER THAN WEARING *THIS* GADGET ANOTHER MINUTE!

WHAT'S OUR PLAN OF *ATTACK*, PROFESSOR?

WHILE UNDER THE INFLUENCE OF LUCIFER'S BEAM, I MANAGED TO PINPOINT ITS *SOURCE!*

OUR DESTINATION IS...THE *SOUTHWEST DESERT!*

AND SO...

AM I SLIDIN' THESE CRATES DOWN TOO *FAST* FOR YOU, JEAN?

WITH ALL DELIBERATE ALACRITY, SIR!

NO, BOBBY--KEEP THEM COMING! HANK AND I CAN KEEP UP WITH YOU!

THE WAY SCOTT *SNAPPED* AT ME A WHILE AGO! HOW COULD I EVER HAVE THOUGHT HE MIGHT *CARE* FOR ME?

BEAST! YOU MAY START LOADING THE *PLANE*, NOW!

MINUTES LATER, A SEEMINGLY SOLID WALL OF THE STATELY SCHOOL-BUILDING RISES--TO REVEAL A SLEEK PRIVATE JET, POISED MOMENTARILY BEFORE ROCKETING SKYWARD...

AS YOU KNOW, I PURCHASED THIS PLANE SEVERAL WEEKS AGO--BUT OUR ENCOUNTERS WITH THE *SENTINELS* AND *MAGNETO* KEPT US TOO BUSY TO USE IT BEFORE!

IT'S BEEN ESPECIALLY FITTED FOR SHORT TAKE-OFFS AND LANDINGS!

YOU KNOW, BEAST, I CAN'T *WAIT* TO GET MY ICY MITTS ON LUCIFER! I DON'T *LIKE* HAVIN' PEOPLE THINK WE'RE *CROOKS!*

NOR DO I, MY FRIGID FRIEND! BUT, MORE THAN OUR *REPUTATIONS* ARE AT STAKE--IF I DEDUCE CORRECTLY!

YOU'RE RIGHT, HANK...

FOR, ALTHOUGH WE DO NOT KNOW THE PRECISE NATURE OF LUCIFER'S *MENACE* TO US...

...IT MAY WELL BE THAT *WE* SIX ARE THE EARTH'S SOLE HOPE FOR *SURVIVAL!*

NEXT ISSUE: THE STARTLING, SINISTER SECRET OF... *DOMINUS!*

20

THE NEXT MOMENT, AS THE PROFESSOR REGAINS CONTROL OF THE SMALL PRIVATE CRAFT, A NEW AND EVEN MORE STARTLING PHENOMENON GREETS THE EYES OF THE STUNNED MUTANTS...

LOOK! THAT BEAM SEEMS TO BE EMANATING FROM AN OPENING IN THE SKY ITSELF!

AND THAT'S NOT ALL! LOOK!

INSIDE THE SHAFT --MOVING AT INCREDIBLE SPEED-- SOME KIND OF MASSIVE SHAPES, STREAKING DOWN TOWARDS THAT BUTTE! WHAT CAN THEY BE?

BUT, NOT EVEN THE TRAINED MINDS OF THE EXTRAORDINARY X-MEN, UNDAUNTED BY THE DIREST OF THREATS, CAN HOPE TO FORESEE THE ULTIMATE, MIND-STAGGERING MENACE WHICH THESE OMINOUS FORMS PORTEND!

I HAVE NO IDEA OF THE EXACT NATURE OF THOSE SHAPES, BOBBY! BUT, THERE CAN BE NO DOUBT THAT THEY ARE RELATED TO THE THREAT WHICH THE EVIL LUCIFER POSES TO ALL MANKIND!

WHAT DO WE DO NOW, PROFESSOR? GO DOWN AND INVESTIGATE?

IN A MATTER OF MINUTES, ANGEL! BUT FIRST --DAWN IS BREAKING, AND I WANT TO OBSERVE THIS AREA BY SUNLIGHT BEFORE LANDING!

FOR, WE ARE NOW PREPARING TO ENGAGE THE ENEMY IN HIS OWN LAIR --AND IT IS ALWAYS THERE THAT HE IS MOST DANGEROUS!

MEANWHILE, NEARBY, OTHER EYES AS WELL HAVE WITNESSED THE AWESOME SIGHT!

THERE IT IS AGAIN-- THAT SAME LIGHT WE SAW LAST NIGHT!

SOMEHOW I HAD ME A HUNCH THAT WASN'T THE LAST WE'D SEE OF IT!

WHAT CAN IT BE, MR. MACK? I'VE NEVER SEEN ANYTHIN' LIKE IT BEFORE!

I DON'T KNOW, SMITH---BUT I SURE INTEND TO FIND OUT! C'MON, LET'S GO!

PORTER MACK DUDE RANCH

CONSIDERIN' THE LACK OF ROADS NEAR BUCHANAN'S BUTTE, WHERE THE LIGHT CAME FROM, THESE HORSES'LL DO US A LOT MORE GOOD THAN THE STATION WAGON!

AND WE'RE NOT COMIN' BACK TILL WE GET TO THE BOTTOM OF THIS! A THING LIKE THIS COULD DRIVE ALL THE CUSTOMERS AWAY FROM MY DUDE RANCH!

I'M GONNA FIND OUT WHO'S USIN' THOSE PHONY SCIENCE FICTION GIMMICKS ON MY PROPERTY!

WE'RE WITH YUH ALL THE WAY, MR. MACK!

2

NEXT, AS CYCLOPS TURNS HIS AWESOME RAY ON THE LEDGE ITSELF...

HELP! WE'RE FALLIN' INTO THE *RIVER!*

MAYBE WE'RE *SAFER* DOWN HERE!

WAIT! WHERE'RE YOU NO-GOODS *GOIN'?* COME *BACK!*

SORRY, MR. MACK, BUT WE GOT US SOME BUSINESS BACK IN *TOWN!*

SO--YER RUNNIN' *OUT* ON ME, EH? YER *FIRED*, THE WHOLE *BUNCH'A* YA!

THAT'S OKAY WITH *US!* AT LEAST, WE'RE STILL AROUND TO COLLECT *UNEMPLOYMENT INSURANCE!*

THEN, AS THE WATER-LOGGED WESTERNERS PULL THEMSELVES ASHORE...

LET 'EM GO! WHO *NEEDS* 'EM? I DIDN'T WIN THE BLUE VALLEY SHARP-SHOOTIN' CONTEST FOR *NOTHIN'!*

I'LL TAKE CARE'A THOSE BLASTED *MUTIES* BY *MYSELF!*

IN FACT, I THINK I'M ABOUT TO GET MY CHANCE *RIGHT NOW!*

WHAT A *BREAK!* THERE'S THE ONE CALLED *ICEMAN*--AND HE DOESN'T SEEM TO KNOW I'M *HERE!*

LOOKS LIKE YOU TOOK THE *FIGHT* OUT OF 'EM, CYKE! THEY'RE MOVIN' OUT!

I'LL JUST *WING* 'IM--AND FIND OUT WHAT THIS IS ALL *ABOUT!*

OH NO YOU *DON'T*, MISTER--!

THANKS, BUDDY--BUT WHY DIDN'T YOU LET *ME* HANDLE HIM?

LET'S JUST SAY I GOT TIRED OF EVERYBODY AND HIS BROTHER TAKING *POT-SHOTS* AT US!

THE *ANGEL!* I FORGOT ABOUT HIM!

HERE'S THE LEADER OF OUR GUN-HAPPY PLAYMATES, ICEMAN! NOW, THE QUESTION IS--WHAT DO *WE* DO WITH HIM?

I DEMAND YOU PUT ME *DOWN*, YOU CRIMINAL! I'M THE *OWNER* OF THIS LAND!

I DON'T KNOW WHAT YOU CROOKS ARE *UP* TO WITH THAT BEAM OF LIGHT OF YOURS, BUT YOU'LL NEVER GET *AWAY* WITH IT!

CROOKS, HUH? IT LOOKS LIKE NEWS OF THOSE NEW YORK ROBBERIES HAS SPREAD *FAST!*

WELL, WE CAN'T STOP TO EXPLAIN THINGS *NOW!* I'VE GOT AN *IDEA*--!

THERE! I'M SURE THE *HORSE* KNOWS THE WAY HOME--AND, BY THE TIME YOU *GET* THERE, THE ICE WILL BE *MELTED!*

HOW'LL I EVER EXPLAIN *THIS* TO THE BOYS BACK AT THE DUDE RANCH?

MEANWHILE, WE'LL BE TRYING TO *SAVE* YOUR SAND-COVERED SPREAD--AND MAYBE ALL OF *MANKIND*, TO BOOT!

5

THEN, OBSERVING THE SCREEN INDICATED BY HIS GLOATING CAPTOR, THE PROFESSOR SEES...

I'M *SAFE!* LUCKILY, MY *WINGS* ENABLED ME TO BREAK THE WHIRL-POOL'S GRIP!

BUT--WHAT OF *MARVEL GIRL* AND THE REST? I CAN'T LET ANYTHING *HAPPEN* TO *THEM* --THEY'RE STILL *DOWN BELOW!*

THERE CAN BE ONLY *ONE* CHOICE FOR AN *X-MAN!* I MUST GO *BACK!*

NO MATTER *WHAT* DANGER LURKS BENEATH THESE SWIRLING WATERS, WE'LL FACE IT-- *TOGETHER!*

A SINGLE, MIND-RENDING SECOND THAT SEEMS AN ETERNITY--AND THEN...

MADE IT! I'M *UNDER* THE WHIRLPOOL--IN A HUGE *SUBTERRANEAN CAVERN!* FROM THE LOOKS OF ALL THESE *PIPES,* THIS MUST BE LUCIFER'S *HEADQUARTERS!*

AND--THERE'S *MARVEL GIRL* AND *CYCLOPS!*

HURRY, ANGEL! I--CAN'T HOLD ON--MUCH LONGER!

THERE YOU ARE--A LITTLE *DAMP,* BUT STILL *INTACT!* BUT, WHAT ABOUT *ICEMAN* AND THE *BEAST?*

THEY MUST'VE COME UP *ELSEWHERE* IN THIS CAVE! WE'VE GOT TO *FIND* THEM!

WAIT A MINUTE, *BOTH* OF YOU!

THERE'S SOME SORT OF *OPENING* RIGHT OVER THERE!

YEAH, I SEE IT, TOO! COULD IT BE THAT OUR MISSING BUDDIES GOT THERE *AHEAD* OF US? IT'S WORTH A *LOOK-SEE,* ANYWAY!

C'MON, CYKE--I'LL GIVE YOU A *LIFT!*

I ONLY *PRAY* THAT NOTHING HAS *HAPPENED* TO THEM!

IF THEY'VE BEEN *HARMED,* JEAN, THERE'S NO POWER OF *EARTH* THAT WILL PROTECT LUCIFER FROM US!

HOWEVER, AS THE GRIM TRIO SET FOOT UPON THE UNDERGROUND LANDING...

IT'S A *TRAP!* SOME SORT OF *TRANSPARENT CAGE* IS CLOSING ABOUT US!

QUICK, MARVEL GIRL! USE YOUR *TELEKINETIC POWER* TO FORCE THE WALLS *BACK!*

I--*CAN'T!* THE FORCE BEHIND THEM IS *TOO GREAT!* WE'RE *CAUGHT!*

9

THEN, ABRUPTLY, OUR SCENE SWITCHES TO WHERE THE BULKY *HANK McCOY* PLOWS DESPERATELY THRU THE MURKY WATERS....

MY LUNGS ARE *BURSTING!* THE VORTEX OF THE WHIRLPOOL HURLED ME DOWN TO THE VERY *BOTTOM* OF THIS RIVER!

I MUST SURFACE *SOON*--OR IT'S *BYE-BYE* BEASTIE!

A MOMENT LATER, THE ANTHROPOID X-MAN'S URGENT WISH IS GRANTED--OR *IS* IT?

-SPUTTER- MANY THANKS, FRIEND, FOR LENDING THE IMPERILED *BEAST* A HELPING HAND!

BUT--*WHAT* A HAND! I STRONGLY SUSPECT I HAVE GONE FROM THE FRYING PAN INTO THE *BLAST FURNACE!*

HERE IS ONE OF THE REMAINING MUTANTS, ROBOT *GAMMA*--THE ONE KNOWN AS THE *BEAST!*

A MOST UNGAINLY SPECIMEN! BUT-- WHERE IS THE *OTHER* HUMAN STILL *UNACCOUNTED* FOR?

WHEREVER HE IS, YOU'LL *NEVER* LOCATE HIM!

AND, EVEN AS HANK STRUGGLES VAINLY TO FREE HIMSELF, THE *FIFTH* X-MAN ENTERS THE FRAY...

GOT TO HIT THAT OVER-SIZED GARBAGE PAIL WITH AN *ICY SURFBOARD* AT *FULL SPEED!*

OTHERWISE, THE BEAST AND I ARE *BOTH* IN *HOT WATER!*

I *DID* IT! THE IMPACT SENT THE ROBOT *SPRAWLING!*

BUT, WHAT ABOUT THE *OTHER* ONE?

KR-A-A-CK!

MANY THANKS, ROBERT! YOUR ARRIVAL WAS MOST *PROPITIOUS,* INDEED!

ALLOW *ME* TO ATTEND TO OUR OTHER *CLANKING COMPEER,* IF YOU WILL!

THE BIGGER THEY ARE, THE HARDER THEY *FALL!*--IF YOU'LL FORGIVE THE *CAPRICIOUS CLICHE!*

-UHHH--!

I'LL TAKE YOUR *WORD* FOR IT! RIGHT NOW, LET'S MAKE OURSELVES *SCARCE,* PAL!

AS ALWAYS, LAD, OUR MINDS ARE *KINDRED SPIRITS!* LET'S *RETREAT,* INDEED!

10

LET'S *DEPART,* MR. DRAKE-BOY, WHILE THE DEPARTING'S *GOOD!* THE NOBLE *BEAST* SHALL LEAD THE WAY!

I'M WITH *YOU,* MR. McCOY!

AND YET, IT ALMOST SEEMS AS IF OUR HAIRBREADTH ESCAPE WAS ACHIEVED *TOO EASILY--*

SUDDENLY...

A *METAL WALL--* DROPPING INTO PLACE!

LOOK OUT! UHHNN--!

AND WE'RE ON A *COLLISION COURSE* WITH IT!

WHILE, IN THE VERY HEART OF LUCIFER'S SUBTERRANEAN STRONGHOLD...

OBSERVE, XAVIER, HOW *EASILY* I HAVE DISPOSED OF YOUR GROUP'S *THREAT* TO ME!

THUS SHALL YOUR ENTIRE *PLANET* FALL BEFORE THE MIGHT OF WE WHO TREAD THE *COSMOS* ITSELF!

THEN, IT'S *TRUE--*WHAT I ALWAYS *SENSED!*

LUCIFER IS AN *AGENT* OF SOME ALIEN, STAR-SPAWNED RACE!

STILL, THOUGH MY MIND CANNOT YET PIERCE THE *MENTAL SCREEN* WITH WHICH HE COMPLETELY SURROUNDS HIMSELF, PERHAPS I CAN *STILL* TRICK HIM INTO PROVIDING THE MEANS OF HIS OWN *DEFEAT!*

YOU *OVERESTIMATE* YOURSELF, LUCIFER! EARTH CANNOT BE CONQUERED BY A FEW GIMMICKS AND A HANDFUL OF ROBOTS!

SO--YOU WISH *FURTHER PROOF* OF OUR POWERS? THEN LISTEN-- WHILE I SPEAK OF ...DOMINUS!

DOMINUS?

YES--FOR AGES NOW, MY RACE HAS PERFECTED IN *DOMINUS* A WEAPON OF INDESCRIBABLE POTENCY!

AND, THROUGH IT, THE ENTIRE *UNIVERSE* LIES WITHIN OUR REACH!

"EONS AGO, WE CREATED THE *ULTIMATE MACHINE--DOMINUS--*AS WELL AS THE COMPLEX ROBOTS NEEDED TO *OPERATE* IT...

11

"AND, WHILE YOUR *EARTH* WAS STILL A MASS OF FLOATING GASES, WE BEGAN TO EXTEND SWAY TO NEARBY WORLDS! ALWAYS THE PATTERN IS THE SAME..."

"WE ESTABLISH OUR HEAD-QUARTERS IN SECRET ON THE UNSUSPECTING PLANET, AND WHEN THE TIME IS RIPE--WE *STRIKE!*"

"SOON, YOUR WORLD--LIKE SO MANY BEFORE IT--SHALL BE BLANKETED BY RAYS DESIGNED TO TAKE AWAY THE *INDEPENDENT WILL* OF EVERYONE ON EARTH!"

IT WAS FOR THIS EXPRESS PURPOSE THAT THE IRRESISTIBLE MACHINE THAT WE CALL *DOMINUS*--AS WELL AS THE INDISPENSABLE ROBOTS THAT ALONE CAN *OPERATE* IT--WERE TELEPORTED TO EARTH THRU BEAMS OF IONIC LIGHT!

EVEN NOW, THE ROBOTS MAKE THE FINAL PREPARATIONS! SOON, YOU WILL WITNESS THE *END* OF MANKIND'S RULE ON EARTH!

YOU'RE *INSANE!* NO MERE *MACHINE* CAN POSSESS SUCH *AWESOME* POWER!

YOU STILL DO NOT *BELIEVE?* THEN, WATCH THIS SCREEN--AND SEE FOR *YOURSELF!*

"BEHOLD THE SCENE OF OUR *LAST* CONQUEST--A PLANET OF THE STAR *SIRIUS!* ONCE IT BOASTED A GREAT AND ADVANCED CIVILIZATION--NOW, ITS INHABITANTS SERVE US AS MERE *AUTOMATONS!*"

AND SO, WITH THAT ONCE-MIGHTY RACE NOW REDUCED TO SERVILE SLAVERY, *DOMINUS* HAS BEEN SENT *HERE!* SOON, YOUR PUNY SPHERE SHALL SHARE THE FATE OF COUNTLESS WORLDS *BEFORE* IT!

THUS IT SHALL *EVER* BE! FOR, IT IS OUR DESTINY TO *COMMAND!*

SO *THIS* IS THE MAD PLAN OF CONQUEST BEGUN A *DECADE* AGO--AND WHICH I HAVE ALWAYS KNOWN I WAS DESTINED TO *COMBAT!*

IF EVEN *HALF* OF WHAT HE SAYS IS *TRUE,* EARTH COULD BE IN THE GREATEST DANGER IT'S EVER KNOWN!

12

WHILE ELSEWHERE IN THE VAST UNDERGROUND COMPLEX...

IT'S NO USE--I CAN'T BREAK FREE! WHAT ABOUT *YOU*, SCOTT?

NEGATIVE! LOOKS AS IF LUCIFER HAS US RIGHT WHERE HE *WANTS* US!

MY WINGS ARE *USELESS* IN A SITUATION LIKE THIS-- BUT I MUST KEEP *TRYING*!

IF ONLY WE COULD RE-ESTABLISH MENTAL CONTACT WITH *PROFESSOR XAVIER*!

CYCLOPS, WHAT OF *ICEMAN* AND THE *BEAST*? WE HAVEN'T SEEN THEM SINCE WE WERE SEPARATED BY THAT MAN-MADE *WHIRLPOOL*!

WE CAN ONLY HOPE THAT THEY ARE STILL *FREE*--AND THAT SOMEHOW *THEY* WILL BE ABLE TO SMASH LUCIFER'S PLAN--WHATEVER IT MAY BE!

WAIT! SOMEONE'S APPROACHING-- *FAST!*

IT'S *BOBBY*--AND *HANK*! BUT, THEY'VE BEEN CAPTURED BY *GIANT ROBOTS*! WHAT ON EARTH--?

PUT THESE MORTALS INTO THE *COSMIC-CRYSTALLINE CUBE* WITH THE OTHERS!

HEAR THAT? MAYBE WE'LL GET OUR CHANCE *YET*!

CAREFUL, ANGEL! WAIT UNTIL THEY OPEN ONE SIDE OF OUR PRISON! THEN--

BUT, BEFORE THE X-MEN'S DEPUTY LEADER CAN FINISH...

UHNNN! WE'RE BEING HURLED *BACKWARDS*!

IT'S SOME SORT OF *INVISIBLE FORCE*--ACTIVATED AUTO-MATICALLY AS THE OPPOSITE SIDE OF THE CUBE OPENS!

WE SHOULD HAVE *KNOWN!* THEY'RE ONLY *TOYING* WITH US!

NOW TO--*HOLD!* WE ARE RECEIVING A MENTAL CALL FROM *LUCIFER!* HE DEMANDS OUR PRESENCE *AT ONCE!*

WE SHALL DEAL WITH THESE *LATER!*

THEY'RE TREATING US AS IF WE WERE MERE *CAGED ANIMALS*--TO BE DEALT WITH AT THEIR *LEISURE!*

PERHAPS THAT'S ALL WE *ARE*--TO *THEM!*

I ONLY HOPE THAT THE BEAST AND ICEMAN ARE ALL *RIGHT!* PERHAPS *TOGETHER* WE CAN MANAGE TO ESCAPE!

THEY SEEM TO BE UNHURT--ONLY *DAZED!* WHAT *HAPPENED* TO YOU TWO?

I'M NOT *SURE*, BUT I FEEL LIKE THE *LINCOLN TUNNEL* COLLAPSED ON ME!

MY SENSATIONS *PRECISELY*, MY COLLOQUIAL COLLEAGUE!

LOOK *ALIVE*, X-MEN! IT WOULD APPEAR WE'RE ABOUT TO GO ON A LITTLE *TRIP!*

13

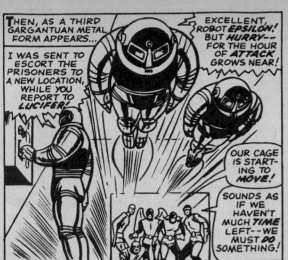

THEN, AS A THIRD GARGANTUAN METAL FORM APPEARS...

I WAS SENT TO ESCORT THE PRISONERS TO A NEW LOCATION, WHILE YOU REPORT TO LUCIFER!

EXCELLENT, ROBOT EPSILON! BUT HURRY-- FOR THE HOUR OF ATTACK GROWS NEAR!

OUR CAGE IS STARTING TO MOVE!

SOUNDS AS IF WE HAVEN'T MUCH TIME LEFT--WE MUST DO SOMETHING!

JEANIE, GIRL, THE BEGINNINGS OF A PLAN ARE TAKING COGENT SHAPE IN MY CALCULATING CRANIUM!

COULD YOU PROJECT A MINISCULE AMOUNT OF TELEKINETIC ENERGY THRU OUR GLASS CAGE?

I THINK I SEE WHAT YOU HAVE IN MIND, HANK! I'LL...TRY!

ONE OF THE FIRST ROBOTS FLIPPED THAT TINY LEVER IN ORDER TO OPEN THE FRONT OF THIS CAGE!

PERHAPS--AS WE PASS BY IT-- I CAN DO THE SAME!

KLIK!

YOU DID IT, MARVEL GIRL!

AND, AS THE FRONT OF THE TRANSPARENT PRISON SILENTLY LOWERS...

I THINK I'VE LOCATED A WEAK POINT ON THE ROBOT'S BACK!

IF I'M WRONG --WE'RE DOOMED!

ZAP!

GOOD OLD CYCLOPS--ALWAYS THE VERY SOUL OF OPTIMISM!

YOU GOT HIM, SCOTT --BUT WILL YOUR BLAST STOP HIM?

THE NEXT MOMENT, THE HIGH-FLYING ANGEL GETS HIS ANSWER, AS THE MONSTROUS CREATURE TOPPLES LIFELESSLY TO THE FLOOR...

HE'S DOWN FOR THE COUNT! YOU MUST HAVE SHORT-CIRCUITED HIM!

THIS IS NO TIME TO PAT OURSELVES ON THE BACK! WHO KNOWS HOW MANY MORE OF THESE THINGS ARE LURKING ABOUT?

ONE THING'S FOR SURE, CYKE-- A CHEERFUL CHARLIE YOU'RE NOT!

LISTEN! WE SEEM TO HAVE SOME SORT OF ALARM!

EEEE EEE EEE

JUST OUR LUCK! KNOCKING OUT THAT TIN-CAN TERROR MUST'VE DONE IT!

WHATEVER THE REASON --WE'RE IN FOR IT NOW!

YOU'RE RIGHT--AND I'VE A HUNCH THE REST OF THEM WON'T GIVE ME SUCH A CLEAN SHOT AT THEM!

EEEEE

LET'S GO! THE BOUNDING BEAST SHALL LEAD THE WAY!

UNFORTUNATELY, THERE'S JUST ONE WAY WE CAN GO-- FORWARD, RIGHT INTO LUCIFER'S OWN HEAD-QUARTERS!

14

AND, IN THE CENTRAL CHAMBER, THE FATEFUL ALARM DOES NOT ESCAPE THE NOTICE OF AN ANGERED LUCIFER...

THAT IS THE SIGNAL THAT ONE OF YOUR FELLOW ROBOTS HAS BEEN DISABLED--DOUBTLESS BY THE INFERNAL X-MEN! GO--HUNT THEM DOWN--AND SHOW NO MERCY!

WE DO OBEY! THEY SHALL NOT ESCAPE US!

EEEEEEE

MUST KEEP PROBING--DEEPER --DEEPER! FOR, THE FUTURE OF HUMANITY HANGS IN THE BALANCE!

SO, XAVIER--YOU PREFER TO PRETEND INDIFFERENCE TO THE FATE OF YOUR PRECIOUS MUTANTS!

THEN, KNOW THIS--I SHALL NO LONGER BE CONTENT MERELY TO RECAPTURE THEM!

THE X-MEN MUST BE DESTROYED!

MEANWHILE, FIVE GRIM FIGURES--TENSE BUT UNAFRAID IN THE MIDST OF MENACE--ARE APPROACHING EVER NEARER...

IT'S--FANTASTIC! WE SEEM TO BE WANDERING THRU ENDLESS CORRIDORS OF ULTRA-SCIENTIFIC MACHINERY!

ALL THAT'S MISSING IS BORIS KARLOFF!

HE MAY POP UP YET!

QUIET, EVERYBODY! TWO MORE ROBOTS --ZOOMING OUR WAY!

OUT OF SIGHT-- QUICK!

THEN, ALMOST BEFORE THE WARY X-MEN CAN TAKE COVER...

--WHEW!-- THOSE BABIES ARE TRAVELIN' LIKE THEY MEAN BUSINESS!

A MOST GRIEVOUS UNDERSTATEMENT, MISTER DRAKE!

WHEN DO WE STOP HIDING--AND START FIGHTING?

SOON, ANGEL-- BUT NOT YET!

ZOOOM

X-MEN! THIS IS PROFESSOR XAVIER! YOU MUST DO AS I DIRECT--WITHOUT QUESTION! WITHOUT HESITATION!

GREAT! NOW WE'LL SEE SOME ACTION! WAIT'LL I GET MY HANDS ON LUCIFER!

WAIT! LISTEN-- THERE'S MORE!

TELEPATHIC THOUGHTS-- FROM THE PROF!

UNDER NO CIRCUMSTANCES MUST YOU ATTEMPT TO DAMAGE THE GIGANTIC MECHANICAL COMPLEX WHICH IS CALLED... DOMINUS!

DOMINUS? SO THAT'S IT! THIS IMMENSE MACHINE ITSELF IS THE DANGER TO EARTH WE'RE PLEDGED TO DEFEAT, RATHER THAN THE ROBOTS!

CHECK, CYKE, OLD BOY! AND HERE'S A PASSAGE WHICH LOOKS LIKE IT LEADS TO THE VERY HEART OF THAT MACHINE! LET'S SCRAMBLE THRU IT AND DO SOME TUBE-SMASHING, WHILE WE'VE STILL GOT THE CHANCE!

NO, ANGEL--THAT'S JUST WHAT THE PROFESSOR SAID WE MUSTN'T DO! HE MUST HAVE SOME SORT OF PLAN--!

15

AT THAT SAME INSTANT...

THAT *TEARS* IT! I'M RIPPING UP EVERYTHING I *CAN* BEFORE LUCIFER'S METALLIC ERRAND-BOYS SHOW UP!

NO--YOU *CAN'T!* THE PROFESSOR SAID THE RESULTS WOULD BE *DISASTROUS!*

BUT DISASTROUS FOR *WHO*--US, OR LUCIFER? SORRY, CYKE, BUT I'M WITH *ANGEL* THIS GO-ROUND!

ANGEL--COME *BACK!* DON'T FORCE ME TO *STOP* YOU!

NO USE! HE WON'T *LISTEN!* THEN-- I HAVE NO *CHOICE*--!

THUS, BEFORE THE UNBELIEVING EYES OF HIS FELLOW X-MEN, THE DEPUTY LEADER *FIRES* ON THE FLYING FORM ABOVE...

--UNHHHNNN--!

HE *DID* IT! CYCLOPS STOPPED THE ANGEL-- JUST BEFORE HE COULD REACH THOSE WIRES!

STUNNED --CAN'T FLY--!

I DON'T KNOW WHAT'S GOTTEN *INTO* CYCLOPS--

BUT, HERE'S WHERE I KNOCK IT *OUTTA* HIM!

OH! I CAN'T SLOW HIM *DOWN* FAST ENOUGH!

NEVER FEAR--FOR THE *BEAST* IS HERE! BETWEEN THE *TWO* OF US, WE'LL BREAK HIS FALL!

AND, EVEN AS HANK McCOY LITHELY CATCHES THE PLUMMETING ANGEL, AN ANGRY *ICEMAN* HURLS HIS OWN FRIGID WEAPON--ONLY TO SEE...

THERE! MY *TELEKINETIC* POWER HAS DEFLECTED THAT CHUNK OF ICE!

THAP!

MARVEL GIRL! ARE YOU *OUTTA* YOUR *TREE?*

ARE YOU GONNA LET HIM GET AWAY WITH RAY-BEAMING THE *ANGEL?*

USE YOUR *EYES,* ICEMAN, LIKE *JEAN* DID! SHE KNOWS I ONLY *DAZED* ANGEL--HE'LL BE ALRIGHT IN A MINUTE!

CAN'T YOU *SEE?* ALL OF *MANKIND* IS AT STAKE--WHILE WE BATTLE AMONG *OURSELVES!*

ALL *I* SEE IS THAT YOU BLASTED ANGEL TO PROTECT THIS *MACHINE!*

NO, BOBBY! HE WAS JUST OBEYING *ORDERS!* PROFESSOR XAVIER KNOWS BETTER THAN *WE* DO HOW TO COMBAT *DOMINUS*... AND *LUCIFER!*

IF, INDEED, IT *WAS* THE PROFESSOR WHO CONTACTED US MENTALLY--WHICH I *DOUBT!*

17

AND, FURTHERMORE, I-- WHAT'S THAT *SOUND* BEHIND ME?

BEAST! LOOK OUT! IT'S ONE OF THE *ROBOTS!*

I DIDN'T *THINK* IT WAS *SOUPY SALES!*

WHILE, BELOW, A MANIACAL LAUGH ARISES FROM THE THROAT OF THE FALLEN *LUCIFER*, FREE AT LAST OF MARVEL GIRL'S TELEKINETIC ATTACK...

GOOD! THE FIRST OF MY FIVE SURVIVING ROBOTS DIVES FOR THE *KILL!*

DESTROY THE MORTALS, ROBOT *DELTA*--AT ANY PRICE!

NOT *ONE* OF THE ACCURSED X-MEN MUST REMAIN *ALIVE!*

HOWEVER, EVEN BEFORE THE ANGERED ALIEN CAN FINISH...

SKRAK!

A NOBLE TRY, MY FRENZIED FRIEND--BUT IT'S OBVIOUS YOU DO NOT POSSESS THE AMAZING AGILITY OF NIMBLE *BEAST!*

HOLY SMOKE! THE ROBOT WAS COMPLETELY *DEMOLISHED*--AND THE MACHINE WAS *UNHARMED!*

BUT, I DON'T *UNDERSTAND!* WHY DID THE ROBOT ATTACK SO *RECKLESSLY* THAT IT WAS *DESTROYED?*

THAT'S *IT*--THE SECRET OF THE PROFESSOR'S *TELEPATHIC WARNING!* --

UH OH! SAVE IT FOR *LATER*, SCOTTY BOY! *HERE COMES ANOTHER ONE*--

--AND, IT'S HEADING STRAIGHT FOR ANGEL! *DUCK*, WARREN!

I--*CAN'T MOVE!* MY WINGS-- STILL *NUMB!*

FIRST, THE *HELPLESS* ONE--AND THEN THE *OTHERS!*

THEN, AS TWO POWERFUL METAL HANDS REACH OUT FOR THE STRICKEN X-MAN...

ZIT!

THANKS, CYKE! YOU CAME THRU IN A *PINCH!*

THAT ALMOST MAKES ME FORGET THAT *YOU* MADE ME SUCH A VULNERABLE TARGET IN THE *FIRST* PLACE!

18

I--CAN'T EXPLAIN THAT *NOW*, WARREN! THAT INTENSE ENERGY-BLAST LEFT *ME* WEAK, ALSO!

QUICKLY, BOBBY-- A *CURVED* ICE SHIELD! IT'S OUR ONLY HOPE!

YOU DON'T KNOW HOW SORRY I AM TO HEAR YOU *SAY* THAT, CYKE-- 'CAUSE HERE COME THE *REMAINING THREE ROBOTS*--MOVIN' *FAST*!

HURRY, ANGEL!

RIGHT! EVERYBODY ON THIS PLATFORM-- ON THE DOUBLE!

LOOK! THE ROBOTS-- THEY'RE FIRING SIMULTANEOUS *RAYS* AT US FROM THEIR *FINGER-TIPS*!

ZZZ ZZZZ

LUCIFER COMMANDS US TO ATTACK WITH *FULL FORCE*! DESTROY --DESTROY!!

THEN, ASTOUNDINGLY...

THOOM!

IT--IT *WORKED*! MY ICE SHIELD DEFLECTED THEIR DEADLY RAYS, SO THAT THEY HIT THE *MACHINE*--AND IT FIRED THEM BACK AT LUCIFER'S MECHANICAL CHUMS!

JUST THINK--IF THE SHIELD *HADN'T* BEEN CURVED, THE BLASTS WOULD HAVE HIT MORE *SOLIDLY*--AND PROBABLY *BROKEN THRU*!

PERISH THE THOUGHT!

BELOW, FOR THE FIRST TIME SINCE THE CONFLICT BEGAN, PROFESSOR X SPEAKS...

YOUR ROBOTS ARE *FINISHED*, LUCIFER! YOUR SCHEME IS *ENDED*!

IT WAS *YOUR* DOING, XAVIER--YOU AND YOUR ACCURSED *X-MEN*! BUT, I SHALL YET LIVE TO HAVE MY *REVENGE*!

WAIT! THAT NOISE--THE *SUPREME ONE* CALLS!

BLEEP.. BLEEP.. BLEEP.. BLEEP..

SLOWLY, HALTINGLY, LIKE A MAN IN A DREAM, THE DEFEATED ALIEN MOUNTS THE DAIS BEFORE A GIANT SCREEN...

AGENT ONE-- WHY HAVE THE ACTI-SIGNALS FROM THE ROBOTS *CEASED*?

IT IS BECAUSE --THEY HAVE BEEN *DEMOLISHED*, SUPREME ONE--BY AN *ADVANCED BAND OF EARTHLINGS*!

I HAVE NO EXCUSES-- I ONLY ASK FOR *MERCY* AT YOUR HANDS!

19

THE NEXT MOMENT, THE DRAMATIC TABLEAU IS SHATTERED, AS THE MASSIVE METAL FIGURE STRIDES OMINOUSLY FORWARD...

OKAY, CYKE--THE PROFESSOR'S LEAVING US ON OUR *OWN*--SO YOU'D BETTER MAKE WITH THE *DEPUTY LEADER* BIT--AND *FAST!*

YOU CAN'T FIGHT AN ENEMY UNTIL YOU KNOW SOMETHING *ABOUT* HIM! SO, THE *FIRST* THING WE'VE GOT TO DO IS FIND OUT THE ROBOT'S *POWERS!*

GREAT THINKING, PAL--BUT WHAT'LL *COLOSSO* BE DOIN' IN THE *MEANTIME?*

ALL RIGHT, X-MEN--YOU HAVE *FIVE MINUTES* TO DEFEAT COLOSSO! THE TIMED PERIOD BEGINS-- *NOW!*

YOU'RE ENTIRELY TOO *BENEFICENT,* SIR!

THOSE STRANGE MULTI-COLORED *LIGHTS*--THEY HAVE AN ALMOST *HYPNOTIC* EFFECT--!

WELL, SOMEBODY HAS TO GET THE OLD BALL ROLLING--AND IT MIGHT AS WELL BE *ME!*

WAIT! YOU'RE FLYING DIRECTLY *AT* THE ANDROID!

FLY AN *EVASION COURSE,* ANGEL--AND BE CAREFUL NOT TO BE DAZED BY THOSE FLASHING *LIGHTS!*

RELAX, WORRY-WARTS! WITH MY SPEED, I CAN FLY *CIRCLES* AROUND THIS--

:UHHHNN!:

BZZZZZTT!

IT GOT ANGEL! HE'S FALLING--

I'M *PARALYZED*-- CAN'T *FLY*--!

SO *THAT'S* HIS MAIN POWER-- JUST ANOTHER CRUMMY *BLAST RAY!*

DON'T WORRY, WARREN! I'LL STOP YOUR FALL *TELEKINETICALLY!*

A SHEET OF *SOLID ICE* ON THE FLOOR AROUND HIM WILL PUT THE SKIDS TO THAT OVERGROWN *TRASH-CAN!*

IF IT WORKED ON THE *SENTINELS*, IT OUGHTTA WORK ON *COLOSSO!*

GOOD WORK, ICEMAN! *BUT*, HE ISN'T *MOVING* NOW--AND I HAVEN'T ENOUGH MENTAL ENERGY TO *PUSH* HIM OVER!

WELL, AT LEAST BOBBY'S *STOPPED* HIM--LONG ENOUGH FOR ME TO RECOVER! HE CAN'T ADVANCE WITHOUT *FALLING!*

HOWEVER, TO THE X-MEN'S SURPRISE...

UH OH! HEAT JETS FROM HIS *LEGS*--MELTING THE ICE! A *PUSH-OVER* THIS CHARACTER *ISN'T!*

A MOST ASTUTE DEDUCTION, MY *FROST-BITTEN* FRIEND!

SSSSS

THEN, THE MOST *POWERFUL*--AND MOST *TRAGIC*--OF THE MUTANT BAND STEPS TO THE FORE...

OUT OF THE WAY, ALL OF YOU! I'M UNLEASHING MY *POWER BEAM!*

IF I CAN DAMAGE A *VITAL SPOT*, THEN THE REST OF YOU WILL BE ABLE TO FINISH HIM OFF!

THE ONLY TIME *I'M* NOT A MENACE TO SOCIETY--IS WHEN I'M COMBATTING ONE!

CAREFUL WITH THOSE BEADY LITTLE EYES OF YOURS, CYKE! YOU ALMOST PULVERIZED THE NOBLE *BEAST!*

THE ROBOT'S MADE OF A MATERIAL THAT *REPELS* MY BEAM--I SHOULD HAVE *GUESSED!*

F.F.F.T!

3

THINGS AREN'T EXACTLY LOOKING *UP!* IF CYKE'S *EYE BEAMS* CAN'T STOP COLOSSO, WHAT *CAN?*

KLUMP!

THUNK!

DON'T *DESPAIR,* LADS! RELIEF IS JUST A *SECOND* AWAY!

BUT FIRST, IT BEHOOVES ME TO GET *BEHIND* MY POTENT PREY!

YET, THE *PROFESSOR'S* TESTS ARE *ALWAYS* CAPABLE OF *SOLUTION!* THERE *MUST* BE A WAY!

CAREFUL, HANK! IT'LL TAKE MORE THAN *RAW STRENGTH* TO DEFEAT THE ROBOT!

THUMP!

FEAR NOT, *FEMALE!*

THWAP!

HAVE I NOT ALWAYS HELD THAT VIOLENCE IS THE LAST REFUGE OF THE *INCOMPETENT?*

I MERELY WISH TO THROW IT *OFF-BALANCE,* SO THAT *SCOTT* CAN HAVE ANOTHER GO AT IT!

IT *DUCKED!* HOW *FRUSTRATING!*

BUT, IT COULDN'T HAVE *"SEEN"* ME—UNLESS THE *PROFESSOR* IS GUIDING IT FROM BELOW!

NO, HANK—I AM ONLY SUPPLYING IT WITH *POWER!* THE ANSWER TO YOUR QUESTION LIES *ELSEWHERE!*

THEN, THE MOMENTARILY STYMIED X-MEN RE-GROUP ON THE FLOOR, AS...

WE *STRUCK OUT* ACTING *SEPARATELY!* IT'S TIME TO SHOW WHAT *TEAMWORK* CAN DO!

SURE! THAT *MUST* BE IT—THE SAME WAY WE MANAGED TO DEFEAT OUR *PREVIOUS* ROBOT OPPONENTS!

BUT FIRST, WE'VE GOT TO FIND HIS *WEAKNESS!*

I'M WITH *YOU,* CYKE—BUT WE'D BETTER *HURRY!* OUR FIVE MINUTES ARE ALMOST *OVER!*

TEMPUS *FUGITS,* INDEED!

OH OH! DON'T LOOK *NOW,* BUT IT WOULD APPEAR THAT COLOSSO IS GETTING *RESTLESS!* HERE HE *COMES!*

AND HE LOOKS *MAD!* THE PROFESSOR MUST'VE EQUIPPED HIM WITH A *TEMPER,* IN ADDITION TO EVERYTHING ELSE!

I MUST BE GETTING *SMARTER,* DEPUTY LEADER! I THOUGHT OF THAT MOVE ALL BY *MYSELF!*

WE CAN WORRY 'BOUT *THAT* IN A SECOND! RIGHT NOW, DISPERSE, ALL OF YOU!

I HOPE I CAN LEVITATE MYSELF TO SAFETY *FAST* ENOUGH TO ELUDE THE ROBOT!

PARDON IF I SEEM *UNCHIVALROUS,* BUT GANGWAY!

WE CAN'T WIN THIS FIGHT BY *RUNNING AWAY!* WE'VE GOT TO MAKE A *STAND* --AND *FAST!*

HOWEVER...

IT'S--NO USE! YOU AND I WERE *TOO SLOW,* SCOTT! COLOSSO CAN USE US AS *SHIELDS* UNTIL THE FIVE MINUTES HAVE ELAPSED!

PERHAPS--BUT DID YOU SEE HOW THE LIGHTS ON ITS HEAD GLOWED MORE *BRIGHTLY* AS HE REACHED OUT FOR US? THAT MAY BE JUST THE CLUE WE *NEED!*

JEAN--THE PROFESSOR'S *BLANKET!* WILL IT TO COME TO US --AT ONCE!

OF COURSE, CYCLOPS! BUT, I *STILL* DON'T SEE--

JUST DO AS I SAY! THERE'S NO TIME FOR *EXPLANATIONS* NOW!

SO! SCOTT HAS FIGURED OUT THE SECRET OF THE ROBOT'S *SENSORY POWERS!*

ONCE AGAIN, HE'S PROVEN HIMSELF A *RESOURCEFUL* LEADER! BUT, THE BATTLE IS NOT YET *WON!*

EXCELLENT, JEAN! YOU BROUGHT THE BLANKET TO US IN *RECORD TIME!*

NOW, LET IT FALL OVER THE *HEAD* OF COLOSSO! GOOD GIRL!

THANKS--THOUGH, TO TELL THE TRUTH, I DON'T SEE HOW *THAT* WILL HELP!

WE'LL KNOW IN A MOMENT WHETHER I WAS RIGHT OR WRONG!

AND, THE NEXT SECOND, ASTONISHINGLY...

HE'S *DROPPING* US! YOU WERE *RIGHT!* BUT--WHAT DID THE BLANKET *DO?*

I GUESSED THAT THOSE *FLASHING LIGHTS* WERE THE SOURCE OF HIS "SEEING" THE BEAST ATTACK FROM BEHIND, SO WE *BLOCKED* THEM!

WE'LL HIT THE FLOOR *HARD!* WATCH YOURSELF!

5

DON'T BE SO *MELODRAMATIC*, SCOTTY, OLD BOY! THE *ANGEL* IS HERE TO GUIDE YOU DOWN *GENTLY!*

AS FOR *JEAN,* YOU SEEM TO HAVE FORGOTTEN HER *TELEKINETIC POWERS* WHICH FREED YOU IN THE *FIRST* PLACE!

THANKS WARREN!

HE'S *RIGHT!* I MUST WATCH MYSELF--FOR SHE MUST NEVER KNOW HOW MUCH I *CARE* FOR HER!

AND, EVEN AS CYCLOPS AND MARVEL GIRL REACH TH GROUND SAFELY...

THERE! THIS EXQUISITE *KNOT* SHOULD KEEP OUR FERRIC FOE'S SENSES CONFUSED A BIT LONGER!

BUT, I'LL NEED *HELP!* WHEREFOR *ART* THOU, BOBBY-O?

RIGHT *HERE,* CHUM--

MY CONCENTRATED *ICE BARRAGE* WILL SLOW DOWN HIS ATTEMPTS TO FREE HIMSELF!

WELL DONE, MY QUICK-FROZEN COMPEER! NOW, THE AGILE *BEAST* CAN TAKE HIS LEAVE!

KEEP IT UP, ICEMAN! AS LONG AS HIS HEAD IS COVERED, HE CAN'T OPERATE PROPERLY! THAT'S WHY HE DROPPED *JEAN* AND ME!

BUT, WHILE THE X-MEN PREPARE THEIR FINAL ATTAC COLOSSUS UNVEILS STILL MORE STARTLING SURPRISES!

WOULDN'T YOU *KNOW* IT! HE HAS *MORE* HEAT JETS IN HIS *HEAD*-- AND THEY'RE MELTING THE *ICE!*

NOT ONLY *THAT,* BUT WE HAVE ONLY *SECONDS* LEFT BEFOR OUR TIME IS OVER-- AND WE'LL HAVE *LOST* OUR FIGHT WITH THE ROBOT

WELL THEN, IT'S TIME FOR THE *SUPER-DELUXE X-MEN SPECIAL TREAT-MENT!* I'LL KEEP POURING ON THE *ICE* AS LONG AS I CAN--

WHILE I ADD MY *MENTAL* POWERS TO THE *PHYSICAL* ONES OF ANGEL AND THE BEAST-- TO TRY TO TOPPLE COLOSSO!

WITH HIS PRESENT PERPLEXED PERCEPTIONS, WE MAY BE ABLE TO DO JUST *THAT!*

IT'S *WORKIN* HE'S STARTING TO *WOBBLE.* DON'T LET UP

I CAN'T TUR MY BEAMS THE ROBOT F FEAR OF HITTING HAN OR WARREN BUT I *CAN* BLAST A HOL IN THE *FLOO* BENEATH ITS FEET!

THEN, WITH A RESOUNDING CRASH...

HE'S DOWN! THAT MEANS WE WON!

AND, WE DID IT AS A TEAM! NO ONE OF US COULD HAVE DONE IT ALONE!

THAT IS TRUE, SCOTT--

THOOM!

AND THAT, OF COURSE, WAS THE POINT OF YOUR BOUT WITH THE ROBOT! ALONE, THE POWERS OF EACH OF YOU ARE FORMIDABLE ENOUGH...

BUT, TOGETHER, YOU ARE ALMOST INVINCIBLE!

HOWEVER, DON'T PLAN TO REST ON YOUR LAURELS! I'LL IMPROVE COLOSSO--AND ONE DAY YOU MAY FACE HIM AGAIN!

KLIK!

IN THE MEANTIME, SINCE YOUR LAST VACATION WAS INTERRUPTED BY THE BATTLE WITH THE MIMIC*, I'M DISMISSING YOU ALL FOR A TWO WEEKS' HOLIDAY!

IF ANY EMERGENCY ARISES, I'LL CONTACT YOU MENTALLY!

GREAT! I'M HALFWAY HOME NOW!

WHAT A CHANCE TO VISIT MY SISTER IN ALBANY!

DID YOU JUST HEAR WHAT I HEARD, BEASTIE?

INDEED, I DID, BOBBY BOY! AND I'M RELATIVELY CERTAIN THAT WE ARE ELATED FOR SIMILAR REASONS!

*IN ISH #19. -SMUG STAN.

SAY, JEAN, HOW ABOUT DINNER IN MANHATTAN, BEFORE YOUR TRAIN LEAVES?

WHY, I'D LOVE IT, WARREN--IF IT WOULDN'T BE A BOTHER--

BOTHER? BITE YOUR TONGUE, GAL!

I PROPOSE, LAD, THAT WE TWO EMBARK FOR GREENWICH VILLAGE POST HASTE!

I'M WITH YOU, PAL!

ONLY CYCLOPS REMAINS PENSIVE, GRIM! I'M BECOMING EXTREMELY WORRIED ABOUT HIM!

IN ALMOST LESS TIME THAT IT TAKES TO RECOUNT, THE FIVE FABULOUS TEEN-AGERS ARE LEAVING FOR VARYING DESTINATIONS...

JEAN AND WARREN--MAKE A LOVELY COUPLE! I ENVY HIM MORE THAN I CAN EVER DARE REVEAL! I--

SCOTT--WHY DON'T YOU DINE WITH US? WE'D LOVE TO HAVE YOU, WOULDN'T WE, WARREN?

UH, YEAH--SURE! HOP ABOARD, OLD BUDDY!

THANKS! I--THINK I WILL!

I KNOW ANGEL DOESN'T REALLY WANT ME ALONG--BUT I CAN'T RESIST THE TEMPTATION TO SPEND EVEN A FEW MORE MINUTES NEAR THE ONE I LOVE!

AND THUS, THE X-MEN DEPART--LITTLE DREAMING THAT THEY LEAVE BEHIND THEM AN ANGUISHED MIND, A SOUL IN TORMENT...

THEY CAN WALK IN THE SUNSHINE--FEEL THE WIND STRIKING THEIR FACES--

WHILE I AM CONFINED TO THIS WHEELCHAIR--A HOPELESS CRIPPLE!

IS THERE NO CHANCE FOR ME? WILL I NEVER WALK AGAIN? I CAN'T ACCEPT THAT FATE! I CAN'T--!

7

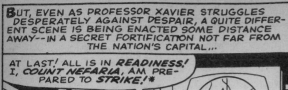

...S THE OFFENDED PASSERBY STRIDES ANGRILY AWAY...

WELL, MR. McCOY, IF YOU'RE *QUITE* FINISHED MAKING A *FOOL* OF YOURSELF!

OH, HELLO, VERA! NO! QUITE--I MEAN, UH--

NEVER MIND! IT WAS A PERFECTLY NATURAL MISTAKE!

WELL, GALS, WE'VE GOT JUST ENOUGH TIME TO CATCH A SHOW BEFORE DINNER! WHAT'LL IT *BE*-- "GOLDFINGER" OR "THUNDERBALL"?

LET'S MAKE IT "*THUNDER-BALL*"! I'VE ONLY SEEN *THAT* ONE *FOUR* TIMES!

TELL ME, HENRY-- WHAT DO YOU *DO* AT THAT PRIVATE SCHOOL YOU GO TO?

OH, MOSTLY I GUESS I HANG AROUND BY MY *FEET*!

HONESTLY! CAN'T YOU *EVER* BE SERIOUS?

THEN, AS LATE AFTERNOON FADES INTO DARKNESS, OUR SCENE SWITCHES TO A FASHIONABLE UPTOWN RESTAURANT, WHERE...

THE FILET MIGNON WAS *DELICIOUS*, WARREN! THANK YOU VERY MUCH!

A PLEASURE, JEANIE! I'M GLAD YOU--AND SCOTT, OF COURSE-- COULD *JOIN* ME!

STILL, WARREN, I WISH YOU'D LET ME PAY FOR MY OWN MEAL! I DON'T LIKE TO *IMPOSE*--!

NONSENSE! WE'LL HAVE NO MORE OF *THAT* KIND OF TALK!

WELL, I SUPPOSE WE'D BEST BE GOING! LET ME HELP YOU WITH YOUR COAT, JEAN!

WHY, THANKS *AGAIN*, KIND SIR!

CAN WE *DROP* YOU ANYWHERE, SCOTTY?

NO, THANKS! I'M...*MEETING* SOME PEOPLE NEAR HERE! I'M LATE *NOW*! SEE YOU IN TWO WEEKS!

MINUTES AFTERWARD, AS A HAPPY WARREN WORTHINGTON III DRIVES TOWARD GRAND CENTRAL STATION...

JEAN'S SO QUIET...SO *PENSIVE*! MAYBE SHE'S FINALLY BEGINNING TO FEEL ABOUT *ME* THE WAY I DO ABOUT *HER*!

OH, SCOTT...SCOTT...

WARREN IS A WONDERFUL GUY--BUT WHEN WILL YOU SEE THAT IT'S *YOU* WHOM I LOVE?

MEANWHILE, TO COMPLETE OUR CONFUSING LITTLE TRIANGLE, LET'S PICK UP ON SCOTT SUMMERS SOME BLOCKS AWAY...

WHY MUST *I*, OF ALL THE X-MEN, BE THE ONLY ONE WHOSE MUTANT POWER MAKES HIM A *POTENTIAL THREAT* TO ALL WHOM HE MEETS?

WELL, HERE'S CENTRAL PARK! MAYBE A WALK THRU IT'LL MAKE ME FEEL BETTER... --SOMEHOW!

I'M NOT *REALLY* MEETING ANY-ONE! I'VE JUST CHECKED INTO A NEARBY *HOTEL* FOR TWO WEEKS! BUT, I KNEW WARREN WANTED TO BE ALONE WITH *JEAN*--AND--

WAIT!

THAT FIGURE --LEVITATING OVER THE TREES! IT'S *MARVEL GIRL*! BUT, WHAT'S *SHE* DOING HERE--

9

A HEARTBEAT LATER...

SHE...VANISHED! OR, DID I ONLY IMAGINE HER?

MY EYES HAVE ALWAYS BEEN A CURSE TO ME! ARE THEY STARTING TO PLAY TRICKS ON ME, AS WELL?

MEANWHILE, IN THE MAMMOTH STRUCTURE WHICH IS GRAND CENTRAL STATION...

...SPECIAL BULLETIN! ONE OF THE MYSTERIOUS X-MEN HAS BEEN SEEN FLYING IN THE VICINITY OF CENTRAL PARK! STAY TUNED FOR...

THIS WOULD HAVE TO HAPPEN WHEN THE METS WERE ONLY FIVE RUNS BEHIND.

A FLYING X-MAN? BUT, ONLY WARREN AND I CAN FLY--AND HE JUST LEFT ME IN HIS CAR!

HER FEMININE CURIOSITY FULLY AROUSED, JEAN GREY HAILS A CAB, AND SOON...

LOOK, LADY, IT'S NONE'A MY BUSINESS, BUT THIS AINT NO PLACE FOR YOU --ESPECIALLY WITH THEM X-MEN AROUND!

THANK YOU, BUT REST ASSURED-- I CAN TAKE CARE OF MYSELF!

AND, AS THE CAB SPEEDS AWAY...

IF THE ANGEL DID FLY HERE AFTER DROPPING ME OFF, I'LL SOON LOCATE HIM AND FIND OUT WHAT'S UP!

BUT, IF IT'S AN IMPOSTOR, HE'S IN FOR IT!

EVERYTHING IS SO HUSHED-- SO TRANQUIL!

YET, WHY DO I HAV[E] THIS NAMELES[S] FEELING OF DREA[D]

SUDDENLY...

TREE BRANCHES-- GRABBING ME!

THAT FIGURE-- IN THE SHADOWS! HIS STRANGE WEAPON MUST BE ACTIVATING THE TREES!

WHO--?

YOU DO NOT KNOW ME, MARVEL GIRL...

BUT SOON THE WORLD WIL[L] REMEMBER THE NAME OF THE PLANTMAN *--AND CRINGE AT ITS MEREST MENTION!

AND NOW, MY FAIR LADY, MY CHLOROFORM GAS WILL TAKE CARE OF YOU!

UHHH--!

THAT GOT 'ER, BOSS!

*LAST SEEN IN STRANGE TALES #121, AS ALL GOOD MARVELITES KNOW! --STAN.

AS, A SHORT DISTANCE AWAY...

FIRST, I SEE MARVEL GIRL--THEN I DON'T! AND NOW, I'M CERTAIN I HEARD HER CRY OUT!

I DON'T KNOW WHAT'S GOING ON, BUT I THINK IT'S TIME CYCLOPS DID SOME INVESTIGATING!

IF THAT WAS JEAN, THEN WHAT HAPPENED TO WARREN?

THEN, GLANCING UPWARD, SCOTT SUMMERS SEES...

SPEAK OF THE DEVIL-- AND THERE'S THE ANGEL!

ANGEL! DOWN HERE! WAIT!

IT'S NO USE! EITHER HE DOESN'T HEAR ME --OR ELSE HE PRETENDS NOT TO! I'LL SEE IF I CAN KEEP UP WITH HIM!

AND NOW, IN CASE THERE IS A MIXED-UP MARVELITE LEFT WHO DOESN'T REALIZE THE X-MEN ARE BEING DECEIVED BY IMAGES, WE SWITCH OUR SWINGIN' SCENE AGAIN...

...LAST OBSERVED IN VICINITY OF CENTRAL PARK!...

CENTRAL PARK? BUT, WHAT WOULD ANY OF THE GANG BE DOING THERE? THERE'S SOMETHING FISHY ABOUT ALL THIS!

I WONDER...COULD IT BE UNUS OR THE BLOB? THEY'RE STILL ON THE LOOSE --AND NURSING AN OLD GRUDGE AGAINST THE X-MEN!

THE PARKING-LOT ATTENDANT IS TOO ENGROSSED IN THE BALL GAME TO SEE ME CHANGE AND FLY AWAY!

24 HOUR PARKING

I'M LUCKY THAT THE METS ARE ONLY SIX RUNS BEHIND!

HIS POWERFUL WINGS PROPELLING HIM ACROSS TOWN, THE WINGED MUTANT SWIFTLY REACHES HIS DESTINATION, AND...

THAT FORM--! IT'S SOMEONE-- IMPERSONATING ME!

WHOEVER IT IS, MUST BE SUPER-POWERED HIMSELF! I'M CLOSING IN ON HIM!

HOWEVER, THE NEXT INSTANT...

HE'S GONE-- IF HE WAS EVER THERE IN THE FIRST PLACE!

BUT I SEE ANOTHER FORM-- NEAR THOSE TREES!

GLEEP!

ALLOW ME TO INTRODUCE MYSELF, ANGEL! MEN CALL ME...THE SCARECROW!

MISTER, I NEVER HEARD OF YOU!* BUT IF YOU'RE RESPONSIBLE FOR THAT PHONEY VERSION OF ME, I'LL--

*YOU HAVE, THOUGH--IF YOU WERE AROUND WAY BACK IN SUSPENSE #51. --SUPERANNUATED STAN.

11

THEN, OUT OF NOWHERE...

WHAT THE--? *CROWS* --PULLING A TIGHT-MESHED *NET* OVER ME!

ANGELS RUSH IN WHERE *FOOLS* FEAR TO *TREAD*, TO COIN A CLICHÉ!

LAUGH WHILE YOU *CAN*, MISTER--THIS THING WON'T HOLD ME FOR *LONG*!

AH, BUT THIS IS NO *ORDINARY* NET, MY FINE FEATHERED X-MAN! ITS FIBRES ARE DESIGNED TO *ADHERE* TO ANYTHING CAUGHT INSIDE!

HE'S *RIGHT*! I'M *CAUGHT* LIKE A FLY IN *FLYPAPER*.

I THOUGHT IT WOULD BE MOST APPROPRIATE TO SEE THE HIGH-FLYING *ANGEL* LAID LOW BY WINGED CREATURES SUCH AS *HIMSELF*!

AND NOW, I'D LIKE TO INTRODUCE YOU TO SOME *OTHER* FRIENDS OF MINE--MEMBERS OF THE INFAMOUS *MAGGIA*!

THE PLEASURE'S ALL *OURS*, ANGEL!

THE *MAGGIA*? I THOUGHT THAT CRIME CARTEL HAD BEEN *SMASHED*!

AND, EVEN AS A SECOND ENSNARED MUTANT FALLS VICTIM TO COUNT NEFARIA'S COSTUMED HIRELINGS, TWO OTHER X-MEN ARE BLISSFULLY UNAWARE OF THE MOUNTING MENACE...

HOW ABOUT AN AFTER-MOVIE SNACK, BOYS-- SODA AND POTATO CHIPS?

YOU TALKED US INTO IT, ZELDA!

MEANWHILE I'LL TUNE IN SOME *MUSIC*!

A LAUDABLE IDEA, ROBERT, MY LAD! THERE'S A *BEETHOVEN* CONCERT COMING ON IN A FEW MINUTES, I BELIEVE!

THAT'S WHAT I *LIKE* ABOUT YOU, HANK! YOU'RE SO *REFINED*!

SUDDENLY, AS THE RADIO WARMS UP...

...AND, ACCORDING TO LATEST REPORTS, THERE HAVE BEEN SEVERAL ADDITIONAL SIGHTINGS OF *X-MEN* IN CENTRAL PARK!...

WHAT? BUT--THAT *CAN'T* BE! ER, I MEAN...WHAT WOULD THE X-MEN BE DOING *THERE*?

MUST BE CAREFUL-- SO THE GIRLS DON'T GUESS OUR *SECRET*!

I DON'T KNOW, HANK! BUT, UH, WHAT DO *WE* CARE?

WE *DON'T*, OF COURSE! STILL, THIS NEWS IS MOST *UNNERVING*! I THINK I'D BEST RETIRE TO OUR *HOTEL*-- AND TAKE SOME *TRANQUILIZERS*!

A POOR EXCUSE IS BETTER THAN *NONE*, BOBBY BOY! MAKE MY EXCUSES TO THE LADIES--WHILE I DO SOME INVESTIGATING AS...THE *BEAST*!

WHERE'S *HANK* GOING, VERA?

TO TH' MOO... FOR A... I CARE...

SURE, BUDDY!

SOON AFTERWARD, A STRANGE FIGURE STALKS HIS PREY AMID THE CAGES OF CENTRAL PARK ZOO...

THAT LAST SIGHTING TOOK PLACE NEAR HERE! BUT, THE ZOO IS *CLOSED* FOR THE EVENING --AND WHY WOULD ONE OF MY SUPER-POWERED ASSOCIATES COME HERE IN *FULL COSTUME?*

THEY CAME FOR THE SAME REASON THAT *YOU* DID, FOOL-- TO BE *CAPTURED!*

-EH?- WHO'S *THAT?*

I AM KNOWN AS...

...THE *PORCUPINE*!!

I BELIEVE IT!

ENOUGH REPARTEE! THIS NERVE GAS WILL STILL YOUR *PRATTLING* TONGUE!

YOUR VOLUMINOUS *VOCABULARY* IS MOST *HEARTENING,* MY *LOQUACIOUS* CHUM!

BUT, YOUR HOSTILE *PERSONALITY* IS STRICTLY FOR THE *BIRDS,* SO--

FSSTT!

SPROING!

ONE BLOW FROM MY *PRODIGIOUS* FEET, AND-- -YEEOW!-

OH, I FORGOT TO *WARN* YOU--

THESE STUDS ON MY BELT GIVE ME *COMPLETE* CONTROL OVER THE QUILLS IN MY SPECIAL SUIT-- ENABLING ME TO *FEND OFF* YOUR PUNY ATTACK!

NOW, *GROVEL* BEFORE ME--AND PERHAPS I MAY *SPARE* YOU!

THEN, AS THE AGILE X-MAN LANDS ON HIS AMPLE HANDS...

I *UNDERESTIMATED* ME, MY FRIEND!

IF THE NOBLE BEAST CANNOT FIGHT ON HIS *FEET,* HE TAKES TO HIS *HANDS*-- NOT HIS *KNEES!* BUT --*WHAT*--?

A SIMPLE *HYPNOTIC DISC*--TO DEFEAT A SIMPLE *FOE!*

AND, MOMENTARILY MESMERIZED BY THE SPINNING DISC, HANK McCOY IS TAKEN PRISONER, AS SEVERAL SINISTER FORMS COME OUT OF HIDING...

HE WON'T BREAK *THEM* ROPES IN A HURRY, PORCUPINE! BUT, WHY DO WE HAFTA *BOTHER?* WHY NOT JUST BUMP 'IM OFF?

THAT I WOULD *GLADLY* DO, CHURL...

BUT, *COUNT NEFARIA* HAS NEED OF HIM-- AND, HE SHALL *HAVE* HIM!

13

MEANWHILE, WORRIED ABOUT WHAT MAY HAVE BEFALLEN HIS FRIEND, BOBBY BLAKE RETURNS TO THE HOTEL ROOM HE AND HANK ARE SHARING...

NO, I'M SORRY-- BUT MISTER McCOY HAS NOT CALLED!

-UH-, THANK YOU!

I DON'T KNOW WHY I LET THE BEAST TALK ME INTO STAYING BEHIND, JUST TO SMOOTH THINGS OVER WITH THE GIRLS! NOW, I'M REALLY GET-TING WORRIED ABOUT HIM!

I'LL SEE IF I CAN LEARN ANYTHING FROM THE NEWS!

BUT, THE ANXIOUS TEEN-AGER NOT READY FOR THE NEWS HE HEARS...

...AND, ONLY MINUTES AGO, POLICE PROWL-CARS SIGHTED THE ICEMAN, MOVING TOWARD THE LAKE AREA OF THE PARK...

THAT SETTLES IT! I WAS SUPPOSED TO MEET HANK HERE...

BUT, I'M NOT LETTING ANY IMPOSTOR MASQUERAD AS ME AND GET AWAY WITH IT! IT'S TIME FOR THE REAL ICEMAN TO G INTO ACTION!

AND, EXACTLY ONE MINUTE LATER...

THIS VACATION WAS UNPLANNED, SO HANK AND I DECIDED JUST TO SPEND THE TWO WEEKS IN NEW YORK, SEEING PLAYS AND MOVIES--AND, OF COURSE, ZELDA AND VERA!

BUT NOW, IT LOOKS AS IF VACATION-TIME IS OVER!

THE HUMAN RACE IS ALREADY DISTRUSTFUL ENOUGH OF US MUTANTS! WE SURE DON'T NEED ANY BAD PUBLICITY FOR TERRORIZING CENTRAL PARK!

WAIT--THERE'S THE BOGUS ME NOW-- STRAIGHT AHEAD!

HE SEES ME! HE'S HEADING DOWN-- RIGHT BY THE EDGE OF THE LAKE!

WELL, AT LEAST I'M SURE OF ONE THING! IT ISN'T UNUS OR THE BLOB*, AS I HAD SUSPECTED!

*LAST SEEN ATOP A SPEEDING SUBWAY IN X-MEN #20, REMEMBER?--STAN.

BUT, AS THE ICY X-MAN ALIGHTS AT LAKE'S EDGE...

GONE--WITHOUT A TRACE! THIS HAS ALL THE EARMARKS OF A FIRST-RATE TRAP!

BUT, IF IT IS, YOU CAN BET YOUR BOOTIES THAT THE ICEMAN WILL END UP THE TRAPPER!

WISHFUL THINKING, YOU WALKING POPSICLE! FOR, YOU'RE ALREADY AS GOOD AS CAUGHT!

WHO THE HECK IS THAT? I CAN'T SEE ANY-BODY--!

OF COURSE NOT, YOU FROST-COVERED JUVENILE DELINQUENT-- BECAUSE I DIDN'T WANT YOU TO!

BUT, NOW IT'S TIME FOR YOU TO MEET ...THE EEL!

I COULDN'T SEE HIM BEFORE--I THE DARKNES NOW, HE'S GLOWING W ELECTRICIT

SORRY I'M NOT TREMBLING DOWN TO MY TIPPY-TOES, MISTER--BUT I NEVER HEARD OF YOU BEFORE!

STILL, I DON'T FIGURE YOU'RE FROM THE WELCOME WAGON--SO I'LL JUST ENCASE YOU IN ICE TILL WE CAN TALK!

YAK, YAK, YAK! YOU'RE AS BAD AS THE BLASTED HUMAN TORCH!*

EEL'S FIRST OPPONENT, IN STRANGE TALES #117. --GUESS WHO.

BUT, THE TORCH DEFEATED ME--BECAUSE MY POWERS WERE STILL NEW TO ME!

SMASHED THRU THE ICE-PRISON WITH ONE ELECTRICAL JOLT!

WHAT HAPPENED TO YOUR BLOCK OF ICE WAS NOTHING, PAL, COMPARED TO WHAT'S GONNA HAPPEN TO YOU!

YOU'LL NEVER ESCAPE HIS NEXT ELECTRICAL BLAST! I--;UHHHNN!-

ZAPT!

NEVER SAY NEVER, EEL! SOONER OR LATER, YOU END UP WITH EGG ON YOUR FACE!

CYKE! WHERE'D YOU COME FROM?

I'VE BEEN WANDERING AROUND IN THE PARK FOR A WHILE--AND I SAW YOU AND YOUR CARBON-COPY COME TO EARTH!

I DIDN'T WANT TO INTERFERE, BUT I DIDN'T WANT TO RISK YOUR GETTING HURT!

BELIEVE ME, I WOULDN'T HAVE HAD IT ANY OTHER WAY!

BUT, HAVE YOU SEEN THE BEAST? HE CAME HERE EARLIER!

NO--BUT I SAW ANGEL AND MARVEL GIRL--OR ELSE THEIR EXACT TWINS! AT THIS STAGE I'M NOT SURE WHICH!

LISTEN! A TWIG--SNAPPING! WE'RE BEING WATCHED!

WATCHED, NOTHING! LOOK WHAT JUST CRAWLED OUTTA THE WOODWORK!

SNAPP!

IT WOULD APPEAR THAT OUR PSEUDO-IMAGE OF ICEMAN HAS NETTED NOT ONE, BUT TWO, X-MEN! AND, IT IS ONLY FITTING THAT I SHOULD BE THE ONE TO MAKE THE CAPTURE!

TURN, BUFFOONS--AND MEET YOUR MASTER!

THE EEL WAS NOT YOUR MATCH--BUT NO MAN THAT LIVES CAN STAND AGAINST...THE UNCANNY UNICORN!

THIS MUST BE HOMECOMING WEEK FOR OBSCURE VILLAINS! WE NEVER HEARD OF YOU, EITHER!

BUT, IF IT'S A FIGHT YOU WANT--I'M IN THE MOOD!

LET'S GET 'IM, CYKE!

15

BLAST FROM MY *EYES* OUGHT TO PUT YOU OUT OF COMMISSION!

WHAT THE--? THE RAYS ARE BEING *BLOCKED*-- BY SOME SORT OF *ENERGY SHIELD!*

PRECISELY, *FOOL!*

IF EVEN MIGHTY *IRON MAN* COULD NOT DEFEAT THE *UNICORN*, WHAT CHANCE HAS A STRIPLING SUCH AS *YOU?*

*IN ISH #56--OF *SUSPENSE*, WHAT ELSE? --SLY OL' STAN.

BUT, I HAVE PLAYED THE *DEFENDER* LONG ENOUGH! NOW, TASTE THE IRRESISTIBLE MIGHT OF MY *POWER HORN!*

NO, THANKS! I'LL TAKE YOUR *WORD* FOR IT!

GOT TO *DODGE* FOR A MOMENT--THEN MATCH *MY* BEAM AGAINST *HIS!*

SO--THE MOST DANGEROUS OF THE *X-MEN* FLEES MY POWER! BUT IT SHALL AVAIL HIM *NAUGHT!*

THIS HAS GONE *FAR ENOUGH!*

AND, AS THE MOST MENACING OF NEFARIA'S HIRELINGS PREPARES TO UNLEASH ANOTHER AWESOME BLAST...

HOLD IT RIGHT THERE, *BUSTER!* I'M PUTTING THAT *POWER HORN* OF YOURS IN *COLD STORAGE!*

WHAT? YOU *DARE*--

LITTLE DOES MY *ATTACKER* REALIZE THAT MY *HELMET*-- DEVELOPED BY MY FORMER COMMUNIST OVERLORDS--HAS DEVICES EVEN FOR SUCH AN EMERGENCY AS *THIS!*

THERMAL UNITS IN HIS HEADGEAR-- MELTING THE ICE AS FAST AS I *CREATE* IT!

I'VE GOT TO KEEP *POURING IT ON*--JUST LIKE I DID WITH *COLOSSO!*

BUT, THAT VERY INSTANT...

YOU CAN *RELAX* NOW, UNICORN! THE *EEL* IS BACK IN BUSINESS!

I WAS *CARELESS* --FORGOT ALL ABOUT MY OWN OPPONENT!

BOBBY! HE'S BEEN STUNNED INTO UNCONSCIOUSNESS! IT'S ALL UP TO *ME* NOW!

THEN, SLIPPING UNOBSERVED FROM THE ENSHADOWED PORT, THE SINISTER FREIGHTER SAILS ALONG THE COASTLINE OF AN UNSUSPECTING AMERICA...

...UNTIL, IN THE MISTY, MURKY HOURS OF DAWN, IT ARRIVES AT THE UNASSUMING BUILDING WHICH SERVES AS THE CAMOUFLAGED FORTRESS OF COUNT NEFARIA...

SO--MY FORCES HAVE RETURNED! AND WITH THEM, ACCORDING TO THEIR RADIO MESSAGES, ARE THE VAUNTED X-MEN!

THEN, THE TIME HAS COME... TO BEGIN!

EXACTLY ONE HALF HOUR LATER, FIVE UNIQUELY-GARBED CRIMINALS GATHER OMINOUSLY ABOUT THE BROODING FORM OF THEIR LEADER, THE INFAMOUS MASTER OF IMAGES...

THIS, THEN, IS THE BAND OF LIEUTENANTS I HAVE CHOSEN TO ASSIST ME SINCE I HAVE REGAINED LEADERSHIP OF THE MAGGIA! FIVE COSTUMED CUTTHROATS --EACH A SUPER-VILLAIN IN HIS OWN RIGHT, WHO HAD BEEN DEFEATED IN BATTLE AND LYING LOW UNTIL I LOCATED HIM!

AND YET, NONE OF THESE MASKED HIRELINGS MAY I TRUST! EACH CONSIDERS HIMSELF A POTENTIAL LEADER OF THE MAGGIA--MERELY WAITING FOR ME TO MAKE THE MISSTEP, THE FATAL ERROR, WHICH WILL GIVE HIM THE CHANCE TO SEIZE THE REINS OF POWER!

BUT, I SHALL NOT GIVE ANY OF THEM TH OPPORTUNITY! FOR, THERE IS TOO MUC AT STAKE--MUCH MORE THAN ANY OF THEM CAN DREAM--FOR ME TO SHOW THE SLIGHTEST WEAKNESS, THE SLIGHTEST HESITATION!

WELL, I DO NOT PAY YOU MERELY TO STAND ABOUT, LOOKING OMINOUS! TELL ME THE NAME AND CONDITION OF YOUR PRISONERS!

MARVEL GIRL-- UNCONSCIOUS BUT SAFE!

THE ANGEL-- CAPTURED UNHARMED!

I CAPTURED THE ONE KNOWN AS THE BEAST--ALSO INTACT!

EXCELLENT--IF MY EXAMINATION BEARS YOU OUT!

CYCLOPS AND THE ICEMAN--SUBDUED BY THE EEL AND MYSELF--HAVE BEEN STUNNED INTO SUBMISSION!

THEN...THE X-MEN'S GLOATING CAPTOR APPEARS!

SO--THESE ARE THE DREADED MUTANTS WHOM THE WORLD FEARS! PERHAPS YOU HAVE BEEN OVER-RATED!

EASY, ANGEL! LET'S LET *HIM* DO THE TALKING FIRST!

COULD BE, MISTER! WHY DON'T YOU *RELEASE* US--AND *FIND OUT?*

A WISE SUGGESTION, CYCLOPS! TRULY, THERE IS NO REASON FOR US TO REMAIN *ENEMIES!* I, COUNT NEFARIA, AM HERE RATHER TO PROPOSE AN *ALLIANCE!*

YOU EXPECT US TO WORK *WITH* YOU --IN THE *MAGGIA*

OF COURSE! WHAT COULD BE MORE *NATURAL?* THE WORLD *DESPISES* YOU-- AS IT DESPISES THE UNDERWORLD GROUP WHOM *I* REPRESENT!

I OFFER YOU THE *SUPREME OPPORTUNITY...FOR REVENGE!*

I PAUSE FOR A REPLY! WILL YOU *JOIN* ME--IN RESTORING THE MIGHT OF THE *MAGGIA* TO ITS FORMER GLORY?

COUNT, I DON'T KNOW *WHAT* YOU'RE PLAN-NING--OR *WHY* YOU THOUGHT WE'D GO ALONG WITH YOU-- BUT I'VE GOT A *BULLETIN* FOR YOU!

YOU'RE *NOT WELL!*

THE BEAST SPEAKS FOR *ALL* OF US, NEFARIA!

SO--THAT IS YOUR ANSWER! I WOULD HAVE PREFERRED THAT YOU JOIN ME *WILLINGLY!*

HOWEVER, YOU LEAVE ME NO CHOICE! FOR, REST ASSURED, MY COSTUMED CAPTIVES-- JOIN ME YOU *SHALL!*

NOW, I LEAVE YOU TO *RECONSIDER* YOUR DECISION! BUT, PONDER *THESE WORDS*

IN A MATTER OF *MINUTES*, I SHALL DO WHAT NO MAN BEFORE ME HAS EVER DONE! I SHALL STEAL AN ENTIRE CITY--THE *CAPITAL OF THE UNITED STATES!*

WHAT? YOU'RE *MAD!*

VERY WELL, THEN! *THINK* ME MAD-- FOR THE *MOMENT!* BUT KNOW *THIS*-- I SHALL *RANSOM* THE NATION'S CAPITAL--FOR *ONE HUNDRED MILLION DOLLARS*--

--AND *YOU*, MY FINE PRINCIPLED FRIENDS, WILL *COLLECT* IT FOR ME!

NEVER! *NOTHING* WILL EVER MAKE THE X-MEN TURN *TRAITORS!*

WE SHALL SEE, ANGEL--WE SHALL *SEE!*

THEN, SCANT SECONDS LATER

AND NOW, LET THE DRAMA *BEGIN!* FOR, IS FAR MORE IMPORTA FAR MORE *CRUCIAL* THAN EVEN THE *X-ME* CAN SUSPECT!

WHAT IS THE DARK, BROODIN SECRET WHICH THE VILLAIN COUNT NEFARIA HIDES? AN WHAT OF THE UNCANNY *UNICORN* AND HIS COSTUME COHORTS? YOU'LL LEARN M ABOUT ALL THESE --AND A HOST OF THE USUAL *MAGNIFICENT MARVE SURPRISES*--IN X-MEN #2. BE HERE--IT'S *YOUR* KINDA YARN, PUSSYCAT!

20

AND, INSIDE THE TRANSPARENT PRISON...

LOOK, OFFICER, IF THIS IS SOME KINDA *ALERT*, HOW LONG IS IT GONNA *LAST?* THIS TRUCK'S LOADED DOWN WITH *PERISHABLE GOODS!*

IF THIS *IS* JUST A TEST, MAC, I DON'T KNOW ANY MORE ABOUT IT THAN *YOU* DO--AND DON'T I WISH I *DID!*

THE CARS ARE BACKED UP FOR *MILES* ALREADY!

MEANWHILE, IN THE CAPITOL BUILDING, AMERICA'S LAW-MAKERS HAVE MUCH MORE ON THEIR MINDS THAN THE *TRAFFIC!*

I DON'T *LIKE* IT! THE PRESIDENT ASSURED US THAT DOME'S NOT OF *OUR* MAKING!

I WONDER--COULD IT BE...*THEIRS?*

WE MUST GET TO THE *BOTTOM* OF THIS, AND *FAST!* I'M CALLING THE *PENTAGON.*

BUT, EVEN AS THE SENATOR DIALS, BOTH THE CIVIL AND MILITARY AUTHORITIES ARE ALREADY ON THE SPOT...

AND I MIGHT AS WELL BE SWINGING A *STRAND OF SPAGHETTI* AS THIS *AX!*

NO GO! THIS PNEUMATIC DRILL WILL CUT *DIAMOND* --BUT IT WON'T EVEN *DENT* THIS STUFF!

ALRIGHT, MEN-- THAT'S *ENOUGH!* WE'LL HAVE TO *BLAST* OUR WAY IN!

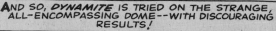

AND SO, *DYNAMITE* IS TRIED ON THE STRANGE, ALL-ENCOMPASSING DOME--WITH DISCOURAGING RESULTS!

WHROOM!

WE STRUCK OUT *AGAIN!* WHAT'S THAT THING *MADE* OF, ANYWAY?

GENERAL, I'VE GOT A HUNCH THAT NOTHING SHORT OF AN *A-BOMB* IS GOING TO SMASH THRU THAT BARRIER!

YOU MAY BE *RIGHT*, CAPTAIN--

BUT, WE *DARE NOT* USE NUCLEAR WEAPONS WITHOUT KNOWING JUST HOW STRONG THE DOME *IS!* OTHERWISE, THE LOSS IN LIVES AND PROPERTY COULD BE *STAGGERING!*

THEN, WHAT IS THERE LEFT THAT WE *CAN* DO, GENERAL?

NOTHING--EXCEPT SIT AND *WAIT!* I SUSPECT THAT WHOEVER CONSTRUCTED THIS DEVICE WILL GET IN TOUCH WITH *US!*

AND--YOU GUESSED IT, MARVELITE--AT THAT VERY MOMENT...

I HAVE GIVEN WASHINGTON--AND THE *NATION*--LONG ENOUGH TO DETERMINE THAT NOTHING THEY CAN DO WILL RID THEM OF MY *CRYSTALLINE DOME!* NOW, IT IS TIME TO PRESENT MY *DEMANDS!*

FOR, IN SO DOING, I SHALL *FORCE* THE X-MEN TO BECOME MY *ALLIES* IN THIS MOST DARING OF ALL POSSIBLE CRIMES!

BUT, *WHY* CAN'T THE FETTERED CRIMEFIGHTERS CONTACT THEIR LEADER TELEPATHICALLY? WE'RE *HOPING* YOU'D ASK--

I'M ALMOST *GLAD* MY X-MEN ARE HAVING A VACATION JUST NOW--

FOR, THIS NEW INVENTION I'M PERFECTING IS SO IMPORTANT I MUST GIVE IT MY *UNDIVIDED ATTENTION!*

THAT *NOISE!* OH, IT'S JUST THE *TELEPHONE!*

I'VE MENTALLY *SEALED OFF* MY BRAIN, SO THAT WHILE I'M WORKING, EVEN THE *X-MEN* CAN'T CONTACT ME! BUT, I *FORGOT* ABOUT SUCH A MUDANE THING AS A *TELEPHONE!*

HELLO, GENERAL NO, AS A MATTER OF FACT, I *HAVEN'T* BEEN LISTENING TO THE RADIO!

WHAT? AN EMERGENCY--REGARDING TH X-MEN? YES, C COURSE I'LL MEET YOU THERE--WITH THE *HOUR!*

THAT WAS *GENERAL FREDRICKS*--WITH WHOM I WORKED AS CIVILIAN ADVISER WHEN WE DEFEATED THE *SENTINELS!*

HE SAYS THAT THE X-MEN ARE THREATENING THE *NATION'S CAPITAL*, AND HOPES THAT I CAN BE OF SOME ASSISTANCE IN *COMBATTING* THEM!

HIS STORY IS *FANTASTIC*-- BUT HE CAN'T BE *LYING!* I MUST CONTACT MY STUDENTS!

ATTENTION, *X-MEN*, WHEREVER YOU ARE! CONTACT ME *AT ONCE!* DO YOU *READ ME?*

NO ANSWER WI MY FIRST TRY THEY MUST B SOME DISTANC *AWAY!* BUT WILL REAC THEM! I MUS

MEANWHILE, IN NEFARIA'S HIDE-OUT NEAR WASHINGTON...

DON'T GIVE UP, MARVEL GIRL! I'VE GOT AN *IDEA!*

IF ONLY YOU COULD *BYPASS* THE METAL BAND ON MY HEAD AND OPEN MY *VISOR* SLIGHTLY, MY POWERFUL EYE BEAMS WOULD FREE US!

I-I'LL *TRY*, SCOTT! BUT, I'M SO *WEAK!*

YOU'VE *GOT* TO TRY, JEAN! THE FATE OF A *CITY* IS AT STAKE!

IT'S *GIVING!* I CAN MENTALLY FEEL THE VISOR *OPENING*, BUT--

THAT *DID* IT! YOU MANAGED PRY IT OPEN JUST ENOUGH SO THAT THE ENERGY BEAM FROM MY EYES *FORCED* I

I'LL TURN THE BEAM ON MY OWN BONDS, THEN FREE THE *REST* OF YOU!

DON'T TAKE TOO LONG, CY I'M GETTING AWFULLY *TIRED* OF BEING THE PO MAN'S *PRISONER OF ZEND*

NEXT, WITH GRIM RESOLUTENESS, SCOTT SUMMERS SWIFTLY FREES HIS FELLOW X-MEN...

PFAP!

THAT'S MORE *LIKE* IT! NOW, LET'S TACKLE *NEFARIA* AND THOSE CREEPS WHO CAPTURED US!

WHAT COULD THE COUNT HAVE MEANT WHEN HE SAID WE WOULD *HAVE* TO JOIN HIM?

WE CAN'T BE *SURE*, JEAN--

BUT, MY GUESS IS THAT HE'S IN THE PROCESS OF *FRAMING* US FOR WHATEVER COLOSSAL CRIME HE'S COMMITTING--FIGURING THAT, AS *OUTCASTS*, WE WILL HAVE NO ONE TO TURN BUT *HIM*!

HOLD STILL, HANK, AND-- *THERE*!

MANY THANKS, LOQUACIOUS LEADER! BUT, WHY MUST THE LONG-SUFFERING *BEAST* ALWAYS BE LEFT TO *LAST*?

OH WELL--C'EST LA VIE, AS THEY SAY!

NOW COMES THE *GOOD* PART! WAIT'LL I PUT THE ICE-COLD KIBOSH ON THAT SLIPPERY *EEL*!

WAIT, BOBBY! LISTEN, ALL OF YOU--WE'RE BEING CONTACTED MENTALLY BY THE *PROFESSOR*! I HAD A *HUNCH* HE'D FIND US SOONER OR LATER!

ATTENTION, X-MEN! THIS IS *PROFESSOR XAVIER*! I HAVE JUST PROBED YOUR LOCATION TELEPATHICALLY, AND AM READY WITH YOUR *INSTRUCTIONS*--

FIRE WHEN READY, SIR! WE'RE ALL *EARS*!

AND SO IT IS THAT, A SHORT TIME LATER, AS THE MALEVOLENT *MASTER OF DREAMS* ELATEDLY OBSERVES A GIANT TELE-SCREEN...

THEY'VE *DONE* IT! THEY'VE AGREED TO MY *TERMS*!

THE SENATE HAS JUST VOTED A *SPECIAL APPROPRIATION*--TO BE PICKED UP BY THE *X-MEN* AT THE EXPIRATION OF THE THREE-HOUR PERIOD!

IT'S FINE AND DANDY WITH *US*, NEFARIA!

OUR ONLY QUESTION--WHAT'S OUR PERCENTAGE OF THE TAKE?

THE MEN! EN--?

NEVER MIND *THAT*, COUNT! LET'S JUST SAY WE WISED UP, AND LET IT GO AT THAT!

AFTER ALL, AS YOU SAID, THE HUMANS *HATE* US! WHY *SHOULDN'T* WE GET REVENGE ON THEM --AND MAKE MONEY AT THE SAME TIME?!

A MOST SAGACIOUS DECISION, MY FRIENDS--

BUT, LET ME WARN YOU OF ONE SMALL *DETAIL*!

I HAVE DESIGNED THE *CRYSTALLINE DOME* IN SUCH A WAY THAT ONLY *I* CAN MANIPULATE THE DIALS TO *DISSIPATE* IT!

IF ANYONE ELSE TRIES, HE WILL BRING *TOTAL ANNIHILATION* TO YOUR CAPITAL!

REMEMBER THAT--IN CASE YOU HARBOR ANY FOOLISH CONCEPTIONS ABOUT *DECEIVING* ME!

6

Panel 1: THEN, AFTER THE COUNT EXPLAINS HIS SCHEME...

INTO THIS *TRUCK!* IT WILL TAKE YOU TO A LOCATION WHERE YOU CAN *ENTER* THE TRAPPED CITY!

NEFARIA'S SO *CONFIDENT!* I HOPE THE PROF KNOWS WHAT HE'S *DOING!*

DRIVEN TO THE SCENE IN A COMMON *MILK TRUCK!* HOW *PLEBEIAN!*

Panel 2: BUT, AS SOON AS THE X-MEN ARE HAULED AWAY...

READY WITH *PLAN "C"!* COMMENCE-- *NOW!*

Panel 3: INSTANTLY, FROM ANOTHER PART OF THE COUNT'S INNOCENT--LOOKING HEAD-QUARTERS, A *SECOND* VEHICLE DEPARTS AT TOP SPEED...

Panel 4: AND, PASSING THE BOGUS "MILK TRUCK", IT DEPOSITS ITS UNSAVORY PASSENGERS AT THE OUTER RIM OF THE DOME BEFORE THE X-MEN ARRIVE...

SO--IT IS *AGREED!* WE SHALL SERVE COUNT NEFARIA *NO MORE!*

THAT FOOL! HE HAS SENT US TO WATCH THE X-MEN--TO BE CERTAIN THAT THEY DO NOT ATTEMPT ANY *TRICKERY!*

EVEN HE DOES NOT SUSPECT THAT WE--HIS *LIEUTENANTS* IN THE NEW *MAGGIA*--INTEND TO SEIZE THE HUNDRED MILLION DOLLARS FOR *OURSELVES!*

BUT NOW--OUT OF *SIGHT!* THE MUTANTS WILL BE HERE AT ANY MOMENT!

DON'T BE TOO FAST TO ORDER US AROUND, UNICORN. REMEMBER, YOU ARE ONLY OUR *PROVISIONAL* LEADER!

PLANTMAN SPEAKS THE *TRUTH!* FOR IF YOUR PLAN *FAILS--*

THEN ONE OF *US* BECOMES THE LEADER AND I KNOW WHICH ONE *I'D* VOTE FOR!

Panel 5: MEANWHILE, JUST TO GET THINGS *REALLY* COMPLICATED, PROFESSOR X ARRIVES JUST OUTSIDE WASHINGTON...

AND THAT'S THE STORY, XAVIER! WE WERE HOPING THAT YOU, AS AN ACKNOWLEDGED EXPERT ON MUTANTS, COULD TELL US HOW THEY MIGHT HAVE CREATED THAT INFERNAL DOME!

IF ONLY HE REALIZED *WHY* I'M AN EXPERT ON MUTANTS, HE'D BE AFTER *MY* SCALP, AS WELL!

I'LL DO ALL I CAN, GENERAL!

BUT, ARE YOU *CERTAIN* THAT THE X-MEN ARE BEHIND THIS? COULD SOMEONE BE *FRAMING* THEM?

TAKE YOUR STATIONS, MEN! WE'VE GOT TO BE READY FOR *ANYTHING!*

Panel 6: *FRAMING* THEM? THE RADIO REPORTS COMING OUT OF WASHINGTON VERIFIED THAT THOSE BLASTED MUTANTS WALKED RIGHT INTO THE CAPITOL AND *DEMANDED* WE RANSOM THE CITY--OR ELSE!

I KNOW, FROM MY PRELIMINARY MENTAL PROBING, THAT THOSE WERE ONLY *IMAGES*, CREATED BY *COUNT NEFARIA* --BUT I CAN'T PROVE IT FOR NOW, SO--

I'M SORRY, GENERAL. YOU'RE RIGHT, OF COURSE. IF YOU'LL JUST GIVE ME A FEW MINUTES TO DO SOME *THINKING* ON THE MATTER--

ALL RIGHT--BUT YOU'D BETTER THINK *FAST!* IF THOSE MUTANTS AN SEIZE THE NATION'S CAPITAL, HEN NO PLACE ON *EARTH* IS SAFE FROM THEM!

LOOK AT THAT, BILL! OUR "MUTANT EXPERT" HAS GONE TO *SLEEP!* TOO MUCH EXCITEMENT, I GUESS!

YEAH! THE POOR GUY!

I HATED TO DISAPPOINT THE GENERAL'S *FAITH* IN ME, BUT I HAD TO GET HIM TO LEAVE ME *ALONE* FOR A WHILE...

IT'S TIME FOR MY INVISIBLE *ASTRAL IMAGE* TO GO TO WORK--

IT IS ONLY IN *THIS* FORM, IN WHICH I HAVE NO SOLID SUBSTANCE, THAT I CAN KNOW ANYTHING LIKE THE THRILL OF *WALKING* AGAIN!

BUT, NO TIME TO THINK OF THAT *NOW!* I'M APPROACHING COUNT NEFARIA'S *STRONGHOLD!*

HOUGH THE X-MEN ARE O LONGER HERE, THEIR MANATIONS REMAIN-- O I KNOW THAT THIS IS HE PLACE WHERE I CONTACTED THEM *EARLIER!*

AND THAT MUST BE *NEFARIA* HIMSELF! I CANNOT PHYSICALLY *ACT* WHILE I AM IN MY ASTRAL BODY, BUT I CAN OBSERVE-- AND *LEARN!*

AH--THE PANEL TRUCK CARRIES THE X-MEN PAST THE FINAL UNSUSPECTING SOLDIERS! AT LAST, MY MONTHS OF PLANNING BEGIN TO BEAR *FRUIT!*

NOW, TO CREATE A MOMENTARY *OPENING* IN THE DOME, THRU WHICH THE MUTANTS CAN PASS TO COLLECT THE *RANSOM!*

WITH THE MONEY, I SHALL RETURN TO MY CASTLE IN CENTRAL EUROPE!

THERE, I'LL RE-BUILD THE *MAGGIA* INTO THE MOST POWERFUL CRIMINAL ORGANIZATION ON EARTH! THEN I SHALL DEAL IN *BILLIONS,* NOT *MILLIONS!*

HE MUST BE *STOPPED!* BUT *HOW?*

UT, AS PROFESSOR X PONDERS THIS PERPLEXING ROBLEM, WE KNOW HOW EAGER YOU ARE TO GET ACK TO OUR HARASSED HEROES, AND SO...

ELL, HERE WE ARE--BUT WHERE'S HE *ENTRANCE* TO THE DOME THAT EFARIA ROMISED US?

DON'T WORRY, ANGEL! IF HE *CREATED* THE DOME, I'M SURE HE CAN *CONTROL* IT!

HEY, GROUP! LOOK ALIVE! SOME-THING'S HAPPENING!

AS SO OFTEN IN THE PAST, BOBBY BOY, YOU'VE PUT YOUR FROST-BITTEN FINGER RIGHT ON THE *CRUX* OF THE MATTER! SOME-THING'S HAPPENING, *INDEED!*

A SMALL *HOLE* SUDDENLY APPEARED-- JUST BIG ENOUGH FOR ALL OF US TO PASS THRU!

AND NOW IT'S CLOSING *BEHIND* US! YOU GOTTA ADMIT--THIS NEFARIA COOKIE REALLY KNOWS HIS *STUFF!*

THIS IS NO TIME TO START *ADMIRING* THE COUNT, ICEMAN! REMEMBER --WE'RE ON *OPPOSITE SIDES!*

IS THAT WHY WE'RE PICKING UP A KING'S *RANSOM* FOR HIM? ALL MY ENEMIES SHOULD BE SO *BENEVOLENT!*

8

AS THE RELUCTANT RENEGADES RACE THRU THE OUTSKIRTS OF THE CITY, THEY PAY NO ATTENTION AS THEIR PROGRESS IS CAREFULLY MONITORED...

BAKER TO ABLE! BAKER TO ABLE! X-MEN NOW PASSING POINT "Y" ON SCHEDULE, HEADED TOWARDS CAPITOL BUILDING!

THIS WAY, MY COSTUMED COMPEERS! LET THE BOUNDING BEAST'S INFALLIBLE SENSE OF DIRECTION LEAD THE WAY!

THEY WOULD BE CONSIDERABLY MORE UPSET, HOWEVER, IF THEY KNEW OF FIVE MORE SINISTER PAIRS OF EYES THAT GAZE UPON THEM, GREEDILY...

WHEN DO WE MAKE OUR MOVE, UNICORN? SHOULD WE FOLLOW THEM TO THE CAPITOL?

PATIENCE, YOU OVERGROWN WEED! THERE IS NO NEED FOR SUCH HASTE!

SURE! LET THE X-MEN DO OUR DIRTY WORK FOR US! THEN, WE'LL STEP IN AND RELIEVE THEM OF THE MONEY!

AND, BEST OF ALL, IT IS THEY WHO WILL BE SOUGHT BY THE POLICE, NOT WE!

A FEW BRIEF MINUTES LATER, ON THE STEPS OF THE BUILDING IN WHICH AMERICA'S LAWS ARE ENACTED...

THESE SPECIAL, LARGE-DENOMINATION CERTIFICATES ARE REDEEMABLE IN GOLD ANYWHERE IN THE WORLD!

LUCKILY, THEY HAPPENED TO BE READILY AVAILABLE--OR WE COULD NEVER HAVE MET THE MUTANTS' DEADLINE!

BUT-- WHERE ARE THEY? IT'S ALMOST TIME!

THE NEXT INSTANT...

SORRY IF I'M LATE, CONGRESSMAN! STRATEGY CONFERENCE, YOU KNOW!

WHAT--? THE ANGEL!

I'LL JUST RELIEVE YOU OF THIS LITTLE BRIEFCASE, IF YOU DON'T MIND!

NO NEED TO FLY AN EVASION COURSE THIS PART OF THE JOB'S A BREEZE!

THIS MAY BE THE BLACKEST DAY IN HISTORY!

THE U.S.-- FORCED TO PAY BLACKMAIL TO RANSOM ITS CAPITAL!

THEN, AS THE HIGH-FLYING ANGEL STREAKS UPWARD...

NOW, I'LL REJOIN THE OTHERS, AND--HEY! SOME EAGER-BEAVER'S TAKING POT-SHOTS AT ME!

DON'T WORRY, CONGRESSMAN! I'LL BRING THE THIEF DOWN!

GUARD, WAIT! DON'T--!

SOMEONE MUST HAVE NEGLECTED TO BRIEF THAT GUARD! IF HE SHOOTS THE ANGEL, IT MAY MEAN THE DOOM OF THE CITY!

SORRY, PAL, BUT I'M AFRAID I'M GONNA HAVE TO PUT YOUR TRIGGER-FINGER OUT OF COMMISSION FOR A LITTLE WHILE!

MY GUN HAND-- IT'S ENCASED IN ICE!

YOU WIN THE CIGAR, CHUM! AND AREN'T YOU LUCKY I'M NOT THE HUMAN TORCH!

THANKS, BOBBY! NOW TO HEAD BACK THE PERIMETER OF THE CITY!

SO FAR, EVERYTHING'S ACCORDING TO SCHEDULE! STILL, I WISH THE PROFESSOR WERE HERE!

PICKING UP THE MONEY WAS *KID STUFF!* WHEN DO WE GET SOME *ACTION?*

I'M SURE HE'S KEEPING TABS ON US *MENTALLY*, MAN! BESIDES, LET'S SHOW HIM WHAT WE CAN DO ON OUR *OWN!*

CHEER UP, ROBERT, M'LAD! WE'RE NOT HOME FREE *YET!*

YOU CAN SAY *THAT* AGAIN, HANK! LOOK--UP AHEAD! SOME OF THE *POPULACE* HAS TURNED OUT TO GREET US!

AND I'LL BET THEY'RE NOT HERE TO GIVE US THE *KEYS TO THE CITY!*

THERE'RE THOSE CRUMMY *MUTIES!* C'MON, MEN--LET'S SHOW 'EM WHAT WE THINK OF *TRAITORS!*

DANGER

WE'RE WITH *YOU,* BUDDY!

BOY--THAT WAS *CLOSE!* AND--I DROPPED THE BRIEFCASE WITH THE *MONEY!*

JUST *OUR* LUCK THOSE GUYS HADDA BE NEAR A *PILE OF BRICKS* WHEN THEY SPOTTED US!

WI SSHH

DON'T WORRY, WARREN! I'VE GOT IT!

THK!

ALAS, WHY MUST THE AGILE BEAST BE CONSTANTLY A TARGET FOR MISDIRECTED HOSTILITIES?

ZIK!

ALL OF YOU--USE *DEFENSIVE MEASURES ONLY!* WE CAN'T HARM THESE PEOPLE JUST BECAUSE THEY THINK WE'RE *CROOKS!*

BUT, WE CAN'T DELAY *TOO LONG!*

PTHUD!

THAT'S FOR SURE! IF COUNT *NEFARIA* GETS TOO *IMPATIENT,* HE'LL CAUSE HIS KOOKIE DOME TO ABSORB THE CITY'S *OXYGEN!*

MEANWHILE, A SHORT DISTANCE AWAY...

THERE'S TIMES LIKE THIS WHEN I'M *REALLY* GLAD I HAVE *WINGS!*

BUT--OVER THERE! A BUNCH OF THEM HAVE HANK *SURROUNDED!*

HANG ON, BEAST! I'M ON MY WAY!

COME AT YOUR OWN CHOSEN SPEED, ANGEL!

IN THE MEANTIME, I'LL JUST SCRAMBLE UP THIS *OVERGROWN TOOTHPICK* HERE, AND ENJOY THE *VIEW!*

HE'S CLIMBING UP THE *WASHINGTON MONUMENT!* STOP HIM!

HOW? HE'S LIKE A BLASTED *MONKEY!*

ON CAREFUL *RECONSIDERATION,* WARREN, PERHAPS I'D BEST ACCEPT YOUR GENEROUS OFFER *AFTER ALL!*

GOING MY WAY?

JUST SO HAPPENS I *AM,* BEAST! BUT, WHAT ABOUT THE *OTHERS?* I CAN'T CARRY THEM ALL AT ONCE!

10

X-MEN--*THIS WAY!* COUNT NEFARIA'S OPENING AN *ESCAPE HATCH* FOR US!

HURRY--BEFORE IT *CLOSES* AGAIN, AND WE'RE *TRAPPED* IN HERE!

LOOK! IT'S THE CREEPS WHO *CAPTURED* US!*

ANY PORT IN A STORM, ICEMAN! BUT, KEEP YOUR *GUARD* UP! I'VE GOT A HUNCH WE MAY BE IN FOR *TROUBLE!*

*LAST ISH--STAN.

THE NEXT MOMENT, AS TEN FLEET FORMS PLUNGE SWIFTLY THRU THE OPENING...

WE *MADE* IT! AND IT'S CLOSING UP *BEHIND* US!

AND NOW, CYCLOPS, I'LL TAKE THAT *POUCH,* IF YOU DON'T MIND! COUNT NEFARIA SENT US TO PICK IT UP FOR HIM!

SORRY, UNICORN, BUT WE'RE DELIVERING THIS LITTLE BUNDLE TO THE COUNT *PERSONALLY!* IF HE HAD WANTED YOU TO HAVE IT, HE'D HAVE TOLD US!

BLAST YOU! YOU HAVE HAD YOUR CHANCE TO SURRENDER THE MONEY *PEACEFULLY*--NOW YOU WILL SUFFER THE *CONSEQUENCES!*

OH OH! LOOKS AS IF THESE COSTUMED CLOWNS ARE PLANNING A KING-SIZE *DOUBLE-CROSS*--AND *WE'RE* FORCED TO HELP *NEFARIA!*

IT'S A *STALEMATE,* HORN-TOP! YOUR RAY-BEAM AGAINST *MINE!*

PERHAPS--FOR THE *MOMENT!* BUT, THERE ARE *OTHER* WAYS!

ZAP!

EEL! THE *REST* OF YOU! *GET THEM!*

BEAST! CATCH THIS AND *RUN,* WHILE I KEEP *UNICORN* BUSY!

WILL DO, CYKE!

NOT SO *FAST,* MY APE-LIKE FRIEND! I HAVE BUT TO TOUCH THE STUDS ON MY WEAPONS BELT, AND THIS *LIQUID CEMENT* WILL STOP YOU IN YOUR TRACKS!

SLOOSH!

HMMM! YOU KNOW, YOU MAY JUST HAVE A *POINT* THERE!

I WAS MOVING *TOO FAST*--CAN'T REVERSE IN TIME TO AVOID GETTING SPLATTERED WITH THAT *GLUE!*

HAVE NO FEAR, BEASTIE-- *ICEMAN* IS HERE!

WHAT--? AN *ICY SHIELD*--BLOCKING MY CEMENT!

MANY THANKS FOR YOUR TIMELY ASSISTANCE, LAD!

STILL, IF YOU WON'T TAKE OFFENSE AT A FRIENDLY SUGGESTION, YOUR ATTEMPTS AT *RHYMED REPARTEE* STILL LEAVE MUCH TO BE DESIRED!

12

WHILE YOU TWO *PRATTLE*, I'LL GET TO THE *ROOT* OF THE PROBLEM-- AND TO THAT *BRIEFCASE*, AS WELL!

-OOOF!- HOW *IGNOMINIOUS*!

TRIPPED UP--AND TO THE ACCOMPANIMENT OF A *PUN*, YET!

DON'T LET IT *WORRY* YOU, BEAST! THE *FLYING* PART OF OUR LITTLE TEAM WILL TAKE OVER NOW!

THERE AREN'T ANY PLANTS IN THE *SKY* TO GET IN *MY* WAY!

IT'S FUNNY--A *HUNDR* MILLION DOLLARS IN CERTIFICATES INSIDE THIS POUCH--AND W TOSS IT BACK AND FORTH LIKE A *PING PONG BALL*!

PERHAPS *I* CAN'T STOP YOU, ANGEL-- BUT SOMEONE ELSE *CAN*!

AN INSTANT LATER, BEFORE WARREN CAN DART TO SAFETY...

-UHHHN!- I WAS *OVER-CONFIDENT*, AS USUAL! I FORGOT ABOUT SCARECROW'S BLASTED *TRAINED BIRDS*!

SUCH A PITY, MY *FEATHERED FRIEND*! BUT, *I'LL* TAKE CARE OF IT FOR YOU!

BEING ATTACKED-- FROM ALL SIDES! I CAN'T HOLD ON TO THE *MONEY*!

VERY *KIND* OF YOU, SCARECROW! HOWEVER, I THINK IT MIGHT BE *WISER* IF I JUST GUIDE IT T MYSELF *TELEKINETICALLY*! DON'T YOU AGREE

THERE! I *KNEW* YOU SEE IT MY WAY!

ANOTHER ONE! DON'T YOU COSTUMED JUVENILE DELINQUENTS EVER GIVE UP?

THEY DON' *HAVE* TO, STRAWFACE

--NOT AS LONG AS THE *EEL* IS AROUND TO *DEFEAT* THEM!

-OHHH!- THAT *DAZZLING LIGHT*!

I MAKE IT A POINT NEVER TO HARM A *LADY*-- AT LEAST, NOT AS LONG AS A BLINDING FLASH OF *ELECTRICITY* WILL ACCOMPLISH THE SAME *ENDS*!

SO, I'LL JUST TAKE THAT POUCH, AND-- *UNICORN!* WHAT ARE YOU--?

-AAARR!-

YOU AND TH OTHERS AR ALL *FOOL* EEL! DID YOU THIN THAT I INTENDE TO *SHAR* THIS PRIZ WITH TH LIKES O *YOU*?

BUT, SINCE YOU HELPED ME *ATTAIN* IT, I SHALL MERELY *STUN* YOU INTO UNCONSCIOUSNESS!

...ND, SOME MILES AWAY, OBSERVING ...S HENCHMAN'S AVARICIOUS ACTIONS, A SOMEWHAT LESS-THAN-...CSTATIC *COUNT NEFARIA*...

SO--HE THINKS I CAN BE THUS *TRIFLED WITH*, DOES HE? HE SHALL *PAY* FOR HIS TREACHERY!

SECONDS LATER, BEFORE THE UNCANNY SUPER-VILLAIN CAN MAKE HIS ESCAPE, HE FINDS HIMSELF HEMMED IN BY...

THE X-MEN! AND A SQUAD-RON OF *ARMY TANKS*-- SUDDENLY APPEARING OUT OF THAT FOG BANK!

LOOKS LIKE YOU'RE *SURROUNDED*, UNICORN!

WHY NOT SIMPLY RELINQUISH THAT BRIEFCASE, SO WE CAN SETTLE THIS MATTER *AMICABLY?*

NEVER! NOT SO LONG AS MY *POWER HORN* HAS ENERGY LEFT TO *DESTROY* THE ACCURSED TANKS! BUT *WAIT*--WHAT'S THIS?

THEY *FADE AWAY* AS MY BEAM TOUCHES THEM! THEY ARE ONLY *IMAGES*--- CREATED BY NEFARIA TO *CONFOUND* ME!

THEN, BEFORE THE STARTLED EYES OF THE TEEN-AGE HEROES...

HE'S FLYING-- USING TINY ROCKET-LIFTS IN HIS *BOOTS!*

I'LL NEVER CATCH HIM AT THAT SPEED! HE'LL BE OUT OF SIGHT IN *SECONDS!*

BUT WE CAN'T QUIT *NOW!* WE'VE *GOT* TO GET HIM!

RIGHT YOU ARE, BOBBY! *LET'S GO!*

...E'LL RETURN TO OUR QUANDARY-STRUCK ...NTET IN A FEW PANELS! BUT FIRST, LET'S SEE ...W PROFESSOR X HAS BEEN SPENDING THESE ...ST, FRANTIC MINUTES...

...S BEEN *THREE HOURS*, ...NERAL--AND THE CITY ...S STILL *UNHARMED!*

I *SUSPECTED* AS MUCH! THE WHOLE THING WAS A *FRAUD*--DREAMED UP BY THE MUTANTS TO *ROB* US!

DON'T BE TOO *SURE*, GENERAL! I--

...SORRY, PROFESSOR ...XAVIER, BUT I'VE GOT ...O TIME TO GAB WITH ...OU *NOW!* I'M GOING ...O ORDER THE X-MEN *SHOT ON SIGHT!*

THEN YOU WON'T NEED *MY* SERVICES ANY LONGER! I'LL BE *GOING*...

A FEW MINUTES LATER, AT A SWANK MOTEL NEARBY...

HERE'S YOUR *KEY*, SIR! ISN'T IT TERRIBLE ABOUT THE CITY BEING *ENCASED*, AND ALL?

ER, YES, *QUITE!* NOW, IF YOU'LL EXCUSE ME...

I'D APPRECIATE IT IF YOUR MAN WOULD WHEEL ME TO MY ROOM AT ONCE! I'M REALLY VERY *EXHAUSTED!*

WHAT A *COLD FISH!* THREE QUARTERS OF A MILLION PEOPLE IN MORTAL DANGER--AND ALL HE WANTS TO DO IS *SLEEP!*

14

AND NOW--SEE? WE **TOLD** YOU WE'D PICK UP ON THE **ACTION** RIGHT AWAY...

ZISH!

WHAT? **AGAIN** THE ARMY APPEARS ON THE SCENE, BEFORE I HAVE GONE A **HUNDRED YARDS** IN THE AIR!

DOES NEFARIA THINK I AM A **FOOL,** TO BE DECEIVED **TWICE** BY HIS SUBTERFUGE?

THAT MUST BE ONE OF THE **MUTANTS!** HE HAS THE **BRIEFCASE!** FIRE AT **WILL!**

:*UNNNHH!*:

BLOOM

MY ENERGY FIELD **PROTECTED** ME--BUT I LOST THE POUCH IN THE **CONCUSSION!**

I SHOULD HAVE **KNOWN!** THIS TIME THE ARMORED UNIT WAS **REAL!**

LUCKILY HE WAS STRUCK BEFORE HE GOT VERY **FAR.**

BUT, EVEN AS THEIR DEPUTY LEADER GRASPS THE PLUMMETING POUCH, THE X-MEN HAVE **OTHER** THINGS TO WORRY ABOUT...

I DON'T **GET** IT, CAPTAIN! IT LOOKS LIKE THEY'RE FIGHTING AMONG **THEMSELVES!**

YOU DIDN'T ENLIST TO **UNDERSTAND,** CORPORAL! JUST DUCK IN THAT TANK AND **FIRE!**

THAT GOES FOR **YOU,** TOO, SOLDIER!

YES, **SIR!**

ALL RIGHT, MEN--GET **READY!** WE'LL TEACH THOSE MUTANTS TO--

HEY! WHAT **GIVES?** THE GUN-BARREL'S **FROZEN SOLID!**

SORRY, DOGFACES! WE'RE ALL FOR **TARGET PRACTICE**--BUT NOT WHEN WE'RE THE **TARGET!**

GREAT GOING, 'ICEMAN! MEANWHILE, I'LL HANDLE **THESE** LADS IN MY **OWN** INIMITABLE STYLE!

WHAT'S **WRONG,** BOYS? A FELLA'D THINK YOU NEVER SAW A **WHITE-FEATHERED CRIME-BUSTER** BEFORE!

SCATTER! ONE OF 'EM IS **DIVE-BOMBIN'** US!

SOMEBODY GET A **BEAD** ON THAT FLYING **FREAK!**

FLYING FREAK, DID YOU SAY?

IT GRIEVES ME THE **QUICK** TO HEAR YOU THUS DISPARAGE MY **AVIAN ASSOCIATE!**

SPLAT

KHA

WHAT THE--?

:*OOOOF!*:--THEY'RE COMIN' AT US FROM **ALL SIDES!**

MEANWHILE, NOT FAR AWAY, SCOTT SUMMERS HAS REACHED THE SIDE OF MARVEL GIRL...

TAKE THE BRIEFCASE TO THE *RENDEZVOUS POINT*, JEAN! I'LL STAY HERE AND HELP THE OTHERS!

I DON'T LIKE TO *LEAVE* YOU--AND THE *REST* OF THE X-MEN--BUT I KNOW I *MUST!*

HOWEVER, UNKNOWN TO THE GRIM *CYCLOPS*, A SECOND GROUP OF GROUND TROOPS IS APPROACHING THE AREA OF BATTLE, FROM *BEHIND*...

LOOK! CYCLOPS IS GIVING THE MONEY TO THE *GIRL!* LET'S GO *GET* IT!

OKAY, MEN-- OUR ORDERS ARE TO CAPTURE THE *X-MEN--DEAD OR ALIVE!*

THOSE COSTUMED KOOKS UP AHEAD AREN'T *THEM*-- BUT THEY SURE AREN'T HERE JUST TO SEE THE *SCENERY!* LET'S TAKE 'EM IN FOR *QUESTIONING!*

OH OH! HERE COMES *TROUBLE!*

WE CAN'T AFFORD TO LET OURSELVES BE STOPPED *NOW!*

AND, AMPLY WARNED AS THEY ARE, THE "COSTUMED KOOKS" PROVE EASIER TO *HAVE* THAN TO *HOLD*...

WATCH IT! THESE BIRDS ARE *MURDER!*

ALRIGHT, PAL, NOW WE'VE *GOTCHA*, AND--

HOLY COW! HE BROKE *FREE!*

HUH? THAT CHARACTER GOT BY ALL *THREE* OF US!

I'M SLIPPERY AS AN *EEL*, YOU MIGHT SAY--THANKS TO A SPECIAL *SILICON COATING* ON MY COSTUME!

OF COURSE, CLOWNS! I AM ALSO AN EXPERT *ESCAPE ARTIST*--NOT A MERE TRAINER OF BIRDS!

WATCH IT, YOU GUYS! THE EDGES OF THIS BUZZARD'S QUILLS ARE *RAZOR-SHARP!*

QUITE SO! THE *PORCUPINE* DOES NOT TAKE KINDLY TO BEING APPREHENDED --FOR *ANY* REASON!

WELL, WE'VE *GOT* 'EM--NOW WHAT DO WE *DO* WITH 'EM?

THE SOLDIERS MOMENTARILY *OVER-LOOKED* ME, BECAUSE OF MY CAMOUFLAGING *OUTFIT!*

THAT GIVES ME JUST THE TIME I NEED--TO GROW MY *OWN* ARMY!

PRECISELY TEN SECONDS LATER...

A JUNGLE-- APPEARING OUT OF *NOWHERE!*

GET BACK INSIDE THE *TANK*, CHARLIE! WE'LL HAVE TO *FIGHT* OUR WAY OUT OF THIS STUFF!

WELL DONE, PLANT-MAN! THOSE *WEEDS* YOU ENLARGED AND BROUGHT TO LIFE WILL KEEP THEM BUSY WHILE WE *ESCAPE!*

OF COURSE! BESIDES, WE HAVE COMMITTED NO REAL *CRIME* HERE!

BUT, THE X-MEN HAVE *ESCAPED*-- WITH THE *LOOT!*

AND WHAT HAPPENED TO THE *UNICORN?*

16

WELL, MARVELITES, WE HOPE YOU ENJOYED OUR LITTLE SUNDAY ROMP WITH NEFARIA'S MASQUER-ADING MINIONS, BECAUSE THAT'S ALL YOU'RE GONNA *SEE* OF 'EM--FOR *NOW*, ANYWAY! MEAN-WHILE, SOME DISTANCE AWAY...

THERE GOES OUR *TRUCK*, BACK TO NEFARIA'S HIDEOUT!

IT LOOKS LIKE THE COUNT'S *LOST INTEREST* IN US, NOW THAT HE HAS HIS HUNDRED MILLION DOLLARS!

DON'T WORRY --HE'S NOT GETTING RID OF US *THAT* EASILY! FOLLOW THE TRUCK, ANGEL!

=SIGH!= EITHER WAY, IT WOULD APPEAR THAT WE MUST *HOOF IT* BACK!

AND, WHILE WE'RE TYING UP LOOSE ENDS, LET'S NOT FORGET THE UNCANNY *UNICORN*, WHO IS STILL IN THE VICINITY...

LUCKILY, I FELL INTO THESE *BUSHES* WHEN I WAS CAUGHT OFF-GUARD BY THAT EXPLODING SHELL!

I HAVEN'T MU POWER LEF IN MY ROCKE SOLED SHOE SO I'D BETTE LIE LOW UNTI THE *TROOPS* HAVE LEFT THE AREA!

AT THIS MOMENT, SEVERAL MILES FROM WASHINGTON...

ANY MINUTE NOW, THE TRUCK WILL RETURN-- BRINGING ME THE INFINITE *WEALTH* I NEED!

THEN WHEN I USE THAT MONEY TO RE-ESTABLISH THE *MAGGIA*, THE WORLD WILL KNOW THE GREATEST CRIME WAVE IN ITS *HISTORY*!

BUT, EVEN AS THE CONFIDENT COUNT SPEAKS, A *NEW* ELEMENT ENTERS HIS FATEFUL GAME-- AN ELEMENT WHOSE EXISTENCE HE HAS NOT *SUSPECTE*

AWRIGHT, BUSTER--WHERE DO YA THINK *YER* GOIN'? *NOBODY* GITS THRU THIS GATE!

STEP ASIDE, UNDERLINGS I HAVE NO WISH TO *HAR* YOU!

I HAVE BUSINES WITH YOU *MASTER*-- THE ONE WHO DWELLS *INSIDE*.

THIS IS JUST A *WAREHOUSE*, BUDDY! *NOBODY* LIVES HERE! SO-- UHH!=

=MMMF! HEY--I CAN'T *MOVE*!

AND, IN ANOTHER SECOND, NEITHER OF YOU WILL BE ABLE TO *TALK*, AS WELL! AS I SAID, I AM HERE TO SEE YOUR *BOSS*--AND I HAVE NO DESIRE TO SEE HIM *FOREWARNED*!

THEN, WITHOUT A FURTHER WORD, THE MYSTERIOUS FIGURE MOVES ON, LEAVING BEHIND HIM TWO FORMS--SILENT, UNMOVING...

AS, ELSEWHERE IN THE DISGUISE HEADQUARTERS OF COUNT NEFARIA...

IT HAS *ARRIVED*! SOON ALL THE POWER, ALL THE GLORY FOR WHICH I HAVE LONGED--SHALL BE *MINE*!

BUT, BEFORE JEAN GREY CAN GIVE UTTERANCE TO HER THOUGHTS...

MARVEL GIRL! ARE YOU ALL RIGHT?

WE GOT HERE AS FAST AS WE COULD!

YES, I'M FINE! HOW DID YOU LOCATE NEFARIA'S HEADQUARTERS?

ELEMENTARY, MY DEAR LADY! ANGEL FOLLOWED THE TRUCK HERE, THEN CLUED US IN!

THANK THE STARS SHE'S UNHARMED! IF ANYTHING HAD HAPPENED TO HER--

BUT--WHERE'S NEFARIA? AND THE POUCH WITH THE CERTIFICATES?

RIGHT HERE! I--WHY, THEY'RE GONE! BOTH OF THEM!

THE COUNT MUST HAVE GRABBED THE MONEY AND FLED--JUST AS WE ENTERED THE WINDOW!

ALL OUR WORK-- FOR NOTHING!

NO, ANGEL--NOT FOR NOTHING!

COUNT NEFARIA JUST BOARDED HIS SHIP DOWN BELOW, AND IS STARTING TO PULL AWAY FROM THE DOCK! BUT, THERE IS NO NEED FOR YOU TO CONCERN YOURSELVES WITH HIM FOR NOW!

MISTER, I DON'T MEAN TO BE RUDE--BUT WHO IN BLAZES ARE YOU?

NO, WAIT, WARREN! DON'T YOU RECOGNIZE HIM? HE--

LOOK! IN THE HARBOR --THE ONE KNOWN AS THE UNICORN!

THE MOST DANGEROUS OF NEFARIA'S CRONIES! LET US SEE--!

AND, GAZING ACROSS THE EVER-WIDENING DISTANCE BETWEEN THEMSELVES AND THE COUNT'S VESSEL, THE ASTONISHED MUTANTS SEE...

IT'S UNICORN, ALL RIGHT! QUICKLY--WE MUST OVERTAKE THE SHIP BEFORE IT REACHES THE THREE-MILE LIMIT!

HAVE NO FEAR, X-MEN--

THE SHIP WILL NOT REACH INTERNATIONAL WATERS! I PROMISE YOU THAT!

THE MASKED FIGURE--IT'S PROFESSOR X! THE HOOD MUFFLED HIS VOICE!

FOR MONTHS, I HAVE BEEN SECRETLY WORKING ON LIGHTWEIGHT, FLEXIBLE METAL BRACES FOR MY LEGS--AND, AT LAST, I HAVE NEARLY PERFECTED THEM!

BUT, SIR-- YOU'RE WALKING! HOW--?

THIS TRANSISTORIZED POWER SOURCE, HOOKED ONTO MY BELT, IS ALL THAT I NEED TO OPERATE THEM FOR SEVERAL HOURS AT A TIME!

THAT'S WONDERFUL NEWS, PROFESSOR! BUT, WHAT ABOUT NEFARIA AND THE UNICORN? SHOULDN'T WE CATCH UP WITH THEM AND RECOVER THE HUNDRED MILLION DOLLARS?

THAT WOULD BE A MOST LAUDABLE SUGGESTION, BOBBY--IF THEY HAD THE MONEY!

WHAT? YOU MEAN THEY DON'T?

NO! IF YOU'LL MERELY GLANCE UNDER THE *TABLE*, YOU'LL SEE--

THE *BRIEFCASE*! THEN, NEFARIA GOT AWAY--*EMPTY-HANDED*!

NOT EXACTLY, SCOTT-- NOT EXACTLY.'

AND NOW, TO LEARN THE MEANING OF XAVIER'S CRYPTIC STATEMENT, WE JOIN AN EXULTANT *COUNT NEFARIA* ABOARD HIS FLEEING VESSEL...

A *HUNDRED MILLION DOLLARS!* WEALTH BEYOND THE *IMAGININGS* OF MOST MORTALS!

BUT, SOON THERE WILL BE *MORE* INGENIOUS CRIMES, MORE RICHES THAN ANYONE HAS EVER POSSESSED! THIS IS ONLY THE *BEGINNING!*

YOU ARE *MISTAKEN*, COUNT-- THIS IS THE *END* OF YOUR CAREER!

FOR, THOUGH MY POWER HORN IS *EXHAUSTED*, I STILL POSSESS THE STRENGTH TO WREST THE POUCH FROM *YOU!*

UNICORN! DON'T-- *WAIT!*

...E HAVE NO NEED FOR ...RIFE! BEFORE US IS ...REASURE ENOUGH FOR ...THOUSAND MEN! WE--

WHAT WITCHCRAFT IS *THIS?*

THE BRIEFCASE IS *FADING FROM SIGHT!* AND WITH IT-- OUR DREAMS OF *WEALTH* AND *POWER!* SOMEHOW, IN SOME WAY, THE X-MEN *TRICKED* US!

AS, BACK IN THE MAGGIA'S ABANDONED HEADQUARTERS...

AT ABOUT THIS TIME, NEFARIA AND THE UNICORN SHOULD BE DISCOVERING THAT I USED THE COUNT'S OWN MACHINE AGAINST THEM, CREATING A *MENTAL IMAGE* OF THE COVETED BRIEFCASE!

IN ADDITION, I ALERTED THE *COAST GUARD*-- WHICH SHOULD HAVE THEM SAFELY IN TOW WITHIN FIVE MINUTES!

NOW, PERHAPS THE GENDARMES WILL STOP ACCOSTING *US* FOR THEIR CRIMES!

MEANWHILE, JEAN, THIS *LETTER* ARRIVED FOR YOU THIS MORNING...

FOR *ME?*

...EN, AS THE FEMININE MEMBER OF THE ...QUE TEAM OPENS THE ENVELOPE AND ...GINS TO READ, A STRANGE HUSH FALLS ...VER THE MUTANT SUPER-HEROES...

...AN--IS SOMETHING ...RONG? IS THERE ...YTHING THAT WE CAN *DO?*

NO, WARREN --NOTHING!

IF IT'S *TROUBLE*, LET US *SHARE* IT!

...O, SCOTT! IT'S *JEAN* ...HO MUST DECIDE IF ...E CAN HELP HER-- ...T *WE OURSELVES!*

IT'S ALL RIGHT, PROFESSOR! IT ISN'T SOMETHING I CAN *HIDE* FOR LONG-- MUCH AS I MIGHT *WISH* TO!

TOMORROW, I MUST *LEAVE* THE X-MEN--*FOREVER!*

NEXT ISH.:
MORE STARTLINGLY DIFFERENT, AMAZINGLY IMAGINATIVE DEVELOPMENTS, AS THE MOST UNUSUAL FIGHTING TEAM OF ALL TIME BATTLES *THE LOCUST!*

AND, IF *THAT* ISN'T 'NUFF SAID-- WE DON'T KNOW WHAT *IS!*

MOM AND DAD FEEL THAT, SINCE WE FORMALLY *GRADUATED* SOME TIME AGO, IT'S TIME I PURSUED A COLLEGE DEGREE...*ELSEWHERE!*

PERHAPS THEY ARE *RIGHT,* SINCE YOU'LL BE ATTENDING *METRO COLLEGE,* WHICH ISN'T FAR AWAY, YOU CAN *VISIT* US OFTEN!

YES...I *CAN!* NOW, EXCUSE ME, PLEASE..I MUST..*CHANGE!*

CHANGE, MY EYE! THOSE WERE *TEARDROPS* I SAW AS SHE RAN UPSTAIRS! PROFESSOR, CAN'T WE...?

NO, WARREN...WE CAN DO *NOTHING!* THIS MATTER IS BETWEEN JEAN AND HER *PARENTS!* WE CAN ONLY HOPE THAT ONE DAY SHE RETURNS ...TO *STAY!*

MEANWHILE, WHEN SHE COMES DOWN, WE MUST TRY TO MAKE LEAVING *EASIER* FOR HER!

BOBBY, BRING ME OUR *PRESENT,* PLEASE!

AND SO, WHEN AN OUTWARDLY-COMPOSED MARVEL GIRL REJOINS THE DECEPTIVELY JOVIAL GROUP...

SAY, YOU LOOK LIKE YOU WERE *MADE* TO WEAR THOSE COLLEGIATE THREADS!

WHY, THANK YOU, WARREN! BUT...WHAT'S *THAT,* PROFESSOR?

YOU DIDN'T THINK WE'D LET YOU GO WITH JUST A COUPLE OF MUSTY *TEXTBOOKS* TO REMEMBER US BY, DIDJA?

PLEASE ACCEPT THIS *CORSAGE,* JEAN...IT'S FROM *ALL* OF US!

THE BEAST *ECHOES* ICEMAN'S SENTIMENTS... THOUGH I SEE NO REASON FOR HIS UNSEEMLY SLUR AGAINST *TEXTBOOKS!*

I'LL TREASURE IT...*ALWAYS!*

I *WON'T* CRY IN FRONT OF THEM...I *WON'T!*

BUT, ALL MY LIFE, I'LL *REMEMBER* THIS DAY...AND BE GLAD THAT I WAS PRIVILEGED, FOR A TIME AT LEAST, TO BE *ONE* OF THEM!

THEN, AFTER THE OTHERS HAVE SAID THEIR FAREWELLS TO JEAN, SCOTT AND WARREN SILENTLY DRIVE THE GIRL THEY BOTH LOVE TOWARDS *METRO COLLEGE,* AS ALL THREE THINK THEIR OWN INNERMOST THOUGHTS...

JOHNNY STORM GOES TO METRO! HE CAN FLY, JUST LIKE *I* CAN! I WONDER IF JEANIE'LL GET INTERESTED IN *HIM?!*

ALL THE X-MEN SEEMED SO SORRY I WAS GOING... EXCEPT *SCOTT!* HE HASN'T SPOKEN TEN WORDS ALL *MORNING!*

CAN'T HE SEE THAT I'LL *MISS HIM...MORE* THAN *ANYONE?*

IF ONLY I DARED HOLD HER IN MY ARMS...AND TELL HER HOW MUCH I NEED HER! BUT I *CAN'T*---NOT UNTIL I'M *CURED* OF THE CURSE OF MY *DEADLY EYES!*

FINALLY, AS THE TORRENTIAL DOWNPOUR CONTINUES, THE SOMBRE, REGAL SEDAN ARRIVES AT THE ENROLLMENT CENTER...

HERE, JEAN... LET ME TAKE YOUR *SUITCASE!*

THANK YOU, SCOTT!

THAT TONE IN HIS VOICE... ALMOST AS IF HE...BUT, I'M *IMAGINING* THINGS! HE *NEVER* CARED FOR ME... AND NEVER *WILL!*

LET'S HURRY INSIDE, JEAN..YOU'LL CATCH A *COLD* OUT HERE IN THE RAIN!

JEAN'S LEAVING HAS STARTED ME THINKING... IS IT PERHAPS TIME THAT *I, TOO,* QUIT THE X-MEN IN PURSUIT OF A MORE NORMAL LIFE? OR AM I DOOMED TO BE NOTHING BUT A SUPER-POWERED FREAK...TILL I *DIE?*

STARTING COLLEGE DURING THE SUMMER IS A GOOD IDEA, JEAN... YOU'LL GET A JUMP ON ALL YOUR *STUDIES* THAT WAY!

AND, WHEN *FALL* COMES, THE *HUMAN TORCH* IS A STUDENT HERE! WOULDN'T HE FLIP TO FIND OUT HE ISN'T THE *ONLY* SUPER-HERO ON CAMPUS!

BUT, HE *WON'T* FIND OUT, WARREN! HERE AT COLLEGE, I'LL BE PLAIN *JEAN GREY*...AND NOTHING MORE!

POOR *ANGEL*...TRYING SO HARD TO CHEER ME UP, EVEN THOUGH HE'D *HATE* THE THOUGHT OF MY DATING JOHNNY STORM!

IF ONLY I COULD HAVE FALLEN IN LOVE WITH *HIM,* INSTEAD OF WITH *SCOTT!* BUT, MAYBE IT'S TOO LATE NOW...FOR *ANY* OF US!

THEN, AT THE DOOR OF THE ADMISSIONS BUILDING...

HELLO, GROUP! *TED ROBERTS* IS THE NAME! MAY I TAKE IT THAT YOU THREE LOST SOULS ARE HERE TO *ENLIST?*

IF YOU MEAN *ENROLL,* FELLA, JUST THE *YOUNG LADY!* WE'RE ONLY...

MESSAGE RECEIVED! NOW THEN, MISS...

JEAN... JEAN GREY!

THANK YOU, TED! THAT'S VERY *NICE* OF YOU!

IF YOU'LL JUST FOLLOW ME, I'LL GET YOU CHECKED THROUGH IN *NO TIME*... COMPLIMENTS OF THE HOUSE!

OF COURSE, IN *EXCHANGE,* YOU HAVE TO SPLIT A *BIG ORANGE DRINK* WITH ME!

I'D *LIKE* THAT, TED...VERY MUCH!

ANYTHING...ANYTHING THAT WILL KEEP ME FROM LOOKING BACK...AT *SCOTT!*

SO..THAT'S HOW IT *ENDS!* BUT MAYBE IT'S ALL FOR THE *BEST*...AT LEAST, THAT'S WHAT I'VE GOT TO KEEP *TELLING* MYSELF!

SO MUCH FOR SMALL TALK *THIS* MONTH...WE'VE A REAL ODDBALL *BADDIE* WAITING FOR YOU... FOR, AT THAT VERY SECOND, MILES AWAY...

THE *SOIL CONDITIONS* ARE IDEAL FOR HATCHING MY *IONICALLY-TREATED INSECT EGGS!* AND SO, THIS IS THE DAY OF...*THE LOCUST!*

THE NEXT INSTANT, AS THE GLOWING, PULSATING "EGGS" STRIKE THE MARSHY SOIL OF THE WHEAT FIELD THEY SEEM TO BURST ALMOST ON CONTACT...

...AND, FROM THE EGGS BURST *NYMPHS*...YOUNG LOCUSTS WHICH *GROW VISIBLY* WITH EACH BITE OF THE MOIST GRAIN...

FEED WELL, MY PRETTIES... *FEED WELL!* NOW, ONLY *I,* YOUR *LEADER,* AM PRESENT TO HEAR YOUR SONG OF *MOUNTING MENACE!*

BUT SOON, THE *WORLD* SHALL KNOW THE MEANING OF THAT SOUND... AND LIVE IN *TERROR* OF IT!

KRUNCH!

KRUNCH! KRUNCH!

3

BUT, MEANWHILE, THE INCREDULOUS FARMER HAS PHONED THE LOCAL AUTHORITIES... AND AS MORNING DAWNS...

BY THE TIME I COULD LOAD MY *GUN*, THE OVERSIZED CRITTERS HAD ALREADY LEVELED MY FIELD... AND *HOPPED AWAY!*

WHAT'S MORE, I'D SWEAR ONE OF 'EM WAS *HALF HUMAN!*

SURE, MISTER! AND AT WHAT TIME DID THE *GOOD FAIRIES* COME FLYIN' BY?

DON'T SHRUG OFF HIS STORY *TOO FAST*, MARV! *SOMETHING* CERTAINLY RAZED THIS PLACE... AND IT WASN'T *PINK ELEPHANTS!*

PERSONALLY, IN THIS DAY AND AGE, I WOULDN'T EVEN BET *THAT* WAS IMPOSSIBLE!

POLICE

A FEW HOURS LATER, AS THE X-MEN GO THROUGH THEIR PACES IN WESTCHESTER COUNTY...

LOOK ALIVE, ANGEL! YOU BARELY CLEARED ICEMAN'S *HOOP!*

KEEP YOUR GOGGLES ON, CYKE! THE WORLD WOULDN'T CRUMBLE IF I *HIT* IT!

TRANSLATION: WITH JEAN ABSENT, THERE'S NO ONE TO HEAP *APPROBATION* UPON HIS PEERLESS PERFORMANCE!

THANKS, BEAST! NOW, IF SOMEBODY'LL JUST TRANSLATE YOUR *TRANSLATION!*

OH OH! HEADS UP, COMPATRIOTS! HERE COMES THE *PROFESSOR!*

I'M AFRAID YOUR TRAINING SESSION IS *OVER* FOR THE PRESENT! I'VE JUST HEARD ALARMING *REPORTS* ON THE RADIO... REPORTS OF *GIANT LOCUSTS* DEVASTATING A SERIES OF FARMS UPSTATE!

IF THIS INFORMATION IS TRUE, THESE HUGE INSECTS ARE POSSIBLY *MUTATIONS*... AND THAT MAKES THEM THE BUSINESS OF... THE *X-MEN!*

BEFORE LONG...

BOY, PROFESSOR OUR HIGH-SPEED 'COPTER CAN REALLY *TRAVEL!* EVEN THE *NATIONAL GUARD* HASN'T HAD TIME TO MAKE THE SCENE YET!

THAT, BOBBY, IS PRECISELY WHY WE MUST MAKE OUR INVESTIGATIONS *QUICKLY!* I WANT TO AVOID ASSOCIATING THIS MENACE WITH THE X-MEN IN THE MIND OF THE *PUBLIC!*

AH, THERE IS OUR QUARRY, DIRECTLY *BELOW!* PREPARE FOR *LANDING!*

HOLY COW... LOOK AT THE *SIZE* OF THOSE *BABIES!*

BUT, THERE ARE ONLY A *DOZEN* OF 'EM, AT MOST!

PERHAPS, FOR *NOW!* BUT, THOSE IN TURN MIGHT BREED COUNTLESS *OTHERS!*

AND *THEN* WHERE WOULD MANKIND BE?

KRUNCH! KRAK!

5

WHILE, UNOBSERVED BY THE MARVELOUS MUTANTS, IN A NEARBY GROVE...

THE X-MEN! I AM NOT YET PREPARED TO *FACE* THEM! BUT, NO MATTER...!

THIS EXPERIMENT HAS SERVED ITS PURPOSE! I SHALL BIDE MY TIME -- AND STRIKE *AGAIN*!

GOSH, IT SEEMS STRANGE TO BE GOING INTO ACTION WITHOUT *MARVEL GIRL*!

NO TIME TO WORRY ABOUT *THAT*, ICEMAN! PROFESSOR XAVIER WANTS ONE OF THESE CREATURES FOR *STUDY*!

NO SOONER SAID THAN *DONE*, DAUNTLESS DEPUTY LEADER!

NOTICE, GROUP, WITH WHAT *GUILELESS GRACE* THE GRANDILOQUENT BEAST ACCOSTS HIS PERPLEXED PREY!

THUMP!

RESTRAIN YOURSELF, INVERTEBRATE! I'M SUPPOSED TO BE APPREHENDING *YOU*!

KUH-PWANG!

HMMM... THIS WOULD SEEM TO BE MORE IN *YOUR* DEPARTMENT, ANGEL! CARE TO LEND AN *ASSIST*?

JUST HANG ON, BEASTIE! I'LL TAKE CARE OF THE *HARD* PART!

THEN, SWIFTLY ASCENDING TO A GREATER HEIGHT, THE WINGED WARRIOR SWOOPS AT HIS TARGET WITH DAZZLING SPEED...

A GOOD *POWER-DIVE* SHOULD GIVE ME ENOUGH FORCE TO *BUG* OUR LITTLE PLAYMATE!

UNDER THE CIRCUMSTANCES MY BIRD-LIKE BENEFACTOR I'LL FORGIVE YOUR SOMEWHAT UNIMAGINATIVE ATTEMPT AT *HUMOR*!

THANKS *MUCHLY*!

BWAK!

THAT *FINISHED* HIM! HE'S DROPPING LIKE A *STONE*!

FOR ALL THEIR SIZE, THESE LOCUSTS ARE RELATIVELY *DEFENSELESS*!

AGAINST A SUPER-POWERED MUTANT, YES! BUT, AN ORDINARY *HOMO SAPIENS* WOULD HARDLY FARE SO WELL!

ALSO, WHAT IF EVERY LOCUST ON *EARTH* BECAME SO LARGE? THAT'S WHAT DISTURBS THE *PROFESSOR*!

AND AS THE HIGH-FLYING ANGEL CARRIES OUT HIS ORDERS...

YOU'RE A FRIEND IN NEED WARRY BOY!

BUT, I'M AFRAID OUR BUDDY STRUCK OUT! THE INSECTS WEREN'T FAZED!

X-MEN... I SENSE SOLDIERS DRAWING NEAR! RETURN TO THE COPTER.. WITH ONE OF THE SPECIMENS!

A PLEASURE, SIR! THE AUTHORITIES ALREADY HAVE A PROPENSITY FOR SUSPECTING US OF UNLAWFUL ACTIVITY!

EXACTLY ONE MINUTE LATER, AS ARMED TROOPS APPEAR ON THE SCENE...

THE FLAME-THROWERS WILL DISPOSE OF THE FEW REMAINING LOCUSTS! IT IS FORTUNATE THEY WERE NOT NUMEROUS!

BUT, WILL MANKIND BE SO LUCKY NEXT TIME?

OKAY, MEN... LET'S MOP UP THOSE SIX-LEGGED MENACES!

FWOOSH!

BUT NOW, JUST FOR A CHANGE OF PACE, LET'S SKIP AHEAD A FEW DAYS ...AND SHIFT THE SCENE TO METRO COLLEGE...

WELL, IF IT ISN'T JEAN GREY! AND HOW'S THE CAMPUS CUTEST COED ADJUSTING TO THE SCENT OF IVY?

IT'S GREAT, TED... ALTHOUGH I'M STILL JUST A BIT... LONELY!

NOTE: NO, THIS ISN'T REALLY JOHNNY STORM AND WYATT WINGFOOT...THEY'RE IN THE HIMALAYAS! WE JUST WANTED TO SEE IF YOU WERE PAYING ATTENTION! ...SNEAKY STAN.

I GUESSED AS MUCH! LET'S FALL BY THE COFFEE SHOP AND YOU CAN TELL ME ALL ABOUT IT!

SOON, IN THE CONGENIAL ATMOSPHERE OF THE METRO STUDENT CENTER...

NOW, THEN, SUPPOSE YOU FILL ME IN ON YOUR PROBLEMS IN ADJUSTING TO AN UNFAMILIAR ENVIRONMENT!

IN CASE YOU COULDN'T TELL FROM THAT SPEECH, I'M A PSYCHOLOGY MINOR IN MY SPARE TIME! I...

LOOK, CHUCK... THERE'S MR. MAD SCIENTIST HIMSELF....OL' DOC HOPPER!

KEEP IT DOWN, MAN... HE'LL HEAR YA!

I WONDER WHY THOSE STUDENTS ARE MAKING FUN OF THAT BEARDED MAN?!

KEEP IT DOWN? WHAT FOR, CHUCK? OL' HOPPER DOESN'T CARE WHAT WE THINK ABOUT 'IM!

HE'S GOT HIS BUGS TO KEEP HIM HAPPY!

LOOKS LIKE YOU WERE RIGHT, BOB...HE'S STILL AS KOOKIE AS EVER!

IT'S PROBABLY A GOOD THING THAT METRO COLLEGE FIRED HIM LAST SEMESTER!

IGNORANT, IMPUDENT FOOLS! WHEN YOU ARE ALL IN YOUR GRAVES, THE NAME OF AUGUST HOPPER WILL SHINE MORE BRIGHTLY THAN ANY OTHER! SCOFF WHILE YOU MAY...FOR THE DAY IS COMING WHEN...

BAH! WHY DO I WASTE MY TIME ON PRATTLING DOLTS? YOU WILL LEARN... ALL OF YOU!

TED--WHO IS THAT MAN? HE LOOKS SO FAMILIAR, SOME-HOW...

THAT'S DR. HOPPER, DOLL! HE LIVES NEARBY AND EATS HERE OCCASIONALLY...

HE WAS A TOP NAME IN ENTEMOLOGY...THE STUDY OF INSECTS...TILL SOME OF HIS CRACKPOT THEORIES GOT HIM FIRED!

DON'T SHED TOO MANY TEARS FOR HIM, THOUGH! HE WORKS FOR RYAN CHEMICALS NOW, I HEAR! WHY?

NOTHING..IT'S JUST SOMETHING ABOUT HIM... SOMETHING IN HIS VOICE...

I MUST STOP LOOKING FOR DANGER...AS IF I WERE STILL ONE OF THE X-MEN!

8

HOWEVER, IF JEAN COULD FOLLOW THE TEMPESTUOUS DR. HOPPER TO HIS *RYAN CHEMICALS* LAB, SHE WOULD SOON OBSERVE...

SO.. IT IS NOT ENOUGH THAT THEY HAVE TAKEN AWAY MY *PROFESSORSHIP*... DEPRIVED MY INSECT-MUTATION THEORIES OF AN AUDIENCE OF *RECEPTIVE MINDS!*

THEY MUST *MOCK* ME, AS WELL... CALL ME "CRACKPOT" AND "MAD SCIENTIST"!

I.... *MAD!!* THAT IS THE *SUPREME IRONY!*

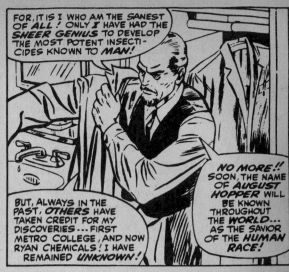

FOR, IT IS I WHO AM THE SANEST OF *ALL!* ONLY *I* HAVE HAD THE *SHEER GENIUS* TO DEVELOP THE MOST POTENT INSECTICIDES KNOWN TO *MAN!*

BUT, ALWAYS IN THE PAST, *OTHERS* HAVE TAKEN CREDIT FOR MY DISCOVERIES... FIRST *METRO COLLEGE*, AND NOW *RYAN CHEMICALS!* I HAVE REMAINED *UNKNOWN!*

NO MORE!! SOON, THE NAME OF *AUGUST HOPPER* WILL BE KNOWN THROUGHOUT THE *WORLD*... AS THE SAVIOR OF THE *HUMAN RACE!*

AND NOW, IT IS TIME TO TEST THE LATEST *IMPROVEMENTS* ON MY NEW FORMULA!

FIRST, I ACTIVATE THIS SINGLE INSECT EGG WITH MY ORIGINAL *MAGNO-RAY!*

FZZZT!

EXCELLENT! JUST AS *BEFORE*, THE NEWLY-HATCHED LARVA BEGINS TO *FEED*... AND INCREASES ITS BULK IMMEDIATELY AS IT DEVOURS ORDINARY LEAVES!

CHOMP! CHOMP!

IT WAS THUS THAT I, IN MY INGENIOUS GUISE OF THE *LOCUST*, CREATED THE SMALL BUT MIGHTY ARMY OF INSECTS WHICH THE ACCURSED *X-MEN* ATTACKED!

BUT, SINCE THAT MEETING, I HAVE *REFINED* THE MAGNO-RAY... AND DEVELOPED THIS *PORTABLE VERSION* OF IT!

BZIK!

AND IT *WORKS*.. AS I *KNEW* IT WOULD! THE RAY *ALONE* NOW INCREASED THAT BEETLE'S SIZE!

NOW, THE CARNIVOROUS BEETLE ATTACKS THE CATERPILLAR! IN THIS WAY, *NATURE* HAS ALWAYS CONTROLLED A BALANCE OF SPECIES!

BUT, THERE WILL *BE* NO SUCH CONTROL ACTING UPON MY *GIANT* INSECTS... AND MANKIND WILL BE *HELPLESS* BEFORE THEM!

THEN, I... DR. HOPPER... SHALL "DISCOVER" THE WAY TO *DESTROY* THEM... AND I SHALL RECEIVE THE PLAUDITS OF A DESPERATELY THANKFUL WORLD!

THUS, AT LAST, I WILL BE GIVEN THE *CREDIT* WHICH HAS BEEN SO LONG DENIED ME! MY FAME SHALL ENDURE *FOREVER!*

MEANWHILE, I MUST *DISINTEGRATE* THESE TWO SPECIMENS... LEST THEY BE DISCOVERED AND MY PURPOSE *THWARTED!*

IN A MATTER OF OF HOURS, MY INSECT LEGIONS WILL ATTACK *ANEW*... MORE POWERFUL, MORE NUMEROUS THAN *BEFORE!*

AND, IF THE X-MEN INTERFERE *AGAIN*... THEY WILL BE RUTHLESSLY DESTROYED, BY... THE LOCUST!

PZISST!

9.

A SHORT TIME LATER, THE MULTI-MILLION-DOLLAR PLANT WHICH EMPLOYS DR. AUGUST HOPPER RECEIVES A FATEFUL VISITOR...

PLANT SUPERVISOR! I'M SORRY DR. HOPPER ISN'T HERE, BUT HE LEFT YESTERDAY ON A SHORT *LEAVE OF ABSENCE!*

I'M SURE HE WOULD HAVE BEEN *HONORED* TO MEET AN AUTHORITY ON *MUTANTS*, SUCH AS YOURSELF, PROFESSOR XAVIER!

I'M *MR. HAMILTON,*

THE PLEASURE WOULD HAVE BEEN *MINE*, MR. HAMILTON! BUT, DO YOU SUPPOSE I COULD SEE HIS *LABORATORY?*

WELL, HE'S USUALLY VERY *POSSESSIVE* ABOUT IT, BUT... I'M SURE IT WILL BE ALL RIGHT IN *YOUR* CASE!

MINUTES AFTERWARD, IN THE LAB WHICH THE AMBITIOUS ENTOMOLOGIST UTILIZES FOR HIS SINISTER STUDIES...

THIS IS DR. HOPPER'S *CASTLE...* ALMOST HIS *HOME!* SOMETIMES HE DOESN'T LEAVE IT FOR DAYS ON END!

HE IS EXTREMELY RELUCTANT TO LET OTHERS *ENTER* IT AT THOSE TIMES... AND, IN VIEW OF THE TRULY FANTASTIC *PESTICIDES* HE HAS DEVELOPED, WE TRY TO RESPECT HIS WISHES!

I SEE! AND, YOU HAVE NO IDEA WHERE I COULD CONTACT HIM *NOW?*

I'M AFRAID NOT! HIS *CONTRACT* PROVIDES FOR SUCH LEAVES OF ABSENCE DURING WHICH HE USUALLY TAKES ALONG HIS *MOBILE LAB!*

IN FACT, FOR ALL WE KNOW, HE MAY BE INVESTIGATING THOSE REPORTS OF *MAMMOTH LOCUSTS* NEAR HERE!

A COMFORTING THOUGHT, MR. HAMILTON!

HMM.. OR *IS* IT? I WONDER..

MY *MENTAL PROBING* OF SOME OF DR. HOPPER'S EQUIPMENT IS BEGINNING TO REVEAL SOME VERY INTERESTING *DISCOVERIES!*

AND *HERE...* THERE ARE SEVERAL *CANNISTERS* MISSING... CANNISTERS WHICH THE LABELS SAY CONTAINED *LOCUST EGGS!*

COULD IT BE THAT DR. HOPPER HAS A FAR MORE *INTEGRAL,* FAR MORE *PERSONAL* PART IN THE MENACE OF THOSE RAMPAGING INSECTS THAN ANYONE HAS *SUSPECTED?*

THEN, AS THE INVALID MUTANT TURNS HIS ATTENTION TO A PREVIOUSLY UNNOTICED WALL...

THAT *MAP...* IT MAY JUST BE THE *CLINCHER!*

THAT LARGE "X" PIN-POINTS THE AREA WHERE THE LOCUST SWARM APPEARED... AND THERE ARE *OTHER X'S* INDICATED AS WELL!

I BELIEVE I'VE SEEN *ENOUGH*, MR. HAMILTON... IF YOU'LL JUST SHOW ME THE WAY *OUT...*

CERTAINLY, PROFESSOR! STILL, I'M SORRY YOU COULDN'T MEET DR. HOPPER! HE'S A *BRILLIANT MAN*, DESPITE HIS, ER, SOMEWHAT *UNBELIEVABLE* THEORIES ABOUT INSECT MUTATION!

I HOPE THE MATTER YOU WANTED TO TALK WITH HIM ABOUT WASN'T TOO *URGENT!*

UH, NO, NOT REALLY! IN FACT, I THINK I'VE *LEARNED* ALL I NEED TO KNOW!

I CAN'T WAIT TO RETURN TO THE SCHOOL.. I MUST CONTACT THE X-MEN.. *NOW!!*

11.

Almost instantaneously, some miles away...

ATTENTION, X-MEN! PREPARE THE HELICOPTER FOR A MISSION, AS SOON AS WE RETURN!

IT'S THE PROFESSOR!

WE'LL BE READY AND WAITING, SIR!

I'VE ONLY BEEN AWAY A FEW DAYS, BUT IT'LL BE GREAT TO GET INTO COSTUME AGAIN!

LET'S MAKE ALL DELIBERATE HASTE, BOBBY BOY!

Soon, when Professor Xavier and Warren return from their productive excursion...

...IN ADDITION, I MENTALLY EXAMINED SOME OF DR. HOPPER'S LATEST FORMULAE, AND FOUND THEY CONTAIN IONIC PARTICLES WHICH WOULD TEND TO STIMULATE GROWTH!

SO, ALTHOUGH WE CAN'T BE POSITIVE, I SUSPECT THAT DR. HOPPER MAY BE RESPONSIBLE FOR THE INSECT PLAGUE!

AND YOU SAY HIS MAP MAKES YOU BELIEVE THAT THE CORN BELT MAY BE THE NEXT SECTION ATTACKED?

YES! I ONLY HOPE WE'RE IN TIME TO PREVENT ANY DAMAGE THIS TIME!

A few hours later...

THERE'S THE UPPER OHIO RIVER! WE MUST BE APPROACHING THE AREA YOU MENTIONED, PROFESSOR!

YES, SCOTT! IN FACT, I JUST MONITORED A RADIO BROADCAST WHICH REPORTS HUGE LOCUSTS JUST A FEW MILES SOUTH OF HERE!

WE'LL LAND A SHORT DISTANCE AWAY, IN CASE ANY MILITARY FORCES HAVE REACHED THE SCENE...

Then, after a landing is made...

KRUNCH!

LISTEN! THE CREATURES MUST BE RIGHT OVER THAT RIDGE!

KRUNCH!

BUT REMEMBER.. IF THEIR HUMAN LEADER APPEARS, IT IS HE WHO MUST BE BATTLED FIRST!

AND THIS TIME HE MIGHT BE EXPECTING US! KEEP YOUR GUARD UP, MR. McCOY!

A MOST SUPERFLUOUS EXHORTATION, MR. BLAKE!

THERE THEY ARE! BUT, THERE ARE DOZENS OF THEM THIS TIME! WHAT CAN WE DO AGAINST THEM?

THE SAME THING AS LAST TIME, ANGEL!..

BUT, THIS TIME, WE'VE GOT TO DO MORE OF IT!

KRUNCH! KRUNCH!

UH OH! TAKE A LOOK ON YOUR RIGHT, CYKE! THIS HAS GOTTA BE THE GUY WE'RE LOOKIN' FOR!

CORRECTION, MY SUPER-POWERED SIMPLETONS! RATHER, IT IS I WHO HAVE BEEN PATIENTLY WAITING FOR YOU!

FOR, IN DEFEATING YOU, I SHALL DEMONSTRATE THE FOLLY OF OPPOSING... THE LOCUST!

LOOK, MISTER, WE DON'T KNOW EXACTLY WHAT YOU'RE TRYING TO ACCOMPLISH WITH THESE GRASSHOPPER PALS OF YOURS, BUT WE'RE HERE TO PUT AN END TO IT!

PRESUMPTUOUS FOOL! DO YOU THINK I WOULD HAVE APPEARED BEFORE YOU, IF I WERE NOT PREPARED TO DISPOSE OF YOU?

THE ONLY DISPOSING YOU'RE GOING TO DO, LOCUST, IS TO GET RID OF THAT NUTTY COSTUME! I....UHHHN!

AWAY, CLOD. YOU SHALL BE THE FIRST TO FEEL THE BITE OF THE LOCUST!

WOK!

OOOOF! CAUGHT ME...OFF-GUARD!

ALL RIGHT, GROUP, OUR BUG-EYED BUDDY HAS OPENED THE HOSTILITIES! NOW, IT'S TIME FOR THE NOBLE BEAST TO GET INTO THE ACT!

HMM...YOU SEEM MORE AGILE THAN YOUR COWLED COMPANIONS...

HOWEVER, AGILITY IS OF NO AVAIL...IF YOU CAN'T GRASP YOUR ANTAGONIST!

WHAT THE..? HE SPREAD HIS WINGS...AND TOOK OFF!

IT'S UP TO YOU NOW, ANGEL!

IT'S NO CONTEST, BEAST! HIS MECHANICAL WINGS ARE NO MATCH FOR MY REAL ONES.

HE'S RIGHT! IT WILL TAKE HIM MERE SECONDS TO OVERTAKE ME!

BUT, THE VICTORY CAN STILL BE MINE!

SUDDENLY...

MY CREATIVE GENIUS ALSO DEVELOPED THIS IONIC STUN-DEVICE, TO KEEP ANY REBELLIOUS INSECTS IN LINE....

HOWEVER, IT SEEMS TO WORK ON ANGELS, AS WELL!

ZZRAPP!

MMMFFF! I'M RECEIVING A TERRIFIC JOLT FROM THAT GIZMO...CAN'T STAY ALOFT!

BUT, AS THE STRICKEN X-MAN TOPPLES HELPLESSLY FROM THE SKY, ANOTHER MUTANT COMES TO HIS AID...

THANKS, MARVEL GIRL!

MY PLEASURE, ANGEL! I'M ONLY SORRY I DIDN'T GET A SHOT AT THE LOCUST!

STICK AROUND, FAIR LADY! YOUR OPPORTUNITY MAY COME SOON!

SOONER THAN YOU THINK, BEASTIE! HE'S FLUTTERING TO EARTH NOT FIFTY YARDS AWAY!

13.

WATCH OUT FOR *FLYING ICE*, ALL! I'M BLASTING OUR WAY *OUT* OF THIS FRIGID FISHBOWL... *NOW!*

WOW! I'M GLAD YOU'RE ON *OUR SIDE*, CYKE!

MOMENTS LATER, AS THE ICY COVERING FALLS BEFORE SCOTT SUMMERS' POTENT EYE-BEAMS...

OKAY, SO WE'RE *OUT!* THAT *STILL* LEAVES THE LOCUST'S *INSECT-BUDDIES* FOR US TO WALTZ AROUND WITH!

DON'T BE SO *SURE!* LOOKS LIKE THE *NATIONAL GUARD* HAS TAKEN CHARGE OF THINGS *HERE*, TOO!

IF THEY KEEP THAT UP, WE'LL B OUT OF *WORK.*

PROFESSOR XAVIER SEEMS TO FEEL *DIFFERENTLY*, BEAST! HE'S REVVING UP THE 'COPTER!

THEN, HE MUST HAVE A LEAD ON THE *LOCUST!* LET'S *MOVE OUT!*

AND, AS THE DAUNTLESS X-MEN TAKE TO THE SKIES ONCE AGAIN, AN AWESOME BUT HEARTENING SCENE TRANSPIRES BELOW...

THEY CAN'T TAKE THIS *FLAME-THROWER*, EITHER! BUT, WHAT WOULD WE HAVE DONE IF THERE'D BEEN *THOUSANDS* OF 'EM, INSTEAD OF JUST *DOZENS?*

THESE *M-2'S* ARE DOIN' THE TRICK! JUST KEEP *FIRIN'!*

FROOM!

WHILE, PASSING SWIFTLY OVER THE SCENE A FEW HUNDRED FEET ABOVE, PROFESSOR X AND HIS SUPER-POWERED STUDENTS ARE PLAGUED BY SIMILAR THOUGHTS..

DEPRIVED OF THE LOCUST'S *HUMAN BRAIN*, THOSE GIANT INSECTS FELL PREY TO MODERN WEAPONS! BUT, IF HE HADN'T BEEN FORCED TO *FLEE*, THE STORY MIGHT HAVE BEEN *OTHERWISE!*

WHAT'S OUR *NEXT STEP*, PROFESSOR?

IF MY MEMORY SERVES ME CORRECTLY, I SEEM TO RECALL THAT THE NEXT "X" ON THE MAP AT *RYAN CHEMICALS* WAS ONLY ABOUT FIFTY MILES FROM HERE! WE'RE HEADING FOR THAT SPOT... BUT, WE MUST ALLOW HIM TO ARRIVE THERE *FIRST!*

AND, *THIS* TIME THERE'LL BE *NO QUARTER!* IT'S THE *LOCUST*... OR *US!!*

SOON, AS THE SEARCHING X-COPTER FOLLOWS THE WINDING OF THE PLACID OHIO RIVER...

THAT *TRAILER*... IT'S PARKED IN A PLACE WHERE THE OWNER ISN'T LIKELY TO BE DOING ANY *HUNTING* OR *FISHING!*

WITH *OUR* LUC IT'S PROBABL THE VANGUARD OF AN *ANTI-MUTANTS CONVENTION!*

STILL, WE MUST BE AT ALMOST THE EXACT PLACE WHICH DR. HOPPER HAD MARKED ON HIS *CHART!* WE'LL SET DOWN QUIETLY NEARBY, AND HAVE A LOOK!

BUT, NO MATTER! ONE STRONG LEAP WILL CARRY ME AWAY, AND... :UNNHH!:

MY APOLOGIES, BUT IT'S ESSENTIAL THAT YOU STICK AROUND FOR A SHORT TÉTE-À-TÉTE!

THAT MEANS A HEART-TO-HEART TALK, IF YOU'RE BEHIND IN YOUR FRENCH LESSONS!

AWAY, YOU BUMBLING OAF!

I HAVE NO TIME FOR SUCH DELAYS!

:OOOF!:

IT'S BECOMING OBVIOUS THIS JUST ISN'T MY DAY!

BUT, IT MAY BE MINE! AT LEAST, THIS TIME HE'S NOT GOING TO USE ANY STUN-RAY ON ME!

SO...THE WINGED X-MAN CLUMSILY SEEKS TO TAKE ME UNAWARES!

DOESN'T HE REALIZE THAT LOCUSTS HAVE GREAT PERIPHERAL VISION?

HERE, ANGEL! THIS COCOON SILK...A TRAIT I BORROWED FROM THE LOWLY CATERPILLAR...WILL STOP YOU IN YOUR TRACKS!

CAN'T STOP IN TIME...I'M GOING TO RAM RIGHT INTO IT!

OF COURSE, YOU DOLT! DID YOU THINK I LEAVE SUCH THINGS TO CHANCE?

SECONDS LATER, AS AN ENSNARED ANGEL TOUCHES DOWN...

THAT HORN-HEADED DO-BADDER REALLY KNOWS HIS BUSINESS! THE STUFF IS LIKE GLUE!

LOOK! HE'S COMING DOWN AGAIN!

YES...BUT TOO FAR AWAY FOR US TO REACH HIM BEFORE HE CAN ACTIVATE SOME MORE SIX-LEGGED TERRORS!

AND, INDEED, EVEN AS THE X-MEN'S DEPUTY LEADER SPEAKS THESE PROPHETIC WORDS...

THE X-MEN HAVE INTERFERED WITH MY PLANS FOR THE FINAL TIME!

THESE TWO EGGS... WHICH HAVE BEEN TRIPLY TREATED BY IONIC PARTICLES... WILL BE THEIR DOWNFALL!

FOR NOW, THE MOMENT HAS COME FOR MY ULTIMATE CREATIONS!

SSSST!

THE NEXT INSTANT, BEFORE THE ASTONISHED EYES OF THE ONWARD-RUSHING MUTANT BAND...

GROW! GROW! GROW! LET NOT ONE X-MAN SURVIVE!

THEY'RE ZOOMING UP RIGHT BEFORE US... MORE ENORMOUS THAN ANY OF HIS OTHER MONSTROSITIES! WE'VE GOT TO HALT THEM!

WHATEVER YOUR PLAN IS, CYKE, CLUE US IN FAST... WHILE WE'RE STILL AROUND!

NOW, HOW DOES A RATIONAL PERSON ARGUE WITH SENTIMENTS LIKE THOSE?

SUDDENLY, THE RESOURCEFUL MARVEL GIRL STEPS TO THE FORE, AND...

HIS ANTENNAE! IT'S THROUGH THEM THAT HE CONTROLS HIS CREATURES! IF ONLY I CAN...

NO! IN DESPERATION, THE FEMALE X-MAN HURLS HERSELF AGAINST ME!

DO NOT THINK TO STIR MY HEART TO MERCY! FOR, STILL I ORDER MY GIANT SUBJECTS TO DESTROY ALL OF YOU!

BUT... THEY ARE LUMBERING TOWARDS ME!

STOP! I, YOUR RULER, COMMAND YOU TO STOP!

IT..IT'S IMPOSSIBLE! BOTH OF MY INSECT CREATIONS ARE ATTACKING ME! BUT, I CAN YET ESCAPE!

IN MY MOBILE LAB...IS AN ANTIDOTE WHICH WILL MAKE THEM SMALL AGAIN!

GREAT WORK, JEAN! HE DIDN'T SEE YOU TELE-KINETICALLY KNOTTING HIS ANTENNAE!

...AND, WITHOUT HIS COMMANDS TO GUIDE THEM, THE CONFUSED BEETLES ATTACKED HIM... PERHAPS BECAUSE, IN HIS LOCUST COSTUME, HE SO RESEMBLES ONE OF THE TINY INSECTS THEY NORMALLY PREY UPON!

WE READ YOU, CYKE! WHAT DO WE DO TO RESCUE HIM? IT WON'T TAKE THOSE THINGS LONG TO TEAR THAT TRAILER APART!

ANGEL'S RIGHT! WE'VE GOT TO HELP THE LOCUST SOMEHOW!

BUT, BEFORE THEY CAN SUIT ACTION TO THEIR WORDS... DISASTER STRIKES...

SNAP!

THE TRAILER'S SNAPPED FREE OF THE CAR...AND IT'S ROLLING TOWARDS THE CLIFF! WE'VE GOT TO USE OUR POWERS TO STOP IT!

WE'LL HAZARD THE ATTEMPT! BUT, YOU'LL HAVE TO FORGIVE ME IF I'M MODERATELY APPREHENSIVE ABOUT THE ULTIMATE OUTCOME!

19

Panel 1: MORE *POWER*, ALL OF YOU! THE MOBILE LAB IS STILL SLIDING TOWARDS THE *EDGE*!

I CAN'T *HELP* IT! THOSE BLAMED BUGS ARE ROCKING THE TRAILER SO MUCH I CAN'T FREEZE THE *WHEELS* SOLID ENOUGH!

IT'S *GOING OVER!* ANGEL.. TRY TO GRAB THE *LOCUST... FAST!!*

Panel 2: AND, ALMOST AS SCOTT VOICES HIS COMMAND...

NO-- *NO!* I CAN'T *FLY*.. MY *WINGS* WERE DAMAGED!

RELAX, FELLA! AS ONE FLY-BOY TO ANOTHER I *GOTCHA*!

HE *DID* IT! WARREN *GOT* HIM!

Panel 3: BUT.. MY MOBILE LAB... PRICELESS, IRREPLACEABLE *EQUIPMENT!* ALL *GONE*... DASHED IN THE RIVER BELOW!

MISTER, IF YOU DON'T SEE HOW *LUCKY* YOU ARE, I'M TEMPTED TO LET YOU *JOIN* IT!

SPLOOSH!

Panel 4: YES, LOCUST... LOOK AROUND AND SEE THE *ERROR* OF YOUR PATH! THE X-MEN COULD HAVE LET YOU *DIE*... YET, THEY SAVED YOU FROM YOUR OWN *CREATIONS!*

PERHAPS... I UNDERSTAND AT *LAST,* OLD MAN! I HAVE BEEN... *ILL!*

BUT, I CAN *YET* ATONE FOR THE EVIL I HAVE CAUSED!

Panel 5: LET THESE DEVILISH DEVICES... MY SOLE REMAINING *MAGNO-RAY* AND *STUN-WEAPON*... JOIN MY OTHER INVENTIONS BENEATH THE WATERS!

I MUST SURRENDER TO THE *AUTHORITIES* AND PAY MY *DEBT* FOR THE *HARM* I HAVE CAUSED!

AND PERHAPS, ONE DAY, THAT HARM WILL BE MORE THAN OFFSET BY THE *GOOD* YOU MIGHT ACCOMPLISH!

Panel 6: THEN, AS THE SOLITARY COSTUMED FIGURE OF DR. HOPPER DISAPPEARS IN THE DISTANCE...

NOW THAT THE THREAT IS OVER, JEAN WILL RETURN TO *COLLEGE!* HOW LONG WILL IT BE BEFORE SHE FORGETS THE X-MEN *COMPLETELY?*

I THOUGHT THAT, IN THIS GUISE, I COULD SOMEHOW *REASON* WITH OUR FOE!

AFTER *THIS* CASE, I COULD *USE* A BIT OF RELAXATION AS A "MERE" COLLEGE STUDENT!

YOU SHOULD'VE BEEN AN *ACTOR,* PROFESSOR!

WHAT OF *DR. HOPPER,* PROFESSOR? DO YOU THINK WE'LL SEE MORE OF... *THE LOCUST?*

Panel 7: IT'S IMPOSSIBLE TO SAY, HANK! WE CAN ONLY HOPE THAT HE HAS LEARNED HIS LESSON *PERMANENTLY!*

FOR, IF THE LOCUST RETURNED --LEADING AN *ARMY* OF GIANT INSECTS, EVEN *WE* MIGHT NOT BE ABLE TO STOP HIM!

AND IF YOU *WANNA* FIND JUST HOW *RIGHT* OLD CHROME-DOME IS-- KEEP FOLLOWING THE ADVENTURES OF **THE WORLD'S STRANGEST TEENS**